COBWEB FOREST
(Cobweb Bride Trilogy: Book Three)

Vera Nazarian

Cover Art Details:
"Sunrise on the Adriatic" by Saxum, 2009; "Swinton Park Tree by Night" by Andy Beecroft (geograph.org.uk), January 14, 2007; "Tree silhouetted in radiation fog" by Andy Waddington (geograph.org.uk), November 22, 2005; "Star-Forming Region LH 95 in the Large Magellanic Cloud," Credit: NASA, ESA, and the Hubble Heritage Team (STScI/AURA)-ESA/Hubble Collaboration, Acknowledgment: D. Gouliermis (Max Planck Institute for Astronomy, Heidelberg).

Interior Illustration:
"Map of the Realm and the Domain," Copyright © 2013 by Vera Nazarian.

Cover Design Copyright © 2013 by Vera Nazarian

ISBN-13: 978-1-60762-126-3
ISBN-10: 1-60762-126-6

Trade Paperback Edition

December 31, 2013

A Publication of
Norilana Books
P. O. Box 209
Highgate Center, VT 05459-0209
www.norilana.com

Printed in the United States of America

Cobweb Forest

Cobweb Bride Trilogy: Book Three

Leda

an imprint of

Norilana Books

www.norilana.com

Acknowledgements

There are so many of you whose unwavering,
loving support made this book happen—
My gratitude is boundless, and I thank you
with all my heart.

First, my dear friends and fantastic first readers:
Anastasia Rudman, F.R.R. Mallory, Jeremy Frank,
Sara Cooper, and Susan Franzblau.

Indiegogo Acknowledgements

And all the generous and wonderful **Indiegogo backers**, you who are amazing friends, colleagues, supporters, readers, fans, and one-time strangers who are now friends:

Benefactor

Anonymous (three)
Anastasia Rudman
Anna Chernyshenko
Brook and Julia West
Lauowolf
Lisa Harrigan
Marian Allen
Nivair H. Gabriel
Robert Brandt
Susan Franzblau
Lady Phantasm
Torbjørn Pettersen

Patron

Alexandra Dimou
Allison Smith
Isa Lavinia
Leslie R. Lee
Melanie C. Duncan
Neile Graham
Nicole Platania
Rita Savage
Sara Cooper
Stephanie Piro

Supporter

April Richardson
Cynthia Ward
Joan Marie Verba
Katy Sozaeva
Mordred

My deepest thanks to all for your support!

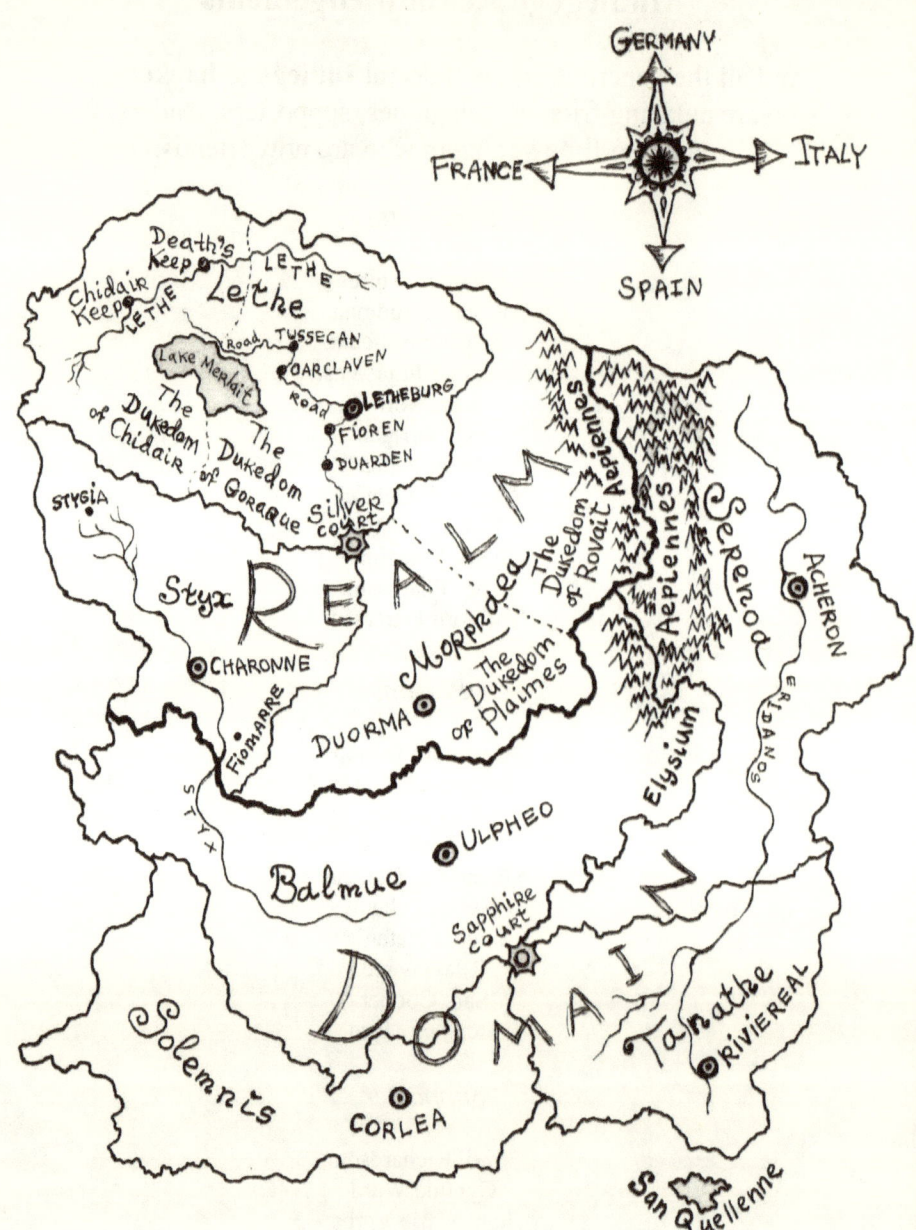

Map of the Realm and the Domain

For all those who have gone before . . .

There is only Love—and Stories.
All else is but a shadow dream.

Cobweb
FOREST

Cobweb Bride Trilogy
Book Three

vera nazarian

Chapter 1

“**L**ord Death,” said Demeter, the Goddess of Tradition, as she filled the sterile Hall of bones with her golden light. “Before another word is spoken, *you* need to drink the water from the River Lethe.”

The goddess had cast aside her dark winter cloak that had been worn by her as the maiden Melinoë, and underneath she was still attired in her dress of pristine whiteness, the one in which she had lain in state as the Cobweb Bride.

And now, as everyone observed her transfiguration, her dress became a fine antique Grecian chiton of gossamer fabric, so delicate that it appeared to be wrought of pure radiance. At the same time, her body grew taller, more statuesque, attaining matronly curves, and her golden hair was now artfully gathered in a headdress, shaped like a braided crown of wheat and harvest sunshine.

The Hall itself—having been eternal monochrome and dull grey for time untold—was suddenly *awake*. It had been swept clean with a sweet divine breath, and given an aura of life. And now, everything glowed. It was like being within the heart of a great cocoon of infinite layers, dreamlike, warm, and fragile . . . like looking out at the world from the inside of an eggshell. For indeed, every bone in the Hall was now translucent, illuminated and backlit, so that one could see nearly through it and observe cream and honey radiance streaming from beyond.

Meanwhile, the obedient sentinel death-shadow belonging to the Cobweb Bride, moved away from the immortal goddess, for it was no longer bound to her. And yet, the death-shadow remained nearby, for it was now an orphan, impossibly separated from its mysterious true owner. It billowed sorrowfully, for it had nowhere else to go. . . .

At the same time, the mortals standing in the Hall—Percy Ayren, Lord Beltain Chidair, the girls, Lord Nathan, and Lady Amaryllis—were all bathed by the glow of the goddess.

The only one still untouched, still remaining in permanent shadow, was a grim man-figure, bearded in the angular manner of a Spaniard, clad in a gentleman's black velvet doublet and hose, and wearing a wide starched collar of lace.

He was Death, his antiquated demeanor hailing from centuries before, out of the depth of the Middle Ages. And his face was a vacant spot, never to be observed directly . . . as though it was not there.

Death stood before the immortal goddess, still holding in his beautiful, sharp-clawed hand the small flask containing the shadowy waters of Lethe. He was motionless, possibly stricken with disbelief, fixed with the impossibility that was taking place all around.

And then Death moved. He lifted the flask—shielding it with one ivory hand from the golden radiance of the Hall, so that the liquid inside was given the amount of twilight necessary for it to physically materialize—and he brought it up to the dark obscured place where, it was assumed, were his lips.

No one saw Death take the swallow, for no one could look upon his face. And yet, it was somehow made clear to all that he drank.

And then. . . .

The Hall illuminated in golden radiance started to grow dark again.

Swiftly the darkness approached, but this time its nature

was different—it was the menacing overcast before a thunderstorm, the gathering of clouds that were not silver but true thick night. It brought with it sudden heightened contrast, a new quality—so that shadows turned from indifferent grey to profound black. And the honey light itself faded by several degrees, approaching monochrome, its warmth reduced into a slightly anemic cream hue. However the warmth could not be effaced completely, due to the presence of the goddess, and thus it still lingered in all things, flavoring them with a hint of life. But the shadows had fundamentally changed, for a new rich black emerged, populating the dim places.

A *black* of the Underworld. . . .

And with the advent of deepened contrast, Death transformed before their eyes.

The figure of the Spaniard darkened, coalesced, gaining in physical presence and tangibility. He was now ebony, a tall living statue cast of antique polished metal the color of midnight. His trappings of a stern gentleman faded into non-existence, revealing bare, coal-dark skin. Instead, he was now clad in a classical tunic that came to flow over his one shoulder, leaving his muscular beautiful torso exposed. The tunic, belted at the waist, was made of a strange unearthly fabric that appeared black one moment, silver the next, glistening like mother-of-pearl and constantly shifting and moving in the light. His powerful arms were now bare of sleeves, and there were wide braces of black iron at his wrists and around the biceps of his upper arms. Laced metal-studded sandals defined his powerful calves.

His hair, coming down to his shoulders in waves of a frozen night waterfall, was such an intense shade of black that it shone with a blue and indigo light.

And his face—at last it was fully visible, with its fine, hard, angled lines of exquisite masculine symmetry not found in mortal nature. His eyes underneath stern perfect brows were fathomless openings into a place without definition or end. A high Grecian forehead, a chiseled nose, austere lips and a clean-shaven chin, all balanced into a striking visage of terrible and mesmerizing intensity.

The god stood before them, feet planted wide, and he glanced about him in incredulity that turned into confident disdain and then just as quickly, sorrow.

"I remember myself . . . and everything else up to the moment of my oblivion, when I confined myself to this halfway place between worlds," he said. His voice—oh, the profundity of its rich timbre, the rumbling echoes that filled the Hall in its wake. . . . "And then I remember only this dreary Hall and the occasional mortals who came here to find me. Since then, what has come to pass?"

"Welcome, Lord Hades," replied the Goddess Demeter. "It has been many days. The world is broken. And your love—she is *broken* also."

And saying this, Demeter lowered her face, and the aura of light softly surrounding her waned, while tears glistened down her cheeks.

The black God, who was indeed Hades, Lord of the Underworld—for Death was merely one of his aspects—observed Demeter with an expression of severe intensity. Once he had gathered himself under control after his initial moment of re-awakening, his face did not betray any emotion. Only his eyes, glittering and fathomless, reflected a moment of pain.

"Tell me, Mother of Bright Harvest," he said. "What has gone wrong? Have we not drunk the water of Lethe as agreed, all three of us, in our designated places?"

Meanwhile, as this dialogue was taking place, the mortals in the Hall stared in fearful wonder at the gods in their midst—gods conversing as if they were not present.

"Yes," Demeter replied, wiping tears from her cheeks with the back of one impossibly lovely hand. "We have all drunk *once*, as agreed. You were the last to drink. And while you stayed here and were eventually diminished, I took my daughter's hand and together we flew to the distant Palace of the Sun. There, she drank her portion—only one sip—and I left her seated on the Sapphire Throne that brings her from the world below and conducts her back there every season. I left her there, for once she was without memory I had wanted her to recognize and learn anew that intimate, sacred place before all else—to remember her divine function. Finally I went to lie down in my chambers, hidden in the heart of Ulpheo—which is my own city, sworn to me ages ago, even though they do not remember me properly now and worship the One God. There I flew to rest and drink my own portion of Lethe."

"And then?"

"And then," concluded the Goddess, "I remember only dreams."

Hades watched her with a stone gaze. "What you say is impossible. Why did you not remain cognizant? Lethe's oblivion does not rob you of awareness and reason, only the *past*. . . ."

"I realize that, but now I know that something else must have occurred that took away my time and consciousness. For I was awakened elsewhere—not in Ulpheo but in the Sapphire Court, in a secret chamber underneath the throne—by this mortal who serves you—" and Demeter pointed at Percy—"and she was the one who broke the bonds of power that held my mind in a web of dreams and my body immobilized and enslaved."

Percy found herself unable to blink from the overwhelming awe that filled her when Hades, the beautiful dark God, turned around and trained his gaze upon her. . . .

At her side, Beltain instinctively placed his strong steady hand at her waist, to support her.

"My Champion . . ." said the God softly, regarding her.

Percy felt herself drowning. Flashes of memory came to her, the incandescent overwhelming white from Death's mindscape, where she had first met Death as the White

Bridegroom, fair and glorious . . . and he had given her a fragment of his heart in a kiss.

"Yes," Hades said, reading her thoughts. "It is my aspect also, the one that every mortal is gifted with, in their last moment before oblivion."

"My—My Lord!" uttered Percy. "I am—that is, I know not what to say or think! Which is the real *you?*"

And surprisingly, Hades smiled. It was a light smile that barely moved his perfect lips and never touched his eyes—for they were utter pitch-black *otherplaces*. "You have now seen my real self in my three primary aspects. There are others—but not to be revealed. I am Death, the grey shadow that lingers in the mortal realm. . . . I am the White Bridegroom who conducts you all to the Wedding. . . . And I am the Black Husband—but only for *one*. . . . In this last and deepest form, none but a few know me. And yet, because the world has been turned upside down and inside out, my true self is revealed before you as it had never been revealed to any mortal soul outside my true kingdom that lies Below. As the Lord of the Dark Harvest, I rule the Underworld. And as the Black Husband I love *her* who is my Consort, my Dark Lover, Persephone whose name you bear, and who is Resurrection."

Percy tore her gaze away from his endless abyss and attempted to incline her head in a bow. "My . . . Lord." She stood, rendered numb, and then became aware that she was trembling. And again she felt Beltain's strong hand upon her back, and now he was also holding her chilled hand with his own warm one, and squeezing her fingers. . . .

"Persephone," said Hades. "Percy, Death's Champion. You have tried to do my will and bring to me my Cobweb Bride. You have done well—as well as possible under the circumstances. But now—the task is still unfinished. The world was never meant to be deprived of my Dark Harvest."

And Hades glanced at the orphan death shadow that was a sorrowful pillar of grey smoke, standing a few paces away.

"But—what can I do?" Percy asked, glancing at the Goddess Demeter. "I thought she was the one! The death shadow of the Cobweb Bride was attached to her!"

"That bond was only an illusion. While I was merely Death, a pale specter of myself, my full knowledge and power were also diminished. Thus, I could not tell the difference, nor recognize the immortality before me." And Hades looked at Demeter with steady regard.

"Then whose death-shadow is it? Where is this infernal Cobweb Bride?"

It was Lord Beltain Chidair, the black knight, who spoke thus, addressing the dark God with a fearless countenance. When the god turned the full force of his gaze upon him, the knight did not even blink.

"You ask *me*, fearless mortal?" Hades said with a surprisingly sardonic shadow-smile. "I may be eternal, but I am not all-knowing like Zeus, my Brother who rules the Skies. I was confined in this place and have no knowledge of events outside this Hall. However, all of you who have been in your mortal world—all of *you* have borne witness to the events unfolding— you yourselves contain the answer. Thus, I need to look within your memories to see." And the god motioned to Percy, raising his sculpted ebony hand and offering it to her. "Come, my Champion, let me look inside you and search for her who is so elusive now."

While Beltain frowned in worry, Percy approached Hades. She took one step, then another. The closer she neared the more she could sense the invisible weight, the darkness thickening, the ghostly oppression around him. . . .

The God of the Underworld took her numb hand into his large, pitch-black own, and she felt a piercing charge of energy pass through her as her skin made contact with his—surprisingly not cold but warm and electric, and indeed impossible to describe.

In the moment of contact, she shuddered, and was instantly submerged into a dream.

Events of the last days raced through her mind with a rapid flickering displacement of twilight and fleeting clouds, sunsets replacing dawns, cities and human figures, and falling snow, in a multidimensional carousel of time. . . . She saw everything, lived through everything again, including her terrifying interactions with the dead and her glorious moments with Beltain. And then she was once again in that secret room underneath the Sapphire Throne, bathed in anemic lavender glow, and she was forcing the veil of energy, and shattering the infinity of cobwebs, releasing the maidens from their stasis—

"There she is, the Cobweb Bride!" said Hades, his voice breaking through the mesmerizing flood of rushing memories. And Percy came to, finding herself upright and back in the Hall of shadows.

The dark God had released her hand and was regarding her.

"You know who *she* is now, do you not?" he said softly.

Percy inhaled deeply and the image from her own memory stood out clear as day in her mind.

Leonora.

How did she not see it before? Lady Leonora D'Arvu was the only maiden among them all to "survive" being freed from the bonds of power. And yet—even *then* she had appeared to Percy to be pale and sickly, as though there was something slightly wrong with her, something off. . . . If it hadn't been for the fact that she had no death shadow at her side, Percy would have eventually recognized her as someone *dead*.

She realized now that Leonora's death shadow had been taken from her and attached to Melinoë instead.

But how? And for what purpose?

"Yes," Percy replied audibly, to answer Hades. And then she added: "We had her, and we let her go. . . ."

She then explained to Beltain and the others what she now knew.

Beltain exhaled in frustration. "The Count D'Arvu and his family have gone away at the same time as we did. They are gone into hiding to escape the Sovereign's wrath—where to, it is unknown," he mused. "They could be anywhere!"

"Well, this is all very entertaining," Lady Amaryllis spoke up suddenly. "But surely there must be a reliable way to catch this annoyingly elusive female Bride creature, once and for all? Why not send out one of those infamous Hell Hounds? Cerberus, is it?"

Amaryllis was the fastidious, disdainful, and sarcastic beauty from the Silver Court, dressed in clothing that had at one point been the height of fashion and was now rumpled and dirty from their recent misadventures. She, together with her companion Lord Nathan (even more disheveled than Her Ladyship) and several young girls, had inadvertently found themselves stuck in Death's Hall after escaping imprisonment in Chidair Keep, sailing in a boat upon the River Lethe, and being "contaminated" by touching the twilight water. Death had told them that they had to remain here until the Cobweb Bride was found and the order of the world restored.

"Indeed! I would really love to get out of this woeful place . . ." the dark and handsome yet woefully unkempt and unshaven Lord Nathan said carefully, echoing her. He then glanced sideways, with a rational degree of caution, at both Hades and Demeter . . . who both seemed to regard the mortals with the same level of curiosity with which he himself might have observed a chattering squirrel.

"Oh, yes! I don't wanna be stuck 'ere forever!" exclaimed a grimy and freckled girl by the name of Catrine.

"Me neither!" blurted Faeline, a small blonde girl dressed in simple village clothing, then put her hand over her mouth and glanced at Hades in abject terror.

The god seemed to observe her fear with amusement—indeed, all of their fears—for a faint smile returned to the corners of his dark chiseled lips.

It was rather curious, thought Percy, but Hades—this grim God of Death, oblivion, the demon Death-Thanatos, the Underworld, and every utter horror known to humankind—seemed to smile and find quite a few things amusing, in the short amount of time that she had been in his divine presence.

And once again he must have read her mind. For the piercing gaze of two impossibly beautiful, pitch-black eyes slithered over her, making her skin prickle and rise in goose bumps.

I am not what you think, Persephone, my sweet Champion. I promise, in the end you will come to know me as I truly am. . . .

Percy blinked, then again found herself trembling. But it was not only fear, no; there was something else, something electric. The same kind of sweet prickling as she felt when she looked at Beltain—

No!

Percy was abruptly horrified at herself. And it was in that moment that she thought she heard divine laughter. In her mind alone Hades laughed, his heavy sensual gaze upon her, slithering dark, overwhelming sweetness.

Do not fear me, not in that way, his rich, low voice sounded inside her head. *And do not fear yourself. You are mine in your soul's essence, and thus you are drawn to me, and you respond to me. . . . You are Persephone, and yet you are not. You can never be her, my one and only love, just as I can never be him, your faithful true lover—this man who now stands at your side. You are thus safe from me, my Champion, safe from me and my regard. And he is safe also, the one you truly desire.*

He is yours. I relinquish you to him for all of your mortal life.

". . . Percy!" Beltain was speaking to her, squeezing her shoulders, and she realized she had lost track of time, yet again, in a strange hallucinatory daydream.

But no, it was all the dark God's doing. He had made it

happen, and she was his instrument, and yet she was entirely her own.

And as she glanced at Hades she saw him barely incline his head in acknowledgement.

"My Champion," said Hades, and this time he spoke out loud so that everyone heard him. "I give you the means now to find this maiden Leonora who had eluded us for so long. Her own death shade will lead you to her. It stands now, lost and forsaken, its natural life bond twisted by dark immortal sorcery, so that it does not know its master."

And then Hades lifted his hand and he pointed to the pitiful billowing thing, the slate-grey pillar of death smoke, and he said, "Come!"

And immediately the death shadow floated toward the Lord of the Underworld, until it stood before him. It occurred to Percy that no one but Hades and herself—and possibly the Goddess Demeter—could actually see what was taking place.

Hades extended one jet-black finger, and he touched the air where the shadow paused. It reacted to him, as though to a jolt of invisible force, by writhing and contracting, then unfurling once more into the vague human shape that it owned.

"It is done now. It remembers itself and its true mortal bond," said the God, while everyone stared in confusion. "You must follow it, as you would a hound, and it will obey you in every manner, as do all the other deaths out there."

"I understand. . . ." Percy reached out with her own hand and called to the vaporous thing with a single thought.

Come to me. . . .

The death shadow immediately responded. Like a soft cloud of darkness it started to float toward Percy.

Stop.

The thing obeyed. It now hung in the air halfway between Percy and Hades.

"I assume there is something there," said Lady Amaryllis

with annoyance. "For I see nothing, and it very well better be something."

"It is here," Percy spoke, looking before her.

"Aha! Well then, splendid!" Lord Nathan grunted and stood up from the bottom stair of the dais of the throne of bones where he had been reclining, and made a show of stretching. "But why in Hades—that is, begging all pardon of Your Divinity—why must this tedious quest be enacted *yet again* by this poor girl Percy and presumably an invisible ghost, when you are both immortal gods with untold powers? Now that you are free, and no longer bound by Lethe's odious water and have your godly minds back, why not simply pop on over there as you gods supposedly do, and just grab this Lady Leonora and bring her here? You are gods, are you not? Or are you drunken louts? What is the point of power and immortality if you must employ peasant girls?"

There was silence.

"I would hush now, if I were you, Nathan . . ." Amaryllis whispered, with a very strange expression.

But Hades did not even turn to look at the insolent mortal. His face was now pensive and cold, like beautiful stone.

Instead, it was Demeter who spoke. "Unfortunately I have no influence over the dead. And Lord Hades has limited powers in the world of the living. Furthermore he must remain here at the source, the twilight place that stands at the entrance between the two worlds," she said, and her bittersweet gentle voice was a warm breeze of ripe summer. "He must guard it . . . and he must prepare now. He must gather all his strength, for the coming struggle with his love."

The countenance of Hades deepened with tragic gravity, and became even more remote, as the golden Goddess continued: "He alone has the ability to stop her. For my daughter approaches even now, with her armies covered in your mortal blood. Persephone, my lost child, comes to destroy and to conquer and to rule—the worlds Above and Below. And as she is now, he must never allow her back into the Underworld."

Percy's mind was reeling.

Persephone, her namesake, the terrible Goddess of the Underworld was one and the same as the Sovereign! She was the terrifying dark queen of the Domain, who had caused untold death and suffering and had somehow become what she was now.

She was *broken*.

Those were the first words that Demeter the bright golden Goddess had used to refer to Persephone of the Underworld. What did it mean?

Apparently the gods could always read thoughts, for as Percy thought all this, Demeter replied again. "Something else had happened to her, child, something after I had drunk the water of Lethe. I still do not know what it is, but *something* changed her. Something else other than her already overwhelming, bitter grief."

"She is wicked! And so frightening . . ." Percy said.

"You do not know my Persephone, none of you!" Hades said suddenly, and his voice rang with angry echoes in the deathly Hall. "She was not like this! She had never been like this! The murder, the destruction—yes, I have seen it all in your memories, Percy, you who are my Champion—and none of it makes sense! She was deep in mourning, yes, and so was I, so was my Lady Demeter of the Bright Harvest—it is why we have drunk the waters of Lethe together, all of us, to *forget*. . . . But now—now I am in mourning yet again, this time for my lost love!"

Percy felt a cold heavy weight fill her chest. There were so many unspoken questions, burrowing inside her. "My Lord," she said. "When I find the Cobweb Bride, and she is reunited with her shadow, will that make everything right again? Will it cure your Persephone? Will it . . . *heal* her?"

"No." Hades looked at her with his tragic eyes. "If you had asked me this question earlier, while I was still under the influence of the River Lethe's oblivion, I might have answered differently. But now my mind is clear again and I have learned the extent of the destruction. Thus I tell you in truth: no. The resumption of the Dark Harvest will only *begin* to heal the world. Whatever had happened to my love, it is something else entirely."

"I believe," spoke Demeter, "that she may be responsible for what has happened to all mortal things, but I do not know how or why. I suspect she herself bound the Cobweb Bride and bound her death to me in paradox of immortality, and thus made all death stop as a result."

"Once and for all, how does that work, exactly? The death stopping part?" Nathan spoke again, rather fearlessly, scratching his wildly tousled head of dark hair. "What I don't understand is how can Percy, Death's Champion, put the dead to rest individually, when death has ceased overall? Why cannot Death—Lord Hades—perform this task himself?"

Hades turned at last, to look in the mortal man's eyes, and Nathan was transfixed.

"You ask, and I will tell you," said the black God. "Death is the Dark Harvest. It is my common and best-known function in the scheme of the world. I reap all of you mortals in a continuous sequence of cause and effect. Imagine a mortal harvest of wheat in the fields of your own world. The peasants come out as one, and the land is worked tirelessly by the masses, in orderly fashion, and the wheat is cut and gathered and loaded onto carts. Imagine next, the first sign of inclement weather. If the harvesters do not finish reaping before the storm comes, they are told to stop and return home, for it is useless to work effectively in the rain while the stalks and chaffs of wheat grow heavy and laden with water and the ground turns to mud. The harvest labor has been halted—indeed, the remaining crops are about to be ruined—but an individual harvester, armed with a scythe, can continue working despite the bad weather, if willing. He or she will not get much done, but will manage to do *something*, nevertheless.

"Such is the situation now—Percy is my Harvester, and she may manually reap individual souls on my behalf. But such reaping is not effective, nor can it maintain the eternal order of things in the mortal world. The Dark Harvest itself must resume, a great mechanism of being. The Cobweb Bride is the rainstorm halting the Harvest, and she is a small cog caught in the gears of the machine, a cog that has jammed and now prevents the entire great mechanism from running."

Hades went silent and looked around him at all the mortals gathered in the Hall.

"It is now time for you to go—all of you."

"What? We can leave also?" Nathan and Amaryllis spoke in near unison. And the four girls, Catrine, Faeline, Regata and Sybil, exchanged glances of excited relief.

"Yes. You were made to wait here in my Hall because Death, my most limited aspect, was not aware of the whole truth. You have been marked and tainted by the waters of Lethe, but nothing prevents you from departing into the mortal world. You will however carry the taint with you—the taint of mortality and the premature yearning for oblivion."

"Good heavens, is that all?" Amaryllis gave a disdainful laugh. "I've been yearning for oblivion and relief from this tediousness of being stuck in the mortal coil for as long as I can recall, Lord Hades—indeed, much longer than a few days or weeks."

"Your propensity for ennui has indeed been stupendous," remarked Nathan, glancing at her. "As for me, I'll take a nice dish of braised beef long before I'd take oblivion."

"Take care, mortal maiden," said Hades very softly, "that you do not yet regret your indifference for life. . . ."

"She does tend to take many things for granted," Nathan

said. And then he added, "Now that it's all decided, when may we depart?"

Percy was about to speak, but Beltain neared her and she again felt his powerful armored frame standing behind her like a wall of safety. "While Death's Champion searches for the Cobweb Bride, what happens here?" he said. "And what of her, the goddess who is Persephone, the one whom we knew as the Sovereign? Her armies ravage our homeland even now, and the Realm falls before her. Is there any hope of stopping her?"

"That, I cannot tell you," Hades said gravely. "Your Realm may fall, and the entire world after it, before she finally comes to knock at my gates here. I can *feel* her even now, slowly approaching. Even *broken* as she is, I feel her, always. Even when my mind was not entirely my own, under the influence of Lethe's waters of oblivion, I felt her as an anonymous *entity* that compelled me to linger in this shadow Hall, at times confusing my yearning for *her* with a yearning for the Cobweb Bride. Now, Persephone is moving north. And she comes for *me*."

"What will she do, My Lord?" Percy whispered. "What does she want, really? Conquering the world seems like such an—*empty* thing."

"Conquering the world is nothing. The world is already hers—has always been. She is hurting, even if she does not know it. She may want simple destruction, or she may want *revenge* for all things she has had to suffer. . . ."

"What things? This is your *wife* and consort that we are speaking of, is it not? Have you been beating her, Lord Hades?" Amaryllis inquired archly. "Seriously, what odious manner of revenge might she want to extract from you? And for what?"

"You do not know of what you speak, O mortal maiden with a bitter tongue," said the God, "and I may not tell you."

"Oh, but Lord Hades, do feel free to enlighten us."

"Amaryllis. . . ." Nathan cleared his throat. "You really ought to desist at this point."

"Will *both* of you, Lordships and Ladyships, shut up

already?" said Catrine, the freckled urchin. "That is, ahem, beggin' pardon—but enough, please! Before the Lord Hades strikes us all down for your big an' fancy fool words! Me, I just wanna be outta here!"

The Lady and Lord of the Silver Court went immediately silent and stared with amazement at Catrine.

Percy took the opportunity to speak. "It is indeed time to go, My Lord," she said to Hades. "How shall we proceed out of this Hall?"

The Lord of the Underworld was again impassive, his beautiful face becoming a mask. He glanced at all of them, at the Hall of bones and sea of cobwebs high overhead, and then he walked up the dais back to his Throne of Ivory. He sat down, pitch-black and unreal upon the ivory, a study in impossible contrast.

Unlike his limited Death aspect, Hades sat upon the Pale Throne like a confident master. Where Lord Death reclined, lingered, Hades dominated the seat. Braced hands came to grasp the bone armrests, and his back was straight against the tall chair.

"Now," the black God said, "tell me where you would go, all of you. And I will send you there in your next blink. First, all the rest of you. Then, leaving for the last, my Champion. Speak now! But think well, before you decide upon your destination."

"Oh dear . . ." Amaryllis said, taking a few paces to stand at Nathan's side. She then looked up at him.

"Uhm . . . where to, my dear?" Nathan said, finding himself suddenly at a loss.

"I suppose we could go home to my Papa's northern estate in Morphaea, or to your family's lovely residence near the court in Duorma—"

"There is no Duorma," said the black knight. And then he quickly related the events of the city's disappearance, as had been described to him by the Duke of Plaimes. "The Kingdom of

Morphaea is in shambles," he concluded. "The Sovereign and her Trovadii army have passed through it on their way north, and the Silver Court is likely besieged."

"Where then shall we go?" Nathan's demeanor was for the first time truly grave and serious.

"To Silver Court, naturally," replied Amaryllis.

"But it is under siege, my dear. We will be in grave danger—"

"Perfect," replied the lady. "It is precisely where I would like to be."

Nathan signed. "It is surely madness, but then, we have always been the League of Folly, have we not, sweets? Well then. To Silver Court!"

"Close your eyes, mortals," Hades said, looking at them with his mesmerizing gaze.

Amaryllis took Nathan's hand, and then they both shut their eyes.

Hades snapped his fingers.

A small funnel of grey wind appeared out of nowhere, moving like a dust devil, and it spun wildly, growing larger. In seconds it arrived behind Hades and his throne, standing behind him like a wall of moving air. Overhead, the cobwebs billowed wildly, everywhere airborne dust arose from the floor . . . and the jet-black, softly curling hair on top of the God's head was now moving like undulating snakes. . . .

Percy had no time to blink more than twice, when Lady Amaryllis and Lord Nathan were simply *gone*.

"Who is next?" Hades said softly.

Regata and Sybil looked at one another, and they stepped forward, fearfully. "Home, Your Divine Lordship," they said. "That would be Letheburg."

"But Letheburg is under siege too! It's surrounded by a dead army," Percy reminded them.

"Yes, my accursed father's army," Beltain added. "Duke Hoarfrost and all the undead rabble of the Kingdom of Lethe have gathered outside its walls. Do you really want to go there?"

"Well, we have nowhere else to go," red-headed Sybil said. "And besides, Grial's there too, isn't she?"

"Oh, what the hell—Hades—I mean, *hell!* That, is, beggin' all pardons!" Catrine said, stepping forward to stand with the others. "Then I'll go to Letheburg too, since my sis Niosta is there with Grial an' all. Isn't that right, Percy?"

Percy nodded.

"So be it," Hades said, bathed in the unnatural wind, and his voice was that of a serpent. "Close your eyes, all three of you."

"Wait!" Faeline exclaimed, and then hurried to stand next to Catrine. "Me too, please, to Letheburg—since I got nowhere else to go, and Chidair Keep and the whole town is all full of dead soldiers, an' besides, I never seen the fancy town Palace there!"

Meanwhile Lord Beltain Chidair shook his head. "You have the whole world to go to, and you choose Letheburg?" he remarked, for the first time in minor amusement. "Why not southern France? Italy? The green isles of Great Britain? Arabia? Imperial China? Anywhere else but this sorry Kingdom of Lethe!"

But the girls were all standing together, some of them clutching hands, and their eyes were squeezed shut.

"Goodbye, Percy! We'll see you some time!" Catrine cried out at the last moment, and her voice was suddenly a fading echo, because Hades snapped his fingers, and all of the girls were *gone*.

Except for the gods, only Percy and Beltain remained in the Hall—and behind Beltain was his warhorse Jack, which the black knight held on a lead.

"And now, you, My Champion. And you, mortal man—take good care of her, or you will answer to me."

At which Lord Beltain Chidair looked directly into the eyes of Hades and said, "I will answer to none but myself, if anything were to happen to her. For I follow her unto the end of the world, and neither you nor all of Heaven could judge me more harshly than I would judge myself, were I to fail her. Fear not, Lord Hades, I will be with her always."

In reply, Hades smiled.

Percy felt a sudden pang of warmth at the black knight's words and the sound of his rich baritone timbre. The sweet warmth poured through her like honey, her breath quickened, the sound of her pulse beginning to race in the temples, and she now looked at the God of the Underworld, ready to proceed. And then she turned to glance at the disembodied death shadow of the Cobweb Bride.

"Yes, call to it," Hades said. "For now I will send you all to the place where the maiden Leonora hides from the world. Bring her back to me together with this pitiful death of hers so that I might unite them at last—but take care not to perform the deed yourself, for it must be done properly by me. You may travel through the twilight shadows from anywhere in the mortal world. Merely think of this Hall, and the twilight will return you to me."

Percy nodded. She reached out to Beltain who instinctively reached for her also, and her fingers were encased tightly in his large warm hand.

"Close your eyes now," said the Lord of the Underworld. At his side, Demeter stood now, right next to the Pale Throne, and her golden aura was permeating the wind and the bones. . . .

But Percy faltered. "Before I go to do your will, My Lord," she whispered, "if it is possible, I would know one thing. *Why* have the three of you drunk the water of Lethe? What have Persephone, Demeter, and Lord Hades wanted to forget so much that you took away your own memories of all things? Why are you in mourning?"

There was a pause. Even the funnel wind seemed to slow down its circular constant motion behind the throne. The gods regarded her.

"We wanted to forget one child," Hades replied after a heartbeat of silence. "Melinoë, our daughter."

And then Percy blinked, and the world went dark.

Chapter 2

Claere Liguon, the Infanta and Grand Princess of the Imperial Realm, stood before the tall arched window of the opulent chamber allocated to her on the upper floor of the Winter Palace of Lethe.

She was slim and fragile—a young girl of sixteen fixed into permanence by untimely death which rendered her into a doll of porcelain and spun glass. Her pale bloodless skin now bore a ghostly hint of a strange, grayish-green patina, and her great smoky eyes sunken in dark hollows imbued her face with ethereal pathos.

She was *dead* and yet she was animate. She was *undead*, for in this broken world there was no death to grant anyone the final oblivion. And thus the dead girl gazed with fixed, unblinking, apathetic eyes at the busy scene in the square below.

Outside was dreary winter . . . and war.

It was late afternoon, and the overcast sky was the color of thinned milk streaked with silver. Already the daylight was being leached from the panorama of snow-covered rooftops far beyond the boundary of the square, and gradually replaced with early bluish shadows.

It was the fifth day of the siege of Letheburg. Endless columns of weary soldiers and carts filled with artillery supplies populated Lethe Square. Infantry ranks of pikemen with torches instead of their usual pole arms, and musketeers in cobalt blue colors of Lethe lingered in formation while waiting for orders, before being told to march to the city walls in order to relieve those who have been fighting upon the lofty battlements for hours, holding back the attacks from below, as the endless army of dead men assaulted Letheburg.

They were thus defending the city for two days now, in shifts—two days straight, around the clock, for unlike the living soldiers, the dead took no breaks and needed no sleep.

The first attack started in complete darkness, with the moon hidden behind a deep overcast, a few hours after midnight of the third day of the siege—just like that, with no warning, and no meaningful reason to explain the timing. The city soldiers patrolling up on the battlements—who had spent the last two nights in a heightened state of alert and had grown somewhat slack and weary of waiting—had the surprise and then shock thrust upon them.

Dark silent shapes started to pour over the parapet walls and immediately there was chaos. Torches and beacons flared into life, fire of every sort was brought out, and a fierce senseless melee commenced, during which the defenders barely managed to beat off the first wave, when the next began. . . .

The city garrison soldiers burned the dead or hacked off their limbs—the only two means of halting their relentless approach. They rained fire and dropped burning bales of straw, poured boiling oil, which they then lit with arrows, and managed somehow to maintain their line of defense.

Yet for how long?

The city resources were limited, and their incendiary resources even more so, because the arsenals were stocked with supplies intended to be used against normal living enemy soldiers—men who could be killed in regular combat and did not require so much flammable material as did these *things* of winter-frozen flesh and bone. . . .

By the second day of this, the King of Lethe, Roland Osenni, was in despair. He hand sent carrier birds with messages to the Emperor of the Realm and to anyone he could think of, requesting assistance. And so far, no one had responded.

And now, Claere, the Emperor's dead daughter, stood witness to yet another closing day of bitter relentless drudgery for these poor soldiers—for war was drudgery of the worst sort, and this war was even more dire. "Normal" war was the kind where one went through the motions and turned off the human portion of the self so that one could cut up, pierce, dismember, shoot, or otherwise *end* other living beings, sometimes with the ease of accident, and if one was lucky enough, then from a distance, without "getting one's hands dirty." *This* war involved methodical precise butchery, a series of intimate and up-close actions that had to be taken—a precise removal of limbs, one after another, or a thorough immolation in flames—in short, a complete eradication of the enemy to the point that the enemy no longer had a recognizable, much less human form.

This was physically intensive, brutal work. The soldiers of Letheburg were not only tired of fighting, they were tired of the unspeakable acts they had to perform simply to stop each undead enemy from repeatedly coming at them. They had put away, for the most part, their normal weapons—arquebuses and muskets, bludgeoning maces, pikes and other pole arms—and instead wielded bladed weapons for cutting and oil-soaked torches. And this was only the end of their *second* day.

Claere watched from the window with her stilled glassy eyes, and she could see the dejected movements of the tiny figures far below in the square, the imperfect formations, the filthy rattling carts that were getting refilled for the hundredth time at the city arsenals and had been driven back and forth through the freezing and melting slush of the city roads to the walls and back.

It was impossible to feel anything but slow malingering despair.

And yet, because she was a thing of stillness herself, a sad, quiet, dead thing, Claere was almost fascinated by the fact that the world still went on around her, and all this was happening, this slow massive engine of war. . . .

War against her own kind.

What makes me any different from those other dead? The ones who stand outside the walls and climb it like ants, relentlessly, united by a single purpose? They come and do not care that they burn or they become stumps without limbs. They just keep coming.

And she thought yet again, for what immeasurable time, *What then is my own purpose? Why am I still here? Is it to stand thus, looking through the window, like an effigy? Why am I here?*

A knock sounded at the outside door of her chamber. It was soft but somehow determined, familiar, and Claere thought she knew exactly who it was, who it would always be.

"Come in," she said, forcibly drawing a breath into her stopped lungs, reviving them momentarily for speech, and it sounded like a wound clockwork mechanism of subtle gears.

He opened the door and came into the room. She heard his footsteps, knowing them without having to turn around. If she had a heartbeat, it would have been racing by now, restarted in the same manner as she activated her lungs. But her heart was stilled—stilled by his hand, oh-so many days ago now—and there was nothing that could make it quicken ever again, not even the agitated fluttering of living *thought* in the flesh prison of her mind.

Her thoughts—they were the last and only things alive.

He stood behind her, not quite near her, yet close enough that she could sense him somehow, maybe his breathing, maybe the sound of his own living, pounding heart.

For there it was, yes; she could almost hear its constant rhythm.

"I thought you might want some company," he said. His voice was soft, but cold somehow, or possibly very much under control.

It was always the same words. For some reason he never knew what else to say, in those initial moments when he entered her room. And he came so often now, it seemed. . . . Indeed, he spent most of the dreary siege days in this room of hers, and frequently a portion of the night or dawn hours—for he slept very little, and she, being dead, slept not at all.

"It is good to see you, Marquis Fiomarre," said Claere, without looking around to actually see him, but "seeing" him nevertheless with every fiber of her stilled, lifeless, cotton-thick, insensate being.

He was silent.

Long moments passed, the late afternoon outside turned blue, and it was she, the dead one who had to move first, to turn around slowly, with a creak of her delicate limbs, and be faced at last with his presence.

He was dark, fiercely handsome in the swarthy way of the olive-skinned southerner, with wavy raven hair, black eyes and black brows, a chiseled nose and a pleasing jaw line. There was some residual bruising along the planes of his face from the heavy beating and punishment he had sustained in the Imperial prison many days ago now, immediately after he had struck that dagger through her heart—just as death had stopped, which kept her in the world of the living.

He was her murderer. And now, in a strangest twist of fate, he was also her loyal companion.

"What news?" she said. Not because she really cared, but because she wanted to hear his voice, more of his cold-yet-intimate voice, in the hollow silence of the darkened chamber.

Soon, there would be no more daylight, and the royal servants would come in to light the fireplace and offer her candlelight, which she often refused. But with his presence here, she might allow it . . . a single candle.

"Nothing new, I am afraid," he replied. "The shift has changed again, and the soldiers from the walls go to collapse and sleep, while the evening shift takes their place."

"How many casualties?"

He sighed. "No one is counting."

"What—what do they do?" she said softly. "What do they *do* once they die? Do they change sides immediately and fight their own regimental brothers? Or do they continue to fight for the city?"

The Marquis Vlau Fiomarre was looking at her with his very dark, very liquid eyes. "I believe it is different with every man. Some turn and become the enemy. Many others do not. I've heard that quite a few Letheburg soldiers, who are slain, bravely stay on the walls to fight. Being dead, they are very useful, for they can stand up on the battlements with no fear of arrows or musket balls striking them, and they can shoot flaming arrows with less haste and hence better aim. Others yet, once dead, retreat from the fighting altogether, and return to the city to their families. Some merely sit in the snow. . . ."

"I am glad," she said, "that they retain humanity—those that do."

"Yes," he replied, never taking his gaze off her.

Another lengthy pause. The servants arrived as expected, and the fireplace was soon turned into a reddish-gold source of warmth. Before they exited, a candelabra was lit in the corner.

"What of the King?" Vlau Fiomarre asked. "Has he been to visit you today?"

"No, only you." Her answer came in a soft measured creak of her lungs.

And suddenly Fiomarre's face turned a shade of red that appeared to be a kind of darkness against his olive skin.

"I—" he said woodenly, as though he were the one dead, "thought you might want some company. . . ."

Claere's face was blank. But her thoughts, oh, her thoughts

fluttered and beat against the dense walls of her body's prison. She could almost feel it then, a living response that she once knew how to make with the muscles of her face . . . a smile. It hovered at the corners of her fixed pale lips. "Yes, I know," she replied. "And I appreciate it."

In another part of Letheburg, on a small cobblestone-paved street called Rollins Way, snuggled between other houses with overhangs, was a little brown building with a shingle up on top. The words *"Grial's Health & Fortune Chest"* were painted on the shingle in large red and black letters, and it swung somewhat crookedly above a friendly storefront window with lacy chintz curtains.

The first hues of twilight started to fill the streets with deeper shadows when the freshly painted red wooden door of the house opened, and out came Grial herself. She was a middle aged but youthful woman, with an extraordinary frizzy head of dark hair that was at present covered up with a large winter hat with a wide brim and scarf flaps wrapped under her chin. Her shapely and buxom figure—usually clad in a stained patchwork housedress with a dingy apron over it—was hidden by a coat. Her face, with its very dark eyes, was handsome, and its expression energetic.

"Well, who would've guessed? Looks like another chilly evening before a chilly night!" Grial said in a sonorous voice that rang brightly and echoed along the street.

Behind her, three girls came out of the house one by one, all dressed for winter in coats, hats or shawls, and mittens. They were all holding large loaded baskets and unlit torches.

"Wait here, dumplings, while I'll come around with Betsy." Grial locked the red door behind them and headed around the corner into the tiny alley and to the back.

Lizabette, Marie, and Niosta nodded, and stood waiting, stomping their feet against the sludge-stained and slippery cobblestones.

"Say, 'Bette, you got a red nose already!" Niosta said teasingly, looking at the somewhat sharp-nosed older girl dressed in a reasonably nice coat with buttons and a stylish hat. Niosta herself was a permanently grimy-looking skinny urchin with a streetwise expression and freckles spotting her nose and cheeks, wearing a ragged hand-me-down coat and a relatively new borrowed shawl from Grial.

"Don't call me 'Bette, rude child," responded Lizabette with minor irritation that was mostly for show and dignity. And then she involuntarily brought her gloved hand up to her face and drew it against her nose, while the white vapor from her breath curled around the glove fabric. "Br-r-r, it is rather chilly already," she observed. "I dread to think how nasty it will be when it gets dark. Especially out there near the walls where the wind really blows."

Next to her, the third girl, Marie, olive-skinned with very black doe-eyes, was small, dark and mousy, dressed in a much-darned old coat, and at present shivering already from the bitter freezing air. "Very cold, yes," Marie responded, speaking with an awkward accent—for she was originally from the Kingdom of Serenoa, a foreigner from the Domain.

Moments later, Betsy, a large creamy-pale draft horse, emerged from the alley, pulling behind it the familiar cart, with Grial in the driver's seat.

"Whoa, Betsy!" Grial said cheerfully, then stopped the cart in front of her house. "All right, ladies, pile in! Be sure to set the baskets down carefully. We don't want anything falling out and landing on those icy cobblestones."

The girls started to bustle and loaded the cart, then climbed in from the back.

"Is everyone ready? Let's get moving then!" Grial struck a flint and then lit two of the torches, placing one at each corner of the cart in the front near the driver's area, to illuminate their way in the darkening city. The torches sprang to life, golden-orange beacons that colored their faces with honey warmth and immediately dispelled the blue and indigo shadows.

And then Grial loosened the reins and Betsy moved forward in a steady and confident walk, on their way to the city walls.

The torches flickered merrily on both sides as they moved through the shadowy streets, and it was a time when city lanterns started to bloom also, as the lamp keepers climbed up to check the oil and trim the wicks then add the flames with long matches.

"Look there!" Marie marveled often. "Oh, how pretty! Such round glass shades around those lanterns! And that one is long and square and all frosty!"

"I like that one!" Niosta chortled and pointed to a corner lamppost of a wider street that had a large black hat stuck on top of the glass and metal frame.

"Some poor fellow will be missing his head gear tonight," Grial said, guiding Betsy past the hatted streetlight. "On the other hand, tonight this lantern is going to be the warmest one in all of Letheburg! Just imagine how envious those other lanterns all around it will be, probably going all silly gossiping about it too—"

Marie giggled and rubbed her nose, and even Lizabette had a smile on her face.

"Say, will we be goin' all around the walls again, Grial?" Niosta said.

"Of course!" said the older woman. "How else will the good soldiering gentlemen up on the battlements get their cinnamon apple pies?"

They turned onto a yet larger street, and suddenly there were clanging noises of metal and voices, as several columns of soldiers jogged by.

"It's so nice and pretty, with the evening lanterns here, that I'd almost forgotten there's a war going on," Lizabette said sadly, as they sat waiting before the street crossing while the columns of soldiers passed.

"Yes," Grial responded, and in the orange light of the two

torches her eyes appeared pitch-dark. "It is always easy to forget the things that are so very wrong that they shouldn't even be happening in the first place. Just stop and look at the lights and the sparkling snow on the roofs and all those stars overhead, and goodness, it's like the bad things don't even exist, if only for just a moment. It's rather nice, I say, to stop now and then and just take in a peaceful moment or two. . . .."

Soon the soldiers had moved on and they could continue also, turning onto the big boulevard and approaching the city walls.

As they drew near, a new sound became audible, a dull roar, constant like the surf, and punctuated by crackle of flames—great bonfire-loud ones—the clash of metal against metal, and harsh male shouts of effort and pain.

It came from the battlements of Letheburg, under relentless attack.

As Betsy pulled the cart closer to the edge of the city structures where began the pomoerium, that last wide vacant space between streets and the outer walls, the girls froze with grim fearful expressions, all beauty of city lights and glowing lanterns forgotten.

"All right, dearies, make ready," Grial said, driving them into the pomoerium that ran like an inner moat all around the city on the inside perimeter of the walls. It was at present filled with soldiers of all ranks and formations, a mess of running men and carts, of sergeants-at-arms yelling orders, and constantly moving traffic in every direction, including vertically, as supplies and men went up narrow stairways and ledges up to the top, and came down, carrying the wounded. . . .

At least, with the world being what it was, they did not have to carry their dead brothers, for the latter walked on their own, some away from the fighting, others assisting the living. No, not all the dead had abandoned the cause of Letheburg.

And right overhead, as the girls stared, there were the city walls, massive and unbreachable. The battlements with their crenelated tops of parapets were silhouetted in black against an infernal ruddy aura of what was a conflagration burning outside, just beyond the walls. It painted the sky angry red against the coming night.

The conflagration, set on purpose by the defenders of the city, was their main defense against the attacking enemy.

Grial drove the cart slowly parallel to the walls, and the girls stared in silent horror at the wounded and the dejected and the utterly exhausted soldiers. But—there was no time to think or contemplate. They were here to do work.

Grial stopped Betsy and the girls hopped out and started unloading the baskets and unpacking the cloths covering them. Inside, the baskets were filled with breadstuffs and pastries, freshly baked—all day by the girls themselves, together with Grial. Lizabette, followed by Marie and Niosta, moved out, approaching each paused or seated man who looked like he needed it, and handed out the food.

The soldiers, covered in soot, tar pitch, smoke, and blood, looked up gratefully and took the apple pies and tarts and pastries and ate them up in hungry instants, wiping the crumbs from their chins and beards. They muttered their thanks, and gave brief smiles, and often waved at Grial who remained seated up in the driver seat of the cart. She in turn waved and grinned, and called out names of individual soldiers—for remarkably she seemed to know everybody.

A few moments later, they got back in the cart, their baskets much lighter than they had been, then Grial drove Betsy onward, for another length of wall, until they came upon more clumps of wearied or wounded. And again they stopped, got out, fed as many people as they could.

They weren't the only women or civilians doing this. The girls noted many others, also armed with carts or large bags and some pulling or driving wheeled kegs and rolling barrels of ale and beer, or dragging big-bellied kettles of hot tea set on top of wheelbarrows. Yet others came with linens and medical supplies to help clean up and bind the wounds of the hurt soldiers.

Every stop they made, it was a marvel that they never seemed to run out of apple pies. "It's got to be Grial's special magic!" whispered Lizabette to the others with a knowing look, as she opened her basket yet again to find a few more pies and tarts on the very bottom—even though she had been certain she had already given out the last one to that lamed soldier with the scowling jaw who merely grunted his thanks as he chewed the apple pie.

The evening meanwhile grew darker, until it was full night. The sky turned black, and the tops of the battlements appeared to be silhouetted against hellfire.

At some point they came to a spot in the wall that had *disappeared* entirely, and here there was a desperate barricade erected, and a very fierce battle going on in ditches just before and beyond the barricades. A cannon was positioned with its great muzzle pointing outward, and it was loaded periodically and made to fire great blazing balls covered in pitch and set aflame. A wave of the enemy dead was pouring in at the barricades, pushing at them, and yet somehow the defenders held their spots, raining fire and brandishing great torches on the ends of poles that once were pikes.

"Grial! Get back, sweetheart, it's too deadly hot here!" someone shouted, and the girls and Grial saw an officer commander look at her—his face badly cut up, grotesque in the infernal light—and gesticulate wildly for them to move off.

But Grial smiled a wide grin and waved. And then she looked at him with her very dark gaze, and next, stared intently at the breach in the walls. Where she looked, it seemed the shadows undulated thicker, and beyond them, the enemy dead roiled, and yet somehow did not make the effort to approach.

Grial looked away then, her face illuminated with the two torches burning on both sides of the cart, and then with the same grin of encouragement she snapped the reins lightly and they again moved on, past the breach and the barricade, and onto the relative safety of the once-again-solid walls. . . .

Another quarter of an hour later, they had driven up to a large angular bulwark section of the walls, with a stairway leading up to the battlements, and here there were three of the very large city cannon positioned permanently, aimed in three directions at the outside. The cannon were firing every few minutes, like clockwork, as the artillery soldiers manning them worked madly to keep up. Smoke and tar pitch was everywhere, and the stink of gunpowder and sulfur was so overwhelming that everyone started to sneeze.

"Is it time for the good luck charm?" Marie cried in order to be heard above the thunderous din.

"It sure is!" Grial cried back.

"Oh, goody!" Niosta chortled.

They stopped the cart near the wall, and this time Grial tied up the reins and told Betsy to stand there like the excellent girl that she was, and she herself got out of the cart also.

The girls, having done this the previous night, knew exactly what was coming.

"Two torches, girlies! Each one of you take two, and follow me!"

They did as told, and everyone, armed with yet unlit torches, carefully stepped through the snowy slush and walked up the very narrow stone stair that ran parallel to the wall and ascended very slowly upward, holding on to the walls for good measure. For indeed, there were no outer walls to contain the stair hewn directly alongside the main wall rock, and one wrong step could cause them to fall a hundred feet. Lizabette, walking up ahead, appeared to be particularly stiff and pale, for she apparently did not tolerate heights too well.

When at last they had climbed the parapet to the very top of the battlements, they ended up in the one of the few secure spots where the enemy fire from the outside could not reach, and only the friendly city cannon spat out their fireballs through narrow special embrasures. Several artillerymen nodded and smiled at Grial and the girls with infinite weariness, then turned away and got back to their labor.

Grial meanwhile, took several paces and stopped in a small clearing well away from the soldiers, so as not to be in their way. Here was the very middle of the great bulwark.

"All right, everyone, gather 'round!" she said, and then struck a flint and lit both of her torches. Next, she extended both torches to each side and lit the torch in the hand of Lizabette on one side and Niosta on the other. The girls, used each of their lit torches to light the other, and finally both in turn extended their hands to light up Marie's torches.

"Well done!" Grial cried out with a smile. She held her torches up, and her face was lit up ruddy and orange on both sides.

"Now, make a triangle, ladies!" she said. "Remember, exactly as we did last night!"

The girls nodded with enthusiasm, every one's expression serious and intent.

"Lizabette, you stand here to my right and face out in the same direction as that big cannon muzzle."

Lizabette nodded and stood so precisely that she was straining.

"Niosta, you get on my left side, dumpling, and you be sure to look out the same way as that other big old cannon that's facing thataway."

"Yes, Ma'am!" Niosta said with a grin and did as told.

"And Marie, you stand right here in the middle, close to the wall, sweetie! Don't be afraid, nothing will fly over it in this exact spot, nothing, I promise you! Now turn and look directly out!"

Marie, the most timid of them all at this point, took a deep breath and did as she was told.

Grial gave them a moment to gather their breath. She was smiling lightly, watching them.

"Now, raise your torches everyone! And repeat after me, three times: *Earth, sea, and sky! Guard and keep us safe!*"

The words were spoken, loudly and enthusiastically. Niosta brandished her torches and even jumped up and down a few times for emphasis. Lizabette stood, fixed motionless, and straight as a board as she spoke each word precisely so. Marie swayed slightly with fear but spoke all of her words nevertheless.

"Oh, well done!" Grial exclaimed again, and then raised her own torches high, brandishing them, her brimmed hat flopping slightly in the wind. And then, curiously, she did something new that was not done the night before—she turned to each of the girls and named them thusly:

"Earth!" she spoke to Lizabette. "Sea!" she called Marie. "Sky!" she named Niosta.

And indeed, each of the girls realized that they had been in fact swaying like the sea, fixed like the earth, or buoyant like the heavenly air.

"Oh!" Niosta said in wonder. "How did you do that?"

"How did I do what, pumpkin?" Grial was grinning at her, and the torchlight danced in her liquid black pupils. "Why, it is all your own doing, you know! I'm just standing here watching all three of you do it yourselves!"

And Marie smiled back, and for the first time forgot to tremble. "Will the magic now keep Letheburg safe, Grial?"

"One should certainly hope so, at least for the rest of this night!" said the older woman. And then she lowered her hands and stuck the torches into the piled up snow, extinguishing them on the stones underfoot. The girls followed suit.

"And on that note," Grial said, "who's up for some apple pie?"

"Me! Me!" Niosta and Marie replied.

Lizabette's brows went up archly. "I thought there weren't

any more pies left!"

Grial snorted. "I certainly beg to differ! Let's go down and look in those baskets!"

They got back to Rollins Way by the time the moon was high up in the partially overcast sky, and everyone was more than ready for bed.

As Betsy and the cart pulled up to the corner near the little alley and the house, Niosta was still wiping her mouth and her pie-stained sticky hands against her dingy coat, and smacking her lips. "Oh, that was darn good! Best apple pie ever!"

She was so busy picking her teeth with a wood splinter that she never looked to see who was waiting for them at the door of Grial's house.

One of the two small shadows leaning near the doorway separated from the wall. And then, "Sis!" cried Catrine. "Jupiter's balls an' entrails! You're alive, Niosta! An' so am I!"

It was indeed Catrine, and next to her, somewhat shyly silent, Faeline.

"Grial!" Catrine exclaimed next, while her sister whooped and came hurtling down the cart to hug her.

"Oh, goodness!" Grial said, halting Betsy and grabbing on to her brimmed hat with one hand in a slap of surprise. "Is that another of my favorite Cobweb Brides? So glad to see you, girlie! And I see you've brought a friend!"

"I'm Faeline, Ma'am," said the blond girl bashfully, stepping away from the wall, and wiping the back of her nose with a mitten. "I'm from Chidair Keep and town. We've escaped the dungeons, and floated on the magic river with lords and ladies, and then got to see Death Himself!"

"Well, gracious be!" Grial smiled, giving her an intent look-over. Meanwhile Lizabette and Marie waved and everyone exchanged greetings and jumbled chatter.

Catrine told them the whole story in a breathless torrent.

Grial listened thoughtfully at the same time as she guided Betsy into the pitch-black alley around the corner and the back yard, with only the two torches on the cart to light the way, and the girls walked alongside in excitement, everyone having forgotten sleep.

Betsy was unhitched, rubbed down and placed in her warm stall, and still Catrine was talking, occasionally interrupted by Niosta and the others.

At last they made it indoors, and were in the cheerful front parlor of Grial's house, seated on the sofa and the chairs.

". . . An' so, there was this nasty-creepy disappearin' water from the River Lethe that makes you forget stuff worse'n a drunken sailor with a bashed-in head, an' turns out everyone's drank it, even some damn fool Gods!" Catrine was saying. "And then the blasted fools drank it again, or should I say the Ladyship who *thought* she was the Cobweb Bride drank it again, and suddenly, smack as anything, there she was! She remembered she was this big ol' golden Goddess, by the name of Dimmeeter! An' then *she* told stink-for-brains Death to drink, an' *he* did—good thing too, since all he remembered was no better than a steamin' bowl of poo—and so he went all black as soot and became this big ol' God of the Underworld, none other than Hades himself! And then, and then—oh, oh! And *then* there was all this stuff about another rotted Goddess by the name of Persephone, who's none other 'an the blasted Sovereign of the Domain! And then, Percy Ayren was there too, *and* the Black Knight, who, it turns out, is not all that bad, an' not too bad lookin' if you know what I mean—"

Niosta and Lizabette and Marie all exclaimed variously at the mentions of the latter.

"—and finally, Hades told us he'll take us anywhere we wanted, so Sybil an' Regata an' Faeline an' me all decided, what the hell, to come here to Letheburg! So we tell the ol' goat where we wanna go, close our eyes, an' next thing we know, we're on a street in Letheburg! Sybil an' Regata took off home to see their folks, and me an' Faeline, we just came here! An' so, here we are! Been waitin' for you for hours! Can't feel my arse from the cold!"

Catrine stopped talking, took a big breath and let it out. She then folded her arms in satisfaction and looked around her with barely contained pride and excitement. Everyone was looking in rapt amazement, while Faeline, who already knew the events, just picked her grimy nails.

Grial had been listening to the tale with interest as she bustled around the parlor adjusting furniture and closing shutters for the night. And now as soon as Catrine was done, she came to a stop in the middle of the room. There was something very unusual in Grial's very dark eyes, and in her intense expression—more unusual even than her normal eccentric mannerisms.

Grial looked at Catrine, then gazed around the room, and exhaled what felt like a long-held breath.

"At last . . ." she said softly, and her face was transfigured.

The seated girls looked up at her.

"At last . . ." Grial repeated, this time in a louder voice. "It is done. At last my lips are *unsealed*."

"What do you mean, Grial?" Lizabette stared at the older woman, for some reason straining to *see* her, to see her strangely set-in-motion visage and her chameleon face with its familiar frizzy mane of unkempt hair. . . . Indeed, for a moment there, did it only seem so, but was it *moving* like snakes?

But Grial was not to be properly seen, not any longer—for now she was *changing* before their eyes.

The cheerful room around them, lit by a few candles, was suddenly thrown into deep shadow. And the nature of the light dimmed a few degrees from golden candle glow to cool silvery moonlight. There could be no moon indoors naturally, and indeed the window shutters have just been closed . . . and yet it felt as if the moon *was* here—*she* rode the sky and somehow shone through the roof and ceiling of the little house, and filled the parlor with her cool radiance. . . .

As this uncanny sense filled them all, Grial appeared to stand taller and straighter. And her patchwork dress with its filthy apron began to dissolve around her, to be replaced by a fine noble cloth of flowing darkness, a classic long chiton that came down in folds around the statuesque woman, to lie at her sandaled feet. Grial's hair was now a perfect ordered crown of curls, symmetrical and severe. And her face was abysmally beautiful.

The strangest thing was, she was still Grial, with her same ancient-young, very black, very wise eyes. The same intimate expression filled them, as she gifted each of the girls with her profound gaze.

And yet she was now someone else.

"Oh . . . *Grial!*" whispered Lizabette.

"You know me as Grial, and it is my mortal aspect," said the familiar stranger. "I have taken the greatest Oath upon the sacred waters of the River Styx, to keep my silence and be diminished and live in the mortal world among you—until the reasons for the Oath are no longer. It has come to pass and it is done now, and my lips are unsealed at last, so that I may speak freely and resume my true aspect."

"What—who are you?" Niosta muttered, while Marie's eyes opened wide and she started to tremble.

"My beloved children, you may now know me as I truly am," said the goddess. "I am immortal, and I preside over Crossroads and Choices and Doorways and all the things that linger Between. I am Hecate."

Chapter 3

As Percy opened her eyes, she felt a powerful cold breeze and the contrast of sudden unseasonable brightness of the dawning sun on her cheeks. She held Beltain's hand, as though he were her last anchor in the world, and he in turn squeezed her fingers tight, fighting a moment of vertigo. And she heard Jack's startled neigh, as the great black warhorse was pulled along with them into whatever supernatural vortex that had brought them here.

They found themselves in a strange place. Neither of them had ever seen the sea up close, but they recognized this was a beach. A vast expanse of vibrant blue-green water lay before them on one side, stretching to the haze-filled horizon where it paled into mauve silver, and on the other, a strip of darkened wet sand upon which they now stood, defined the boundary between water and land. Beyond the strip of sand was more sand, piled up in dunes, and they formed a general incline rising inland, dry and crumbling, and the powder that comprised them was of a bleached cream hue.

Wherever this was, Death—who was Hades—had brought them here for a reason.

Somewhere in the vicinity was the Lady Leonora D'Arvu, the Cobweb Bride.

And her death shadow hovered above the sand right next to

Percy and Beltain, obediently having followed them also.

"Where are we?" Percy said, hearing her voice sound faint and small and blown about by the crisp salty wind from the sea. Her woolen shawl ballooned with the wind and filaments of her hair were swept wildly up in the air, so that she had to hold the shawl down with one hand under her chin.

"Are you all right?" Beltain examined her intently with his clear slate-blue eyes. He still held her hand, gently moving his fingertips against her palm in a calming manner he might use with a wild creature, and the warmth at the point of contact between them served to give her an immediate focus.

Percy blinked, narrowing her eyes at the rising sun that floated on the eastern horizon directly over the strip of wet sand, so that it appeared to rise halfway between land and sea. "Yes . . ." she said in a dreaming voice. "And you?"

"Everything seems to be intact," he replied, with a touch of relieved amusement, letting go of her hand to tuck away his brown wisps of wavy hair at his forehead and adjust the tight coif hood that was part of his chain mail hauberk over his head. And then he glanced behind him to observe that Jack was equally unharmed.

The wind was very strong here—coming in sharp gusts then relenting, then sweeping them again, full body, so that they were bathed in sea air, inhaling spray and the scent of seaweed and salt.

"This far south, at the edge of the great sea. . . . What a wonder this is!" Beltain inhaled deeply and stared at the boundless panorama of water. "I believe we must be in the Domain once again, very likely the Kingdom of Tanathe. It alone touches the sea. Or maybe not—Solemnis too might share some of the southern shoreline. In any case, we are very far away from home."

Percy took in a deep breath of sea air also, feeling it sting her lungs, and looked out into the distant horizon. "I no longer know where home is," she said. "I don't think it's Oarclaven."

And then she turned back to look at the black knight, her earnest gaze meeting his.

He gazed back at her, intense and serious, and completely open to her. She noticed how, most recently, his eyes seemed to turn darker-colored than normal when he looked at her, the pupils expanded and deep, overtaking the surrounding slate-blue irises. With such deep dark eyes he looked, rarely blinking, and so very *intimate*.

Percy realized that it was for *her* alone that his eyes became thus, different, deep, vulnerable. And the awareness of it brought a peculiar heat to her cheeks.

"It does not matter where home is now," he said. "Since the land itself is uncertain, and places can fade away and disappear at any moment."

"Oh!" she said. "Yes, I did not even consider—for a moment I'd forgotten. Oarclaven may no longer even be there! And what of my parents and sisters? Where would they be? But—you're right, it doesn't really matter, not any of it, not now. First, I must finish this task given to me."

And Percy turned to glance at the death shadow, and she spoke to it. "Go," she said, both with words and with thoughts. "Go find her who is yours alone. . . . Go!"

And the death shadow billowed then started to drift softly along the strip of wet sand in the direction of the sun and then turned inland.

Percy and Beltain followed, choosing to walk on foot for the moment, their winter-shod feet sinking in the sand as it became dry and lost its resistance. The black knight led his warhorse behind him.

They emerged about a quarter of an hour later past the sandy beach and found a path leading up a chalk-white line of low cliffs punctuated with ravines, onto more fertile land, and then gentle rolling hills. The earth here was an even mix of red clay and rich black soil, and the pale cream sands gave way to grassland. Tough heather and weeds grew in abundance, shrubs covered with leaves—a thing unheard of in Lethe during winter—and there were strange obelisk-like shrubs that were neither tree nor bush, but something that Beltain called "cypress" for he had read of it in books that his mother had given him to study, so many years ago.

Percy watched him talking, and thought with new admiration how this man who was known to all as a warrior was also someone who did not eschew learning, and actually read and studied. Not many other such military men were inclined to read a bit of parchment much less entire volumes—as he described his mother's library. Indeed, Percy would have very much liked to meet this woman who had borne and raised such a son as Beltain, and regretted with a strange pang of sorrow that she never would, since the Duchess Chidair was long since deceased.

After another half hour of walking, they encountered a small roadway, and here Beltain lifted Percy up onto the saddle and mounted after her, wrapping his arms closely around her with pleasing protectiveness, and letting Jack take them forward the rest of the way.

The death shadow of the Cobweb Bride moved before them steadily, and Percy often reached out to it with her *death* sense and tested its bearing, and kept it on a reasonable path in the general direction where it *wanted* to go—such as this road.

When the sun rode the clear cornflower-blue sky close to noon, the road meandered northeast and finally started to climb up another gentle hill.

On the topside of the hill began a plateau, filled with verdant trees and fruit orchards. And in the middle of the plateau rose a prominent castle of white stone surrounded by a town settlement. Bright white square houses with roofs of the same chalk as the cliffs filled the vista on both sides, and greenery was everywhere.

At the same time the road finally had traffic. A few peasants dressed in light shirts and jackets moved along in carts pulled by donkeys and occasional draft horses, some covered with wide-brimmed hats, and the women in colorful kerchiefs.

The sight of the black knight in his imposing suit of armor, and his giant warhorse caused quite a few stares. Indeed, pitying eyes followed Percy who was seated up in the saddle before him, seemingly locked in the circle of his metal-clad arms. Likely they thought she was his victim and prisoner. . . .

"What town is this? And what castle?" the black knight inquired of one pedestrian.

The peasant raised his head hidden by a wide straw hat, and his wrinkle-surrounded eyes widened with alarm at being addressed.

"I mean you no harm," Beltain said, wondering for a moment if maybe his language was unrecognized. "Tell me, good fellow, where are we?"

"San Quellenne, Mi-Lord," the peasant replied in a heavy foreign dialect.

"Ah . . . so we're in Tanathe?"

"Yes, Mi-Lord." This was obviously a man of few words.

Beltain then pointed at the castle. "And what is this?"

"San Quellenne, Mi-Lord, San Quellenne *Castille*."

"My thanks." Beltain nodded, seeing that not much more could be gotten from this conversation, and the peasant raised his hat, and was again on his way.

Percy meanwhile observed that the death shadow moved steadily in the direction of the white-roofed town and castle. "I believe," she said to Beltain, "that the Cobweb Bride is in there."

He nodded, and they continued on the road, past growing traffic.

It was interesting to note that there was no sense of war here, no soldiers marching, no urgency; nothing to indicate that this part of the Domain was engaged in military conflict. Indeed, it felt the opposite—such overwhelming serenity, a gentle peace and lack of tension. If anything, the black knight on horseback was likely the most threatening thing these people had seen for days.

And as for the local dead, Percy could *feel* a few of them in the vicinity, but nothing out of the ordinary. Apparently the peasants of Tanathe had resigned themselves to the situation as best they could, at least for the moment. Occasional dead old men and women sat on the side of the road and were calmly ignored by everyone. Percy even saw one practical pedestrian leading an overladen *dead* donkey bearing a heavy load of baskets, its poor quadruped death shadow plodding just a few steps behind.

They reached the edge of town in a few minutes, and soon enough moved past whitewashed houses and cheerfully strung laundry lines flapping with bed linen and coarse shirts and pants, past back yards overflowing with green trees and climbing vines.

Percy was starting to grow very hot, bundled as she was in her winter coat and shawl, which she slipped from her head to her shoulders and over her coat, letting her head with its plainly gathered braided hair breathe in the pleasant mid-noon air. And as for Beltain, his dark armor attracted the sun—even if it was the merciful sun of winter—and she could see streaks of sweat sheening his forehead and rolling down his cheeks. She had long since removed her mittens, and he his heavy gauntlets, and both longed to divest themselves of the rest of their unsuitable attire.

"I would think the Count D'Arvu and his family would either acquire a house in a better part of town, or maybe find themselves a place in the castle," the black knight reasoned.

"There!" Percy pointed down a small side street from the main road, leading into a large affluent courtyard covered in forest green ivy and a house that had three stories and appeared finer than many of its neighbors.

Because the death shadow of the Cobweb Bride was now *pulling* at her, pulling strongly in this direction, Percy was certain. . . .

Beltain said nothing, merely guided Jack into the smaller street. Soon they stopped before an archway of closed double gates of wrought iron, beyond which could be seen a long approach-way with a gallery of cypress on both sides, and then a fine façade of a building in the distance, framed with tall trees.

Beltain picked up a small metal mallet and struck the brass bell that swung from the top of the gates.

The sound of the bell chime had a high soprano cadence, beautiful and echoing into the distance. They waited for several moments then Beltain struck the bell again.

At last, a man appeared far among the greenery, walking hurriedly to the gates along the approach-way. He was dressed simply and wore a straw hat similar to many of the peasants they had seen on the road and in town. Up close he was revealed to be an older man with a dark weather beaten face and a grey beard.

"Is this the residence of Count Lecrant D'Arvu?" inquired the black knight.

The man stopped on the other side of the gates, squinting his eyes and peering at them through the grillwork, and did not reply immediately.

"No such here," he said curtly after a long pause, his face retaining a blank expression, and turned to go.

"Wait!" Beltain said. "I am a friend of the Count. Please inform him that Lord Beltain Chidair of Lethe together with Percy Ayren is here to see him on an urgent matter."

The man paused, considering. Then he nodded and said, "Wait here." And he turned around and half-ran, half-walked back to the house.

Having paused before the gates, the death shadow of the Cobweb Bride billowed in a fine grey smoke stack in Percy's supernatural vision. It was straining to move forward now, like a bird caught in a net. . . .

The Count D'Arvu received them inside the great house within minutes. The same servant returned, this time with a completely different, friendly demeanor, and they were taken through the gates and up the walkway into the house—leaving Jack in the purportedly trustworthy care of two stable-hands—and then, past the cool columns of stone up a dramatic staircase and into a small but elegant and comfortable parlor with furnishings upholstered in faded cream silks and brocade.

Count Lecrant was a middle-aged man with a dark complexion, his face lacking vanity and his dark hair lacking the artifice of a wig worn inside his own residence. He was still vigorous for his years, dressed in plain clothing hardly different from that of his servant. The moment he saw them, he walked spryly toward Beltain and Percy, his face taking on a warm expression.

"My dear Lord Beltain! And Percy, my dear girl!" he said, taking the knight by the hand and then taking Percy in a similar manner, with the difference that he brought her hand up to his own lips for a proper courtly greeting worthy of a *lady*.

Percy was so amazed and chagrined that for a moment she said nothing while the men exchanged greetings as though nothing was amiss.

"However did you find us? And how did you manage to be here so swiftly?" the Count asked. "I admit to being amazed, for when we parted ways at the Sapphire Court, our two parties were headed in opposite directions!"

Beltain explained briefly that they had traveled with the help of nothing less than the gods. He then cast one careful glance at Percy, not venturing to explain their reasons for being here just yet.

Percy meanwhile, was observing the behavior of the death shadow that was waiting obediently at her side, as she had told it to wait. But at the same time it was vigorously pulling at her, *pulling* to be reunited with the Cobweb Bride.

"How is the Countess Arabella and—and Lady Leonora?"

Percy inquired, deciding that directness was the best way to proceed.

The Count's expression momentarily changed from warm amiability to something a bit more uncertain. "They are quite well, thanks to you, naturally, dear girl. We've had a very hasty ride here, and to be honest, have just arrived ourselves early this morning. Again, I marvel how you've found us, for I have just acquired the keys and the lease to this house, and no one but a trusted handful knows we are here—certainly no one up in the San Quellenne Castle knows, nor any of the local nobility. We have taken such great care, you know—"

And the Count went on to describe the intricate plans he had laid in place many months earlier, for just such a possible need to escape from court and its increasingly dark politics. Even before their daughter Lady Leonora fell ill and was hidden away by the Sovereign several weeks ago, and then freed by Percy from the Sovereign's secret chamber filled with sorcery and cobwebs—even before that, the Count had made arrangements to procure a residence in distant Tanathe, and to have all means ready for his family to uproot themselves and travel, just in case things became dire and such a last resort became necessary.

"And thus, here we are," he concluded. "My wife and daughter are still resting upstairs, and I do think the journey has taken its toll on them—Leonora especially. My poor child has suffered such an ordeal, and she is particularly weak and very pale, and has no appetite. I should be concerned about her recovery, but it will come later, soon as we get the change to rest and recuperate—"

Percy and Beltain exchanged glances.

"Ah, but do forgive my lack of hospitality!" the Count D'Arvu said loudly, recalling himself as host. "You must be parched and famished, and I will order a room prepared for you—though you must forgive the fact that our own belongings are hardly unpacked, and the carriage stands in the back while the servants unload and make the rest of the house ready for all of us."

And the Count rang a bell to call his servants and ordered refreshments to be brought up in haste.

"I am armored for war, and it would be some relief to the girl and myself to remove our winter clothing," said Beltain, deciding to let Percy be the one to make the first mention of their true reasons for being here, in her own good time.

"In that case, off you go, my dear Lord Beltain, I will not keep you in your plate and chain mail! A change of clothes and refreshment will find you upstairs. By the time you are restored, we can dine together, and the women of this household will be up from their sleep and ready to properly receive you."

Percy took a firm hold of the death-shadow of the Cobweb Bride with her mind and directed it to move closely at her side. She then followed Beltain and two maidservants leading them up yet another flight of marble stairs to the upper third floor where the corridor of bedchambers was located. The house was an older venerable villa, erected around a solid framework of cool stone and with solid soundproof walls of sufficient thickness and clever masonry to retain a pleasant temperature indoors regardless of weather outside.

The maids took them to a large airy bedchamber where the furniture was covered with sheets, and then bustled to make the room ready.

There was a grand four-poster bed in the middle of the chamber and Percy looked at it with sudden warmth in her cheeks. Meanwhile, Beltain seemed to be no less affected by the implications of the single bed, as he turned his back to her and began to remove his plate armor with the assistance of a valet who had swiftly arrived after the maids, to offer his services.

"Would you like me to take that, Miss?" said a young maid, pointing to Percy's coat and shawl.

Percy knew better than to argue. She was soon down to her coarse burlap and wool dress, and the maid ran off somewhere then returned with a light cotton dress which she set on the bed. The material was not costly fabric but ordinary country clothing that a simple country lady or even the maid herself might wear.

Before anyone could protest, two sturdy wooden bathtubs were brought in, one after the other, by four burly servants who looked as if they had been borrowed from country fieldwork.

Next, came endless buckets of water, steaming hot, and finally the baths were ready. Two maidservants came to stand in the middle of the room between each tub, holding up the ends of a large opened sheet to create a curtain of privacy. The valet helped Beltain disrobe further and enter his bath, while the same was done on Percy's side with a maid.

Even though she had gone through a similar bath service at the Silver Court once before—though admittedly this was much simpler and countrified—Percy still blushed when disrobing, and still felt the awfulness of revealing her threadbare underclothing to anyone.

But sinking into the heaven of hot water made her forget everything else—even the ever-present billowing death-shadow of the Lady Leonora that stood patiently waiting a few steps away in the corner of the room, invisible to all but herself. . . . The bliss of the warmth, the overwhelming relaxation after relentless events of so many days, was a pleasure unimaginable to Percy. She hardly even noticed when a maid came to help her wash her hair, because she was utterly groggy with sleep.

The maids with the privacy curtain had also gone away while she was not looking. The next moment she opened her eyes and focused, Percy could see Beltain a few feet away, seated in his own bath. He seemed to sense her scrutiny immediately because he too turned his face in her direction . . . and she saw the blooming of his soft smile and the intimate look of his slate-blue eyes.

Percy felt such a breathless pang of joy in her heart at the sight of him, with his wet curls of slick hair and the water running down his face and his great bronzed shoulders, and his mesmerizing kind eyes, that she felt herself flushing beyond any heat the bathwater held.

She smiled back a him shyly, and quickly turned away, and then the next moment the maid poured a bucket over her face, so it was all for the best anyway.

An hour later they were washed clean and dried and clothed into a fresh set of simple but well-made clothing from the D'Arvu family personal or guest wardrobes. Beltain was now clean-shaven and wearing a white linen shirt with loose lace-trimmed sleeves, dark pants, and buckled shoes that were likely fashionable at some point at the Sapphire Court, but now were sufficiently ordinary so as not to provoke undue foppish attention. It was fortunate that the clothes fit his very tall and large muscular frame, for they certainly must have belonged to some other gentleman than the Count who was a much smaller man.

Meanwhile Percy had her hair swept up in a simple but attractive knot arrangement and was attired in a light dress with a tightly laced and somewhat revealing bodice that left her neck and shoulders and some of her chest frightfully uplifted and exposed. After the maid was done lacing it from the back and left her to her own devices, Percy spent several futile moments attempting to pull up some of the fabric higher over her bulging bosom and tucking it around the armpits of the sleeves, while Beltain stood watching her with amusement. It only made things worse when Percy realized the direction of his gaze upon her and the fact that his eyes once more seemed so very dark, and their dilated pupils overwhelming the irises, as he stared at her—to be precise, certain parts of her, in particular.

"How can ladies wear such peculiar dresses?" Percy muttered, because she felt she must say something to cover her embarrassment.

But in reply he continued to *look* at her, so that Percy felt herself on fire. And then he said, "You have never been to a Court assembly, my sweet girl. The ladies there are always close to naked. Your dress is quite demure and you look—very *well* in it."

And then Beltain smiled.

Percy's heart had no time to even begin racing because in the next breath he offered his arm to her. "Come," he said. "They are waiting for us downstairs, and you have an important task ahead of you."

Percy exhaled with a shudder and nodded. She then took his arm, feeling an immediate outpouring of honey warmth at the place where their arms touched. And then she called upon the nearby death shadow to proceed after them.

The D'Arvu family had gathered in the parlor. The Count had not bothered to change for dinner. Seated on a brocade-and-silk upholstered divan, the gaunt and dark-haired Countess Arabella was dressed far simpler than Percy had ever seen her to be, as a country matron. Next to her, Lady Leonora their daughter wore a flowing girlish dress of mauve silk and linen that emphasized the pallor of her skin and offset her chestnut curls.

The moment Percy saw Leonora, pale and stiff-backed, and with an apathetic glassy stare, she had no remaining doubt that the young woman was dead. And oh, her death shadow! How quickly it flew to be at her side! It was as though an invisible string of power was jerked, tossing it forward across the distance, and setting it next to her rightful mistress, at long last. . . .

The culmination of all things was now at hand. But first, the formalities had to be observed.

"Come, my friends!" said the Count, to his guests and then,

turning to his wife and daughter—"We are blessed to have our dear friends in our midst once again, and so soon!"

Beltain bowed, and Percy curtsied very carefully. The Countess arose from her seat and rushed forward to take Percy in a very unexpected motherly embrace. "Welcome, dear child, you are always welcome in our home, wherever it may be!"

The Lady Leonora turned her face to the visitors and then arose somewhat stiffly and curtsied also. Her chestnut hair was sweetly arranged, and she was attempting to smile, but her facial muscles were struggling to form the movements necessary, and the result was neither here nor there.

It pained Percy to look at her and see her for what she was, even though neither her parents nor she herself had any idea of her true condition.

After everyone was once again seated, a small pause ensued.

"Percy Ayren, I must thank you again for saving me," Leonora said, her voice measured precisely and slightly monotone.

"Lady Leonora," said Percy gently. "I only wish I could have done more. . . ."

And then Percy steeled herself and clenched her hands at her sides, and continued, "I wish—I wish I did not have to say this, and—and things had turned out differently. Maybe, if I had gotten to you sooner—"

"What do you mean, my dear?" Count Lecrant had been looking away at something else in the room, cheerfully ready to summon the servants for pre-supper refreshments, but the tone of Percy's voice made him turn back and look at her with attention.

But Percy was looking at Leonora, unable to take her eyes off her, and her expression was unnaturally composed, controlled somehow. None knew it, but she was watching the maiden and her death, how they were together, how close to its seated mistress the shadow stood. . . .

"I am so sorry to say this now, dear Lady Leonora, but I must. We have come here, returned to see you so soon, but not for a happy reason. As you remember, we thought we had the Lady Melinoë with us, she who was the Cobweb Bride. We took her to see Lord Death in his Keep. But we—that is, I, everyone—was mistaken. The death that was attached to her was not her own—"

"What are you saying?" the Countess D'Arvu interrupted, paling.

Lady Leonora had grown absolutely motionless. She regarded Percy with her glassy eyes.

"I am saying, the death shadow at Lady Melinoë's side belonged to someone else—another lady—it belonged to *you*. I am sorry, Lady Leonora, so sorry, with all my heart, but I had to return, and bring the death back here, to you. Your own true death stands now at your side, waiting. . . . You are the rightful Cobweb Bride. And I must return you to Lord Death, so that the world can be set aright once more. Will you come with me, My Lady?"

The room had become as silent as a grave. The afternoon sun came in soft dappled patches through the window and upon the old marble of the floor.

And then Lady Leonora, motionless as a doll in her flowing silk, opened her lips and evoked the mechanism to expand her dead lungs, and uttered in fierce gasps: "*No* . . . not dead . . . I am *not* dead! It is not true!"

And the Count and Countess, also agitated, made exclamations, while the Countess clutched her daughter's hand, saying, "My child cannot be dead! Look, see how rosy her cheeks are! And I can feel her heart beating, surely it is beating!"

Percy stood up and approached, then gently touched Lady Leonora's hand also. "You are cold, My Lady. And I feel no pulse, nor hear a heartbeat. I am so sorry. . . . As for your cheeks, they are rather pale already. Any remaining pink is but the last shadow of your former health, and it will not last long. . . ."

Leonora jerked her hand away from Percy, while her death shadow flickered in response to Percy's touch. The lady drew backward, sinking deeper against the divan pillows like a stiff plank of wood. "No!" she said again, clutching at the seat and cushions then putting her hands up to claw at her face. "No! I am not dead, I cannot be!"

"This is a terrible mistake!" the Count D'Arvu added. "No indeed, my daughter is perfectly healthy!"

"But your death is right beside you!" Percy insisted. "I can see it!"

"That is a lie!" Leonora's fixed gaze hardened and her brows arched downward with effort. From her seated position she glared at Percy with a dark maddened expression, then looked around her at both sides of the divan, past her mother, as though searching for any sign of ghostly death in her proximity. "No!" she said yet again, her chestnut ringlets of curls trembling. "No and no! You lie now! I know not why it is that you are really here, what horrible lies you've brought to torment me, but you will *not* have me! I refuse! I will not die! I will never go with you!"

And with a cry, followed by some other incomprehensible exclamation, Leonora got up once again, her hands and arms shaking with awkward jerking motions, and she ran out of the parlor.

Her death shadow followed her.

Chapter 4

Lady Amaryllis Roulle and Lord Nathan Woult opened their eyes . . . and found themselves in a low-lit but unusually busy corridor of the Imperial Palace at Silver Court.

"Ah!" Amaryllis exclaimed, as a liveried servant carrying something in a wooden box crashed into her shoulder rather painfully, nearly knocking her against the hallway wall, and making her let go of Nathan's hand.

"Oh, a thousand pardons, My Lady! I must be terribly blind!" the servant exclaimed in abject confusion, for his way had been entirely clear only seconds ago.

"It is of no consequence," replied the lady with tired magnanimity, but then suffered a pang of mortification as the servant took a good look at her and noted her disheveled appearance, her horrible tangled hair, and the dirt stains on her face and dark red travel clothes.

His expression changed from groveling to suspicious and then haughty.

But then he took in the terrifying sight of Lord Nathan, wild haired, overgrown with a black beard, and even more filthy in attire. The servant's jaw fell open, but just then Nathan said: "On your way now, good fellow! Stop gawking, scram!"

And the liveried servant fled.

The next few passerby in the hallway, also servants, heard

the interaction and gifted Amaryllis and Nathan with similar glares, before hurrying away.

"Are you all right, dearest?" Nathan inquired. He considered for a moment taking the lady's hand, but refrained.

"Dear Lord in Heaven!" Amaryllis whispered in icy fury, clutching her filthy brocade skirts. "I am mortified! To be seen looking thus, and then to be disdained by *serving staff!* Fie! I must now kill myself!"

"Now, now," said her dear friend and companion. "Killing yourself, nowadays that is an empty threat if ever there was one, unless you've managed to become Death's Auxiliary Champion while he was not looking. Considering we have been through hell and Tartarus, literally—well, at least its front parlor—I dare say no one would blame us for the stains on our clothing after days in a Chidair dungeon—"

"I do not *care!*" the lady cried. "I must be on to my quarters immediately, where I shall bathe for two days straight, have these clothes burned, the chamber fumigated, and then eat something that is not *gruel*—and you too! Speaking of fumigation!"

"Well, yes, naturally, my dear. But do you not think it might be important to attend the Emperor first and let him know what we know?" Nathan glanced at a pair of running servants that passed them just now. "Lord knows, but this entire Palace might be under siege, or worse, getting sacked this instant by that mad Goddess Persephone and her army!"

"The goddess and her army be damned!" Amaryllis hissed, and began walking in a general direction of her Palace quarters. "It can all wait till after I am fit to be seen in public. Nathan! If you see anyone we know, warn me, so that I might turn around and hide my face, and you can block me with your brute nightmarish figure—"

"Well, certainly, yes, but—"

"But what?" Amaryllis cried, turning to glare at him. "Think, Nathan, we know *nothing*. Nothing, really! What good are we to the Emperor, but to tell him that Death and a few antique Grecian gods have come to our mortal coil and are having an insane quarrel that is going to tear apart the world and us with it? Seriously? What can we tell His Imperial Majesty that will not have us made into a laughingstock worse than we already are?"

And she continued on her way.

"Amaryllis, you do underestimate what we know," Nathan said, swiftly matching her rapid pace with his longer stride. "I really think the Emperor needs to see us now, exactly as we are—no baths, no rest. *Now*."

"And why is that, Nathan?"

"Because," he replied, "for once, in the greater scheme of things, we can make a difference."

Within a quarter of an hour of walking past a myriad corridors, rushing servants, and occasional harried nobles, Amaryllis and Nathan were ushered into a small elegant parlor in the Imperial Quarters of the Palace.

Here a man of advanced middle years with a dark beard met them, attired in expensive but subdued clothing. He frowned slightly, squinting at the unsightly but vaguely familiar pair—for in the dirt and disarray, the horrific stained outfits, and Nathan's unkempt wild hair and beard he could hardly recognize two of the most foppish and brilliant young members of the aristocracy.

"Dear Heaven, is that you, Lord Nathan Woult?" said the Duke Claude Rovait eventually. "You look a fright! What in God's name has happened to you? Where have you been? And oh, my dear Lady Amaryllis!"

The lady and gentleman curtsied and bowed before the distinguished Duke Rovait who was one of the Emperor's closest advisors. Amaryllis's usually pale, elfin features were flaming mulberry with a blush of mortification.

"I beg pardon of Your Grace for our dire appearance,"

Nathan hurried to speak. "But we come straight from having escaped a Chidair dungeon up north where we've languished for days, and then Death's Keep where we languished an unspeakable number of hours that felt like centuries. We request an audience with His Imperial Majesty, for we have news to impart that might be considered significant."

The Duke frowned. "Go on. . . . Before I allow you an Imperial Audience on such short notice and at such an inopportune time, I need to know what this is about. As you can imagine, the Emperor has an overwhelming number of concerns to deal with—"

"Are we besieged?" the Lady Amaryllis interrupted. "What has happened here at Court that we have missed during our absence? Is the Sovereign here yet?"

The Duke glanced at the lady with a grave countenance. "So you *do* know that we're at war?"

"Yes, I imagine it is the inevitable outcome of all this horror," Amaryllis retorted.

"You claim to be newly sprung from a northern Lethe dungeon. How did you manage to get here, inside the walls of the citadel? No, there is no siege, but the Silver Court is on lockdown. No one can enter or leave without our knowledge or permission."

"That is precisely why we must speak with His Imperial Majesty," said Nathan.

"Well?"

"The answer is rather unbelievable," Amaryllis spoke again. "And it involves Death—who, it turns out, is not merely an apparition but a *god*."

The Duke Rovait's frown increased.

"In short, we were brought here, by unnatural means," Nathan said. "Death, who is Hades, Lord of the Underworld, sent us here—through air, or shadows, or some kind of wind tunnel—or Hades himself only knows what, but it involved neither carriages nor horses."

"Lord Nathan," the Duke interrupted sternly. "I am not going to pay you the discourtesy of asking if you are in your cups. What you are saying is beginning to sound like bad drivel. Is this supposed to be some kind of exquisite jest on your part? If so, it is in poor taste."

"Your Grace!" Nathan exclaimed. "Do you honestly think I would let myself grow this monstrous beard and come to be in such a foul state merely for a lark?"

The Duke stared at both of them, glancing from one to the other with thoughtful severity, then relented. "No, I suppose not. Knowing the two of you, I must regretfully admit the possibility of what you say. But only so far! Give me something more, something tangible the Emperor can put to practical military use—"

"You require strategic information?" Lady Amaryllis said with intensity. "Well, Your Grace, here is one—our former dearest friend, the Lady Ignacia Chitain is a Balmue spy of the Domain, and has been, it appears, for years on end."

"We are aware of it," the Duke replied calmly.

"What? You *knew?*" The expression on the lady's face was outrage.

"We have learned it recently," the Duke continued. "In fact, just as our suspicions on her behalf were supported by observation, the three of you happened to disappear shortly afterward, so for a while there it did not look good for *all three* of you."

"What?" This time it was Nathan who exclaimed. "But we'd been captured by Chidair! We had gone to play at Cobweb Brides—an idiot adventure, I admit—but it all ended in the Chidair Keep with dead soldiers taking us, locking us up, and feeding us pig slop. Amaryllis and I here had nothing to do with any of Ignacia's treason!"

"Yes, we also know that now."

"Ignacia has betrayed *us*, and our friendship as much as she betrayed the Imperial Realm," Amaryllis said with cold fury. "She had turned on us and gone over to Duke Hoarfrost's side, with promises of some kind of beastly Alliance with the Sovereign—who incidentally is immortal—"

"What?" Duke Claude Rovait stopped Amaryllis's tirade with a raised hand. "What did you say about the Sovereign? She is *immortal?*"

"Well, yes. She is the Grecian Goddess Persephone who has apparently lost her mind—or whatever it is that goddesses possess up there in the cranial region—and it has made her commit supposed atrocities."

"Well now, this is indeed interesting news; this we did *not* know," Duke Claude Rovait mused. "If what you say about Rumanar Avalais is true, then it explains some things remarkably, including her uncanny charismatic influence upon so many, despite her cruelties. She has indeed been pursuing a political course of action that had no apparent logical pattern to it, and not a solid hint as to motives. Indeed, the gradual brewing of hostility between the Realm and the Domain was observed by us over the years with much puzzlement, and more and more it became a mystery tied to her *person.* We suspected sorcery and the dark arts. But now—with the cessation of death, with potions of the land completely disappearing, chaos and unrest and soon-to be universal hunger, as our meager food supply dwindles—"

"Now you have a mad goddess on your hands," Nathan concluded with an exasperated sigh. "So, when can we expect her to besiege the Silver Court?"

The Duke watched them both with a closed expression. "That is the strangest thing," he said. "She and the Trovadii army have come . . . and *gone.* They came upon us the night before last, arriving in the late evening from the direction of Morphaea, and they did not stop. . . . Instead of surrounding the Imperial citadel, they simply passed around us, the undead multitudes streaming outside the walls, and then continued onward, north, and into Lethe. It was as if the Sovereign did not consider the Emperor a threat at all, to such an insulting degree that she did not bother to pause and make war with us!"

"Oh, I am certain I know where she is headed," Amaryllis said. "If what Hades said is true, then she seeks Death's Keep and plans to take her armies and enter the Underworld—how or why, I have not the faintest notion. As for our own mortal world—I fear we are in for some very bad times."

"Well, my dears," said the Duke, "it appears that you will have your Imperial Audience after all."

Dawn bloomed softly, staining the lower edges of the starlit black sky of night with mother-of-pearl at the eastern horizon over the great ancient city of Charonne.

The ethereal first light gathered its riches over the capital city and over the entire Kingdom of Styx. It pooled with broken shards of mirror-clarity in the rapidly moving waters of the dark and wide river that flowed only a mile-and-a-half west of the city walls—the River Styx that never froze, not even now, in the heart of winter.

An invading army camped on the snow-laden distant western shores of the river, from horizon to horizon, as far as the eye could see in the dawning blue twilight. Hundreds of tents had been erected, morning campfires were already smoking, and a hive of soldiers wearing the olive and black colors of the Kingdom of Solemnis moved around the tents. At even intervals all along the shoreline, the great engines of siege were lined up in monolith formations, their dark silhouettes sharp against the paling sky, their wooden towers and catapults pointing across the river at the bulwarks of the city walls where the defending cannon faced them in turn from embrasures, silent for the moment.

This was an army of mortal living men, and thus, they had to eat and sleep, and wage ordinary war. King Frederick Ourin of Solemnis, which was one of the four Kingdoms of the

Domain, had sent the entire force of his battalions north, into the enemy territory of the Realm, all upon the orders of the Sovereign. They had been told to wait at the western shore of the river, to block the city from any outside access in the west, but not to engage until further orders, and not to cross Styx. This has been days ago. . . . And as yet, no new orders were forthcoming.

And thus the Domain army sat in readiness, while the defenders of Charonne observed them from the height of the bone-pale walls.

More than fifty feet above ground level, up on the battlements, musketeer and arquebusier marksmen wearing the crimson and black colors of Styx leaned in readiness, manning their long-muzzled firearms through every merlon embrasure and along every crenel. Behind them, amid flickering night torches, paced sergeants-at-arms and various infantrymen with pole weapons at the ready, and suppliers moved small wheelbarrows and loaded carts. At one such point near a sizeable bulwark facing west, several high-ranking officers were gathered, and in their center stood a slim youth dressed in a full suit of battle armor, his plates shining to a high polish and trimmed with gold. His crested helmet sported black and crimson ostrich plumes and his visor was raised, revealing the face of a grave and frightened youngster of no more than fourteen.

His Majesty, Augustus Ixion, the young King of Styx, recently orphaned and recently crowned, was here at dawn, to observe and take stock of his city's defenses. At his right stood a tall, vigorous man with a handsome face and artfully styled dark hair, bare of helm and heedless of the cold dawn, with filaments of his hair flying in the morning breeze. He was Andre Eldon, the Duke of Plaimes, from the Kingdom of Morphaea. Together with his King, Orphe Geroard, and the ragged remainder of the Morphaea army, the Duke had arrived here in Charonne only two days ago, under the cover of night and in inclement weather, to join forces with Styx against their common enemy. It has been a miracle they managed to enter the city from the eastern side without being intercepted and destroyed by the Solemnis forces. But so far, Solemnis showed no interest in crossing the river. And besides, the Morphaea men were so few in number that their arrival was easily overlooked and their reinforcements were mostly a boost to morale.

"I wonder what it is that makes them wait now . . ." mused the Duke of Plaimes, as he raised a long spyglass to stare at the roiling vista below, across the silvery waters of the River Styx. "Especially since the Sovereign and the Trovadii are well on their way deep into Lethe by now. One would expect Solemnis to be done here quickly then hurry to rendezvous with the Trovadii, coming together from the west and east at some point, but where?"

"Likely, Letheburg, where Hoarfrost sits," replied Bruno Melograno, one of the garrison officers in their company.

"Yes, but why? Why Letheburg? It is incomprehensible to me. Why drive past the most attractive prize of the Realm that happens to be the Imperial Seat at Silver Court and cast away the opportunity to take the Emperor, and instead enter the northern wilderness?"

"Maybe the Sovereign wants to surround the Realm along its outer perimeter and cut us off from all our foreign borders?" Bruno Melograno pointed at the line of the camped enemy army across the river. "Even now, see how they choose to stay on the other side of Styx? There is no solid tactical advantage to it, since the added distance of the river makes artillery close to useless, except for the heaviest cannons. Their catapults will likely have the required reach to hit the walls and beyond, but other projectiles will fall short, miss all targets and likely drown in the river itself. If I were their commanding officer, I would cross Styx and camp on the eastern shore, closer to our walls. This way they still have plenty of safe distance between our artillery and their men, but at least they will have better chances of breaching us."

"Agreed," said Duke Andre Eldon. "So what is their reasoning? What are they waiting for? An invitation?"

King Augustus Ixion took a deep steadying breath and his boyish voice revealed only a slight tremor. "If they think to frighten me and my city simply by their extended presence, they will not succeed."

"No, Your Majesty, indeed they will not. But generally speaking, it is a good thing to be *somewhat* frightened—just a tad, just enough to be on alert. . . . Nothing wrong with a healthy dose of awareness of reality, and the resulting caution," the Duke replied in a steady matter-of-fact voice, as he continued to observe through the eyepiece of the slender brass telescope tube. "As long as fear is then transformed into useful actions."

"Do you think," the youth said, "that they will attack today?"

"Anything is possible. Your garrison is as ready as it can be, and My Liege and I are both at your service. I will personally stand at your side when it happens."

Augustus turned his pale blotchy face with its acne-blemished skin and bright blue eyes at the older man. Then he glanced at the other officers surrounding him. "I thank you, Your Grace, and all of you who are here. I am ready for them," he said bravely.

In that moment as the young King spoke, something unusual was taking place beyond the city walls of Charonne.

The nature of the sky itself seemed to change. But it was not the normal gradual brightening from blackness to pallor and a consequent fadeout of the stars. . . . Instead, the twilight seemed to pause momentarily, suspended for a few long moments in a perfect in-between state—while the stars hung fixed in the rich navy velvet of the heavenly zenith, almost black in the highest spot. And then the light at their back—coming from the east, from the direction of the city interior and beyond it, began to fade again—as though something had *reversed* the dawn itself.

As they looked out over the parapet walls at the western countryside and at the expanse of the faintly glittering river, at the same time, directly behind them, coming from the opposite direction, night was *returning. . . .*

No, it was not possible. It could not be.

The reversal happened quickly—far swifter than had been the normal blooming of dawn. In about ten breaths, there was an in-rushing of darkness, as first the heavens directly overhead became the same rich black they had been half an hour ago, and then the edges closer to the eastern horizon followed, darkening.

Meanwhile, the river and the army across it in the west were now in full darkness, their many beacons of campfires scattered like golden dots to mark the land.

"The sky! What in the world?" an officer exclaimed. "What is happening?"

"Lord protect us!" another man spoke, making the holy sign of God.

The soldiers manning the walls all trained their attention to the impossibility before them in the heavens. Marksmen were looking up, looking around and behind them, standing up and away from their firing posts in confusion.

But the Duke of Plaimes kept the spyglass raised, sweeping the horizon in all directions and was now once again aiming it in the direction of the river.

There, the lights of the enemy army were winking out, one by one. . . . In their place, a dark whirling mist arose, to obscure them entirely—and indeed to obscure most of the western half of the River Styx, so that nothing could be seen beyond its halfway point, much less its remote western shore.

At the same time, as they continued to observe all around them—with their only source of light being their own torches that were now cleanly burning in absolute night darkness—the men standing up on the battlements of Charonne looked up at the black sky and watched the stars go out overhead, as quickly as did the distant campfires.

It made even less sense. If it was night again, where were the stars?

The dome of the sky in its entirety was now a strange, uniform, homogeneous thing of darkness, a veil of mist, black as pitch.

Indeed, if one were to look out and around the city walls at the overwhelming mist-darkness surrounding them from all directions, Charonne no longer seemed to be situated in any place recognizable as being a part of the mortal world. . . .

Meanwhile, from the vantage point of the invading Solemnis across the River Styx, the soldiers of the Domain witnessed the same impossible phenomenon that seemed at first glance to be a reversal of dawn. The sky in the east faded, and a sudden black mist gathered over the middle of the river, blocking all view of the city beyond the other shore.

The mist stood up like a tangible wall of darkness, rising higher and higher into the expanse of heaven, while the air shimmered like a winter mirage.

For a quarter of an hour it stood thus. And then, as though touched by the capricious breath of the gods, the curtain of mist dissipated, and with it the eastern sky was revealed to be full of ordinary morning light.

However, the soldiers continued to stare in unrelieved wonder. Before them the wide and rapid River Styx had been diminished into a narrow stream, its girth reduced by half, and its eastern shore was now just a hundred feet away.

And beyond it, the land was a flat and snow-filled wilderness of brush and sparse trees, with nothing else for infinite leagues in the distance.

There was no trace of Charonne, the ancient city.

Chapter 5

Vlau Fiomarre awoke with a start, from yet another dream in which he saw *her* alive. She lay next to him, warm and glowing, her heart beating solidly in her chest, her blood coursing through her veins, a healthy rose flush on her delicate skin. Her great smoky eyes, open wide, were looking at him with soft receptiveness. . . .

Claere.

He found himself, as always, in her chambers, fully dressed, having fallen back against the cushions on the sofa, where he had nodded off yet again—for he was almost never sleeping any more, not properly in a bed. He existed in a chronic state of exhaustion, something within himself always preventing him from attaining the true moment of peaceful release necessary to accept sleep. Thus, sleep came upon him in stealth, taking him by force when he least expected it—such as now, here, in her presence.

While she—she stood silently near the window, as always looking out at the world outside, the distant rooftops of Letheburg, the street lanterns coming to life like golden fireflies among the early heliotrope dusk.

Vlau inhaled deeply and rubbed his eyes, then sat up, groggy from the lucid dream.

There had been a knock on the door. The sound had pulled

him out of the stupor, while Claere slowly turned her head, casting a single glance at him where he sat, and then said softly, "Come in."

The door opened and two liveried Palace guards entered, followed by the King of Lethe.

Claere Liguon turned, full body, away from the window and stood watching the newcomers. Her expression was the same nebulous mixture of infinite patience and resignation.

Vlau Fiomarre stood up, with a short bow before the King.

"I trust Your Imperial Highness is as well as can be," King Roland Osenni said in a tired voice, coming to the point, as was his usual manner. "I regret that it has come to this but I am left with no choice but to request your services."

"Your Majesty," the Infanta acknowledged him with a slow inclination of her head. "What . . . services?"

The King motioned with a weary hand at the window. "Out there," he said. "Up on the parapets. I want you to go out there and talk to Hoarfrost. Attempt to talk some sense into him, for it might make a difference coming from one such as yourself. From one—uhm—*deceased* royal to another deceased vassal."

"But—what am I to say?" Claere's expression did not falter, but Vlau's eyes—oh, they were fierce with reproach and intensity as he stared at the King.

"Say whatever you like. Think of something—anything, to get him to reconsider this siege. You, my dear, are Liguon. And if there is any shred of reason and loyalty left in Hoarfrost's rotting brains—no offense—he might heed your words. He certainly did not bother to heed mine—not that I was able to stand up there for any length of time necessary to have a sentient conversation with that boar. At least you are in little danger of coming to—any further *harm*."

There was a brief pause as Claere considered this. And then, "Yes," she said. "Yes, of course. Take me there and I will do what I can."

In that moment, the Marquis Fiomarre opened his mouth,

and without looking at the Infanta, dared to address the King directly. "Begging pardon of Your Majesty, but this is madness. Even if Her Imperial Highness believes she has the means of ending the siege, surely she does not seem to realize that as soon as she shows herself up on the city walls she will be subject to enemy artillery fire, as much as any man, dead or living. Her fragile body will be torn asunder, and she will be shot at—"

King Roland Osenni turned a frustrated face at Fiomarre and glared at him. "Enough! How dare you, Marquis!" he said. "You forget yourself. Your presence here is tolerated only as a favor to Her Imperial Highness. Your opinion is neither heeded nor wanted."

Vlau bowed his dark head curtly before the King, then straightened and looked him directly in the eyes with an indomitable gaze. "I will not speak again. And yet—Her Imperial Highness cannot go out there alone. Indeed, she will not last up there long enough to say a single word!"

"Well, in that case I suggest you do something to make sure that she does!"

"I will stand at her side and shield her . . ." Fiomarre replied.

"Excellent! And now, be silent!" The King went furiously silent himself and then looked from one to the other, the young man and the dead young woman. His dark frown eased when he noted the tragic sunken eyes of the Infanta and the fragile look in them. "My dear child," he said. "Again, I deeply regret the necessity of this, but we have run out of options. And so far we have not heard from either His Imperial Majesty, your illustrious Father, or anyone else whom we contacted for aid against the enemy."

Claere nodded slightly, moving her delicate neck like clockwork. "There is no need to explain, I understand what is required of me."

The King nodded. "Good, good. . . . I am glad you see the

necessity behind this. For obvious reasons, Your Imperial
Highness being as you are, there is hardly any chance of
additional harm coming to you, and we will take all necessary
precautions to keep you guarded, naturally. . . ."

"Yes, I thank Your Majesty." Her voice was steady and
gentle, with no indication of reproach.

And yet, the King felt a momentary crawling sense of cold
draining his cheeks followed by a flush of chagrin, and he again
considered her, this tiny slip of a girl-child, this pitiful *thing*,
nothing more than a dead upright corpse—

"A carriage awaits downstairs," was all he could mutter. "If
you would take a few minutes to get ready, of course—"

"No," she said. "I am ready now."

And the Infanta threw a single empty glance at the Marquis
Fiomarre, nodding to him. She then walked out of her chamber,
following the King of Lethe and his guards.

His pulse racing wildly, Vlau Fiomarre came after her.

The ride through the city was brief and uneventful. The well-
appointed royal closed carriage took Claere and her silent
companion Vlau Fiomarre down the long driveway of the Winter
Palace into Lethe Square and then along Royal Way lined with
rows of filigreed brass street lanterns, and eventually through the
winding lesser streets of Letheburg. There was little traffic other
than the military convoys and formations of infantrymen moving
to and from the city walls. There were also the endless carts
carrying the wounded. . . .

Claere watched through the carriage window the nature of
the fading daylight, a deepening blue of the sky as early evening
came into being. Soon, the scalding golden glow and noise of
flames from somewhere ahead, signaled the proximity of the city
walls. When they arrived at the walls and the carriage stopped,
she paused only to allow Vlau to take her gently by the arm and
help her down onto the snow-swept ground of the pomoerium,
the wide empty space just before the great walls began.

Overhead, the battlements were silhouetted black against a blazing red-gold inferno that was burning just outside of the city—it was their main line of defense.

The Infanta stood with her fabric shoes in the snow, her dead flesh knowing no sensation of cold, wearing only a light velvet cloak given her by the King to cover her thin plain dress. And she looked up at the crenellated tops of the parapets, the flickering torches, the shadows of running soldiers . . . all eerie wild movement, a constant roiling overhead.

Vlau Fiomarre stood at her side. His hand continued to hold her arm, to steady her, since as always her brittle dead body had a hard time keeping balance.

There were several guards accompanying them, and a pair of trumpeters. They came forward, with one captain ahead of them. The captain bowed before the Infanta, and in the thickening dusk she barely saw the liquid glitter of his eyes, the vapor curling on his breath, and his wary cool expression—for he was not particularly trustful of the dead, even the friendly ones, and yet it was perfectly understandable.

"This way, Your Imperial Highness." The captain pointed at a narrow stairway that was carved directly into the wall, rising parallel to it all the way up. He started walking up the stairs, and the Infanta followed, with Vlau directly behind her. He had released her arm, but was close enough to be her shadow, and to catch her if she lost her fragile balance and started to fall.

It occurred to Claere that if she fell down those stairs, tumbling down many feet from any point along the rising stairway that had neither rails nor handgrips, she could simply lie there in the snow, feeling no pain, knowing only a possibility of broken limbs.

No, she told herself, *I will not fall.*

And Claere Liguon slowly and gingerly took each step up the slippery iced-over stones, until she had reached the upper landing.

Vlau, a few of the guards, and the royal trumpeters, came
after her.

Up on the battlements, the blazing golden-orange inferno
was terrifying. The crackle of the flames, the black stifling
smoke, the stench of gunpowder and coppery tang of blood, all
of it filled the senses.

Good thing she was *dead* and could sense any of it only
through the distance of a thick veil of cotton. . . .

"This way." The captain's voice was gruff. He was moving
along the walkway in front of her, stepping over and around
seated wounded soldiers and fallen weaponry, past embrasures at
which tired marksmen sat, holding longbows and dipping arrows
into tar and pitch, setting them ablaze and then letting the arrows
fly into the distance. Every few feet there were skirmishes as
ladders were upturned and grotesque silhouettes of dead men
tossed back over the walls.

They came to a wider area of the battlements just before a
large bulwark.

Here the trumpeters moved forward, past a mess of
overturned supply wheelbarrows and stacked kegs of gunpowder
next to a stockpile of large round iron cannonballs.

"Wait here, Your Imperial Highness," the captain said
loudly, over the din around them. "But not too close to those
barrels of black powder, they are flammable. Indeed, let us have
you move in this direction, right here, yes—"

Claere obeyed, taking a few paces in the direction shown.

In the same instant there was a blast of trumpets directly
behind her.

The two trumpeters of the King of Lethe lifted their
regimental instruments and played a bright parade fanfare of
extended major notes that was somehow more terrifying than the
sound of the artillery fire or the crackle of the inferno below the
walls. And then in the resulting momentary pause of silence,
they raised well-trained heraldic voices to call out into the airy
expanse:

"Ahoy there! Heed this now, Duke Ian Chidair, known as Hoarfrost! Cease fire and come forth to parlay with the Imperial Grand Princess of the Realm!"

Their voices rang with echoes and a well-practiced long range.

They repeated the parlay call three times at least, before a deep rude voice was heard in reply, coming from somewhere below, off in the distance of at least fifty feet. It seemed to be powered by bellows.

"So, the King of Lethe sends out a little girl to do his dirty work? Ahoy there, little girl!"

If Claere had a living heart, it would have been beating wildly right now. Instead, she made the effort to pull in the freezing air into her own lesser bellows of lungs, and then she stepped forward to look over the parapet wall at the chaos below.

Vlau Fiomarre immediately lunged forward to stand before her, blocking the outside, shielding her with his living body from view of the enemy.

But she put her hand up and placed it on his chest, and pushed him backwards slightly, away from the edge of the parapet. "No, Marquis . . ." she mouthed the words without remembering to use the held breath within her lungs to make her speech audible.

Vlau frowned but allowed himself to be directed backwards, and his handsome face, infernal in the firelight, was a study in repressed agony on her behalf.

Claere saw his look, but did not acknowledge it. Instead she turned her back on him with a strange proud movement that was both mechanical and somehow reminiscent of grace.

And she looked out past the parapet at the scene below.

At first glance there was almost nothing distinguishable, nothing to see past the raging wall of orange flames of at least twenty feet in height, and beyond it, the pitch black moving shapes of dead men—an infinity of them, crawling like ants before the walls.

And then she saw him. Unlike the others around him, he stood motionless, a giant, thick as a stump, with a barrel chest and a wild tangle of hair and beard, all of him frosted with ice and cast into demonic shadows by the flames.

"Duke Hoarfrost!" she uttered, and her voice creaked and broke at first, then became louder, stronger. "I am Claere Liguon, Grand Princess of the Realm and I am here to speak with you. Will you speak with me honorably?"

"What shall we speak of, little girl? Tea and biscuits? Terms of your surrender?"

"First, I would know what it is you want with this city."

In response came a bark of mechanical laughter.

"I want to take it, naturally!" Duke Hoarfrost exclaimed.

"But why?" said Claere. "It is not yours to take."

From below came more laughter.

"And neither is it *his* to keep! Letheburg falls to me now, little girl, because I will *have* it. And no living man or dead one shall stand before me! Tell that to the King who hides from me! Tell him, I will come for him and drag him by the beard through the streets of his city! I suggest you open your gates now, and spare yourself the trouble of the long and ugly siege! How much longer can you last? Your fuel will come to an end, your fires will go out, long before your measly food runs out, and then, what will you do? Because I promise you, by the time I am done with you, you will wish for a much quicker death!"

Claere pulled in a deep breath and replied. "I am dead already, Duke. And you are a villain, forsworn to your Liege Lord."

There was a brief pause.

"Dead, you say? So, you are dead too, little Princess?" he said. "Ah, I see how it is! In that case, my sympathies to you on your own untimely demise. But it is not so bad now, is it? No more pain, no more needs, no troubles of any sort, eh? Come now, admit it, girl! We are better off this way, you and I!"

"If there are no more needs," Claere said, "then why do you need Letheburg?"

"Ha-ha-ha! I like you, clever little Princess! Little Imperial whelp who would do your Emperor Papa proud! I see why old Lethe sent you here to talk, why you're a sharp one, aren't you! But clever words will not be enough!"

"Duke Hoarfrost, you have not answered my question."

In reply, he suddenly roared. The peculiar mercurial change in his manner was terrifying. "Answer you? *Answer you?* Why should I do anything now? I am *dead!* A goddamned dead man, and so are all these poor bastards around me, and so are *you!* What answer needs there be but that we're all dead, and death is everywhere and nowhere, and we are all rotting in our meat carcasses, biding our time—this extra impossible time given us—and I'll be damned if I don't take each precious fool moment and use it to the fullest! Now what say you to this, Your *Imperial* Highness?"

And suddenly several arrow shafts zipped through the air, one of them moving right past Claere's head, a hairsbreadth away.

But the Infanta did not even flinch. The arrows clattered on the top of the battlements, and only Vlau's startled exclamation a few steps behind her quickly cut short was any indication of their acknowledgement.

"No, no, damn you, don't shoot!" exclaimed Hoarfrost, waving angrily at the archers in his ranks. "Don't shoot just yet, boys, for the girlie and I are not done talking! Don't want to make a pincushion out of her just yet—that can come later when we sack the city—"

"Your words are overconfident," said Claere, looking in his general direction, looking down blindly into the fire and darkness below, because the rising pitch and black smoke were causing the film of ice on the surface of her frozen eyes to melt and cloud over, so that suddenly she could barely see anything. "Why are you so sure you will take Letheburg?"

"Ah, because I know something you don't!" He cackled suddenly.

A strange cold sense came to her, moving inside, entering her past her thickness of cotton, past the layers of distance formed from the fabric of her dead flesh. Claere felt a strange pang, a moment of true fear.

"And what is it that you know?" she said, her measured voice ringing out brightly against the constant crackle of flames.

"I know that even now *someone* comes who will make sure that the gates of Letheburg fall open. . . . And once they do, the city is mine. It has been promised to me."

"Who is it that comes?"

"Ah, but it is a surprise! You must wait and see, girlie!"

"I must do nothing of the sort," Claere said. "You are bluffing. And even if you have reinforcements, so does the King of Lethe. My Father, the Emperor of the Realm is on his way here even now, and he will put down your rabble army—"

"And who is bluffing now, Your Imperial Highness? You know very well no one is coming—no one will rescue you. Your Emperor father has enough to occupy him, and soon, he too will fall! Death! Death will come to all of you, all of the others still breathing within these walls!"

"Why must there be death? Why must you persist in this evil? What happened to your oath and your honorable word given to serve the Realm?" Claere was speaking, but she knew with every word it was a lost cause.

"My *oath?*" the Duke roared. "My oath of allegiance to any mortal man has died alongside me! Enough blathering now, girl! Begone from your walls before I change my mind and rain some pretty fire of my own in your direction! Now, run to your coward King and tell him to expect guests very soon—the whole lot of us! Tell him to prepare a Great Feast!"

But she was no longer listening. Her hollow eyes dark with

despair, Claere turned away from the edge of the parapets. She moved with awkward motions—her face glistening with the sheen of melting rime from the hot smoke that had been bathing her, but the joints of her body frozen stiff in those long moments she had been standing still—and she walked directly toward Vlau Fiomarre.

He stepped forward, reaching for her arm automatically, and his gaze was aflame. "Your Imperial Highness—you did all you could. . . ."

"Aye, that she did indeed," said the captain who had brought them here. He had been silent all this while, together with the other soldier guards and the trumpeters. But now he gifted Claere with a look of honest approval.

"Yes," said the Infanta. "I am done speaking with him. Take me back now."

And the captain complied.

B ack inside the Winter Palace, with the evening fully upon them, Claere and Vlau were delivered to the Infanta's own quarters, and then the King returned briefly to hear what had happened between her and Hoarfrost. Claere spoke evenly, telling what had come to pass in as neutral a language as possible.

"Unbelievable! What a madman! He is a blackguard and villain indeed to have insulted Your Imperial Highness and the Imperial Crown so damnedly!" King Roland muttered. Shaking his graying head, he paced the room before her, helpless and impotent in his complex union of terror and rage.

"He is not going to relent, I am sorry, Your Majesty," Claere said gently.

"No, he is not; yes, yes indeed, we see that now." The King stopped pacing, rubbed his forehead. "As for the *surprise* he is referring to, it is of course the war with the Domain. We have received some terrible news this morning, carried by Imperial birds, news that the Silver Court has shut its gates and fortified its own walls, and that the Sovereign of the Domain has invaded the Realm. Morphaea is razed and they have entered Lethe."

"War? What—what is happening, then? What does that mean for Letheburg?" Claere's attention focused for the first time.

The King glanced up at her with a gaze that did not fully meet her eyes. "I am afraid, my dear child, that Your Imperial Father may now be delayed and preoccupied at home, and Heaven only knows when any assistance from him can be expected. Unless Goraque comes to our aid, we are on our own."

"I—see." Claere uttered.

"Well, yes, then, and so it goes. Meanwhile, you have done well, Your Imperial Highness, as well as can be expected, out there. If any more news is forthcoming, you will naturally be informed." The King ended the conversation, and then left them in a chamber having grown dark with evening, and not a single candle lit.

As soon as the last guard and footman exited, taking the candlelight with them, and the door was closed, Claere paused in the twilight and then again approached the window. There, the lights of Letheburg were a sprinkling of golden dots in the distance, and the sky was still not fully black but an interim shade between heliotrope and deep indigo.

Vlau stood silently, watching her slim silhouette.

"Marquis . . . it is late, and you should have something to eat," she said suddenly, without turning to look at him.

"I—" he said, his voice cracking, for her words reminded him that he was indeed hungry and parched—or at least that he *should* have been, for he genuinely did not remember the last time he ate or drank at all. "I am not—"

"No," she said. "You *are*." And then, with one brief glance in his direction—and he saw only the glass reflection of her eyes while all else was silhouette—she moved to the side-table near the wall and rang the bell to summon a servant.

When a maid arrived a few moments later, somewhat startled by the summons, for in the last few days the servants had grown accustomed to the Infanta never seeming to require *anything* of them, Claere requested candles and a proper fire to be lit in the fireplace, and then a hot supper service "for the gentleman only."

The servant hurried to carry out Her Imperial Highness's orders, and soon the room was properly illuminated and warmed for the first time in days.

"Why are you doing this?" Vlau whispered out of hearing range of the servants.

Claere, who had placed herself stiffly in a tall-backed chair near the window, now regarded him with her great sunken eyes. "Because you spend more time in here than in your own chamber, Marquis. It is only right that the room is made comfortable for one such as yourself—with human *living* needs."

"Then I am sorry! I should go—" Angry inexplicable color flooded his cheeks and he started to rise.

"No, stay," she said in a commanding voice.

And he obeyed her.

"I am rather glad you are here," she said evenly. "But if you are to continue, you must eat and drink and rest. It benefits no one if you languish and starve."

"What does it matter if I eat?" he said. "When more deserving others could use the dwindling food that will be wasted on me."

"It matters to me," she replied.

He watched her with his dark unblinking gaze.

The servants arrived in that moment with his supper tray. There was a large platter of blue veined and aged cheeses, fresh baguettes of bread, a steaming-hot salted ham roll baked in flaky pastry, pears poached in port sauce topped with sweet cream, and apple tartlets in honey. Another servant carried a decanter of deep red wine to be imbibed with the blue cheese.

Vlau watched them arrange the serving table, set out the delicacies, pour the wine, and then make their bows and depart, after Vlau nodded to the footman server that he did not require his presence during the meal.

"Please, eat," the Infanta said. Her hands were folded in her lap and she looked at him in expectation.

The sight of her gentle smoke-colored eyes in their hollowed sockets, trained upon him, evoked a painful spasm in his chest, which then continued downward, twisting his gut. Indeed, eating was the last thing he wanted to be doing. And yet, he was dried on the inside, hollowed out himself, empty, parched, dead . . . he had forgotten what it was like to taste and swallow. Only his mind was fevered, hot, burning, fertile with the moisture of life, like a river. . . .

Vlau picked up the goblet of wine and brought it to his lips—while she continued looking at him and he at her, their faces illuminated by warm candlelight. And for some reason neither one of them could make the supreme effort to break the bond of their gaze.

Vlau swallowed, and the cool bittersweet liquid was a vibrant shock. The wine filled his mouth with living force, and he knew sudden wild thirst—his body remembered it, the sensation of needing to drink. He then started to swallow the liquid in gulps, and it went down inside him in a torrent that for some reason did not seem to fill him, was not quite enough to satiate the bottomless need of his desiccated innards.

What is wine but the blood of death? The fevered nonsense words sounded in his mind. *What is blood but the wine of life?*

He drank the entire goblet and put it down, momentarily breaking the connection of their gaze. He breathed deeply while the wine coursed inside him, warming his blood.

"Now, eat," she reminded him and continued watching his every move.

Vlau nodded and forced himself to pick up the knife and cut

into the flesh of the pastry and the cheese. His lips parted and he ate, his motions once more mechanical and senseless at the beginning. But then his body took over—it recollected the burst of flavor, the virile juices filling his mouth, the sudden ravenous hunger. . . .

The fireplace and the candlelight together had warmed the room entirely by the time he was done eating, and the large tray with its dishes was mostly empty. Meanwhile, outside the great glass window, the sky stood pitch-black over Letheburg, while the stars emerged like sugar sprinkles, and the street lanterns were a sea of glowing spilled droplets of candied amber. So easy to forget that just a bit further off in the panorama of the city, outside the scope of the window, the distant walls stood up silhouetted against an orange inferno, and the relentless enemy continued to storm the parapets. . . .

Vlau Fiomarre felt a slow groggy relaxation coming over him, a pleasurable fullness of a solid meal and the warm buzz of wine. He did not recall the last time he had eaten so well and drunk so deeply—maybe that supper meal at Grial's house was the closest approximation, except he recalled eating warily and in a hurry, hardly tasting anything and being on his guard the whole time.

But now—now was a strange suspended moment of animal comfort, an impossible magical time.

He glanced up and saw her watching him still, steady and serene. There was a tiny, barely formed smile on her lips.

And he could not help it. He smiled at her in return, warm and satiated and mindlessly *present* in the moment. . . .

"How was the apple tart?" she said, with a small nod of her head at the tray.

He blinked, recollecting himself because he was warmly mesmerized by the ethereal appearance of her smoke-hued great eyes. "Ah, delicious."

"You know," Claere Liguon continued, "I used to love

berry tarts. I would always ask for them for supper and with tea and even at breakfast—even though I was sickly and could hardly finish a single one. When I was about seven or eight, I still remember the one time I was punished by my tutors, and sent to bed without a raspberry tart and custard because I refused to properly read and memorize the stupid chapter about the high office and governing differences between the elected Doge of Venice and the hereditary King of France. To make matters worse, after I was left alone, lying furious in my bed, I secretly named him the 'Dog of Venice' in a perfectly horrid little girl's revenge. To this day, when I think of the government of Venice, *La Serenissima*, it is with irritation and a thought to canines, and yes, with some wistful thoughts of raspberry tarts."

She made a small sound that was almost a laugh, and continued smiling at him.

Vlau glanced at the tray, his first impulse being to offer her a tart, for there were a couple of them remaining on the dish. And then the impossible darkness of reality, the realization struck him. *She* could never eat a tart again.

And oh, how bitterly he wanted to laugh at the simplicity of it, and then cry, and scream, and crawl out of his own skin and simply not be. . . . She would *never* again *eat*—she would not—because of what *he* did to her.

His countenance transformed, vertigo striking him, and his full warm stomach was now filled with rocks. Indeed, knives were cutting him. . . .

"Oh, no, no!" she said, noting his new terrifying expression and recognizing its cause. "I did not mean to make you feel uncomfortable, Marquis! Please, do not mind my careless words, it was just a passing silly memory! I was making small talk—"

"There can be no small talk between us," he blurted, and his wonderful meal was now a boulder inside him. He regretted it already, regretted having even a bite.

"It does not have to be this way," she said. "I was certain— I'd thought that by now, some things were in the past—"

"How can any of it ever be in the past?" he exclaimed, and stood up, pushing back the supper table with brutal force so that the fine china dishes clattered.

The fragile smile left her lips.

In that moment the servants arrived to clear the supper service. As they removed the leftovers of his meal, Vlau stood coldly, wanting to speak, to look at her directly, but frozen in a strange mindful pride.

As soon as they had taken away the dishes, raked the coals in the fireplace, and the door closed behind them, the Infanta said, "Please do me the courtesy of sitting down once more, Marquis."

"It is wrong," he said coldly, remaining standing, and no longer meeting her eyes. "I should not be here."

"Maybe not," she said. "But did you not say once that there would be *no guilt?* Do you not remember how you said it yourself?"

He frowned, the candlelight emphasizing his black brows, the shadowed hollows of his lean cheeks with their growth of dark stubble, giving him an even more fierce demeanor. "Yes," he whispered. "I said it then. And I was a fool for having said it. But now—"

"Nothing matters any more." She said the words softly and then stretched out her hand—thin and white, delicate skin over bone—pointing him back to the sofa. "Please . . ." she whispered. "If you go and leave me now, it would mean that nothing had changed indeed, and that your hate continues to burn at me and my family. If you go—" and her voice went silent.

"What?" he said, permitting himself once more to look at her. "If I go, then what?"

"Then I will be all alone in this room, in silence, with the candles softly dying and the fire eventually all gone out, in the dark . . . in the *grave.*"

And at that word, his heart was stilled. He heard her, and he sat down once more, where he had been, across from her in her high-backed chair.

"I will . . . stay," he said. And his eyes did not blink—could not—for they were welling with liquid, and if he blinked, it would pool and run . . . and she would *see* it.

"Thank you," said Claere, and her hands were once more folded in her lap.

There was a long pause of silence. The fire crackled in the hearth, and the light of the candelabras cast a soft buttery radiance at the well-appointed furnishings of the chamber, the brocade of the upholstery and the fine curtains.

Outside the glass window, in the darkness, against the mosaic of city lights, snow began to fall. Large white snowflakes floated down near the window, and brushed the glass with their cobweb pallor before sinking away out of sight.

"Tell me a story," said Claere suddenly. "Tell me your favorite story of childhood, the one told to you when you were a little boy. The one that made you laugh and smile just before you fell asleep."

Hearing her calm, soothing voice, his stiff posture eased somewhat. Vlau inhaled a deep breath, and then sat back against the fine cushions of the sofa. He tried to think—he thought back to what curious tales of magical desert kingdoms and flying carpets and clever genii his mother used to tell him and his sister and brothers as they lay down each night—back in the early days. Then he remembered one in particular, and with it a fragile warmth returned to his insides, slowly filling the dark places, turning eventually into a soothing flow of comfort and security and long-forgotten laughter.

And he started telling the story.

It was several hours past midnight. The candles in the candelabras had burned down into puddles of wax, and the wicks had ceased smoking a while ago. The fireplace too had faded into ruddy coals which had winked out one by one, until the room was submerged in darkness—all but for the light outside the window where the *sfumato* moon was a delicate blot of haze in the sky, while below everything was *chiaroscuro* contrast as the city lanterns continued to cast their cheerful golden dots into the sea of deep blue all around.

Claere sat motionless in the tall-backed chair, sometimes gazing out through the window at the twinkling cityscape of night. But mostly she looked at the man who was on the sofa, fast asleep. He had slid down against the cushions and pillows, at some point having fallen asleep while seated upright, but now was lying back, with his head lolling on one shoulder.

She watched his face slackened in sleep, seeing possibly for the first time how he could appear when not harboring a tense frown on his handsome features, or not glaring with intensity. And what she saw was a young man with circles of exhaustion under his eyes, a soft cast to his features, woefully unshaven cheeks and longish raven-black hair tousled around his forehead and ears.

Claere looked at him with a kind of gentle, painful, previously unknown affection that tugged at her and made her almost *feel* the place within her chest where once she had a beating heart.

Here was her murderer, the man who had struck a knife blade into that very place in her chest, and she should be feeling hatred and a desire for retribution. Instead, she could only look at him and feel pity, sympathy, and overwhelming excruciating warmth.

Earlier that night, after she had asked him for a story, just to get his mind off their grim reality, he had complied and started speaking. He talked non-stop, telling one tale, then another, and the tales turned into history and the story of his siblings and parents and his ancestral home, and outrageous childish pranks, and the grapevines laden with fruit so ripe it was nearly black, and the hot summer sun in a vibrant blue sky. . . .

His voice had been like music, its rich expressive cadence, its narrative, both soothing and invigorating in a strange dichotomy of living imagery. It filled her imagination with a distant world that was no longer—a world of happy innocence and bright colors, of fragrant breezes and dappled sunlight.

He talked thus, deep into the night, as the candles burned down, and he was eventually burned out along with them, his passionate words quenched, and his memories cast forth before them like a jumbled deck of cards. She listened to him, responding occasionally in her soft voice, nodding at other times, smiling when it was called for, but mostly allowing him to vent his intensity in the quiet solitude of this room. Finally he went silent, and paused, saying that he needed to rest his eyes, and then he exhaled in peace and was asleep in an instant, like a young boy.

Claere exhaled also, letting go of the mechanical breath she had held in reserve in her lungs so that she could make human living speech and hold a conversation with him. She then sat thus in stillness and silence, letting him rest, and watching his living peace . . . it was almost her own peace, or so she could let herself imagine. For, he had stayed in the room with her and thus made it a place of the living instead of her solitary grave.

And for that alone she was grateful.

As the fireplace burned down and the darkness in the room deepened by the time the moon finally sank beyond the horizon—though never reaching full pitch-black, for the city lights were too bright for that—there was nothing, no sound left, only his regular deep breathing. She listened to its comforting rhythm and watched the endless armies of snowflakes coming down outside the window.

At some point she wanted to rise and approach him, to sit down at his side—to look closer at the sheen of his olive skin and to observe his eyelids over eyes that occasionally moved rapidly in sleep, long dark lashes fluttering against his cheek.

But she refrained, for on some strange human level she did not want to frighten him, recalling herself, knowing full well what she now was—nothing more than an animated *corpse*. How would he feel, what jolt of primal terror, were he to wake suddenly and see her thus leaning over him, or simply nearby, staring at him with her cold, fixed, *dead* eyes?

And as Claere pondered this, seated primly in her chair—exactly as she had been for the last several hours, never having moved even a finger since he had fallen asleep—he suddenly awoke with a shudder and came to himself in the soft imperfect darkness.

"Ah!" he muttered, then said thickly in a sleep-laden voice, "Claere. . . ."

He had never once used her given name before, only called her "Liguon" or "Your Imperial Highness," in each case speaking with disdain or with hints of mockery. Indeed, he had never spoken in her presence like this, not with this strange, raw inflection, and revealing such peculiar vulnerability. . . .

Such *need*.

"Claere!"

This time, because his utterance was a desperate cry—*he was calling her!*—she got up, stiffly and awkwardly, and moved to cross the distance in the room between them, and she leaned slightly over him, keeping her dead balance with some difficulty. "Yes, I am here . . ." she said, after refilling her lungs, and shaping the words into a whisper.

But he was sitting up now, his shadowed face wild with the moment of transition between waking and sleep, an instant of incomprehension and then sharp awareness.

Awareness of *her*.

With a gasp he moved forward then, toward her in the darkness. . . . And in the next instant she felt his hands taking rough hold of her own in a powerful desperate grip that would have been painful, had she been able to feel anything beyond a remote discernment of physical contact through the usual cotton thickness of her dead flesh.

Then he was coming down before her, falling, falling—kneeling on the floor, in the shadowed darkness, grasping her legs, her feet, the folds of her skirt, a mess of his limbs enclosing hers while somehow she remained standing upright. From the floor, he looked up at her, his upturned face faintly illuminated by the night's glow seeping from the window, his black liquid eyes in agony. Finally her gripped her around the waist, pulling her small fragile body close to him as she stood stiffly. And stilling thus, he placed his forehead against her solar plexus, and then slid lower, against her silent womb. . . .

He held her thus—she, cold and brittle, he, burning and pliant and shaking with sobs, his face running with hot tears that stained the front of her simple dress, pressed against her, wallowing. "I am . . . sorry! *So sorry! Forgive me!*" he cried hoarsely over and over, gasped, choking on his tears and breath, shaking, shaking in a fever. . . .

Until she reached out and put her small cold hands on his head and stroked his dark soft hair.

"Claere!" he said, looking up at her. "Take my life, Claere! Please! Please, *take it!*"

He grasped her hands and this time pressed his warm trembling lips against the coolness of her wrists, her fingers, her arms, staining her lifeless doll's skin with his scalding tears, like burning drops of liquid wax falling upon brittle parchment.

And suddenly, fiercely, he put his hand up on her left side, fingers splayed just below her chest, in that spot where he had once plunged steel, and which was now cold and silent. "It was here," he whispered, "yes, here . . . it went in, and—and I hurt you . . . *here!*"

"Hush," she replied. "It is no matter now."

"Claere! My life is yours! All of me, I am—*yours!* Please . . . forgive me!"

"I've forgiven you a long time ago." Her voice was soft and

serene as the snow falling outside the window.

"But how could you? *How?* What manner of mad, holy angel are you?"

"How could I not?" She looked down at him with her great gentle eyes of glass and smoke.

"But no, oh, do *not* forgive me! Never!" he ranted suddenly. "It is hell, my place is there, in the deep dark pit! From its bowels I will *love* you with my last breath, even as I burn, as I am twisted and torn and consumed with black flames and rent asunder, over and over unto eternity, for hurting you—"

"No, please stop!"

"I cannot—I cannot live anymore," he said, his hand upon her mortal wound. "Not with what I've done to you. Life had ended when I put the dagger here—your life and *mine*."

"I know," she said, her gaze upon him never faltering. "And yet, my life had never *been*—not for that weak, sickly girl that I had been. I was dying inside, since birth, and you *transformed* me. For that alone, I can only love you, Vlau."

"You . . . *love* me?" His breath had stilled to the point that now he too was like a dead man, motionless, fixed in the impossibility, looking up at her in hunger, in disbelieving wonder.

"*Vlau*," she said. "My poor Vlau.'"

Chapter 6

S now was falling.

It had continued falling all through the night and into a weak, pale overcast dawn. The protective wall of roaring flames that had been set to burning intentionally all around the city walls by the defenders of Letheburg, was being softly eroded and quenched by the gentle blanket of whiteness coming down from the sky. Lower and lower the fire-moat burned, sputtering and in places going out altogether.

The inferno had been the city's main line of defense, keeping the onslaught of the dead at bay. And now they were about to lose its protection.

There was despair and chaos up on the battlements. In many places where the fires were particularly low on the ground below, the dead were now aggressively scaling the walls, and the living could hardly keep up with overturning their ladders, poles, and grappling hooks and casting them back down.

Making matters worse, Hoarfrost's army had taken the few days of siege to erect and position towers and catapults. And now, the first heavy projectiles loaded with tar and pitch were being sent into the city, set on fire from the very flames readily burning in the defensive fiery moat around the walls. The fires they started on the outskirts of the city interior were now a new cause for distress, as the remote outer neighborhoods of

Letheburg burned, wooden structures of the older houses going up in flames, while the more recent buildings of brick and stone holding up better but still charred and damaged. The only thing saving them from a major citywide fire was the same culprit that crippled their defensive firewall beyond the city walls—the falling snow.

King Roland Osenni was awakened from his troubled slumber, soon after first light, by his advisors informing him of the new disaster.

"Begging Pardon of Your Majesties, but what must be done?" they asked him as he lay abed next to his wife, Queen Lucia, and squinted at them.

The soul-weary King momentarily considered just pulling the bed canopy curtains around them, hiding under the warm softness of the royal bedcovers, and pretending none of this was taking place. Queen Lucia opened her eyes, groaned and listened in despair while her spouse was briefed on the ugly details— catapults firing, safety fires going out outside the city while new fires were springing up inside, and now—*burning* city blocks, in addition to a few new *disappearing* city blocks.

"And so, I am afraid we are not going to be able to hold them off much longer," concluded one aged military advisor in an old-fashioned powdered wig and with a thick white brush mustache.

King Roland frowned, rubbed his forehead and held the bridge of his nose. Then he muttered in a sleep-weakened cracking voice. "Ah, what an abomination this is . . . this war, these endless dead, this everything! What do you suggest, Lord Granwell? What can we do?"

Lord Granwell bowed with a resigned expression. "The troops are on their last strength, even as they toil in shifts. Our resources, especially the flammable materials and kindling to keep the fires burning, are running out. Truthfully, there is very little that can be done, Your Majesty—"

"So what are you saying?"

"Regretfully, it appears very likely that Letheburg might not hold out much longer."

The King felt a debilitating wave of cold in his abdomen. He sat up in the bed. "So soon . . ." he whispered. "Ah-h-h. . . . I had thought we would manage at least a few weeks, at least until some reinforcements arrived. Indeed, our dwindling food was my greater concern. How did this happen?"

"Well, Your Majesty, having the dead attacking 'round the clock was unprecedented, and no one could have prepared for such a peculiar manner of warfare narrowly limited to using ordinary fire as opposed to the more traditional artillery and flammables such as black powder and explosives."

"There has to be something! Something more that can be done!"

"I am afraid, Your Majesty" Lord Granwell said carefully, biting his upper lip with its thick white mustache, "that the carrier birds sent to Goraque had prompted no reply. We might try sending again today, after the snow slows down—"

"Yes, yes, do it!"

"There is another thing, Your Majesty. There is a notion being discussed up on the battlements that the next step in our defense might be to employ sorcery and the more *positive* of the occult arts—in conjunction with common prayer, naturally, since I do believe the Archbishop will be saying a series of extended masses all throughout the day—"

"Grial!" Queen Lucia exclaimed suddenly, interrupting Lord Granwell. "Oh, we must send for Grial!"

"Oh Heaven, no! Not that nuisance of a woman!" the King muttered.

"Actually," Granwell said in a diplomatic tone, "Your Majesty might be interested to know that this very same Grial person has been indeed seen up on the battlements every night— doing quite a bit of good for the soldiers, it must be added. They do seem to love her, Your Majesty, and a morale boost can work wonders to keep them going. Furthermore, it is rumored that she might indeed be up there doing more than just passing out pies and rolls, if one might venture to surmise—"

"That's it, my dear, we must summon Grial immediately," Queen Lucia persisted. "I know she can help! I am certain of it!"

The King sighed, untangled himself from the bedding, pulled up his long fine silk sleeping shirt up past his knees and started to get out of bed, while his valet rushed forward with the royal silk slippers. "Very well," he said. "Lucia, my dear, I capitulate as always to your pleasure. Send for that ridiculous woman."

Snow was falling.

Ebrai Fiomarre rode through the countryside, a dreary white landscape of uniform pallor and contrasting black shrubbery, with only occasional traces of a road underfoot. It was a deceptive serenity, he knew, for even now, underneath the snow they crawled, slowly and inevitably, the endless *dead.* . . . At times, like mushrooms breaking through cracked earth, the snowdrifts churned, and broken man-shapes would become visible. Limbs appeared, clawing bone-white hands, damaged torsos, heads barely recognizable as human, and there would be a transient flicker of color from bits of their coat fabric— pomegranate for the Trovadii, sienna brown for the Balmue, a scattering of tan and teal of Morphaea. . . . They came in the wake of the Sovereign's main army, these pitiful and broken dead, some aimless, others single-minded and thus dangerous.

Did they even know where they were crawling, or why?

Ebrai steeled his heart and paid them minimal attention. Instead he drew his nondescript grey cloak and hood closer about him from the relentless ice-wind, and held on to the reins with his leather gauntlet. Although he wore no full suit of armor to draw less attention to himself, there was a fine chain mail hauberk underneath his plain unmarked surcoat, and beneath it a thick warm gambeson. And attached at his waist was a discreet and compact sword.

For the moment he rode a sturdy grey gelding that he had procured from his Imperial contacts just outside Silver Court, after a hurried exchange of intelligence and a change of horses.

He had been moving carefully in the wake of the Trovadii Army, keeping just half a day behind their progress through devastated Morphaea and now Lethe. As soon as the Sovereign and her armies had swept past Silver Court, he made his rendezvous a mile outside the citadel walls in a small cabin surrounded by sparse forest and knee-deep snowdrifts. Here he was told to continue executing his directive, which at present meant following the Sovereign's original command to find the village girl from Oarclaven, and use this as the means to maintain his proximity to Rumanar Avalais.

"It is Our Will," the Emperor's words were conveyed to him, "that you seek the opportunity to find the Sovereign's greatest weakness and vulnerability, if such exists, and to use it to our immediate advantage. There is no longer any necessity to bide your time. When the first opportunity arises, you must act upon it."

Ebrai understood very well what this meant. He was to destroy the Sovereign. Before the Event of death's cessation it would have meant a simple solution—assassination. But now that there was no death, things had become exceedingly complex.

Ebrai had fewer *clean* options remaining. Capture and isolation of Her Brilliance in a remote and secret prison cell where she could be left to rot in anonymity was the least distasteful, and also the least likely possibility. Had it been anyone else—anyone a bit more ordinary, more *human*, and less tainted with something he was certain now was dark sorcery— then he would have started making plans for capture and abduction and come up with a solid method long before he even caught up with the Trovadii.

But now—now, Ebrai was at a loss. He rode, thinking grimly on the fact of the Sovereign's undeniable charismatic effect upon all those who served her—including himself. In her presence, the loss of personal will was astounding. . . . One look from her, an almost tangible caress of her blue-eyed gaze, and Ebrai had to make a superhuman effort to keep himself in control and retain focus of his true secret mission. To *capture* the Sovereign would have been an extraordinary effort considering the loyalty of her men, but at least it was a remote possibility. However, to *keep* her held and contained after the fact would have been impossible. Ebrai imagined numerous scenarios where the Sovereign seduced her guards, both male and female, with a look or a voice, bribed them with a smile, and consequently all doors were opened before her.

No, there was no way to hold and keep her, he finally admitted to himself.

The ugly options remained. Taking her captive and immediately cutting off her limbs, beheading and separating parts of her flesh in separate locations. Burning her body until it was no longer recognizable as such. . . . Or else, drugging her and keeping her thus unconscious round the clock—but here again, the charismatic effect of her as the innocent victim might cause her guards to become attached, sympathetic, and then become lax. And then her dose of drugs would be tapered off, reduced intentionally or not, and one day she would make her escape. . . . Finally, there was the option of breaking her mind—driving her to insanity with privation and torture. . . .

The more Ebrai thought, the more horrified he became. Not only were the solutions gruesome and morally reprehensible, but there was also the very strong probability that whatever method was ultimately used by him in the name of the Imperial Crown of the Realm, it would create a martyr.

There had to be another way. . . .

And Ebrai suddenly had a sharp stroke of inspiration. The

girl from Oarclaven! The one who supposedly could send the dead to their final rest! All he had to do was continue his mission, find her, then tell her the truth and convince her to play along while he took her with him before the Sovereign. There, he would strike Rumanar Avalais a killing blow, and the girl would simply finish her off by performing whatever miracles necessary in order to send the Sovereign off to the devil below, once and for all.

Such a marvelous solution it was to their problem that Ebrai felt better for the first time in what felt like months and years of his clandestine post and service ordeal.

Of course the supremely difficult details were still to be worked out, and carrying out this operation together with some untrained village girl was going to be a challenge, but it was the best option before him.

Ebrai exhaled a sigh of relief and gripped the reins with more confidence than he had in months.

As he rode across what might have been a small ravine, emerging carefully on the rise, past occasional crawling shapes of the broken dead, he saw before him a definite road.

And across from it, only about fifty feet away was a camped army, consisting of at least several hundred men, infantry and a company of mounted knights. They had made no fires and were near-silent, snow falling upon them as they sat in clumps, apparently taking a small rest in their march to chew dried meat and bread, and thus there was no warning to be had.

Ebrai slowed, pulling up his horse, his mind racing swiftly, but he was completely in plain view, and there was no avoiding it.

Fortunately, he also saw their banners, red-and-gold, with a familiar crest of Goraque. These were men of Lethe, and he had nothing to fear as long as he acted forthright.

"You! Halt!" A nearby soldier guard had seen him and challenged his approach. Heads turned, and a few seated men sprang for their weapons.

Ebrai calmly raised one arm in greeting, keeping the other visibly on the reins, and spoke in a loud measured baritone. "Peace be with you, soldiers of Goraque! I am alone and I am on your side."

"Who are you?" said one dark bearded knight, immediately approaching on foot, his iron-plated boots sinking in the snow. "Quickly, your name!"

"My name is of no consequence," Ebrai replied. "However, my mission on behalf of the Emperor is. I am headed to Oarclaven—"

"Why should we believe you if you refuse to give your name?" The knight had stopped across the road from him, and folded his arms. "You're not going anywhere."

Ebrai simply pointed to the ground near the knight's feet, where an arm suddenly emerged out of a snowdrift.

"There's a dead man crawling at your feet, about to pull you down. You may choose not to believe me. Or you might want to back away—"

"Ah, *merde!*" the knight stepped back, while a few foot soldiers approached, carrying long pikes, and they unceremoniously prodded the corpse away with the sharp ends.

"These damn things keep coming up and they are everywhere," muttered the knight, wiping snowflakes from his nose and beard and watching his men deal with the dead man. However his stern expression loosened and he nodded at Ebrai. "If you're really on our side and have useful news from the Emperor, the Duke will want to see you."

"By all means." Ebrai nodded in turn. He then directed the gelding to cross the road toward the knight and soldiers. The horse snorted in displeasure, shook its head, scattering the fresh snow powder frosting its mane, and carefully stepped around the spot with the floundering corpse and the pikemen.

"By the way," said the knight tiredly, starting to walk alongside Ebrai and his mount. "If you must know, there is no more Oarclaven. For that matter, most of Goraque is gone too, up north, and to the east especially. There's nothing there; hardly any of our land left before the foreign border begins. You can now see the Valley of the Rhine, they say, and the Holy Roman Empire. . . ."

Ebrai took a deep breath, exhaled, once more feeling the compounding weight of the new complications. Following the walking knight, he slowly rode through the spare camp, greeted by halfway indifferent stares of the Goraque soldiers.

The knight was talkative. "We're making our way toward Letheburg now, collecting reinforcements, and whoever you are, you might consider joining us. The city is under siege, and we are told the Sovereign's armies are headed that way. Indeed, we watched them pass only hours ago, as we lay low in hiding, in the forest just a few miles back."

"I've been following the Trovadii, yes," Ebrai responded. "They swept past Silver Court and did not stop. They are moving north."

"I am sure His Grace the Duke Vitalio Goraque will be curious to hear all this and anything else you have to say."

"I have no doubt. . . ." Ebrai spoke, looking up at the sky, for in that moment the overcast thickened and the flakes sped downward in thick flurries.

"Aye, it's really coming down now," muttered the knight, seeing the direction of Ebrai's gaze. "Just our luck."

S now was falling.
      Great big flakes swirled, blanketing Rollins Way, on the other side of the glass window and past the bright chintz curtains of the cheerful parlor of Grial's house.

Hecate, also known as Grial, sat in a wooden rocking chair with her back to the window, looking as mundane and human as she had been for so long that it had almost become a habit. Even her frizzy hair was back, and her dingy patchwork housedress with it grease-stained apron. Only her eyes were different, darker than black, filled indeed with the weight of immortality.

"Well, girlies," she said to the room full of very attentive, truly mesmerized girls who were attending her every word, and in some cases still shaking in residual holy terror. "In about ten minutes, there will be a knock on the front door. I am about to be summoned to see the King in the Winter Palace, so I am going to pop on over there right now to save everyone some precious time. Time is in very short order, dumplings, so there's simply no excuse to waste it, not even to let nature run its temporal course."

"Oh, goodness, yes, Your Divine Grace—that is, Your Sacredness, o Great Goddess Hecate—" began Lizabette, stammering and sitting very primly on the sofa with her feet together and her back straight.

"Now, now, phooey," said Hecate. "I told you to stop that nonsense. I am still Grial as far as all of you are concerned. 'Grial' is a perfectly lovely name, and it is definitely *one* of my names, so please, do be kind enough to use it. Now then, there's the big kettle of potato soup still not done boiling and needing a few chunks of Gorgonzola to be stirred in toward the end, so please be on the lookout for it, Marie. And Catrine, have yourself and Niosta a few apple tarts from the pantry, top right shelf, but don't touch the one just below it—oh, might as well bring the whole platter out for all of you to have while I'm gone. Faeline, be a dear and stop hyperventilating, that's it, just remember what I told you, breathe through the right nostril, then the left, and count to ten. . . ."

And saying this, Hecate patted down her kinky wild hair, tugged at the apron around her waist, and then, as the girls continued staring in her, she pointed at the door and added, "As soon as that knock comes, simply tell the dear man from the Palace that I am already there."

"Yes, Ma'am!" Niosta said breathlessly.

But Hecate was already gone, while the empty wooden

rocking chair continued to creak and rock a few more instants without her.

S now was falling.
    Queen Lucia Osenni sat morosely in a deep wingchair near the window in her Royal Spouse's study and watched its endless white descent, thick and relentless, from a winter sky that was a dreary cocktail of milk and ashes.

The whole world outside was grey despair. Indeed, they were being smothered by a veil of overcast that seemed to have taken over the heavens permanently. It was mid-morning and yet the level of light was that of dusk, so that the street lanterns had to be re-lit to burn in the daytime. Meanwhile Letheburg was being inundated with the white powder, piling on the rooftops and streets. In just a couple of hours it was ankle-deep, and lord knows how bad it would get by evening. By then, it would also be too late for their citywide defense of the walls, as the struggling black-smoke fires that were at present still burning, sputtered into nothing.

For the moment, the exhausted garrison soldiers continued to trudge back and forth on their shifts to hold down the defense of the city. She could see them as dots of dark cobalt blue in the Lethe Square below. Wheeled carts were moving along with difficulty, sinking deep and getting stuck in the icy ruts, and in most cases replaced with freight sleds to glide over the fresh powder. Torches flickered with weak golden light, struggling to stay lit in the snowfall. . . .

Queen Lucia looked away, glancing at King Roland as he was occupied with a large map of the city, spread out on the desk, and arguing with several advisors. Whatever futile strategic nonsense they were considering or planning, she was certain, would do little good now.

Instead, Queen Lucia counted down the minutes until Grial got here. . . . All their hopes lay with Grial, she knew on some odd instinctive level. She would arrive and *she* would say or do or reveal something useful, even if at first the King always protested and frowned at her "devil suggestions."

And speaking of the she-devil—a liveried servant announced Grial's arrival, in what seemed to be an impossibly short amount of time elapsed since the courier had been sent through the snow to fetch her.

The King grunted and frowned, granting his reluctant "audience," while the Queen immediately stood up from her seat with hopeful excitement.

Grial entered unceremoniously right after the servant, and the general babble of voices in the room quieted while all the distinguished military advisors stared at her, many over their noses or through the lenses of their pince-nez.

"Your Majesties!" Grial exclaimed, nodding with her head once to each Monarch in the remotest kind of courtesy possible, and put her hands together, rubbing her palms on her filthy apron that normally made His Majesty queasy. "Now, how may I be of service?"

"Grial!" Queen Lucia smiled and came a few steps forward, but then relented, seeing her husband's stern glare.

"Mistress Grial, hmm, well—yes, I realize this is frankly ludicrous, to expect this of you, but I am being told you might have some *unusual* means of assisting our city defense." The King coughed to clear his throat and spoke the words reluctantly, setting down the map markers in the form of tiny tin soldiers. He then folded his arms and looked at her.

"Unusual means, Your Majesty?" Was it only a trick of the light, but Grial's black eyes seemed particularly dark and bottomless today, despite her smile. The nature of the expression in those eyes made the King want to shudder.

But Roland Osenni got himself under control and got to the point. "Unusual, yes," he said. "As in, sorcery. *Witchcraft.* The thing that you do, woman! Don't make me come out and say it!"

"Well, Majesty, apparently you did just say it, and so

naturally I must respond." Grial looked around the chamber, from the King to the Queen to all the advisors, and then she continued, in a bright ringing voice. "Here is the thing, about sorcery and witchcraft. It's all about using one's true will and desire and the energy at hand to make something happen. Something very *powerful*."

"Go on," the King said.

"Here we have Letheburg. An entire city surrounded by sturdy and tall walls of stone. And we have a great big army of thoroughly nasty dead men camped outside our walls, trying to get inside."

"Yes, yes, we already know all this!"

"So what we must do," Grial said, "is make the walls impossible for the enemy to breach or scale—using the will and the power at hand."

"Yes, that's exactly it—whatever it is you've just said!" said the King. "Now, proceed to make yourself useful, and do it!"

"Do what, Your Majesty?"

"Oh, for heaven's sake, Grial, do your infernal sorcery!"

Queen Lucia clutched her hands together, and then added, "My dear, you really ought to ask her gently, I dare say, and maybe use the word 'please'—"

In response suddenly Grial cackled. Her raucous laughter came ringing through the chamber, and lasted at least long enough to make King Roland want to cover his ears and gouge her eyes out, or maybe gouge his own eyes out—or exactly ten breaths. "Oh, oh, oh dear!" Grial said at last. "My dear Majesty, how you do make me chortle so! Begging pardon, of course, but surely you don't expect *me* to do any of this sorcery on behalf of Letheburg?"

"What?" said he, frowning once more. "What now?"

"Why, Your Majesty, this kind of magic may only be performed by the one who is in charge. The one who is ultimately *responsible* for Letheburg, the guardian or the caretaker, the steward or the lord, the ultimate ruling authority. In other words, Majesty, someone such as Yourself."

The King glared at her. "What are you saying? I thought you were already performing some kind of binding spell up on the parapets every night! I am told this with great assurances of certainty! Or are my men addled?"

"Goodness, I am merely spreading good cheer up there!" Grial put her hands on her hips, shook her head, and cast her gaze about the room. "Really, now, gentlemen! Did you honestly think I was doing sorcery when I was supplying the good soldiers with my famous apple pies? Why, the girls and I spend every day covered in flour, baking and rolling the dough—"

"Enough!" the King roared. "I knew this was a terrible and foolish mistake calling you here. There is no such thing as sorcery, and all of this has been for nothing—"

"Ah, but I wouldn't say so, Your Majesty, not quite for nothing!" Grial stopped moving and froze, and her gaze upon him was like the weight of an invisible hand holding him down. "There is indeed sorcery and magic, and yes, wonder and *power* in this world . . ." she said softly.

They heard her utter the words, and everyone present felt each tiny hair rise along their arms, together with a chill. The room had grown as silent as the grave.

"The one who rules this city must go up on the battlements. This person must walk the entirety of the walls in a great circle, beginning and ending in the same spot, then proceed to stand up there, holding two torches raised up to the heavens, and look out beyond the walls to face the enemy. This individual must stand thus, one whole day and one whole night, and never waver, using all the will and power in their heart to create the true wall of safety and protection around Letheburg. After that, no one will be able to breach the city, for as long as the true ruler remains within the walls, or simply wills it to be so."

When Grial finished speaking, the abysmal silence

continued. King Roland stood, plunged in thought, and a deep frown was crippling his features.

"So you're saying I must go up there, and stand with torches a whole day and night while some kind of magic happens, and all the while I get shot at by muskets and arrows and heaven knows what other hellfire that they're sending our way?" the King said eventually.

"Why, yes, Your Majesty. But it's not all that different from what the good soldiers are already enduring up there as they aim and fire and strike and chop and throw down the corpses back into the fire below, while keeping themselves safe as best they can. At least all you would have to do is merely stand there and look out, after taking a nice leisurely walk around the entirety of the walls."

"Damnation!" King Roland burst out. "Is there no other way?"

"Not really, I am afraid not, Your Majesty."

"And how would I know that the sorcery is working?"

Grial smiled, and the smile filled her face, but never quite reached the depths of her so-very-dark eyes.

"You would know it worked," she said, "because by the end of the day and night you and this city would still be alive and standing."

Another long pause of grim silence.

"Wait!" said the King. "You say that only the ultimate figure of authority, the—uhm—highest ruling *personage* may attempt this feat of sorcery? Could it be interpreted to mean the one who is highest ranking?"

"It could, Majesty, it certainly could."

"Well then!" King Roland Osenni exhaled in profound relief. "While it is obvious that I am the King of Lethe and ruler of this fine city, it cannot be forgotten that we have an even higher authority in our midst! Naturally I speak of Her Imperial Highness, the Grand Princess Claere Liguon, who is the Emperor's own daughter and Heir to the Crown of the Realm!

Why, it is clear as day that she and none other must be the one to perform this deed of sorcery!"

"Oh, Roland, are you certain? Why, the poor dear is but a child!" Queen Lucia spoke up, with an uncertain glance to Grial and then back to her spouse.

"She is certainly a capable Grand Princess, and she is *of age*, if you might recall, having recently turned sixteen—"

"But she is *dead!*" Lucia said.

"Even more reason why she should be the one to do this *dangerous* procedure," the King said firmly. "No further harm can come to her, if she takes care to keep away from burning projectiles, and if she is properly guarded—as she most certainly will be. Her Imperial Highness has already demonstrated an excellent diplomatic ability in her attempt to parlay with the villain Hoarfrost. Now she can demonstrate her ability to *rule*."

"Wonderful! It is settled then, Your Majesty!" Grial said in her ringing voice. She looked at the King unblinkingly, with a curious smile.

"It certainly is settled. You, Mistress Grial, will now proceed to show Her Imperial Highness how it is all to be done. And so, let us not waste another moment here."

And with those words the King wiped the palms of his hands against his jacket and sent servants to inform the Infanta of her new duty and fate.

S now was falling.
    Outside the window of the moving carriage the air was thick with the illusion of white blossoms descending from heaven, delicate petals swirling, and the streets of Letheburg appeared to be ghostly shapes of pallor. Occasional dark lines of building corners came into view and angular roofs jutted out, and then came lines of street lanterns burning in rare bright spots through the veil of snowfall.

Claere Liguon sat next to Vlau and across from Grial in the

carriage. They were headed once more toward the city walls.

Half an hour ago, Claere had been in her chambers in the Winter Palace, seated on the sofa, her soul isolated in the prison of her dead flesh, as always. Only now that same soul was a strange, *joyful* prisoner, brimming with a sense of completion . . . a soft wistful serenity, and a rush of impossible wonder.

Everything was different now, after what had happened between *them* in the darkness before dawn.

He was at peace with *her* at last, even though he was never to be at peace with himself.

He loved her.

After their moments of shared intensity—the confessions that had happened just before the first light, awkward, bittersweet, perfectly forthright for the first time, and at long last—after he had wept and wanted to die, and offered up his life to her, Vlau had fallen asleep once more in exhaustion. Only this time, his head rested in her fragile lap, and her fingers, cool and brittle like china and stained with his tears, were cradling him gently, stroking his soft dark hair . . . even though she could barely feel its touch.

And then came the knock on the door, shattering their illusion of peace, and once more the Royal Summons.

Claere felt something like a distant *memory* of having a heart, and then having that same living heart torn out of her by the disruption of their impossible, illusory, *soft time* together. Vlau came awake into grey dawn and into both exultation and despair, for he glanced first into her eyes, and there was everything in that look, all of him. "Claere . . ." he whispered. And then they faced the summons together.

This time, fortunately, they saw a familiar and welcome face. Together with a liveried royal servant, Grial, of all people, entered the chamber.

Grial was dressed as always in a colorful shabby dress and stained apron, and her kinky strands of wild unruly hair stood out past her attempt at a head kerchief.

But even as Claere looked at her, there was something decidedly *different* in Grial's very dark, very black eyes. . . . Whatever it was, however, Claere had no time to consider.

"Good morning, Your Imperial Highness! And Vlau, my dear young fellow!" Grial exclaimed, and her raucous loud voice for some reason acted like a warm soothing balm.

"Grial!" said Claere. "Oh, I am so glad to see you! What are you doing here?"

"Well, dearies, my heart is entirely aflutter to see both of you!" said the older woman, advancing to the sofa and suddenly putting both her hands on each one of their shoulders. "But, it appears that we have a very long day ahead of us, dumplings! Up you go, right now! To the battlements we head immediately, on the fine orders of His Royal Majesty—and a fair amount of orders there have been indeed, I dare say! An order here, an order there, and it all comes down to this—Letheburg needs *your* help, young lady, and a Grand Princess is the only one who can provide it!"

"What?" Claere almost forgot to draw the requisite amount of air to operate her lungs, and at first it came out in a creak. "*My* help? What do you mean, Grial? What does the King command? The battlements, again? Is it the Duke Hoarfrost?"

"No, girlie, thankfully it is not that stubborn old lump of a Duke, not this time. Instead, I am going to show you a little bit of—well, how does one call it?—oh yes, I do believe it is called *magic*. But, fear not! Because magic and sorcery is in truth all nonsense and silly posturing while following a complicated recipe, and ordinary smart people are rightfully cautious of all that woo-woo, as well as any sane person should be! Thus, no—while His Majesty might expect me to show you spells and sorcery, what I am going to teach you instead is the magical power of your *desire*."

Grial proceeded to describe with her usual manic energy

and enthusiasm what was expected of Claere—how she was to circle the entire walkway around the city battlements, then stand up and hold the torches, and of course how she was to dream and think and use the power of her imagination *just so*, and in a *very particular* way.

While spewing forth this equally disturbing and comforting torrent of chatter, Grial took both Claere and Vlau by the hands and practically dragged them after her, first however ordering Vlau to grab his warm cloak, and use the privy next door to Her Highness's chambers, since it was going to be a very long day and night. Grial then told the Palace servants to hurry and fetch some freshly baked rolls for the young man to eat on his way— since there was no time for a sit-down breakfast.

A short time later they descended the many Palace stairways, exiting outside into a pale grey world filled with flurries of snow. Next thing they knew, they were stepping into a carriage surrounded by a military convoy, and sitting down on velvet-upholstered cushions across from each other. Grial wore her usual simple coat and her wide-brimmed hat, while Claere had her new velvet cloak courtesy of the King, and Vlau was dressed in a barely adequate wool jacket worthy of a lower servant.

Vlau however did not seem to be aware of anything else around them, and did not even notice that he held Claere's cold little hand in a tight merciless grip—not until they were seated and being driven through the city.

Claere broke the silence at last. "Why me?" she asked. "Why does His Majesty want me to do this thing?"

"Because," Vlau said with intensity, answering in Grial's stead, "you are the only one who can."

"Oh, well said, young man, well said!" Grial nodded at Vlau with a smile of approval.

In a matter of minutes it seemed, they approached the city walls. It was soon apparent how badly these fire-ravaged neighborhoods had suffered since morning, for even the new blanket of snow did not sufficiently cover the smoking ruins of wooden houses and the piles of rubble resulting from the projectiles cast by the catapults. Soot and grey smoke was everywhere, mixing with the snowflakes, and so were the garrison soldiers, carrying out their grim duty and moving rapidly to perform the needed tasks in this broken military hive.

Their carriage stopped at the pomoerium space before the walls, filled with wounded soldiers and supply carts and smoking rubble, and the small convoy of the King's elite soldiers accompanying them led the way. Claere recognized the same captain who had taken them to parlay with Hoarfrost, and this time he bowed to the Infanta respectfully, then nodded to Vlau. Following him, they again ascended to the battlements, engulfed by an auditory sea of shouts and hoarse cries of agony and the familiar crackle of the flames. Except, now the flames beyond the walls had gone down to a low simmer instead of a roar, the orange glow had been replaced with a thick curtain of black smoke, and the Letheburg soldiers were engaged in fierce melee fighting along nearly crenel and merlon of the parapets.

Overhead the sky was slate and silver, and beyond the walls, a chaos of dark crawling shapes of the dead silhouetted against the falling snow.

"Stay well back, Your Imperial Highness!" the captain cried hoarsely, walking with his long sword drawn. "Stay as far away from the outer edge of the exterior wall as you can—" And then he turned with a fierce cry and parried a strike from the mace of a burly dead soldier who had scaled the parapet right next to him.

"Oh, my . . ." Grial shook her head as she stood just behind Claere and Vlau, watching the hell unfolding.

"What is your name, captain?" Claere said, raising her mechanical voice above the din.

"Brandeis, Highness!" the captain replied, having cut off the limbs of the enemy soldier, casting him back over the walls, and continuing to walk ahead of them.

"Captain Brandeis, would you have a sword to spare, for this man here who is at my side?" And Claere nodded in the direction of Vlau who gifted her with a look of gratitude and intensity.

In moments, a spare sword was procured, and Vlau Fiomarre was properly armed for the first time in days—indeed, for the first time since he had struck his love down with the dagger—

No, don't think, don't think. . . .

"Now, then," Grial said, as she waved to a soot-covered soldier here, and another group of tiredly grinning musketeers there. "I think it is time to start."

Claere stilled for a moment, gathering her will and her thoughts and her strength. She looked out over the walls at the distant horizon of haze and snow and enemy chaos. "I am ready," she said. "What must I do?"

"First, the easy part, dumpling," Grial said with a smile. "You take a nice leisurely walk all around the city, *your city*, and I'll be right here beside you. As you walk, imagine that you are drawing the line of a great city-wide circle directly into the ground below. Make it take root and continue downward underneath you, many, many feet down, deep below, through the walls of stone itself. See that the line is drawn by every footstep you take and it is shaped and marked in the stone beneath your feet by the very shape that is your body, its death shadow and its once-living reflection, all moving endlessly forward. . . ."

As Grial spoke, in a voice that was both resonant and sing-song, for a moment Claere thought she saw, in a purely strange instant of doubled vision of soot, snow, and smoke, *someone else* in Grial's place—a tall statuesque woman dressed in an ancient flowing garb, with her dark hair braided in a stern regal crown, and her face impassive and beautiful in its immortality. . . .

The vision lasted an instant only—then once again Claere

was seeing Grial, and none other. And thus she started walking forward, her thin frame held tense and straight, in a balancing act to keep her dead body upright. She looked below her feet and before her, allowing herself, *her mind*, to soar suddenly—to transform into winter air, into in a butterfly flurry of snowflakes, and into the many gusts of ice wind all around as the world tilted and then straightened again in vertigo, for the ground was up and the sky was below, and everything, everything was *hers*.

Thus did Claere Liguon, the Grand Princess and the Infanta of the Imperial Realm, together with her ethereal death-shadow, circle the city of Letheburg, making it her own.

Like a second loyal shadow, holding a drawn sword, Vlau Fiomarre walked closely behind her.

In their wake, Hecate silently followed.

S now was falling.
It had covered the whole world it seemed, and piled tall on the parapets of Letheburg, adding white caps to the tops of the merlons and filling in the space in the crenels, which however was quickly swept away by the struggling bodies of soldiers, both living and dead, in the endless melee.

Claere was done circling the city and was back in the same spot where she had started, in the center of a wide portion of a bulwark. It was long past noon, and torches had been employed along the length of the battlements, both for illumination and for re-igniting the fires below and keeping the dead at bay.

The invisible circle of power stood around Letheburg, a psychic wall that she had wrought.

It was definitely there.

It rang.

She could hear its crystal resonance on a strange superhuman level. Had she been alive, the hairs along her flesh would have risen. . . .

All along, Vlau had been right behind her. He had had

occasion to use his sword blade in her defense at least a dozen times as they walked. At one point, while four of the King's guard appointed to the Infanta's defense struggled to fight off a dead giant in torn chain mail who had once been a living knight—a thick-necked monster with bulging muscles and the strength of five men—Vlau stepped between the King's soldiers. With odd elegance and spare movements he did an intricate and fiercely violent figure with his sword and then swung it like lightning. Fueled by the impossible swiftness of the stroke, Fiomarre's blade cut through the neck muscle, sinew, and bone of the frozen corpse like butter. Soldiers paused to stare as the dead giant's head rolled several feet and rested in the snow, its maddened eyes fixed upon them, rotating slowly in their sockets in impotent fury. The enemy's headless torso continued to fight, but now without the head's guidance it was mostly ineffective, so Vlau simply gave it a powerful shove in the abdomen, sending the beheaded body flying like a boulder back over the parapet.

"Impressive," Captain Brandeis said to Fiomarre. "Where did you learn that move?"

Vlau's expression was impassive and perfectly focused as he first glanced to make sure that Claere was unharmed, then turned back to the captain. "I did some fighting at the southern border of Styx," he said vaguely, then resumed his vigilance at the Infanta's side.

That had been an hour ago.

Now she glanced at him occasionally from the corner of her fixed glass eye, seeing his soot, his grime-spattered clothing, his worn features, dear and familiar to her in their relentless intensity. And always she saw his eyes, fathomless and deep as winter, as he returned her intimate look. Indeed, it seemed that whenever she turned to glance at him he was already staring at her, his gaze *consuming* her. . . .

Claere forcibly made herself focus on her task and not to think of *him* yet again.

"It is done . . . I can feel it," she whispered at last, coming to a stop in the middle of the bulwark with its relative clearing, away from the thick of the battle and the pile-up of detached human limbs, endlessly twitching like snakes.

Grial, who had been also walking behind them discreetly, a few steps behind the King's guards, now came to a stop likewise. "Ah, the circle is there indeed, Your Imperial Highness! You did a fine job of it!"

"I thank you, Grial, for your wisdom and all your help in this. What now?"

As Claere spoke, at the far end of the bulwark where they stood, near the edge of the distant wall, a small keg of gunpowder exploded. The impact sent a portion of the wall boulders crashing down together with a whole merlon, and leaving a gap of several feet in the top section of the parapet. Agonized screams were heard as Letheburg soldiers struggled, died, and then "awoke" and loyally resumed fighting on the side of the city. Orange flames burst forth, and at least a dozen dead enemy soldiers started to pour over the wall and onto the battlements. Immediately, garrison soldiers responded, coming to defend the spot with all they had.

Grial paused, silhouetted against the roaring flames, and she observed the melee taking place only fifty feet away from them. "Now, Highness, you simply *stand*. And you make the circle strong with your will and your heart."

And Grial took two lit torches from the nearest King's guard—for they were in a semi-circle around them, the King's guard soldiers and Captain Brandeis, standing protectively around the Infanta, while Vlau Fiomarre with his sword, immediately at her side, was the last line of defense—and she gave the torches to Claere.

"Hold these up, Highness, and stand straight and firm. Hold the fire in your mind and think of it as what makes up the circle of defense around Letheburg. It is not the fire burning in the outer moat below, but the invisible fire up *here*, which courses along the parapet walkway perimeter even now, in the very place where you have trod the stones around the city."

Claere took the torches and stood as straight as she could imagine herself able—even though the act of balancing her atrophied flesh was a great effort. Her thin arms shook slightly, but she was dead, and she felt no pain of straining muscles, only the intensity of *effort*.

"That's it . . ." Grial watched her with a soft smile. "Now, look out beyond the wall, and imagine in your mind, the entirety of Letheburg, contained within this circle of inner fire, this circle of *you*. Nothing can breach it."

"Yes," Claere whispered. "I see it."

"Good. Now, stand, dear heart. Stand here for as long as you can. And you—" Grial pointed to the King's guards and their captain—"you are now free to go. Your task is done here, for Her Imperial Highness will do the rest."

"But—" Captain Brandeis said. "What of my orders? Who will stand to defend Her Imperial Highness while all this is happening?"

"I will." Vlau Fiomarre stepped forward, and positioned himself on the outside of the Infanta, between her and the outer wall of the bulwark. "I will guard her with my body."

"But it is not enough!"

"Ah, but it is!" Grial smiled and pointed to a large burning projectile that came hurtling in their direction in that very moment. It sailed over the parapet, moved about twenty feet into the air space over the bulwark, and then seemed to have met an *invisible wall* of something in the air. The flaming thing crashed against the invisible something, then bounced backward, and capsized close to the outer edge of the wall.

"Nothing can get through now," Grial said. "Nothing and no one *uninvited*—for as long as she stands."

Captain Brandeis and the guards, and indeed all the Letheburg defenders in the vicinity, looked in wonder at what had just come to pass. They witnessed sorcery, or maybe a genuine impossibility.

The captain blinked, his eyes watering from the newest blast of rising smoke, then nodded in acquiescence. "Then I must inform His Majesty at once," he said in a new voice of hope, signaling his convoy of guards to follow. He bowed deeply before the Infanta, gave a nod of respect to Fiomarre, then hurried away, walking back the way they had come with newfound energy, stepping over rubble and twitching body parts.

Meanwhile, everywhere along the battlements, commanding officers were calling their men to step away from the walls, ignore the attacking dead, and retreat behind the invisible demarcation line of supernatural safety.... Soon, military trumpet calls came everywhere, signaling retreat and long-needed relief for the city. The bulwark and the battlements were now empty of the defenders of Letheburg, but filling with the unopposed enemy dead that massed forward but could not breach the invisible wall.

Claere remained standing as she was, torches held aloft, straining with her gaze into the freezing-cold wind.

"Well, my dears," Grial said cheerfully, "I am going to head back home for a while, to do a thing or two that needs to be done, but I promise I will return in a few hours! You, dear girl, keep that chin up, keep those torches up, and keep being yourself!"

"I will, Grial," said Claere. "Thank you."

"And you, young man—" Grial turned to Vlau who stood like an unshakable post at Claere's side—"You might consider coming along with me for a bite of dinner and some hot tea to warm you. She will be perfectly safe—"

"I thank you, but no," he replied, turning his dark beautiful eyes momentarily to glance at Grial. And then he turned away and continued standing next to Claere, sword in one hand, his feet planted in a deceptively casual stance.

"As you wish," Grial said, with a strange little smile, then adjusted her wide-brimmed winter hat and headed away along the walkway, and back down into the city.

After she was gone, it seemed the wind had grown colder, its gusts harsher, and the snow was whirling in cruel funnel flurries. Vlau stood motionless, relentless and stoic, face turned into the wind. His exposed skin had lost all feeling and his extremities were numb, snow powdering his raven hair with sterile pallor. He was a dark, tall counterpart of Claere with her upright posture and her torches that flickered wildly but refused to go out despite the gale.

Half an hour had passed, maybe more. It was hard to tell in the strange afternoon dusk, and the slate-grey dome of overcast heaven. Vlau had blinked and briefly closed his eyes, his lashes sprinkled with snowflakes, and it seemed an eternity of silence had passed. . . .

After a few more silent moments of winter, of whistling wind and horrible stumbling dead, beating themselves in grotesque futility against the invisible wall of power just a few feet away from Claere, she spoke to him, without turning around to look. "Vlau . . ." she said gently. "Please go back and get some rest. I will be fine here."

"No," he said in a voice cracking from the cold. "I cannot leave you."

"But it will only be for a little while! And look how freezing it is getting! The wind is picking up and there is no end to this snow—"

"Claere," he said, and there was so much intensity in his voice that she had to turn around at last and look at him. "Claere, I will never leave you. Never. I may not, even if I could, even if I wanted to."

"What are you saying?" she whispered.

"I am saying, I *cannot* leave, my Claere. For . . . there is no more need. Now I will never leave you again."

And he took one stiff, frozen step to close the small distance between them, and he touched one of her hands, even as she continued to hold up the torch.

His fingers upon her hand were like ice.

If she were to look closely upon them, she would see their bluish grey color, the absence of movement of blood under the skin.

And if she were to look at him with the eyes of *sight*—at his elegant shape, his well-formed broad shoulders and his slim waist, his proud posture and his stilled dark eyes—if she could look thus, she would see a familiar new shadow at his side.

A death-shadow of billowing smoke, similar to her own.

But there was no need to look, for in her heart she already *knew*.

Snow was falling.

Chapter 7

Lady Leonora D'Arvu had escaped everyone and now sat upon a stone bench in the garden of the villa, in the cool late afternoon approaching dusk. Vestiges of sunset still stained the western horizon with streaks of persimmon and rust, and the breeze had cooled enough to require a shawl, but Leonora did not feel the need for warmth.

Instead she attempted to take deep perfumed breaths of evening air, and to listen to her own heartbeat. . . . It was there, surely; to hear it, all she had to do was focus on the familiar pulse in her temples, in her inner ear, the sound that had been with her for as long as she could remember, since the first self-aware moments of infancy and childhood. Indeed, it had been with her even when she first started seeing the impossible wonder of *her*, the infinite and eternal woman with the *sky blue eyes*—

No!

She focused on her breath. She inhaled and exhaled, and her lungs worked like mechanical bellows. But then, if she stopped thinking about it, stopped thinking about breathing, so did her breath.

It stopped.

There was also silence in her temples, no soft regular rush of blood to mark her time.

Nothing.

The fragrance of the ever-blooming acacia blossoms was overwhelming even in winter, and the trees surrounded this garden spot in a private alcove. Branches clustered with large dark green leaves hung low and spread around and above her like swaying green fingers gently reaching for her.

From her vantage point the whole world was filling with the rich purple of approaching twilight.

She felt sudden panic. There was a sharp moment where the trees and the blossoms and the purple air all seemed to press down on her, and she felt she could not breathe, and her lungs had then stopped indeed, and her chest was utterly silent, and she was clutching the stone bench beneath her with fingers that had somehow grown "thick" and senseless.

No!

"Lady Leonora. . . ."

Percy Ayren stood before her, a plump peasant girl in a simple light dress. Percy's expression was profound and very attentive, her eyes filled with murky things, like the gathering twilight, and her knotted hair, the color of shadows, framed her round plain features, lending her an otherworldly gravity.

Leonora looked up at her with frightened eyes, and once again she had forgotten to breathe, and thus she was *not* breathing. . . .

"What—what is happening to me?" Leonora said, making the effort to move the air through her mouth and shape the words.

"I am so sorry," Percy said. "I know this is an impossible thing, and what you are feeling is beyond anything you know. It is unimaginable and it is unfair. I am so sorry!"

"Am I really dead?"

"Yes. . . ."

"And that thing—that whatever you call it, death-shadow—it is at my side?"

"Yes. It is right here. It stands waiting."

Leonora glanced to the right where Percy pointed, willing herself to see, but there was nothing, only the side of the stone bench. Another surge of panic came to her, this time a numbing horror, so that she could almost feel a chill, but did not *quite* feel it, only vaguely sensed things around her through the remote thickness of cotton.

"Why can I not see it? Why is it that *you* can?" she spoke at last.

Percy sighed. "May I sit with you, My Lady?"

Leonora nodded and the girl sat down on the bench beside her. She then told her a long peculiar story of visiting Death in his Keep, and the quest for the Cobweb Bride.

Leonora listened, in particular responding to the part of her own rescue from the chamber of cobwebs underneath the Sapphire Throne. Memories of it had haunted her all day, all sleepless night since their long carriage ride, since her liberation from the debilitating soft morass of—

Whatever it was, Leonora could not remember. She only saw vague snatches of spinning images . . . the strange beautiful blue eyes of the Sovereign, her sublime face hovering close over her. But most often she saw only the gossamer whiteness of cobwebs.

"What was done to me?" Leonora whispered. "How did I die? Why do I not remember?"

"It might be of some use to give you the water from the River Lethe to drink," said Percy gently. "Unfortunately I have none with me—it can only be obtained at Death's Keep, and indeed the whole underground river flows there—"

"Oh, God, the water of Lethe!" Leonora's eyes, vulnerable and tragic, suddenly became wild. "I remember it! That was many weeks ago, indeed, months! Oh, what am I saying, maybe years! I was so young then, maybe fourteen—but no, how could that be? I am seventeen now, so how could it be years when I only entered her service when I was sixteen? In any case, there was a goblet of very strange water, at the Palace of the Sun. Her Brilliance the Sovereign had called it the water of Lethe and instructed me to keep it in my own quarters until she called for it, and to allow no other Lady-in-Attendance near it. I was told to watch over it and make sure no one touched or drank even a drop, for it was dangerous—"

Percy listened closely.

"It is a very strange story, and the time it seems to span makes very little sense, now that I think about it—years, months, weeks?" Leonora continued, while her retinas were seared with the imprint of *sky blue eyes.* . . . "Her Brilliance had been somewhat indisposed, or possibly saddened somehow, for many days this past spring—or was it two springs ago? Maybe three? No, that is nonsensical! We all noticed it but it was very subtle and hard to put into words. Indeed, it is always difficult to tell moods with Her Brilliance because she is such a delight and brings such joy always—what am I saying! Even now, I think of her as radiant and kind and beloved, when she did all this horror to me! But no, let me continue. And so, she kept me late one evening and instead of retiring for the night, she instructed me to fetch the goblet and to carry this same goblet with her into the Hall of the Sun, and there she sat down upon the Sapphire Throne. . . ."

"Please go on," Percy said, because Leonora went silent, her words fading, and her eyes appeared lost.

"Yes, she sat upon the throne. No one else was in the hall with us, not even her personal guards. I had thought it very strange at that time, but of course I loved her and obeyed her every command. And thus, she sat on the Sapphire Throne for long moments so that the moon rose and I was growing weary of standing motionless before her. Indeed, her face, now as I remember it, it was so sad! So impossibly sad, as I had never seen her to be, not ever. It was sad and somehow *real.* Her expression—it hid nothing. No duplicity. And it was tragic, and her eyes—her beautiful *blue eyes*—they appeared strangely dark in the moonlight, and they glistened with tears.

"Then she turned to me and asked me to give her the goblet. And she told me that whatever happened next, I was not to tell anyone, and if the *worst* happened, I was to simply turn around and leave the chamber. What 'the worst' meant, I did not know. . . . But I was terrified. And then, I watched her drink."

"How many sips did she take, do you remember?" Percy asked.

"Oh yes! She drank the first sip, and then sat back. And her face became relaxed with utter peace. She looked at me, and her eyes held no recognition, and then she looked at the goblet in her hands, as though considering it. . . . Moments later, she must have made some decision because she lifted it to her lips again and she drank another sip, or possibly a gulp. And immediately her face contorted. 'No, no, oh, no!' she exclaimed, and she started to weep, clutching the goblet loosely so that I was afraid it would fall, and its liquid sloshed around from the trembling of her fingers. I had never seen her thus! Oh, what indescribable rending sobs filled her, and she shook and she wept, sitting on the throne, painted by the moonlight! And when I asked if there was anything I could do, she cursed me, and then the very next moment begged me for forgiveness . . . and then she took a deep breath and she drank again—"

"For the *third* time," Percy whispered with sorrow.

"Yes, and for the fourth and more!" Leonora's speech cracked and she pulled in more air into her lungs to continue. "Indeed, she drank down the whole goblet!"

Percy was stunned. She sat clutching her hands in her lap while Leonora paused again. The dusk around them turned from purple to deep indigo. Somewhere behind them the villa lights bloomed forth and candlelight spilled from windows, while the garden lanterns outside were also set to burning by discreet servants.

"She should have died . . ." Percy said at last. "Anyone else in her place would have died, for Death told me that one cannot have more than two sips of the water of Lethe. The third sip means such unimaginable death that it takes you beyond all things and casts you from the world."

"Oh!" Leonora looked at Percy in new fear. "How then—"

"She is immortal," Percy said. "She is the Goddess Persephone. My understanding is, she drank death, but death could not take her, and thus an *impossibility* was created, a paradox. And it *broke* her."

"She is a goddess?" Leonora's expression was disbelief. "But why did she do this senseless thing? Knowing who she was, what did she think—"

"I think she wanted to die. Desperately. She drank on purpose, because she was looking for a way out."

"A way out of what?"

"Out of the universe. Out of being. Out of performing her divine function."

Percy rubbed her forehead. "In truth, I do not know—at least I have only an inkling, but I am not certain. But tell me, My Lady, what happened next, after she finished drinking the goblet?"

Leonora frowned with the effort of remembering. "I am not sure, but I think, after she was done drinking, she handed the empty goblet back to me, and her eyes—they were now perfectly *empty*. No—that is, they were cognizant and intelligent and aware, and she recognized me perfectly. But she was suddenly hard and cold and insensate, and yes, she was *wicked*—as though she no longer had a heart or a shred of sympathy. As though she, or any living soul inside her, had in fact *died*. Indeed, the first words out of her lips were, 'child, what an ugly face you have.'"

"You say this," Percy mused, "as though her wickedness was a new thing?"

"Oh but it was indeed!" Leonora spoke hurriedly. "Her

Brilliance was suddenly different, had become someone she had never been before. I was only seven—oh lord, why do I keep seeing myself at that age in her presence? That is ridiculous! No, I mean, obviously, I must have been sixteen, for surely this all happened only last spring—and yet even now I *feel* like I had known her all my life—"

"She was different, you say. Which suggests that indeed the water of Lethe had caused her to be what she is now. Caused her to perform acts of cruelty for occult reasons and whatever she thought she was doing when she took you and the other maidens in that chamber, robbing all of you of will and life—"

"No, oh, no! I admit, I do not understand any of it," Leonora said. "I am suddenly very confused, not only to be told that My Liege, the Sovereign is, as you say, an immortal goddess—which is a bizarre impossibility—but I am confused by my own memories and my own place in this whole thing. Why is time and my recollection of it so distorted? Why do I see myself before her both when I am a child and then later, as a young woman? As if the entirety of my life has been a jewel preserved along a string, covered in unnatural cobwebs. . . . Could it really be some kind of sorcery?"

"That, My Lady, I do not know," Percy said thoughtfully.

"Or maybe I am just an insane madwoman! A dead one!"

"I do not think," Percy said gently, "that you are mad. But it is likely that you have been harmed considerably by whatever had come to pass—the events that you in fact cannot recall. Those same events that have made you into the Cobweb Bride."

Leonora got up from her seat, holding herself up with rigid awkwardness. She stood, balancing stiffly on her feet, her knees trembling from the effort. "I cannot speak of this any more . . ." she announced coldly. "You must forgive me—I remain grateful for your help in rescuing me, and you are always deeply welcome in this house, but—but I cannot—" And with those words Leonora hastened away toward the lantern lights, returning back into the villa.

Percy got up and returned to the house also.

W hen Percy entered the guest boudoir given to them by the family D'Arvu, Beltain was waiting for her.

Warm candlelight made the large airy chamber comfortable, while outside the windows was an ink-blue evening sky.

"Percy!" he said, and stood up from the deep chair in which he had been seated, still fully dressed. "How did it go?"

"Not well . . ." Percy sighed, and looked up, seeing his familiar grey-blue eyes, and immediately feeling a warm energy surge between them, invigorating her. She stood before him, suddenly a little awkward, remembering all kinds of things that had nothing to do with Leonora or death or the entirety of the world around them. And then she said, "I do not think Lady Leonora is ready to be Death's Cobweb Bride. Nor do I think she might ever be—or at least not in a long while."

He nodded, his countenance turning serious, the softness that was directed at her retreating as he focused on what was being said. "She does not want to die. Or rather, she is dead, but she does not want to accept whatever it is that happens after the soul leaves the mortal flesh—the *end*. For that, I do not blame her."

"I do not blame her either. But unless she agrees to accept her fate, the world will continue broken as it is."

Beltain took a step forward and he stood directly before her, so that Percy had to look up even more, while her breath quickened slightly, because she could feel the warmth of his body radiating at her, even without them touching.

"There are other things she told me. . . ." And she related the conversation with Leonora, while speaking softly into the shirt on his chest.

"So we have a mad, damaged goddess . . ." Beltain mused. "I admit, I am still coming to terms with the notion of the classical gods and goddesses living in our midst and the One God allowing it—or sharing the universe with them. Now, it may be that what Lady Leonora has just told you might explain much of this immortal Sovereign's violent behavior, but not all. Given what appears to be possible, what does she want *now?* What *can* she want or expect from the world, from all of us in it?" And he placed his hand on Percy's bare arm, near her shoulder, his fingers splayed, and moving lightly against her skin.

Percy shuddered with the shock of his touch and looked up at him.

Beltain was looking down at her with intensity, his head leaning in, until his face was directly over her cheek and the wavy locks of his soft brown hair tumbled against her neck. She felt his warm breath on her cheek, and then he whispered, "Sweet Percy . . . let the gods be mad as they may, but . . . I must steal a kiss."

"Oh!" she said.

He kissed her mouth, hard.

She knew the now familiar yet still impossible-to-believe pressure upon her lips, and she turned into it so that there was no space between them, no breath, no skin.

Soon, both his hands held her face between them, tilting her head back so that she felt as though she was swooning into the floor, into the ground, into the earth itself, while he *opened* her, consumed her from above and from the inside, and her gaze was turned heavenward, and *he* was the dome of her sky, its entirety. . . .

They came up for air, and both were shuddering with exultation, with heat and lassitude in their limbs.

"My sweet love," he said. And his eyes, so near her own, were molten and dark, and soft and oh-so-vulnerable.

Percy placed her hands upon his chest and she leaned into him. She rested the side of her face against him, feeling the linen of his shirt, and through it the heat of his skin and deeper yet, the steady beat of his heart.

And then he gently disengaged himself and stepped back. The bed was just two paces away. "It is getting late . . ." he said, standing and looking at her without end, with the candlelight warming the planes of his face. "You must rest now, Percy, and so must I, for none of us know what will come tomorrow. Now, go on and lie down on the bed, it is all yours . . . while I will stay in the chair."

Percy looked in uncertainty from him to the great bed with its soft and plush coverings, its many grand pillows with tassels and the delicate linen sheets. "What do you mean, My Lord?" she said. "You need to lie down properly. Come and sleep in the bed, there is so much room!"

"I—" he said. "I am afraid. . . ."

Her lips parted. "Afraid of what?"

He was silent, his gaze brimming with leashed intensity.

"Beltain!" said Percy. And as she said it, she was cognizant that for the first time she was using the black knight's given name, and doing so entirely without permission. Not that any of it mattered any more.

"If I lie down next to you, Percy, I am afraid that I would— I would not be able to hold myself back. That I would *do* to you what a husband does to his *wife*. . . ."

And saying that, he blushed darkly, his cheeks and forehead and neck burning.

She stared at him, and started to flush also. She bit her lip and averted her gaze and looked down at the soft bed coverlet, at the fringe on the pillows and the tassels . . . and then her lips started to quiver with a tiny little smile.

"Get into bed, Beltain," she said. And she looked up and gazed directly into his eyes.

"You—" he said softly, looking at her in amazement. "But you are so young. . . ."

"I am not! I am not young at all! I'll be seventeen at the end

of May, and that's only a few months from now! Besides, half
the girls my age back in Oarclaven are already wed, with babes
in their arms! And yes, I know all about that, they told me
plenty! Besides, how old are *you* anyway? Not all that older than
me, I venture, five and twenty, no more! Now, get into bed, or so
help me, I will thrash *you!*"

He shook his head and gasped, but then the beginning of a
grin was taking over, and then he started to laugh, his baritone
ringing with warmth.

"Oh, my sweet, sweet Percy . . ." He chuckled, then went
silent, but his lips retained a malleable softness, and a smile. "I
will lie down at your side, but I will not touch you in *that* way,
nor harm you, for you know not of what you speak. . . . I would
not impose on your dear body, not at such a time when the world
is falling apart and I can offer you little to nothing in return, not
even my family home. Even the good ancient name of Chidair is
tainted now, so I must first set it aright before anything else. And
you are quite young indeed, and you may not want me, or a child
of mine, when all is said and done. Thus, let us only sleep now,
beloved. We shall lie together as friends. Come!"

In response Percy stepped forward and turned her back to
him, saying, "Well then, it will be as you wish, Sir Knight, you
ninny—big strong man with your big strong arms and your fool
of a brain—as long as you lie down properly and not on some
idiot chair. But first, I need to put on my nightshirt, and so you
will have to undo these horrid laces at my back instead of one of
the maids, all of whom I think have gone to bed, and I would
hate to bother the poor girls at this hour, because I dare say they
have plenty to do around the house without having to undress the
sorry likes of me—"

And in the next breath, his fingers were at her back, and she
felt their strong touch, and coursing waves of honey-weakness
poured into her at every point of contact. And then she realized
that his fingers were also trembling. . . .

Percy awoke in the first glimmer light of dawn diluting the thick pitch-black night darkness. The candles had long since gone out, and she was lying in his arms, while he slept, breathing deeply, his body great and warm all around her, and she could feel his virile heat through her long cotton nightshirt.

He had kept his word, and steeled himself all night, lying at her side without touching her at all, not even her hand. . . . And only toward morning, when his sleep deepened, did she come to lie with her head against this chest, her face pressed against his heart, and his arms came to wrap her in an unconscious embrace, even as he slept.

She did not want to move, not ever. This was the only true perfect moment of her being, the only thing real—this one instant here and now, with *him*.

But Percy took a deep shuddering breath of regret, and then she gently disengaged herself from his arms—the arms of deity, her heart's one god—for such he had become to her. And she softly slipped from the bed without waking him.

She stood and dressed, and watched him lie there, beautiful in his abandon . . . listened to his sweet breathing.

Oh, how she wanted to kiss his muscular arms, his bronzed shoulder, the side of his neck, his parted lips—all of *him*.

But she could not—she must not. For he would wake.

And she had to go.

Percy glanced at her beloved one more time. And then, in the thick twilight before dawn, she glanced in the darkest corner of the chamber where the shadows stood thickest. And she walked into them, willing herself to travel, to fade from this place, and to emerge *elsewhere*.

Death's Keep.

Chapter 8

The mist was a grey curtain, and then Percy was walking through a pale cobweb forest. The web filaments were all around and she blinked, her lashes trembling, her skin filling with primeval unconscious shudders of revulsion at the strange faint touch.

She knew this place . . . it was the Hall of bones, the grand sepulcher with columns curving upwards into arches of ribcage, and overhead swayed the endless ocean of webs and a strange dark starry sky that was neither true sky nor true stars.

Only a few steps away before her, through the veil of cobwebs, began the dais of Death's Ivory Throne.

It stood empty, with no one seated there.

Percy blinked.

And then in the next blink, she saw him. Dark and beautiful and pitch-black, with skin the color of jet, and ebony eyes, and hair so black it had a bluish tint, dressed in a tunic of swirling silver and darkness, Hades sat upon the Throne.

"Lord Death . . ." Percy said, feeling suddenly all alone—for indeed, for the first time of the many times she had been here in Death's Hall, she truly *was*. "Lord Hades."

The dark God's face had been averted, as if he had been looking into eternity, and she had somehow interrupted his brooding thoughts.

"You have come back, my Champion," said Hades, Lord Death, turning his head and training the impossible, fathomless black eyes upon her. "But you do not have my Cobweb Bride."

"No," Percy said, "I am sorry, I do not. I am truly sorry, Lord Death, but the Lady Leonora is not quite—ready to accept her fate. And I am afraid but I cannot force her to it—at least not yet."

"Ah . . ." Hades spoke sadly. "No one is ever ready for their fate. Such is the paradox of mortality that to be ready for death is to not be alive. Indeed, the moment one of you mortals decides they have had enough of living is when they are no longer mortal. But ah, what am I saying?—I may not divulge such occult mysteries to your kind—not even to you, my Champion. See how weakened I have become . . . even now, as I sit and wait for *her* to come to me, to arrive here in this forsaken Hall, the limits of my divine function fail me, my tongue is loosened, and I am made to speak secrets of immortality. Enough!"

"I am not sure I understand," said Percy. "But I wanted to tell you what I have learned of your—of the Goddess Persephone." And Percy repeated the events told her by Lady Leonora.

Hades listened, looking into space filled with the gossamer of cobwebs, and past her, and his divine visage showed nothing.

"So this is what she did . . ." he uttered at last. "My only love drank the water of Lethe thrice and more, in secret, long before she had been given to drink a mere sip by the Mother of Bright Harvest, blessed Demeter! My love was already harmed beyond mending long before we knew it—long before we tried to help her in her despair! Ah, woe! This I had not known!"

And Hades leaned with his pitch-black muscular arm on the Throne of ivory, and he rested his forehead in his hand. His silken filaments of midnight hair moved in an invisible wind, and at times appeared to be ghostly serpents.

"If I might ask, My Lord Hades, what exactly happened to

cause all this? How come the gods to be broken in the first place? How can it even be?" Percy knew that the questions she asked were daring and were likely not to be answered.

But the Lord of the Underworld gifted her with an intimate look of his heavy eyes, and he started to speak.

"You mortals think that gods are eternal, inviolate, and powerful. Truth is, we are like glass—fixed, limited, and fragile—for we are defined by our divine function. Glass is unyielding, but it is easily broken if forced to bend or to take on another shape, unless it is first returned to a molten state through fire. When a god deviates from his function, he is vulnerable to the forces of the Universal Scheme, and shatters like glass from the conforming pressures of the surrounding universe. It is said that gods are molded and forged—and once we are fixed into the final shape of our function, we may only perform it and none other."

"What a strange thing!" Percy said.

Hades wore a bitter smile.

"I will tell you this dark story, my Champion, for the world has little time left, and I might as well. It started long ago—far longer than you mortals can know or even imagine, for time works differently for us. We gods ride time in all directions while you follow a straight linear path of your own making, a path that you yourselves believe leads forward, but in truth simply marks an endless circle. There are as many circles as there are individuals. Each circle is different from the others— offset in a unique manner, a tiny bit or a great distance, in every conceivable direction and being of every size—and when all of the circles are put together and superimposed, they give shape to the Grand Sphere that is the universe—an eternal thing of *infinite plurality* that we gods both observe and maintain while you mortals merely tread and fill with both wonder and woe all of which then comes with you on the journey.

"Do not be discouraged by the ultimate circularity of your path—it is so vast that you have no way of grasping it. Nor should you be bothered by it, but take comfort that there is no end—for circularity is fate, or the promise of continuity. Instead accept the glorious reality that along each point in your path you have the ability to make different choices—for that is your free will. Indeed, both gods and mortals travel the circles—you do it unknowingly, while we do it with intent. And it *changes* you, while we gods remain the *same*.

"And thus, a long time ago, at some point along the circle which she and I both travel, Persephone, the Goddess of Resurrection—she who is my consort and my only love, and who keeps the world itself moving—Persephone paused for one moment in her divine *function* and looked back at herself. And seeing herself thus, from a strange alien perspective of *other*, of someone else looking at herself from the outside, she realized some things that should not be realized, not even by the gods. And she knew a moment of *doubt* in herself and her function, and with it a moment of being abysmally *alone*. It was not true, of course, for the concepts of *aloneness* and of *union* are both an illusion of moving time. But it was just enough to throw Persephone slightly off balance, and to give her cause to desire more for herself than she already had.

"You might wonder—how can one who already *has* the entire world feel they need anything more? But it was such a small thing, fueled by a tiny bit of curiosity, and a bit of self-reflection, and Persephone did not think it would make any difference in the greater scheme. And thus, Persephone, continuing to think along the lines of 'self" and 'other,' decided to take a tiny bit of the world and *keep* it entirely for herself. It was not enough that she already had everything, since that all-encompassing 'everything' also had to be shared with all the rest of the universe, the gods and the mortals. No, she wanted something completely her own.

"And Persephone gave birth to a child in the Underworld."

"Melinoë," Percy said astutely.

Hades nodded. "Yes." He continued looking at Percy, and his steady gaze was rich and mesmerizing, and with it came vertigo, and a strange sensual overpowering flood of warmth that made Percy flush and think of Beltain.

"My ... Champion," said Hades softly. "I must explain some things to you now, things that may be difficult for you to fathom because of your innocence. But they must be divulged before you can even begin to understand."

"I—" Percy's blush deepened further, the longer she looked at the dark God, falling in and out of sensual vertigo, drowning and then rising again in her mind. It seemed she was stranded at the shore of a great sea, with sweeping waves coming every few breaths to pull her under, then releasing her once more into the moist sand to regain her footing and stand upright on unsteady legs, feet sinking into the shifting quagmire of land yielding to water. . . .

Percy blinked, steadying herself on the inside, steeling herself for a loss of innocence and the gain of revelation.

"It is thus," spoke the dark God. "All the gods have their specific eternal functions. Persephone and I, we create the cycle of life and death—a circle in itself, an overlying Grand Pattern of movement that shapes the nature of all others—and hence we power the engine of the mortal and immortal world. We are mated, she and I. And our act of union every season generates and restarts new life . . . along the infinity of circles and worlds and indeed the entire Sphere of the universe.

"A long time ago, before we had attained our functions, I emerged out of my personal half-life and darkness into the world of light and saw Persephone for the first time—a young radiant goddess, in a field of blooming flowers underneath a blue sky. I saw her and she saw me, and we recognized ourselves in the other, just as the sun and moon appeared in the heavens in that exact instant—for indeed we gave them physical form. I saw her light and she saw my darkness. . . . And immediately we were thus bound by abysmal inviolate desire, need, and love—the thing that brought us together and unknowingly fixed us in the scheme of the world. It was then I took her to me—took her *down* with me Below.

"It had to be done. For I am of Below, and she was of Above, and by taking her, I *transformed* her, deepened her into her true self, so that suddenly she was *both*—both Above and Below, both light and dark, and thus complete and full to overflowing with the *energy* of the world."

"You took her to the Underworld! You stole her away from her divine grieving mother! Oh, I do know that strange sad story. . . . My own mother had told it to my sisters and me many times," Percy whispered.

"But no, you do not know the full of it, not the true story," Hades replied. "For I 'stole' her only in a sense of mythic metaphor, stole her from her former self, as much as she allowed herself to be stolen and *changed* by the act of love. . . . For she desired me as much as I burned for her, if not more—even now I wonder which one of us it was that looked at the other first in that blessed ancient field of flowers older than time. And in truth, as she was changed, so was I. No stories ever tell this secret part, but I too had become *both*—I was now a deity of both Below and Above.

"Furthermore, it is how Death was born—Death the White Bridegroom—for he is my Above aspect, and he exists only for the mortal world, for all of *you*—not to cause pain and destruction but to bring relief and transition into the light. It was inevitable and it was the birth of our common *function*. You see, this happened so long ago, that there is no way to describe it all in your mortal reckoning. All you mortals know is the fearful simplified story told infinite times and transformed by the imperfect act of telling—transformed almost as much as we have been. . . . Which in itself is an impossibility, for gods cannot change, but we were, by each other."

"So you're saying that Death did not exist until you met

Persephone?" Percy stared in amazement.

"Yes. And neither did the mortal world exist as you now know it to be. Everything was new back then, primeval, raw, formless as clay and fire, as titans and giants existed with the gods in virile strife, and ancient divine wars were fought for meaningless supremacy. And Persephone and I, coming together as we did, refined our separate functions and created the way things are now."

"What of Melinoë?"

Hades momentarily averted his gaze, as a wave of old grief returned. "Persephone and I come together every autumn season. When we love, as a result of our union we recreate life for each spring. Our function made it so that Persephone has to be Above and Below for half of each year, in order to make the cycle happen. She sits down on my Dark Throne in the Underworld and—and she emerges on the Sapphire Throne in the mortal world—"

His words faded strangely, and Percy saw that his perfectly black eyes were brimming full of liquid, and it made their darkness change in nature, attain a strange pallid gleam, like a film of quicksilver on the surface.

"This is the part that will change you, and take away your innocence," Hades whispered. "You see, in order for Persephone to move from one world to the other, from Above to Below, and back again, she has to *die*. To enter the Underworld, my love dies in the mortal world. And to come back, she has to die *again*.

"When autumn comes to the world of light and leaves turn the color of flames, and the Bright Harvest ripens and is gathered by her divine mother Demeter, and all you mortals celebrate the fruits of plenty, it is when Persephone sits down on the Sapphire Throne and dies for *you*, in order for the cycle to begin again. As she dies, the world receives the entirety of her life force in the great sacrifice that precedes the coming of winter. She is dissolved and her life spills over into the universe. It fills the expanses of physical matter, of earth, sun, and stars, and it makes the universe resonate with completion, with the stately slowing *movement* of light falling into the profound deep. Only then, when all is done, the earth lies fallow, and the song of the spheres is sung, her essence sinks gently beneath, into the depths, until it emerges Below. It is then that she is given divine form again and awakes in the Underworld, seated on the Black Throne. We are reunited, we are—we—" His words again failed.

For a brief moment he too seemed to sink away and dissolve with the memory, and then he resumed: "And afterwards, when it is time for spring, she sits down on the Black Throne—only this time she is full to overflowing with the new seed of mortal life—and she closes her eyes and dies again, for all of you, exploding forth in a fountain of birth and rising into the mortal world, to bring all things to fruition and to begin the new cycle of light. This time her energy seeds the earth with the new life force, enacting the great resurrection that is the coming of spring. Over and over she dies, twice every season, and she has been dying thus since time untold. . . ."

"I did not know! I am so sorry. . . ." Percy looked at the dark God with compassion.

But Hades continued. "It *hurts* her to die. Each time it happens, it hurts her, and it destroys her completely. Even I cannot imagine how it is, for an immortal to be destroyed thus and recreated anew, what immeasurable agony. For, it is such a perfect dissolution of will, of self, and of power, that there is no mortal equivalent. And Death—my own aspect—cannot help her in this. My poor long-suffering love—she is the only one who may not be conducted by the White Bridegroom into the light. I can only stand by and watch her passing. It is my curse!"

Hades wept silently, his face stone, and the cobweb forest of filaments floating in the air all around them stopped moving, so abysmally still the Hall had become.

"And now, I will at last speak of Melinoë," he uttered suddenly. "Now that you know what Persephone must go through over and over, unto eternity, now you can better understand the beginning of my story where I had told you how Persephone has once paused and questioned her function. One season—over a hundred of your mortal years ago—before emerging Above, Persephone lingered in the Underworld. Instead of sitting on the Black Throne, she stood in the dark resplendent chamber and she pressed her hands lightly upon her richly filled womb and she *birthed* a fine delicate girl of shadows. Out the child came, pouring down between her legs like a ghost, or a bit of gentle vapor, barely moving the fine fabric of her long chiton in passing. She was such a tiny infant, but perfect in every way, except that she was half smoke and half tangible.

"Now, you must know that *nothing* has ever been born before in the Underworld—it is an impossibility, the Underworld being the original barren place, the home of death. And yet, here she was, a girl of shadows, imbued with peculiar life.

"Persephone exclaimed with delight, and she handed me the child, and told me to care for her and look after her until she returned. And then Persephone sat down on the Black Throne as usual, and for once she sighed with contentment, and then closed her eyes and died and then was gone. I admit, I was stunned and still filled with amazement at the circumstances, but now there was also joy at this new wondrous responsibility—my paternity I had never expected, for there had never been room for children in the strange confines of our divine function. I will only say now that the girl of shadows grew and flourished, keeping me wondrous company in the long days while I waited for my love to return Below.

"When Persephone was back, we named our child Melinoë. We cherished her and gave her wonders of the Underworld to eat and drink and play with. For although the Underworld is only a small place—consisting merely of a palatial *house* of seven chambers, and all around it is pure darkness and the bowels of the earth—it has enough riches and sparkling black diamonds to buy all the Kingdoms of the mortal world. Suffice it to say, our daughter grew and thrived, and as seasons passed Above, she became a young woman. She was always shadow-pale and faint and not quite tangible, and yet she was more real for us than any creature of the mortal earth. And as Melinoë spent time with me while her mother was away Above, she asked me questions of both worlds. There was only so much I could answer through the years, and eventually all answers had been exhausted. At last, Melinoë told us that she wanted to see the mortal world for herself.

"Both her mother and I were reluctant at first, and I had my deepest suspicions that this shadow daughter of ours would not survive the journey or the destination. But Melinoë grew sadder every season, and at last Persephone's heart could not bear it. Neither one of us could deny our child anything for long. And yet, before allowing her to go, I consulted with the other gods. I asked my brothers, Zeus of the Sky and Poseidon of the Sea, and they in turn asked all the lesser gods. One of our divine sisters, the Goddess Hecate—she who rules Choices and Entrances and dark mysteries of the deep equally as she rules the sky, the firmament, and the sea—she strongly argued against allowing Melinoë to visit the world Above. Hecate has wisdom and sense, and her knowledge is thrice as profound as any other deity. I was convinced, but apparently my beloved was not.

"And thus, on the day designated to be the one preceding spring, Persephone sat down on the Black Throne and she seated Melinoë on her lap, and with arms wrapped around each other, my two most beloved ones died together, and were dissolved, gone from me—while I watched, with a feeling that was the precursor of despair.

"What I learned next was my worst fears justified. Apparently Persephone awoke on the Sapphire Throne, carrying spring into the mortal world, but Melinoë did not awake with her. Instead, the girl of shadows dissolved into a fine black

powder, like granules of ebony sand. She poured and crumbled
all around her mother's lap, falling on the seat and the floor and
staining the fabric of her mother's chiton. It lay there, the
beloved dust of our child, and Persephone was stricken with
madness. She railed and wept and fell upon the ground and
attempted to collect the ashes of Melinoë. Gathering them the
best she could into a clay vessel, she then spent a barren and
terrifying spring and summer, followed by a barely fruitful
autumn, until she arrived back into the Underworld, holding the
vessel with Melinoë's remains. Here, I was witness to
Persephone's darkest mood, and my own despair, as we
mourned our child and attempted to do anything and everything
to bring her back to us. Seasons passed, then years. Persephone
did not quite recover, and as she grieved she grew darker and
more lifeless, while the world Above suffered her frugal springs,
and the Underworld bore her desolate winters. At last—and here
is where you will recognize the story—at last Persephone's own
mother Demeter and I devised together a means of alleviating
her pain, and it involved the drinking of the water of Lethe.
Only—we did not know that long before we came to this notion,
Persephone herself had tried to cure her mind, and failed, and
instead, as witnessed by your Lady Leonora, she apparently
damaged herself completely."

Percy regarded the dark God with thoughtful gravity.
"Could it be possible that the water of Lethe acted differently
upon her than it might upon other gods? For, according to your
own description, she is the only immortal who also dies on a
regular basis—and I am sorry, My Lord Hades, but I don't
understand how it is even possible. How is her death enacted?
What is her death? And is it possible that because she is unique
in that way, her drinking of Lethe had such a dire result?"

"It could be so," Hades said. "Though it is not known how
any other immortal would react to three deadly swallows of
Lethe, for none had ever attempted it—at least not to my
knowledge. However, I suspect—because Persephone is already

subjected to absolute death and dissolution twice a year, she is somehow more vulnerable to such damage if it is done to her by any other means than the process of her divine function. The overdose of the water of Lethe must have destroyed her immortal soul. . . . And because her soul is the essence of sacrifice and compassion and resurrection, all such things are now broken, and the pattern of the world itself is damaged. Without her soul, Persephone is now a mockery of herself, a dark empty husk, hollow on the inside, with a place that cannot be filled no matter how many armies she commands to destroy the mortal world, or how many lives she takes."

"Was it Melinoë's death that brought about the creation of the Cobweb Bride?"

"What happened after Persephone drank the water of Lethe in secret, is this," Hades said. "Demeter and I decided that the only way to heal Persephone was to make her forget our daughter, her very existence. But—not only was *she* to forget the child, but all three of us would, we who knew of her being and suffered the most. We were aware that some of our memories might inevitably return—yes, even those very memories of Melinoë we were trying to suppress—simply because of who we were and what divine functions we had to perform. But we were willing to make the sacrifice for the moment. The other gods meanwhile were instead to take a great inviolate Oath upon the sacred waters of the River Styx to never speak of her to us or to anyone else for as long as we remained without our memories. And in addition, Hecate was to take the jar containing Melinoë's poor beloved ashes and she was to hide it from us and from the entire world, and to never speak of its location.

"Persephone meekly agreed to this arrangement—that alone should have been a warning to us that something was wrong with her, that she was willing to give in so quickly. Well, it was done, I am told, according to plan, and then Hecate assisted us and made sure that we drank the water of Lethe properly—just one sip to forget, and no more. First, Demeter accompanied Persephone from this Hall where we all came together originally to agree upon our plan, to her own Palace of the Sun. And there, on the Sapphire Throne, she made her daughter take one sip—all along without knowing that Persephone was practicing a subtle deception on us, that she was already *changed* and soulless, the damage done, and the excess lethal water would have no effect on her whatsoever.

"Apparently Persephone played her deception well, because Demeter was satisfied, and then proceeded to her own quarters in Ulpheo to drink her own portion, supervised in turn by Hecate. Next, Hecate left Demeter in a blink to come here, and she made sure I myself drank the one sip of water while seated on my Ivory Throne in Death's Keep—this very same neutral place that is neither properly the mortal world nor the Underworld, nether Above, nor Below, but an interim Shadow. It was important that we do this in such order, and that I lose my memory while locked in my Death Aspect and not the other, in order that I re-learn the things of the world without compromising the natural course of death and mortality. For, had I forgotten Death while in the Underworld, things would have been dire indeed for the world Above. Besides, I would remember 'Hades' eventually, when the time came for Persephone to come to me in our natural cycle—or so we all thought."

Hades sighed, and gave a bitter smile. He then shook his head with its raven hair, and again there was the illusion of his locks turning to serpents as they swept lightly.

"What happened then?" Percy asked gently.

"What happened next was not at all what we had expected. It turns out, Demeter without her memory is an innocent gullible fool who knows nothing of her divine function. Even worse, it turns out that Death without his memory is a grim idiot, who also has no notion of the Underworld, or of his true ability. Couple this with the fact that now Persephone is a soulless madwoman who has planned all of our ruin in advance, and what we have is a grisly hopeless mess not worthy even of you mortals much less gods!

"The moment Demeter and I lost our memories, Persephone apparently went directly to her mother, fetched her from Ulpheo, and did something to her, encasing her in bonds of twisted energy. What else was done, I have no notion, for I was, as you know, not 'myself.' That part remains a mystery—the details of what my poor broken love enacted to bind her own divine mother and those maidens, and to stop the course of death itself by creating the Cobweb Bride. She must have used intricate dark energies to separate Leonora from her death, and then attach that death to Demeter. This caused the grim *event* you all know as the cessation of death. For, through that one small thing the entire mechanism of life and death was halted. . . . Indeed, by creating the Cobweb Bride, Persephone halted the whole process of living movement—our complicated divine function."

Percy listened to this retelling of what she *thought* she already knew. And suddenly a frightening new thought occurred to her. "If death has ceased, and all the dissolution that goes with it has paused, does it mean that *life* has ceased also?" Saying this, Percy stared with growing horror directly into the dark God's eyes.

His eyes—they were tragic.

"Yes . . ." he replied softly. "Now at last you know the true extent of the damage to the world. Nothing can die, and nothing can be *born*. No new crops in the fields, no flowers, no new buds on trees, no new infants to the animals . . . or to you mortals. Not a single new living thing can come into this world now! All is halted! And you thought that not being able to slaughter your food animals, or boil your meat and cook your food was bad enough! Now you know that there can be no new food to replace what is already gone! That which was here at the last Harvest is still viable, for it carries the last of Persephone's life energy. But after death has ceased, so has life."

"No new children born to anyone . . ." whispered Percy, thinking of her own life and its possible joyful course with Beltain.

"I grieve for you, my beloved mortal Champion," Hades said. "And no, you may not conceive with *him*, the man you love, not until the world returns to its proper course. And now the possibility that the world will ever be healed completely is very unlikely."

"Wait, My Lord Hades! What do you mean?" Percy felt panic take over her mind, as the impossible notions rained down upon her like dark blows. "I thought that uniting the Cobweb Bride with her true death would at least begin to heal the world—as you had spoken earlier? But, oh, no . . . no, I *understand* at last. *Life* itself is broken."

"Yes—as you indeed know at last," Hades said. "If the Cobweb Bride accepts her fate, it will only resume death and dying. Mortals will indeed begin again to die as they always have, true. But it is only *half* of the divine function—*my* half. Persephone's half still remains damaged, if not completely beyond repair. Persephone must come to me in love in order to create new life. But now—she comes to me in soulless desire, in disdainful hatred and despair, and I wait for her, terrified to the depths of my immortal being of what will become of us, and of the whole world, if—or *when*—she and I come together in union, whether it be here in the temporary place of Shadow or Below, in the Underworld."

"Oh . . . My Lord!" Percy put her hands up to her mouth.

"The worst of it," Hades continued, "is that even now I know she will come to me. That alone is inevitable, for, even broken, we are mated eternally. All I can do now is attempt to hold her back. For, she must not enter the Underworld—if she does—it is where we are—"

Hades grew silent.

"My Lord Hades," Percy said. "If there is anything I can do

now to help, please tell me what is to be done. I will try again to bring the Cobweb Bride here—"

"No," he said. "Do not bother, not yet. She is not ready. Instead, you must do another thing for me—for Persephone and myself and the entire world—go to Hecate on my behalf. And bring to me the jar of ashes of my daughter Melinoë. It may be the only thing that could help now, the last resort."

Percy did not pause even for an instant. "Yes," she said, "I will do it, gladly! Only, how and where do I go? And how will I know Hecate?"

But the dark God smiled. "Fear not, for you know her already. Now, close your eyes, my Champion. And I will send you to her directly."

Percy nodded, then took a deep breath and closed her eyes.

And the Hall of bones faded around her.

The moment that Percy was gone, a mortal man stepped forth from the shadows of one great ceiling-high bone column in the Hall, and he approached the dais of Death's Ivory Throne, moving fearlessly through the cobwebs.

The black knight, Lord Beltain Chidair, had been listening to the entire exchange. For he had awakened in their guest boudoir in the D'Arvu villa in Tanathe just in time to see his beloved Percy step into the shadows and disappear, and he followed her immediately, and ended up here.

Beltain was going to call out to Percy and make himself known, and reproach her for leaving him in secret for no good reason, when he heard their conversation, the secrets of Persephone the Goddess and the whole sorrowful story of her loss and madness.

It stunned him, to learn most of this. Hopeless despair was now added to his worry on Percy's behalf.

"So, mortal man," Hades said to him, from his seat, glancing with narrowed eyes at the black knight. "You have been listening. Well, what have you learned?"

"Everything!" Beltain exclaimed in leashed anger, and stood before the Lord of the Underworld, ripping cobweb filaments away from himself in futile disdain.

Hades laughed. His deep voice rang in bitter hollow echoes in the infinite Hall. But there was no mirth in it, only darkness of the tomb.

"You have heard only what I have told her who is my Champion. Would it surprise you to know that I have spoken only in the language of her innocence and divulged just enough of the apex of the mountain, the tallest peak, to make her grasp the greater scheme? But know this—the bulk of the mountain reposes in the darkness of opaque mist, and while its tallest peak is visible, the roots of it go deep, the base of it is wide, and the foothills span the world. Thus, there is that much more of the *deep darkness* that had been left unsaid. Do you understand me, mortal man? For I speak to *you* now."

Beltain listened, his slate-blue eyes unwavering upon the dark God.

"There is infinitely more I have not told her, nor could I ever speak of it to such as herself," Hades continued. And there was a reflection of black flames licking in his pitch black eyes.

"But you can speak of it to me." Beltain nodded at last, and a dark flush started to rise in him, for he understood the secret depth of the dark God, and his meaning.

"Yes."

"Then tell me everything—all of it—that you have not told my Percy. Before I go after my love, before you send me after her, I must know."

"Come closer," said the dark God.

Beltain took a step forward, then another.

Hades regarded him with a suddenly lidded gaze, and he whispered, "Take my hand mortal man, touch it, so that you will know."

Beltain reached forward and placed his large strong fingers

upon the midnight skin of the god, upon his slim great fingers with their sharp claws.

Inferno of black fire . . . Ice shock and scalding flames . . . Agony and desire!

It seared him, and Beltain drew back involuntarily, letting go of the Lord of the Underworld and his utter hell. For Hades was burning, and at the same time he was encased in ice—the god was locked in a paradox of intensity, sharp like a razor's edge and extreme.

Such was the dark God's inner state of relentless, unrelieved, perfect *desire*.

And knowing it, Beltain felt himself burning also, burning in the dark flames and fierce in his own virile fury. For it came easy to him, this intensity, and it was his already, had he only known it. It took Hades's touch to awaken him to what was already inside.

"Now you know my secret, mortal," spoke the pitch-black God. "It is my nature and my curse and my infinite pleasure that I contain this eternal desire inside me, for all of my days, and all of my nights, as I wait for *her* who is my one true love. Only with *her* can this hell desire be quenched. And only for *one night*."

"What?" Beltain stood before the God, reeling with his own desire, and in such agony of need that he was uncomprehending of what was being said.

"I have told your Percy of our union and the seasons, and how Persephone dies to bring the fruits of our union up Above into the mortal world. But now I tell you of what it is that happens between us, between Persephone and myself.

"The moment in which Persephone appears in the Underworld is the heart of autumn. I instinctively know the instant of her arrival, and I wait for her in the chamber, standing before the empty Black Throne until she materializes like rich pungent smoke from the sky—which in the Underworld is the nether side of the earth, and the roots of only the most ancient trees come to pierce it from above. Her scent arrives first—it is the breath of mortal air and distant extinct summer, a warmth of the fading sun, a crispness of an apple and the pungent juice of a pear, and the ruby seed of the pomegranate.

"My immortal heart begins to beat faster, as the ripe scent of her fills the dark chamber and turns to musk. Soon, her womanly shape is congealed from the tang of the well-plowed fallow earth and the rich smoke of burning wood, and she takes on physical form. When she is Above, Persephone is in her light Aspect, with her ruddy-gold hair and her blue eyes, her alabaster skin. But when she is Below, she is all exquisite darkness. Her hair deepens to bronze and then brown, with silken highlights of the fur of the fox and the bear and the bark of a maple, until it is near black, with only the shadow of rust remaining. Her skin darkens like sandalwood, and then sweetens to chestnut, and her eyes turn from blue sky to brown earth on a night illuminated by a harvest moon. She is like the wood and the forest floor, and she is beautiful, and she is desire itself given female form. . . .

"She opens her eyes and takes her first breath of subterranean darkness, and I am smitten all over again, as I gaze into her eyes. We look at each other, and she rises and comes to me silently. We stand, touching our hands only, locking our gazes, and we do not dare to embrace, not yet—for such is our restriction and secret sorrow. We may not come together yet, not until the heart of winter.

"Thus, we spend our days Below, in talk or silence, in contemplation or laughter, always in near proximity of each other, indeed, close enough to touch, so close that our breaths mingle and we can see the dark pupils of our eyes. We pass time together and we wait. We are waiting for the culmination, for the one night our union is allowed to take place.

"I admit it is a long dreary season, even as it harbors the pending joy of our togetherness, as autumn deepens into winter, and we know with every fiber of our being, every pore, even as we burn together and apart, the slow approach of the Longest Night."

"All these days and nights, you do not share a bed with her?" asked Beltain, regarding Hades in surprise.

"No," the Lord of the Underworld replied. "For, we dare not—the same way that you dared not lie down with Percy this last night, and it took all your inner strength to abstain from her body. . . ."

"I—" Beltain looked away, frowning with intensity. "I wanted to—"

You wanted to plunge inside her and to move in sweet agony until you died. . . .

He was not sure if the dark God had spoken those words, or if it was a lustful echo of what was ringing inside his own mind.

"Why can you not be with your own wife?" the black knight asked then, to distract himself from the scalding flames inside. "How can the laws of the immortal world prevent you so cruelly from this rightful union?"

"Ah, but it is not the laws of the world, but we ourselves," Hades said. "Persephone and I both know what happens between us, and that it can only happen once, and only in the deepest coldest season, else the intensity of our passion will rip the world asunder.

"And thus it is, that as we fret away the time, and weather the winter, all the while our *need* for each other grows into a single point of absolute desire, sharp like the tip of a needle and the point of a knife. What I tell you next, mortal man, is a divine mystery. And the reason I tell it to you is the same that I gave my Champion Percy—there is not much time left in this world, and I am weakened, and the truth of things may be imparted to whomever would listen.

"The divine mystery is that as winter deepens, so do we, in our unresolved desire. We burn, and in flesh we are turned to coals, the blackest of black, like a hole in the universe, and thus I become my final darkest Aspect, the Black Husband, and she becomes my Black Wife. It is the deepest point of our need and the nadir of our ability to resist our union—the dark point of the universe, just before the end of the cycle.

"What comes next is the Longest Night of the year and the heart of winter. On this night, at last Persephone and I enter our intimate chamber, the deepest and smallest one of the seven in the Underworld. The chamber is hewn directly from the rock of the earth, has walls of black diamond, and is furnished with nothing but a resplendent bed, covered in ebony silk and satin and strewn with pillows. Two torches burn in two sconces on each side of the bed, and the bedposts rise into a canopy of gossamer black silk upon which are affixed small splintered diamonds that serve as subterranean stars.

"We enter the chamber together, wearing robes of flowing darkness, and we cast them aside. Persephone stands nude before me, and her breasts are heavy and weighted like anvils, her womb is the hungry abyss, and her wide hips are black iron. I stand before her and I am all pitch-black night. My muscular body is the side of a mountain, my bursting seed is incandescent, and I am the diamond rock of which the earth was hewn and which supports the weight of the mortal world.

"We reach for each other and we lie on the bed, and at last we do *not hold back*. There is nothing that can be said, for the world ends right there and then, the torches in the chamber go out with a hard snap of rising vacuum, iron grinds with iron, and we are one thing of desire, an impossible *mutual intensity*. I have no memory of flesh, even though our flesh meets. I enter her and I start moving within her, for a brief time. And then I *come*.

"There is a reason it is called the Longest Night. What for your mortal kind is but a few gulping moments of animal ecstasy, is an extended state of sacred elevation for the gods. In your temporal sense, I come for hours, and she too convulses around me in her own dark pleasure. And our pleasure is such that no mortal words can express. I pour my occult seed inside her all the while, enough to restart the mortal world. . . ."

"When it is done, Persephone, Demeter's true offspring, is fertile Mother to All Things. Her womb is full to bursting, quickened with enough virile life force to perform her task when she is reborn Above. As she rises from our marriage bed, her belly is already rounded, even before the new day comes, and her breasts are great and pendulous with the milk of plenty.

"This moment, when we have just come apart and are about to separate again for more than two interminable seasons, is the soft gentle moment of utmost, bittersweet despair. For a brief span, this is the time when our desire is at its lowest and has been satiated, and our burning need retreats to a low simmer in order that we might perform the last part of our divine function. The Longest Night is over and although it is still deep winter, my love must leave me now and ascend to the world Above, to prepare the world for spring. As the Father of the new life, I stand up and help her put on the robe, and I take her to the chamber of the Black Throne. We kiss one last time, and as I taste her succulent lips, already she is lightening, paling, shedding the rich chthonic darkness of her underground coloration, even as she sits down on the throne and prepares to die into mortal life.

"She looks at me one last time, and her brown eyes of the woodland doe are now aerial blue. She closes them, and exhales softly. . . . And then she gasps for breath and shudders in the death throes and agony of her sacrifice—an impossible immortal transformation, a material dissolution of her in every sense. She fades away; her flesh turns to vapor and a memory of smoke, for she is torn apart at the fine level of pure immortal energy. And finally there is only one sharp point of light that comes to an infinite focus in the place where her divine center is, between her heart and her swollen womb, in her solar plexus.

"Afterwards, the Black Throne is empty. I stand there, empty also, drained of all joy, weary and barely satiated for a brief moment. My deepest color, that of the Black Husband, has now faded into a softer darkness—my skin is no longer matte black vacuum that swallows all light, but has attained its normal reflective sheen gently hued with silver, washed by her light—and I am back to my usual self, the Lord of the Underworld. All points on the surface of my flesh are still aroused, still impossibly alive. But now I am all alone in the subterranean silence of my intimate realm. The Underworld is suddenly closing in on me, stifling me in its intimacy, in my own counterpart to her agony—the loss of her for another two seasons.

"I look up, casting my gaze at the ceiling of black diamonds and primeval tree roots and bare ebony rock, where, in the infinite distance overhead through the layers of the earth is the world Above. I know she has been carried away there, together with the divine energy product of our love and the living seed from my body, the only portion of me that emerges Above always. And I imagine her, coming back to life and waking up on the Sapphire Throne, its heliotrope and lavender and blue hues surrounding her in a living cocoon of light, of splintered rainbows, as though she is in the cradle of her own eye. She stretches her supple body, bares her fecund breasts, spreads herself wide and *exudes new life*, while the world receives her fierce bounty in the aptly named Hall of the Sun.

"And then, as I think of it all, I begin to burn again. My desire for her is back, from a faint low simmer to the hell inferno. It will remain thus, only ever growing, until she returns again in the fall and the cycle begins anew."

Hades became silent.

Beltain, listening to the voice of the dark God, had almost ceased breathing. In the new silence of Death's Hall, he now regarded Hades with a measure of understanding and compassion.

"And now you know the truth, mortal man," spoke Hades at last. "You know I cannot resist her, and after our brief union, for the rest of the time I burn for her who is my Black Wife. Here is a lesson to you—do not envy the gods; pity us, for we are fixed in our divine function, while you are free to do as you please. We *must* be wise whereas you *may* be fools."

Beltain watched the stilled face of Hades, the bitterness in his immortal eyes.

"Furthermore," continued the God, "this time, this season, the Longest Night has not even been *consummated* yet! Persephone, my broken love, has not performed her divine function, has not died on the Sapphire Throne and did not come to me in the heart of autumn. Instead, all these months, she has remained Above, enacting destruction upon the world and setting in motion the rest of the events you already know. Indeed, on that very same night that could have been our Longest Night, the Cobweb Bride was robbed of her death and the world's death had stopped. Thus, I burn in the hottest black flames now, weakened by my own excess of virile force, and the Longest Night is still here, malingering, waiting to be enacted, and it will never come to pass. Each day and night is the same moment in the heart of winter! Can you not feel it, mortal man?"

Beltain nodded, feeling the undeniable truth of what was being said. The winter seemed particularly brutal and unending this year. . . . And now he knew the reason why.

"What will happen now, Lord Hades? Where have you sent my Percy?"

Hades straightened in his seat and looked at the black knight with sudden weariness. "What will happen now is the *unknown.* I will send you directly after my sweet Champion, fear not, at least in that regard. But I had to keep you back in order to impart to you this dark side of things. You must know this and be ready for what comes ahead."

"I have heard enough, Lord of the Underworld," Beltain said, blushing once more. "You have made me look inside my own self and now I see the burning darkness inside me also. And it makes me afraid of what I might do, of what I might be capable of."

"Hah! Good!" Hades stared at him with his very black eyes. "It is good that you are afraid of desire, because it is what can rip this world asunder, and very likely, ultimately will. But at least now, mortal man, do not say you have not been warned properly!"

"I say only this—send me after my Percy, *now*. And I will study this desire and find a way to subjugate and control it."

In response, Hades's bitter laughter rang in echoes through the Hall of bones.

"Controlling your dark desire is the task of a lifetime, brave mortal! Take it from me who struggles with it every waking moment and yes, even in my dreams—you are much better served controlling its individual urges. Let the underlying fire burn low and steady in you, for it powers you to true action. Without desire, you will be nothing. Do not subjugate it, and yet, do not be ruled by it, only *inspired*. And now, enough revelation! Close your eyes, Beltain Chidair, and go to join your love!"

Beltain shut his eyelids, and saw in the last instant how a gale wind arose around the Ivory Throne and the pitch-black figure of the dark God faded out of existence, his hair standing up wild with coiling snakes, and the cobwebs trembling.

In the next instant, Beltain faded out also.

Chapter 9

Percy opened her eyes and found herself standing in the snow. Lord Hades had sent her to a very familiar place, a narrow street in Letheburg before a freshly painted red door of a storefront with a cheerful window and a slightly lopsided shingle hanging overhead. Yes, this was Rollins Way, and this was Grial's house.

Brr, it was cold! Early morning, just after dawn, and the dusk of night and dreary overcast hanging heavy in the dark grey sky. And Percy was wearing only a light summer dress from Tanathe, while all her warm winter clothing was back at the D'Arvu villa . . . and so was Beltain.

She had left *him* behind.

Starting to shiver in the freezing air, she stood gathering herself, sharply aware that she had left Beltain more than a hundred miles away. It was a strange protective impulse that had made her briefly run to Lord Death and leave her beloved behind, as if she wanted to spare him any unnecessary trouble and effort. After all, she had planned to return back to him immediately, as soon as she was done telling Lord Hades what she learned. . . .

But now, she had this new task to perform on behalf of Hades. And without Beltain at her side, she experienced a peculiar new, pronounced feeling of being alone. Percy had been solitary for as long as she could remember, even when surrounded by her family, and it was rather ordinary to be thus—and to be satisfied being thus. But since Beltain, she had become acutely aware of the difference of her life *before* and *after*.

She was locked in a moment of indecision—had she done the right thing to leave him, even for a few hours? Indeed, what would he think? Would he worry on her behalf?

Percy admitted to herself that in some ways she had simply bolted. It was simply too much, this overwhelming sense of *love*, of being wanted, of *union* with another. And her reaction was in part a kind of primal senseless panic. Because, on a small secret level, she was also afraid of the extent of her own feelings for him.

But now, here she was, in front of Grial's house, likely the best possible place to be for a girl who had lost her mind in the way that she had, over *him*. Grial would help in so many ways. And surely, Grial would direct her toward finding the Goddess Hecate.

Percy inhaled a stinging lungful of icy air, and knocked on the red door. "Grial! Hello there! Anyone home?"

A few moments later there was a fumble with the latch, and Lizabette opened the door, wearing a plain woolen housedress and a kitchen apron covered with flour. Her face was still puffy from sleep. There was a bit of flour there also, on her cheeks and chin and the tip of her sharp nose.

"Percy Ayren!" she exclaimed, and her expression was more than her usual slightly supercilious one, with the addition of nervous darting eyes. She glanced behind Percy to see if there was anyone else there with her.

"Morning, Lizabette," Percy said, holding her arms around herself and rubbing them. "May I come in, please? It's freezing, and I need to talk to Grial."

"Come in, by all means," Lizabette said, stepping aside to let her in. "I am not even going to bother asking what in Heaven's name you're doing, dressed like that, without a coat or shawl, or how you got here—for I am sure this has something to do with the horrid Cobweb Bride business and the odious Death's Champion business. However, I am going to prepare you in advance for what you are about to learn—"

"Is Grial in the kitchen?" Percy interrupted her, as they walked through the cheerful front parlor, and there was Marie, folding blankets and pillows on the sofa.

"Percy!" Marie exclaimed with a smile and a look of happy surprise. However she also exuded an additional high-strung nervousness that was beyond her usual timid self.

"As I was saying," Lizabette resumed. "You need to prepare yourself—"

"Percy! Persephone Ayren!" Catrine and Niosta, followed by Faeline, came running out of the kitchen, all wearing aprons and flour in their hair and on their faces. They looked half-crazed because they had been giggling, and apparently someone must have *thrown* flour, because there was no other explanation for the amount of it in Niosta's curly dark hair that now looked like an unkempt version of a powdered wig.

"Oh, for shame!" Lizabette exclaimed, seeing the flour-covered Niosta, and forgetting whatever else she was about to tell Percy. "I leave you for a second and you all go crazy! How can you find it in yourselves to waste all that precious flour, with the world falling apart, and no more sustenance to be had soon! We'll starve, and you are playing with the last of our food!"

"It ain't your food," Catrine retorted. "It's gonna be pies an' tarts for the soldiers."

"Even more reason to conserve it! Now, check the cinnamon and sugar sauce in the pan, make sure it did not boil over—did you stir it properly, Faeline?"

"Where's Grial?" said Percy, interrupting Lizabette's tirade.

There was abrupt silence. They all stared at Percy, and then Niosta put her hand over her mouth, and her eyes were very big. "Oh, Lordy, Lord, she doesn't know yet, does she?"

"Know what?" Percy stared at them and felt a sudden bolt of alarm. "Where is she? Where's Grial?"

"Grial is not Grial . . ." Catrine uttered cryptically.

"What?" Percy was beginning to frown, and it was all becoming ridiculous. All of them had the strangest expressions; even Lizabette was being all weird.

"Grial is an immortal goddess!" Marie suddenly announced. "She transformed into a beautiful ancient goddess and told us her true name was *Hecate!*"

"And now she's up on the city walls, doing some magic stuff for the King an' the city of Letheburg! And Claere the dead Princess is with her!" Niosta added, wiping flour from her eyes with the back of her hand.

Percy was stunned. "Oh . . ." she managed to say, then took a step and almost tripped on someone's abandoned clog shoe in the middle of the parlor.

"We're making apple pies for the soldiers!" Faeline said. "The Goddess Hecate told us to keep making pies, even though after last night's sorcery the city is now protected against the dead army and the soldiers can get some rest! But they can still use a bite to eat! I bet you anything they'll become magical pies when Hecate gets back—"

"So . . ." Percy mused, while her mind was racing. "Grial is Hecate. No wonder Lord Hades told me *I know her already*. Lord in Heaven! But it makes a wild kind of good sense, after all. We all thought Grial was a sorcery woman, didn't we?"

"Aye, we did!" Niosta said.

Lizabette nodded. "It was certainly a shock, but it made perfect sense. And now, what an honor! To be here, in the kitchen of an actual Grecian immortal! I admit, I am still mortified and at the same time elevated spiritually—"

"Do you think she will return shortly?" Percy asked, taking a seat on the sofa.

"Dunno," Catrine said. "Could be any moment! She's been gone all night after popping in here briefly for suppertime. Said that the city walls were all safe now, and all thanks to her Imperial Highness, Claere!"

"And then she left again," added Marie. "She said not to wait up—"

In that moment there was a loud brash knock on the door.

The girls started, and Lizabette immediately started to wipe flour off her apron and pointed to the others meaningfully to do the same.

"That doesn't sound like Grial—I mean, Hecate!" Marie whispered, and her expression was frightened.

"Yeah, that's 'cause she doesn't use the door any more!" Niosta said, stomping her feet to get more flour off her head.

"I'll get it. . . ." Percy stood up and went to see who was knocking.

She opened the door, and there was Beltain. His hair was tousled as if he had forgotten to pat it down when rising from bed in a hurry, and he was dressed lightly in the same summer clothing from the day before, but seemed heedless of the cold despite wearing a thin linen shirt. His handsome face was expressionless like stone, a hard countenance filled with what she recognized as anger.

"Oh!" Percy exclaimed, and felt an immediate pang of almost painful affection at the sight of him.

"Percy!" he said in turn. And immediately his face came alive.

"What are you doing here?" She stared at him in a mixture of overwhelming joy and guilt.

"I could ask the same of you! I awoke when you were leaving, and I followed you through the shadows. I was there when you talked to Lord Hades. . . . And then he sent me here directly, after you. Why did you go without me, girl?" He spoke in haste, with emotion. And his anger, she understood, was not directed at herself, but was merely a form of worry.

"I am sorry . . ." she mumbled. "I did not want to disturb

you, and I simply had to speak to Hades and tell him what Lady Leonora said—"

"And this could not wait until I was up and at your side?"

"I think I was—afraid," she replied. "I don't know what made me rush like that, and I am so sorry! Truly, I did not think! I am an idiot, My Lord!"

She had wanted to say "my love," but felt a little strange uttering it in front of the girls. Because the whole lot of them came out, peeking through the door, until Lizabette said, "For Heaven's sake, have His Lordship come indoors already! You're both standing neither here nor there, and letting in the freezing cold! And yes, you *are* an idiot, Percy Ayren."

Beltain stepped through the doorway into Grial's parlor. "So, is Mistress Grial here?" he asked, glancing around him at the girls and the spots of spilled flour on the floor.

And they all told him. For the next several minutes they were speaking all at once, regaling him with the unbelievable information about Hecate who was Grial.

Beltain and Percy both listened, and Percy finally said, "I am here because Lord Hades wanted me to see Hecate about something."

"Yes, I know," Beltain said softly. "I heard."

"Goodness, have a seat, Your Lordship!" Lizabette fussed meanwhile. And Marie started to clear the pillows and bedding from the sofa.

"Anyone want some tea?" Catrine asked, heading into the kitchen.

"Tea! Ah, now that's a perfectly splendid thing on a chilly morning like this, dumpling! Let's all have it!"

Grial's sonorous ringing voice sounded from the back of the parlor, and the rocking chair was suddenly creaking with motion. . . . Everyone started and turned at the sound of it, and there she was, Grial, or better to say, Hecate, even though she was in her mortal aspect, seated in the wooden rocking chair, and smiling at them with an eccentric grin.

Percy looked and did not know what to say. The same familiar dark eyes, warm and comfortable, the same wildly frizzy hair, the plan coat, her funny wide-brimmed winter hat with its knitted scarf earflaps. . . . Hard to reconcile all this with the notion that this indeed was *Hecate*.

"Percy!" said Grial or Hecate. "How good to see you again, my dearie! Did Hades send you to me now?"

"I—yes—how did you—" Percy stuttered and was even surprised at herself and her own dumbfounded reaction. Considering how many gods she had met already, why was it so odd to meet Hecate? Maybe because this was motherly Grial, someone she had come to care for and trust like a friend, and it made it oh-so much more peculiar?

"H-Hecate . . ." Percy said. "I am glad to see you, and please forgive me, but I don't know if I should call you—that is, what should I call you?"

"My dear Persephone Ayren," said the Goddess, looking at her with her very dark human eyes that were both warm and unreadable, containing somewhere in the very back a bittersweet sorrow. "It matters not what you call me, because I am still Grial, just as you are both Persephone and Percy. So let's make it simple! Now, tell me, what has happened with the Cobweb Bride? Any progress there? Have we found the poor creature yet?"

And Percy told her the events of the last few days, shyly skipping the part about her new intimacy with Beltain. But as she carefully gleaned over those personal events, it seemed that Grial read precisely through her words and saw into her secret mind and heart. Indeed, a very warm sense of profound understanding emanated from the ageless goddess, as she glanced at Beltain and Percy. Even Beltain, seeing Grial's wise appraisal, started to blush and averted his normally steady blue eyes.

". . . And so I am told to ask you for the jar that has the

ashes of Melinoë," Percy concluded. All the girls were staring in rapt curiosity.

There was a pause of silence. Outside the window was a grey overcast morning. Hecate looked at Percy thoughtfully, while her chair continued to rock softly. *Creak-creak.*

"All right, I will let you have it, my dear child," Hecate said. "Now, go to the kitchen and look in the pantry, top shelf—no, second shelf from the top. Should be a blue ceramic jar with a cork stopper and a bit of gold glaze. Bring it here."

Percy nodded and carefully went back to the kitchen, where Catrine was filling the teakettle. She rummaged around the pantry, and found the jar as described—large, cornflower blue like the summer sky, glazed with an iridescent sheen of soft gold. It was indeed stoppered with a wide cork. Percy carefully lifted it and carried it into the parlor.

"That's it," said Hecate. "Now, take it to *him*, and be careful not to drop it. Though, I've never opened it myself, so cannot guarantee its contents. My poor divine sister, Persephone—not you, but the Lady of the Underworld—she claims that it contains the ashes of her shadow child—death's true child. But now, knowing that she was already *damaged* when she had agreed to give up her daughter, now I can hardly know what to think. Thus, I know not what is inside that dratted jar. . . ."

"Is it possible that Melinoë's ashes are not there?" Percy asked.

"Everything is possible." Grial's eyes watched Percy, unblinking. "But now, you must hurry, dearie. No time to waste! You must be gone from here, from this place, from Letheburg itself! And you must not come back unless you absolutely must!"

"Why is that?" A strange minor chill ran down Percy's back.

Beltain threw her a concerned glance.

"Because *she's* coming!" Hecate said softly, and her eyes

appeared momentarily to be staring into space, as though she was not present in the room—as though she was listening to something from beyond, from a great distance that no one else could hear. "Persephone is coming here, in her mortal aspect of the Sovereign, and she will be at the walls of Letheburg within the hour. I have done all I can to fortify this city, and Claere, the dear girl did all the rest. But even with the magical wards set in place, Letheburg, or what's left of it—what with all the portions that have disappeared and gone down Below—may not stand against the immense army and the *power* of the Goddess of the Underworld."

"Oh, no!" Marie made a small, terrified sound, Lizabette stifled an "eek," and the other girls became very still, like cornered deer.

"Go, child!" Hecate said, rising from her seat. "She must not find you here! For, among other things, she wants *you* now, and your ability as Death's Champion. And whatever happens, she must *not* have it!"

"I—understand," Percy said, clutching the jar, while Beltain took a step closer to her and placed his hand on her arm.

"And you, young man—" Hecate turned to the black knight. "You take very good care of her, now, you understand? Do not let her slip away again, for the world depends upon *both* of you to remain together! Hear that, Your Lordship? Never let her out of your sight, sleep with one eye open in case she bolts again, and don't make me send the puppies after you, because Cerberus has a mean bite!"

"I assure you, I will guard her with my life," said Lord Beltain Chidair with an intense look.

"Precisely!" Hecate said. "Now, I don't want to see the two of you in this city ever again! Or at least not while everything in the world is broken. Now, back to Hades you go! And give my divine brother my warm regards! Normally I would send some apple jam too, but that will have to wait for another day."

And Hecate clapped her hands together.

The world shimmered and was gone.

Percy and Beltain were back in Death's Keep.

Duke Ian Chidair, known as Hoarfrost, stood on top of a twelve-foot square platform erected for him by the dead, a platform of wood and rock and compacted snow, balanced atop another platform with wheels, so that it could be dragged around the city walls perimeter, not unlike the siege towers. It allowed him to observe the entirety of the battlefield and the countryside for leagues around the city of Letheburg, to see the low banking fires still burning in spots around the city walls, and mostly a blackened stretch of scorched earth, shaping a moat around the outer pomoerium.

The dead army had scaled the walls in numerous places, but along each spot they were met with an invisible wall of resistance—a wall that had not been there before last noon.

"What's this, new blasted sorcery!" railed the Blue Duke, his barrel-chested torso covered with a new layer of snow and ice, so that he looked even less a human man and more like a thing carved of frozen water and wood and bracken debris, with a wild brush tangle of hair like an untrimmed hedgerow. "The King of Lethe in his cowardice has no other means of keeping us at bay! First fire, now this invisible witch fence! But never you fear, Osenni, I will find a way past this latest obstacle you set before me, and then I shall drag you from your Palace and your throne like the old wine sack that you are!"

At his side, a few steps away, near the edge of the platform, stood Lady Ignacia Chitain, wearing a fine fur-lined cloak of ermine, with the hood raised closely over her face against the chill wind. She was the only living being outside the city walls, if one was to discount the young boy who handled her carrier birds—and naturally he was never to be counted. All around was the wallowing dead army.

Lady Ignacia had grown strangely inured to the horrifying

sight of dead grotesques everywhere she might turn. Men with
damaged skulls and deep head wounds, missing limbs, cloven
torsos and other mortal damage to their bodies, were moving and
working to enact Hoarfrost's military orders. Their wounds had
long since bled out, and were now encrusted with a strangely
beautiful, delicate-pink, crystalline layer of frost.

Frost reigning over what had once been blood. . . .

The situation was hardly tolerable in every sense, but
Ignacia could only wait for the arrival of her liege, the Sovereign
of the Domain. In the meantime, her one task was to keep
Hoarfrost docile enough when it came to her own person, and to
keep him from inflicting mortal damage to her own body, in a
latest outburst of madness. It was a precarious situation at best.

The time was no more than a few hours after dawn, and the
sky overhead was grey monochrome infinity. There was no sun
to observe through the thickness of cloudmass, and the day
promised another snowfall.

"Damn you, rotten cowards!" Hoarfrost cried in the
direction of the city walls, taking in a deep swig of air to balloon
his lungs. This was in response to seeing a large catapult-hurled
boulder come crashing against the sorcerous wall and bouncing
back, only to land a few feet from the ranks of the dead army
outside the city.

"As soon as Her Brilliance arrives, this so-called sorcery
will have no chance against her or you, Your Grace," said Lady
Ignacia in a soothing tone.

Hoarfrost whirled to stare at her. "So you say now, little
bird!" he barked. "But you've been saying it for days, and yet,
where is she, this marvelous Sovereign of yours? How much
longer must we wait? I'd hoped to have the city two nights ago,
and would've had it too, if not for this new infernal witchery!
They were weakened, hardly able to keep us back, and even the
snow had quenched their firewall. . . . But now, this!"

Ignacia blinked, gathering herself to reply with something

comforting and innocuous. But then her gaze happened to span south, and she noticed something at the distant grey horizon.

Movement. . . .

And blood.

She stilled, her breath catching in her throat and a kind of mesmerizing excitement coming to her, for she recognized the seething line of red at the horizon for what it was, the pomegranate color of the Trovadii vanguard.

"She is here!" Ignacia said, continuing to look south and never blinking.

"What did you say?" Hoarfrost swiveled his torso in the direction of her gaze.

"My queen comes . . ." whispered Ignacia in a rapt voice. "See the moving army, there on the horizon! The Sovereign is here!"

"I see blasted nothing!" Hoarfrost said. "But then, what is one to expect to see out of these dead marbles? I expect we shall see them when they approach closer. Wait, ah, I do see! Something crawling in red, yes! She comes in blood, does she not, your Liege?"

"It is the color of Trovadii."

"And a fine sight for dead eyes it is! About time!"

Meanwhile, the southern horizon was filling up with the red incoming tide. It surged closer, resolving into tiny figures, into precise formations, divisions of cavalry and infantry, and a distant peculiar hum which then became subdued thunder. There was no other sound, not a birdcall, not a creak of a branch, but the strange dull pounding.

They were deep bass drums. The sound they made resonated in the earth and did not echo, because of the dampening snow cover, but it vibrated richly, making the ground tremble. . . .

Or maybe not.

Those were not merely drums, but the pounding of feet in unison, heavy and lifeless limbs like tree trunks set in motion, as the infantry came. And the cavalry, heavier rumble, came in counterpoint.

"Make room, boys! We have company!" Hoarfrost exclaimed, motioning to his own men to part and group alongside the perimeter of their siege. The Lethe dead obeyed him, and there was a slow stirring in the ranks all around, as waves moved in a semblance of order.

Lady Ignacia finally tore her gaze away from the approaching Trovadii and glanced around. She looked up at the city parapets and saw the dead there, massing thickly against the wall of invisible force, and they had all turned around and were staring downward at the newcomers approaching from the south. Beyond the thicket of the dead, up on the battlements, within the safety of their sorcerous wall, the living defenders of Letheburg observed warily the commotion below.

As soon as Percy and Beltain were gone, Hecate adjusted her funny Grial hat, patted down her coat and said to the girls, "Well, dearies, it seems like *she* is here already, and so I am needed back up on the city wall fortifications."

"Who is here, your divine—Hec—that is, I mean, Grial?" Lizabette asked.

"Why, Persephone," Hecate replied. "And I don't mean our Percy Ayren, but the other one, the immortal with the nasty dead army. You know her as the Sovereign of the Domain. She is now at the walls of Letheburg, and things are about to get a little hot under the collar."

Marie made a small, terrified sound and bit her knuckle, while Catrine, Niosta and Faeline all looked at her with wide eyes.

"Are you—are you goin' to be fightin' her, Grial?" Niosta wiped streaks of leftover flour from her freckled nose.

Hecate made a very loud typical Grial-cackle of laughter. "Goodness gracious! Me, fight? Why, that's a real lark now, girlie! What do you think I am, an armored cavalry knight? No, I think there's going to be some pointed conversation, and then possibly a bit of posturing, and diplomatic strong language. And then, just then, which I dearly hope to avoid, there may be a show of *power*. But fighting? Gracious, no, I certainly hope not!"

"Why is she here?" asked Marie.

"Aye, what does she want here in Letheburg?" Catrine added. "Ain't there some other fancier place for her to go? Like the Emperor's Silver Court?"

Hecate shook her head slowly and continued pushing her frizzy hair around the hat's brim and the scarf flaps. "Apparently not. They say she went right past the Emperor and his Court and headed straight here."

"So why Letheburg?"

"You do ask a very fine question, ladies." Hecate looked around them, gifting each girl with a penetrating gaze of her black eyes. "And thus, I am afraid I will have to tell you. But you must promise me to keep this to yourselves and mum's the word—or is it chrysanthemum?—as far as the neighbors are concerned."

They all nodded, with very serious, attentive expressions.

"You see," Hecate said very solemnly, "there could be two very good reasons why Persephone wants Letheburg. One of the possible reasons was just removed from the premises, and hence from the city environs, by Percy Ayren, in a blue jar. . . . The other reason—" the Goddess paused. "The other reason is still here, unfortunately. And it cannot be taken away so easily. It's *this*." And Hecate sighed and wearily pointed at her old wooden rocking chair in the corner of the parlor.

The girls stared uncomprehending.

"Beg pardon?" Lizabette said, glaring at the chair and then back at Hecate.

"You mean—your *rocker?*" Niosta said in absolute disbelief. "She wants your ole' rocker?"

The Goddess sighed again and nodded. "Yes, ladies, believe it or not, she wants this old thing. But—let me explain. This is not just any old rocker. It is a very special one. It is as ancient as the oldest wood you can imagine, and it is much more than it seems. You see, my dears, this old chair is the only *other* remaining *immortal seat* in this mortal world, a means of divine transport from Above to Below. In short, it is a Throne to the Underworld."

There was complete silence. And then, one by one, the girls slowly stepped back and as far away from the chair in the corner as possible. Marie, finding herself backed to the wall with its colorful wallpaper, whimpered. . . .

"Now, now!" said Hecate. "Nothing to be afraid of, everyone! It's just a rickety old chair, as far as all of you are concerned. You've sat in it dozens of times, all of you, isn't that so?"

"Yes . . ." Lizabette responded faintly.

"Jupiter's balls! I was just sittn' in it today!" cried Niosta.

"Precisely! And nothing happened, pumpkin. So there you have it, perfectly safe for mortals. It's only when one of us immortals takes a seat that we can travel *downstairs*, if you get my drift. And yes, this very unusual throne belongs to me. . . . Now, there are two other such thrones in the mortal world, the first one being Death's Throne of Ivory in the great shadowed Hall of his Keep, and the second being the Sapphire Throne in the Palace of the Sun in the Domain. The Sapphire Throne belongs to Persephone, and she uses it normally. But I am afraid that something has happened to it—it is now just as broken as she is. I *felt* it happen in the same moment when death stopped, a fatal crack, a profound *shutting down*—for I am aware of all things that give passage to other places. Indeed, for a hundred years the Sapphire Throne somehow endured and functioned with an earlier hairline crack the making of which I felt also— that first crack came about the instant when Melinoë was brought Above from Below. But now—the Sapphire Throne no longer has the power to transport the gods."

"Oh!" Faeline parted her mouth in comprehension.

"Yes indeed, you see how it is!" Hecate said. "And because Persephone very likely intends to get to the Underworld, she wants to have the use of this Throne of mine, in case she cannot get past Lord Death and forcibly use *his*."

"Oh dear . . ." said Lizabette. "Cannot you take this chair away somewhere else and hide it?"

Hecate licked her lips and smiled. "This chair cannot be removed from this room," she said. "You are welcome to try! You can certainly move it around the parlor, and turn it every which way, to get comfy as you sit. But you cannot remove it *outside*. It has been here a very long time. Indeed, if I recall correctly, far longer than Letheburg!"

The girls observed and listened in rapt amazement.

"And now, ladies," Hecate suddenly changed the subject, "it is time for me to head on out there and meet the inevitable— you all stay indoors, keep up the pie making, and be sure to get plenty of hot tea to keep you warm, and keep that fireplace crackling. It's going to get very *chilly* today!"

And before any of them could blink, Hecate was gone.

Chapter 10

Percy took Beltain's familiar warm hand, and squeezed it, and at the same time shut her eyes. . . . And the next moment they were in Tanathe.

They had just left Death's Keep. Hades, seated in his usual manner on Death's Throne, had simply received the blue jar from Percy, placing his slim ebony fingers with their sharp claws around the glazed thing of pottery, his hand closing around it gingerly. And immediately the jar faded before their eyes into nothing.

Hidden away into Shadow. . . .

"I thank you, my Champion," said the dark God raising the gaze of his heavy and somehow empty eyes. "But now you must return and complete your task. The Cobweb Bride awaits—go to her. And this time, bring her here to me. Do this one last thing. . . . For if you do not, the world will fade and collapse that much quicker."

He motioned with his elegant hand wearily—indeed, Hades seemed even more stonelike than usual, and somehow diminished in his aura of rich darkness—and then the Hall dissolved around them and they felt the sudden blast of fresh lukewarm morning air of Tanathe.

At first glance they appeared to be in the garden of the D'Arvu villa. But something was different. The air was moist, rich with the smell of the sea. . . . Meanwhile, the sounds beyond the trees of the garden were the splash of water against rock and the cries of seagulls.

Percy glanced around her, seeing a not-so-distant mirror-bright shimmer of a great body of water through the dappled sunlight of the tree branches. "Oh!" she said.

"Wait, Percy!" Beltain took her hand and drew her to him, so that she turned and took a step toward him, placing her other hand on his chest. She felt his warm skin and the strong beating heart through the fine linen fabric. The morning light played through the trees and cast a gilded shimmer over the planes of his face, its new stubble, and the heart-wrenchingly beautiful dear eyes, open as the sky.

"Percy . . ." he said. "Before we go in there, promise me one thing—you will not leave me again, not like that. Please, promise!"

She gazed up at him, drowning in his gaze, and feeling the boundaries of the air and the flesh shimmer and become translucent in a moment of vertigo. "I will never leave you, Beltain." Her words came out effortless, but at the same time a bittersweet sense was inside her, somewhere deep, and she was not sure why.

"No matter what happens," he said. "Even now, I know not what is happening—or what will happen—what has come to pass here, for I can feel that something is different here, something—"

"Yes," she said, putting her hand up to stroke his cheek gently.

He leaned in closer to her, and his mouth pressed against her forehead, sealing, branding her skin with a warm sacred touch.

They stood, fixed in a moment of nothing but sun and living silence and the nearby splashing waters of a world that was inexplicable and unreliable, and a mystery, even a few feet beyond the reach of their senses.

"My Lord . . ." she whispered, her face against his chest, tears beginning to well in her eyes. "My . . . Beltain."

"My *Lady*," he replied. "Always." And then he raised his fingers to softly wipe her eyelashes, and in the next instant his lips were upon her shut eyelids, like a soft gentle dream.

Just behind them a seagull cried harshly, bursting through the greenery, and its rending screech made them come apart.

"I am not sure what has happened here," Percy said. "I am almost afraid to know."

They walked carefully through the garden, along a small gavel path, and emerged near the façade of the house. The gatekeeper's small house was only a few feet in the distance, before the long drive past the front gates began. But as Percy happened to turn in that direction, instead of the scene of a small street past the gates and neighbor houses across the road, she saw a short beach, with waves lapping at the roots of solitary remaining trees and shrubs, and beyond it open water and the sea, stretching to the horizon. . . .

The street with the houses was gone. And so was most of the town of San Quellenne.

"This is truly hard to believe, even now, seeing it," Beltain said, gazing past the driveway and the gates, at the newly created beach. "But the street must have disappeared as all the rest of things. We've seen this everywhere, land fading into shadows— the strange occurrences we have encountered all over the Realm and now the Domain."

"We must go inside! I hope the D'Arvu family is still here. . . . Oh! Leonora! What if she—" And Percy tugged Beltain by the hand and rushed toward the house.

Inside was dark and cool, and the door was unattended by any servant. Percy's footsteps rang against the stone floor, as she rushed into the main parlor, and to her relief saw Count Lecrant seated in his chair, fiddling with a piece of carved wood and a knife, while a pair of servants moved soundlessly through the room at their tasks.

"My Lord!" exclaimed Percy, with a swift curtsy. "You are here! And what of Lady Leonora?"

"Percy, child!" said the Count with a lukewarm semblance of a smile coming to him, seeing her and Beltain, and rose from his seat, dropping his carving. "Ah! Lord Beltain! The servants did not find you in your room, so we thought the two of you had disappeared the same way as has everything else around here! I am very glad to be mistaken!"

"What has come to pass here?" Beltain asked. "We were gone briefly in the morning to—walk in the garden," he added, not willing to reveal the real details. Percy glanced at him with gratitude in her eyes.

"It appears, we cannot seem to avoid this same blight that has been happening all over," said the Count, no longer bothering to hide his despair. "I am told by servants that most of this town had gone overnight, blocks and entire neighborhoods fading one by one, and so has the majority of the countryside south of here, all the way to the shore. Indeed, you can see the waters lapping across our street! There are a few half-drowned trees if you walk out further, and a number of spots that appear to be water-bound islands, isolated and cut off by the sea from the rest of land. It is intolerable! Even the castle of San Quellenne is now a small island plateau on a rise, and, I am told, everyone in the neighborhood that's still left here is getting ready to depart—where to, it is uncertain. But we must go also—I suppose, we must, and we shall—"

"Where *can* you go?" Percy said. "Indeed, My Lord, where can anyone go to escape this? Since every and any part of the land might disappear next!"

"That, I know not." The Count D'Arvu sighed deeply, and nodded to one of the servants. "Go fetch the Ladies," he said with an empty, world-weary gaze. "My noble spouse and daughter—they have gone down the street—the part that is still here, still above water—to listen to a group of townspeople and the local Lady—the Lady San Quellenne, who has called them all out to gather in the marketplace—what's left of it. I believe they are discussing what is to be done now. I—" he paused. "I did not choose to accompany them in this particular matter. For, what's the use? We cannot escape, any of us. Not any more. We've run so far already, and apparently we cannot run away from the world itself. Thus—we must depart immediately—or we must not. . . . Oh and yes, I do know that my daughter is *dead*. I see it very clearly now."

Count Lecrant became silent, and turned away. He sat down and picked up his piece of wood, the knife, and resumed the whittling handiwork.

Percy and Beltain exchanged glances.

"So you do understand, Count Lecrant, about Lady Leonora's condition?" Percy looked at him, speaking in a soft voice. "I am so very sorry. Abysmally sorry. . . ."

"Yes," the older man replied without looking up from his task, "so am I."

Percy understood him in that moment, for it was clear he had given up.

There was a loud splashing of water from the direction of the street, and a small makeshift raft of a few planks of wood tied with rope floated by, with an old woman and two children seated upon it, and a small sack of their belongings. The greenish waves were lapping at the raft and it floated low and did not appear that it would remain seaworthy for much longer, as it swept past them and the abbreviated beach and onward down the street.

"I'll go look for her," Percy said suddenly. "The Lady Leonora—I will go to her now."

Beltain nodded and they simply walked past the Count who never looked up, out of the parlor, and outside into the daylight.

Through the trees, the sea was an expanse of shattered mirrors in the sunlight, and the balmy air swept around them, imbued with a bitter tang of salt.

Percy reached out with her death sense and she searched for the presence of Leonora's death shadow.

There it was, somewhere out there, nearby.

Percy went after it.

They walked rapidly along the street-turned-beach sandbar, a few blocks into a smallish plaza that was the center of town, normally the site of the marketplace.

A few emaciated stray dogs ran past them along the streets and alleyways that opened as they passed. One of the dogs was dead, with a tangled mange coat, and Percy could see its wistful death shadow following from the rear as the dog lagged behind the others, yet followed them unfailingly with its last recognized instinct of "pack." The living dogs did not pay attention to it for as long as it kept some distance, but once it got too near at one point the closest dog growled slightly and the dead one stayed back the same distance, watching them with sorrowful eyes.

A small crowd of townsmen, about three dozen, had gathered to the side near one of the rows of stalls, and in the center on a pale grey horse sat a young lord in a light hunter's hauberk, with a sword belted at the waist. Brazen hair was gathered in a long plait and pulled back from a deeply sun-bronzed elegant face, that of a youth. At the youth's side, atop a bay horse was a lady, mature and matronly, seated in a large comfortable side-saddle, and wearing a wide brimmed straw hat over a long thick braid of dark hair.

The young lord was gesticulating and speaking, and his voice was that of a maiden—brash and commanding, yet a maiden nevertheless.

Percy blinked from the sun as she and Beltain approached the gathering, and saw the two D'Arvu women, the Countess and her daughter Leonora, at the edge of the crowd.

"—and it will require all of you to make use of whatever wood at your disposal to make rafts, and do it as soon as possible, by tonight!" the maiden-dressed-as-a-lord was saying loudly. "We don't have much time, for tomorrow more of the land might be gone, and the sea will take us. It has already closed us off completely from the rest of the mainland, and I expect it will only get worse."

"But Lady Jelavie," a man spoke up from the crowd. "How are we to make enough rafts for everyone? If we pray, mayhap the Good Lord will hear us and keep us safe."

"Have we not been praying all along?" the armed Lady Jelavie exclaimed, sweeping strands of brazen hair that the breeze moved into her eyes, bright with energy and anger. "Father Suell has grown hoarse from saying Mass and the church candles are burning, day and night. If the Good Lord has not heard our prayers by now, I don't expect more praying will make any difference. Indeed, how much prayer is required before one is heard—"

"Jelavie, please have care how you speak," said the older matron lady.

"My Lady Mother, forgive my words, but I am only trying to help these people."

"What of the ill and the elderly?" someone else said. "How will they stay afloat on makeshift contraptions? I doubt, My Lady, that we could manage—"

"Not to mention, there is very little binding rope to be had! The rope maker lived in the part of town that's now gone, and he and his shop with it!"

"It is unfortunate, but you are welcome to whatever stores we have in the Castle," said the older matron lady. "Take what you need, come. We have left the gates open for you."

"Oh, Your Ladyship, thank you!"

"Aye, Lady Calliope, thank you indeed!"

But the matron raised one hand up in a tired informal gesture. "It is the least we can do. San Quellenne will not let its people perish, even if these are the last days, and the world itself ends around us."

"What do they think to do?" Percy whispered to Beltain, as they approached the edge of the crowd discreetly. "Rafts will not be enough to save them and take them inland! Not all of them and their belongings and their poor animals!"

He nodded, with a grave look. "From what we can see, the sea is vast, and is likely thus in all directions, surrounding us. This part of the land has become a small group of islands. Any boats they might've had available along the old shoreline are now gone, so they must make rafts or new boats if they are to leave anywhere. They would never reach the distant northern land otherwise. And even with rafts or boats, it is questionable." Beltain pointed. "Look there, see the haze in the north? I think that's where solid land begins, the farthest place that the sea has not swallowed yet. They need great ships, not flimsy boats made overnight."

"Beltain!" Percy took his hand in a sudden energetic clasp and glanced into his eyes with the warm living gaze of her vaguely swamp-hued eyes. "I have a mad notion how to save these people—all of them. And it will not require rafts."

It took but an hour to convince Lady Calliope San Quellenne that this stranger, this peasant girl who called herself Death's Champion, was not entirely mad, but was someone who could help in this strangest predicament of their lives.

"My Lady!" said the girl, stepping forth from the crowd, "Begging pardon for what might seem like impertinence, but I am Percy Ayren, and I am come from very far away. But I believe I can help you."

She began speaking and the things that came out of her lips were the stuff of stories and nonsense—or would have been thus only a few weeks ago, if not for the impossible events of the most recent days which the Lady San Quellenne had herself witnessed.

"I can walk into the shadows and emerge in Death's Hall,"

said the girl. "And I can take all of you and your people there. It is a neutral grey place, and Lord Death himself will send you onward to where you might want to go from there—at least I think he can be convinced to do so. Indeed, Death is the one who sent us here."

"And why exactly *are* you here?" asked Jelavie, astride her horse and at her mother's side. "Why should we believe anything you say?" For once the Lady San Quellenne did not disapprove of her daughter's outspoken commentary, and shared the sentiment.

At the edge of the crowd, a pair of nobly-dressed women, one of them likely the mother of the younger, were staring very worriedly, watching the stranger girl. Lady Calliope had noticed them previously, for they too were strange new faces here in town, but now she astutely noted there was some kind of connection between them and this girl who had emerged with her strange claims.

Meanwhile the girl paused for a moment before replying to Jelavie's apt question. She was plain and stout and simply attired, and as she glanced around the crowd, Lady Calliope saw her being observed intently by a tall imposing young man with a composed handsome face who towered over most of the men present. He had the look of a nobleman, and he too was a stranger she had never seen before—what was it suddenly? They had not seen so many new faces over a matter of weeks in San Quellenne as seemed to be gathered here now. . . .

The girl named Percy looked around the crowd and then she said, "I can help your dead to pass on. If there is anyone here who has a relation who needs relief from mortal pain—I can grant it."

The townspeople were all speaking, and it was suddenly a sea of angry voices raised.

"What dark things are you saying, girl? This is blasphemy! We are presently cursed with no death, 'tis true, but what can someone like you do?"

"I already told you who I am," she replied in an even voice that suddenly got strong—while the young nobleman took a step closer toward her, glancing at her protectively. "As Death's Champion, I have been given this ability to help you. Is there anyone among you who will give me a chance?"

"What, and let you defile our poor dead even more? You are mad, girl!" a ruddy-faced townswoman cried hoarsely. "My husband has been dead for days now and I am glad to have him with me for the extra work he can put in! I've no one else to help, what with five heads to feed and two infants, and he doesn't even need to eat! Not so bad to be dead, yet still be here with us, I say!"

"Aye!" other voices responded. There was a tumult of more angry whisperings in waves.

Suddenly a young boy's voice sounded. "Can you help my bird?"

The boy stepped out of the crowd of adults, jostling past a few townspeople. He was no older than seven, olive-skinned and tanned to a bronze, his skinny arms poking from the sleeves of an oversized white linen shirt, and his head was a tangle of unruly black hair that dearly needed combing. Who else would it be, thought Lady Calliope, looking at her youngest son fondly.

"Flavio!" exclaimed his sister, Jelavie, giving him a hard flashing look. "What are you doing?"

The boy stretched forth his hand and in its palm was a tiny, feathered shape of a young seagull. He stood before Percy and showed her the creature, feebly moving its broken wing.

"I found it right there, near the water," said the boy. "The dogs were going to grab it, but I grabbed it first! It's dead, and cold, and I think its neck is crushed."

"Are you sure it's dead?" said a man standing nearest to the boy, craning his neck to look.

"It is dead," replied the girl called Percy suddenly, staring intently at the creature. Her expression was full of compassion.

"I can see its death shadow next to the little body."

There was more talk in the crowd.

From her seat in the saddle, the Lady San Quellenne looked down at the girl steadily, evaluating her. "So, you can see the dead among us, is that so? Who do you see, then? Who is dead here?"

Percy looked up at Lady Calliope, and there was a small pause, while the warm breeze blew, stirring their hair, and only a hundred feet away was the sound of lapping waves, just beyond the plaza.

"Well?" said the Lady San Quellenne.

"*You*," said Percy Ayren. "You are dead, My Lady. I am sorry to say. . . ."

Perfect silence. Lady Calliope froze.

Next to her, seated on the other horse, the young Lady Jelavie started and then made a little sound. "What? *Mother!*"

There was a commotion among the townspeople. Stunned gasps. The two strange noblewomen stood watching the proceedings, and one of them made a small stifled sound.

"The bird," Lady Calliope said slowly, never looking at her daughter, indeed, never looking at any of them. "Put it to rest, now."

Percy Ayren nodded, then gently averted her gaze from the Lady San Quellenne and merely with her glance seemed to reach out to the poor broken thing stirring in the palm of little Flavio's hand.

The soft breeze carrying with it a scent of salt from the sea stirred the seagull into a ball of moving feathers, and tangled the boy's dark hair even more than it already was.

When the breeze passed, the bird was motionless.

Flavio gasped. "Oh!" he said. "I felt it rush away, like a magic spirit bird! It is really dead! It is—"

And then he looked up to see his mother's *dead* gaze upon him. And it sank in at last. He scrunched up his face into a contorted mess and then began to bawl.

Seated on her own horse, a mere handshake away from her dead mother and her mount, Lady Jelavie San Quellenne was crying also, silently, her shoulders shaking, and great streaks of water running down her cheeks, while her face remained stern and proud and stonelike.

Lady Calliope San Quellenne made the conscious effort to pull in the air into her lungs, and parted her lips, and spoke the words that had to be said at last, eventually, today, *now*. . . . "It is true, I am dead. I have—*died* four days ago. Just an hour past midnight—remember how very ill I had been that night? I died . . . but I was not sure at first, since I had been so ill for so long. But then, when I stopped hearing my own heart, and stopped needing to breathe or sleep or eat, I knew it then."

"W-why did you not say anything, mother?" Lady Jelavie uttered between sobs.

"What is one to say upon such an occasion? Announcing one's own death is not something that any of us have much experience with. . . . The world has become an impossible thing. And I did not want to frighten any of you, not when so much misery was here already. And then, places started disappearing. . . . I thought it best to wait, and make myself as useful as I can be, for all of you."

Lady Calliope turned at last, moving her neck slowly, to see her daughter's grief. "Please, child, no more," she said. "Think, how many dead mothers are fortunate enough to speak to their daughters and console them? It is a new thing, and it is a strange blessing, even while it is also a curse. Come, stop the crying this instant—and you too, Flavio, my little heart."

The murmuring townspeople in the crowd began taking off their hats and whispering condolences to their Lady.

She in turned listened to their words lovingly. "I thank you, my beloved people of San Quellenne. And now, I relinquish myself and all that is mine to my daughter. Lady Jelavie is now the rightful Lady San Quellenne."

"*No!*" The young maiden cried. "I refuse it, mother! You are my Lady, and—and you are here, with us, and you are—"

"No, dear heart," said her mother. "My time is now in the past. I am but a corporeal ghost—fortunate and blessed enough to witness the transition, as no others could—those who had died over the generations, long before me. For no other San Quellenne Lord or Lady throughout history was as blessed as I, not until these past few days and the strange stopping of all death."

The dead Lady San Quellenne turned to look at the strange girl called Percy, whose coming here has precipitated this day of revelation. Percy was standing very quietly, looking at them all with a gaze of profound sorrow.

"I believe you, and what you say, strange girl," Lady Calliope said to Percy. "I believe that you can save us all, and lead us—as you say—through the shadows. Then, do it. Please. Help us! Help them!" And she stretched one pale arm to sweep it in a circle encompassing the crowd and the street and what was visible of dry land around them.

Ad Percy Ayren nodded, seeing her, and seeing the now softly weeping young boy, and his sister, still wearing a face of stone, but the kind of stone that stands under a waterfall and has been drenched with the aerial spray, and has been made shining and eroded and forever marked. . . .

"Tonight, just before twilight comes," Percy said. "Have your people get ready, and come here to this street. Dress warmly. Come with your belongings and your animals, I beg you not to leave them behind, not to abandon them. . . . Do not tarry, do not be late, or you might miss the shadows, and then it may be too late, for the shadows themselves might come to you and fade this remaining land away."

"These people will be here as you say," replied the lady.

"I will wait for you," Percy replied.

The Lady San Quellenne noticed how Percy seemed to look

out beyond the crowd, to the back, where the two strangers, the two women with their unfamiliar faces, stood, watching her. They locked gazes with the girl for an instant. And then the younger one of the two women slowly averted her stilled, dead eyes.

Percy and Beltain returned to the D'Arvu villa to wait, while the afternoon deepened and the quality of the light outside warmed into the precursor of sunset.

They had followed Lady Arabella D'Arvu and the Lady Leonora as they made their way back along the street that was now the seashore, walking several steps behind to grant them privacy. Leonora turned a few times and cast her bird-like fixed glance at Percy, then looked away.

Within the villa, the count was where they had left him, seated alone in the parlor and his eyes were closed, while his woodcarving was set aside. He was not sleeping, for at once he opened his eyes and he glanced at them all and spoke quietly to his wife.

They consulted in soft weary voices, while Leonora stood in the middle of the room, straight-backed as a pillar of salt. Her faint death shadow billowed at her side, next to the real shadow on the floor cast by the sun in the window.

Percy and Beltain approached and Percy spoke evenly, addressing all of them. "Will you come with us tonight, as I lead the local people from here?"

Lady Arabella turned with a nervous expression on her thin sunken face. "We—we have not decided—that is, we need to think—"

"You cannot stay here. . . . The town is an island now, completely cut off from everything. There will be no food, no means of leaving again, unless you decide to fashion a raft or boat," Beltain interrupted, looking at the Countess and then the Count. "I urge you strongly to think well on this now. The Kingdom of Tanathe in its entirety may not be here tomorrow."

"But it would mean going to Death's Keep!" The Countess began wringing her hands in distress. "My Leonora cannot—must not—she must not be forced to this—"

"I promise you," Percy said, "I will not force the Lady Leonora to anything against her will. Even in the presence of Lord Death, she will have her choice."

"I—"Leonora's voice sounded. "I will come. But—no, I cannot die, not yet. My Lady Mother and My Lord Father, I cannot have you stay here and perish because of me. We will go to this—this *otherplace*. I will see Death and look upon him, and I will think. . . ."

"Then, it is well, and it will be for the best, My Lady." Percy looked upon Leonora kindly.

The count nodded and then called his servants to gather their things yet again. Only this time, he directed them to leave most of their unpacked belongings behind, and choose only what was most essential.

"Will it be cold where we go?" he said wearily.

"Yes, it is Lethe, in the Realm. Death's Keep is to be found from there, though I do not think you will necessarily end up in Lethe once we go there," Percy spoke.

Beltain meanwhile went to gather his own armor and knight's attire, and to get Jack ready to ride.

When sunset approached, they walked to the marketplace, leading horses behind them, and followed by a few servants carrying small items of personal value.

The town of San Quellenne was a place of ghosts, suspended. In the fading cream-yellow sunlight trees moved in the breeze, with flowers that had been the same for days, neither ripening to fruit nor falling off. Leaves fluttered like lifeless eternal parchment.

The D'Arvu family walked slowly through the sparse dappled shadows made by the trees, casting farewell glances at the place they had wanted to make their home but now had to abandon after only a day. Percy and Beltain followed them, keeping slightly back, with Beltain fully armored in his black plate and chain mail, leading Jack behind him. Percy had her winter coat on, even though the balmy air made it stifling hot and beads of sweat were on her forehead.

Seagulls raced through the sparse trees around them, emerging through the branches clustered with greenery and on the other side where was the sea, casting themselves with hunger into the aquamarine waters and trying to hunt for fish that would not die in their beaks. They were all starving slowly, Percy thought, watching the maddened birds in their futile plight, sending up plumes of white spray as they struck downwards at the surface of the seawater.

On the street that was a beach, a few small animals emerged, lean nervous squirrels, and packs of dogs with despair in their eyes. A small, skinny orange-and-white tomcat peered through the shrubbery. They scattered from the approaching men and women, and yet followed the passerby with famished looks.

When they arrived at the market plaza, quite a few people had already gathered there, sitting on sacks of their belongings in the middle of the wide-open space. As soon as they saw Percy, every eye was upon her and their murmuring voices ceased.

The sun cast long indigo shadows as it sank into the west, the top of its bloody orange sphere like an egg yolk floating at the horizon. Slender tree branches stood out in layers of silhouette against the sunset, and the sky faded from blue to damson.

The denizens of the Castle of San Quellenne arrived last of all, the Lady San Quellenne and her daughter and son, all dressed simply—except for Lady Jelavie who wore a ruddy surcoat with a family crest over a suit of light armor, polished white metal, with a helm in the crook of her arm—with a few servants leading horses, and donkeys pulling a cart loaded with all that ever meant 'home.'

Lady Calliope headed directly toward Percy. Her long dress

of pale cotton billowed around her, without sleeves to cover her pale flesh that death had leached of any residue of tan, and only simple open sandals were on her feet. She wore no straw hat this time, and her hair, rich russet with highlights of pale metal was gathered in a simple plait, and a small band of shimmering sun-gold sat on her brow, which upon closer perusal turned out to be a simple coronet of braided silk ribbon. Her eyes were dark rich brown, a warm hue, even in death. "It is difficult saying goodbye to the place were you lived all your life. So many memories. . . ." Her measured words came in an even, calm voice, riding her breath.

Percy met her gaze and said, "Again, I am so sorry. I also left my small home village, though it does not compare to this green beautiful place."

"Let us wait then, and see if any more people come."

Percy nodded silently. Beltain caught her glance and there was patient strength in his slate-grey eyes. They stood thus, waiting, while the crowd gathered and the sunset faded.

"How much longer?" asked Lady Jelavie, approaching Percy. She glanced briefly in the direction of the black knight, appraising his new armored look.

"Soon," Percy pointed to the long shadows. "As soon as the sun is gone, and twilight starts thickening, there will be some shadows that serve as *passageways*."

"How can you tell them apart from other shadows?" Jelavie was looking at Percy with a hard gaze, and her brown eyes, the same hue as those of her mother, were not warm at all.

"I can feel their difference," Percy replied, matching her gaze with her own steady one. "It is like grey mist. And then I move it apart by imagining it to be thus, and it becomes a *space* that can be entered."

"Ah, I do not quite believe you," the lady dressed as a knight said. "How do we know you are not leading us into an enemy trap? The Domain and the Realm are at war, even if we know not why, nor do we like to make war ourselves, and Lord knows what awaits us on the other side—dark sorcery! Will you enter first?"

"I will enter first," sounded a rich baritone, and they both turned to look at Beltain.

"You are an enemy knight of the Realm," said Lady Jelavie, looking up at him insolently. "I see by your armor you are of a high rank. Will you slay our people as we pass through this sorcerous passageway of shadows and smoke?"

"I am Lord Beltain Chidair, and I give you my word of honor you will not be harmed. If I had wanted to slay your people, they would be dead already," he said softly, looking back at the lady with an unblinking stare. That same basilisk stare had cowered quite a few opponents on the battlefield.

But Lady Jelavie was undaunted. Her slim hands in their elegant steel-braced gauntlets reached for the length of sheathed sword at her side. "Do not think, Lord Beltain," she said, "that San Quellenne goes like lambs to the slaughter. I *promise* you, your treacherous task will be far more difficult than you imagine."

"Jelavie, please, stop. . . ." Her mother had come closer once again, moving with weary stilted footsteps that had grown more pronounced in awkwardness of stiff limbs, now that she was no longer hiding her condition, and Percy observed the soft resigned sorrow, a strange delicate sheen of it on her features.

Jelavie frowned, but immediately nodded to her mother, and looked away from the black knight.

In the next few moments, the sun sank beyond the horizon.

It was the beginning of true dusk.

The people in the marketplace shivered, glancing round them, for they too seemed to realize that the time of leaving was almost upon them.

In all places where the trees and buildings stood close together, branches clustered to obscure all vestiges of sky's glow, shadows were gathering thickly. Soon, in a strange manner of a wavering mirage, the air began to warp, and Percy sensed an almost tangible pull at her death sense.

"There!" she said, pointing to one end of the plaza, where the darkness had developed a rip into another place and the air was suddenly thick like mist. Already, nothing could be seen through it on the other side and beyond into the distant trees, only the mist itself existed, and it was a curtain of unrelieved grey.

The people of San Quellenne started moving, rising from their seated positions on the ground, picking up their belongings.

"Tell them to line up in single file, or in pairs, no wider," Percy said to Lady Calliope San Quellenne. And then she looked at Beltain, and he met her gaze and nodded silently, his eyes intent upon her. The great back warhorse at his side made a snort as Beltain led him, alongside Percy, to the edge of the clearing and toward the curtain of grey mist. He paused momentarily, staring at Percy with a haunted look. "I am going ahead, and I will wait for you on the other side."

"Yes, and please take care of them as they pass. I will follow you all as soon as the last one of them goes through—"

"I will go directly after him, the first of my people!" Lady Jelavie was standing behind them, holding the bridle of her pale grey stallion, almost of the same hue as the shadows.

"Of course. . . ." Percy noted how the lady had unconsciously spoken the words "my people," as though she were their liege already.

The black knight simply nodded, and said, "Follow me." He turned and walked into the mist, with Jack stepping behind him, and they were dissolved into nothing.

Percy felt a sudden twinge of the same peculiar sense that she had discovered recently, a sensation of being left completely *alone*. She missed his presence in an instant, as if a part of herself had gone forward and left her behind.

She did not dwell on it however, and stood aside, allowing

Lady Jelavie to move past her.

The young lady knight cast one look behind her, and the blue-twilight of the town of San Quellenne, its shapes fading already into the coming evening. She saw a line of townspeople behind her, and somewhere far in the back stood her mother, holding Flavio by the hand.

Jelavie waved at them, and then exclaimed loudly, "I am going now, follow me, everyone! Stay together, and be on your guard! And Mother, Flavio, be sure to come quickly, do not tarry!"

The Lady San Quellenne merely gazed at her, never taking her eyes away, and there was a small gentle smile on her lips as she nodded at her daughter, just once. The little boy meanwhile, waved energetically with his hand and looked excited to be going on an adventure.

Jelavie turned her back on them, took in a deep breath, and then stepped bravely into the mist, holding on to her horse.

She was gone, faded into nothing.

The townsman standing right behind her with a satchel and a large bag, paused only for a moment in indecision. He glanced at Percy standing there. But she smiled at him lightly and said, "Go on, it is very easy. Just a few steps, a little mist, and you will be on the other side. I've done this many times now and I still have the nose on my face to prove it."

The man relaxed at her words, and nodded, then took a step forward and passed through into the mist. He was followed by a family with small children, several other men and women. And then one by one they all came.

Percy stood and watched as townspeople and peasants of all ages walked past her, in a quickly moving line, carrying belongings and tools of their trade, leading pack animals, small carts and wheelbarrows, and glancing at her with careful occasionally mistrustful looks, while at other times they were looks of hope. Quite a few of them had death shadows accompanying them. . . . A priest passed by, dressed in a long habit and carrying a bag with holy items from the church. He glanced at Percy, then recited a prayer and stepped forward into the mist.

In minutes, the marketplace plaza emptied.

The last ones remaining were the family D'Arvu and their servants, and the Lady San Quellenne and her son.

"We will see you on the other side, Percy Ayren," said Count Lecrant, giving Percy a fatherly pat on the shoulder. "Thank you, my child, yet again for saving us. For, I do know what you are doing. . . . *Thank you.*"

She nodded, somewhat flustered, watching the D'Arvu servants begin to pass through, single file.

Lady Leonora and her mother paused momentarily. Leonora gave Percy a troubled stare, then said resolutely, "I am going." And she stepped into the mist.

The Count and Countess D'Arvu started to follow, when Lady Calliope's voice sounded. "Flavio San Quellenne!" she said to the boy. "Take this nice lady's hand now, and go on ahead of me."

The boy, gently pushed forward by his mother, turned around and stared at her with a questioning look, and at the same time a look bursting with excitement.

Lady Calliope leaned down, with unreadable eyes, and gave his forehead a light kiss. She then pointed Flavio to Lady Arabella D'Arvu. "Go on now! I'll be just a moment, then right behind you."

Lady Arabella paused only an instant, her look briefly startled, then wordlessly took the boy's hand in her own and smiled warmly at him and then looked up and smiled somewhat wistfully at his mother.

"Go on, Flavio, my heart!" his mother said, standing next to Percy.

The boy made a chortle of delight and then ran forward, pulling Lady Arabella behind him. The Count D'Arvu followed them, and they were swallowed by the mist.

Percy and the Lady San Quellenne were the only ones left.

Percy looked at the lady before her, and she could see everything in her expression, all the things she had held back before the others.

"My Lady," Percy said softly. "You are not coming. . . ."

Had the woman been living, she might have sighed. Instead she merely watched Percy with unblinking resigned eyes, completely at peace, in the blue cooling twilight of San Quellenne.

"No, I am not. How can I, when this—*all* of this—is me? For I am San Quellenne. I can never leave."

"But what if everything, all of San Quellenne is gone? Would you risk disappearing into the unknown alongside it, all of it?"

For a few long moments the lady spoke nothing. She glanced around her at the town, the trees, the deep violet sky overhead beginning to fill with stars in the east. And then she pointed to the south where a faint glimmer of the sea was visible, ghostly waters moving with white-capped waves of phosphorescent foam. . . .

"Do you know," Lady Calliope said, "that there used to be an island there once? Only a few days ago—back then, more than a few miles out there where the land used to be just yesterday, yes, beyond it, beyond the original beach? Yes, there was the Island of San Quellenne. Just a few times a year, when the tide receded, you could wade to it along a sandbar. . . . But most of the time it was surrounded by deep water. It had tall white cliffs, and on top of the cliffs, a garden of paradise, so green and lush it was. There was also Saga Mountain, a pale white peak, covered with wild shrubbery and heather and honeysuckle. My husband was buried on Saga Mountain. He lies there, in the shadow of a cedar tree—that is, he lay there. For Saga Mountain was the first thing gone. And then the island."

Lady Calliope paused, her gaze straining to the south. "So

as you can see, I cannot leave this place, not ever. Even though I know not where *he* is now, where the island is, where anything is, this it is the closest I can be to him, here in San Quellenne—for as long as it remains. And then, I go with it."

Percy held her lips tight and her own breath, then she uttered, softer than a whisper, "Would you like me to put you to rest?"

Lady Calliope San Quellenne nodded. "Thank you. Do it now, swiftly. For if the shadows come—the other shadows, they that steal the land away—then you will have no time to return after our people. And I would not hold you back. . . ."

Percy watched her, for long profound moments. "Where would you like to . . . rest?"

The Lady San Quellenne smiled then, and pointed south, to the edge of the plaza with a copse of trees, through which was visible the glimmering sea. They walked there, and it was a small rise, then below it, beyond the trees, the beach began.

"Lie down now, My Lady, and . . . close your eyes. . . ."

But Calliope San Quellenne shook her head. She came to a stop before a great tree with a wide gnarled trunk, and she sat down, leaning with her back against it. Her long cotton dress billowed in the mellow cooling breeze, and she pulled it over her feet, and then folded her hands in her lap. "No," she said. "I will not lie down, nor will I close my eyes. . . . Let the last thing I see be the horizon and the water. . . ."

"As you wish." Percy stood at her side gently, and they looked out together into the watery distance.

"I am ready now . . ." said the Lady San Quellenne after a few moments had passed.

And Percy reached out to her with her thoughts, no longer needing to touch. While the air rang with familiar tolling darkness, she gently took her death shadow and gave it soft passage inside the body of the one who had been Calliope San Quellenne.

The breeze enveloped them then, as though the island itself issued a soft farewell gasp, and in that moment Percy knew she was entirely alone at last.

It was time to go for her also, for now Percy could feel the preternatural sensation of fading all around, as the last of the landscape began to warp, and was being *taken*.

And thus Percy turned her back to the sea and returned as quickly as she could to the plaza where the grey mist marked the spot of the passageway into which the people had gone.

Her last few steps she ran, for she could feel the land being consumed around her by forces beyond this world, and the stars overhead were warping, pulled apart into splinters and shards of light, and the ground under her feet was quicksand. . . .

As she entered the safety of the mist, she knew that behind her, the land that was San Quellenne and the rest of Tanathe was gone entirely.

Chapter 11

King Roland Osenni of Lethe carefully ascended the stairway along the parapet wall to the top of the city battlements. He was flanked by guards who watched his every step upon the ancient iced-over stone stairs, moving close enough to catch him in case he slipped.

Once on top, the King and his guards were greeted by the curious sight of a constantly moving wall of the dead pushing up against an invisible barrier that existed halfway between the inner and outer parapets and was present along the entire perimeter of the walkway. There was nothing to mark its existence in the floor of the battlements or up in the air, not even a discoloration of vapor. The only thing that delineated the barrier were the actual dead bodies crushing against it as though there was an invisible wall of glass erected to keep them away.

The bodies were so thick that it was impossible to see beyond them and properly look over the outer walls and down below.

"Careful, Your Majesty," one of the soldier captains remarked. "You must not attempt to reach out beyond the sorcerous boundary, for on this side there is nothing preventing us from stepping across—only *them*. Once your limbs pass the boundary, even by accident, you might be in danger of being grabbed by these accursed corpses."

"I see," said the King, adjusting his expensive long fur coat closer about him and patting down his fur-lined hat, as though there was some concern that the edges and bottom of his coat or the top of his hat might move of their own accord toward the zone of danger and thus imperil him.

"This way, Your Majesty," another captain said, and the King followed him, keeping to the inside of the walkway, and trying not to see the horrifying faces of the dead and their gaping wounds and their stirring damaged limbs, leering at him less than a foot away.

They walked for several minutes until they reached one of the southern bulwarks of the battlements. Here, the walkway widened into a flat area where several angled structures protruded, containing city cannons pointing out at the enemy. The cannons were silent and unmanned, for they were in the zone beyond the boundary, and that portion of the bulwark was full of the dead. There was also a stockpile of ammunitions and barrels of black powder and other supplies which fortunately lay near the inner parapets and were thus within the safety of the magical warded zone.

Here, in the middle of the bulwark, close enough to touch the invisible boundary that she had herself created, stood Claere Liguon, the Infanta of the Realm. Her back was turned to the city and she looked out, facing the sea of the enemy dead. At her side stood her familiar companion, the disgraced Marquis Vlau Fiomarre, the same man who had killed her. . . . Their two forms were still and upright, both equally lifeless, frozen almost, it occurred to the King.

After she had marked the boundary of the city by walking the entire circle of the walls, Claere Liguon had been standing here thus all day and all night with two lit torches upheld. Now, in the wintry pallor of the overcast mid-morning, the torches had long since gone out, and she had lowered her arms and placed the torches on the ground at her feet. But she continued standing in place, silent and statuesque. And the marquis stood at her side.

"I am glad to have received your message, Your Imperial Highness. . . . Wonderful news! Now, my dear, how are you faring?" the King said, after clearing his throat.

The Infanta turned to him slowly. "It is done, Your Majesty. The city has been warded, with the help of Grial." She drew in a deep breath, and spoke with a creaking voice and a sound of shattered ice in her lungs.

The King saw her white face dusted with a fine sheen of frost, like a delicate porcelain doll frosted with infinitesimal specks of crushed glass. Her great smoke-grey eyes sat deep in their sockets and were shadowed and particularly lovely, so the King felt a pang of guilt mixed with compassion.

"But now, I am sorry to say, the enemy is here in full force," she said. "I just witnessed the arrival of a great army below the walls. They are wearing the red heraldic color that I am familiar with as the color of the Domain. I assume the Sovereign is here. Admittedly it is difficult to see from here, especially since we many not approach the edge of the exterior wall to look. But at least we are safe within the city—at least for the moment."

"True, true!" the King said hurriedly. Then he motioned to the ranking soldiers around him. "What of the army out there? What reports do we have now?"

"It is as Her Imperial Highness says, the Trovadii army is here, stretched as far as the southern horizon. They have spread around in a great semi-circle, and Duke Chidair's rabble is now but a small crowded circle directly around us."

"Here, Your Majesty, a spyglass might help," another officer remarked. He then assisted the King to step up on a raised portion of the inner bulwark and thus to see better over the walls beyond.

The King stood up, balancing carefully, and a circle of guards stood all around below, ready to catch him, while a long brass telescope was brought to him, fully extended for a viewing of at least a league's distance.

Roland Osenni glanced through the eyepiece, training it at the grey mass of snow and tiny dark moving specks of the dead soldiers below. He could see very little at first, for the daylight was poor, and distance and the enlargement only inspired confusion. Eventually a garrison soldier pointed the end of the lens in the proper direction precisely, and King Roland Osenni could at last see the face of his enemies up close—in particular the enemy newly arrived.

About two hundred feet below, beyond the quenched remains of the scorched earth that was all that was left of the firewall, stood a fine regal carriage trimmed with gold, attached to a splendid team of white horses. Before it stood a statuesque woman, wearing an ermine-lined cloak of dark shimmering sable on the outside, sweeping the ground at her feet. A hat of similar sable fur trimmed with gold sat atop a small platinum courtly wig that lent a piquant air to her impossible beauty—for that much could be seen even through the imperfect lens of the spyglass.

The woman was conversing with the burly monster that was none other than Duke Hoarfrost. And there was a third person, a lady dressed in sage green who stood in attendance.

"Ah-h-h." said the King, watching them. "It is indeed Rumanar Avalais, the Sovereign, damn her. Wish I could hear what is being said."

He then swept the spyglass in a slow panoramic circle, and saw the extent of the Trovadii army. It was worse than he thought. Rows upon rows of perfectly aligned infantry, formations of cavalry, and banners of the Three Armies, stretching in pomegranate red to the horizon . . . indeed the whole of the Trovadii were camped out below his city's gates.

It occurred to the King in that surreal moment that "his city" was not precisely the term he might use any longer, for the dead Infanta had appropriated his authority—for better or worse—even as she wrought the warding defense boundary for Letheburg. However, these were technicalities. He would proceed as usual for now.

"How many are there, would you say, captain?" he asked the nearest officer.

"Hard to say, Majesty," the man replied after a pause. "Though, I can see the banners of all three of their Field Marshals. First Army there, dead center, see the Spiked Sun. And southwest, quarter turn, there's the Second Army banner of the Coiled Serpent. And on the southeast, there's the Third Army, Black Rose. So I am estimating eight to ten thousand, give or take a hundred. Plus, there's Hoarfrost's local rabble, about two thousand at least."

The King exhaled loudly. "Not good. No, not good at all. Now, the question is, will this magic, this blessed sorcery of ours hold? Where is Grial? I would ask her—"

"Your Majesty! Here I am! How might I serve, now?" A loud familiar voice rang out, sonorous and grating at the King's nerves and yet quite welcome for the moment.

Grial stood bundled in her coat and winter hat, just a few feet behind the guards surrounding the King up on his lookout pedestal.

"There you are, Grial," said His Majesty, again clearing his throat in some minor vocal discomfort that curiously made itself known during circumstances such as these. "I would know— how well this magic of yours would hold out against *that accursed woman* and her army?"

"Ah, but Majesty, this is not my magic! It belongs to our dear Imperial Highness, Claere. And as for how well it can hold out, well, we'll just have to see, will we not?"

"Well, is there anything else that you can do now?'

"Not in particular, Your Majesty. The next move belongs to her who stands below."

Hoarfrost stood and watched the blood-red army surround him and his men from all sides, with the sound of drums and feet striking the snowy ground in unison. He had to admit, the formations were impressive, and the discipline worthy of envy—for he was yet to achieve such polish and orderly lines in his own haphazard local men. And had he not been thoroughly dead and thus lacking a heart to beat loudly in his chest and echo in his temples, he might have experienced an alarming sense of being closed in, even though these were the forces of an admitted ally. . . .

At some point, as he observed the various Field Marshal banners and divisions, suddenly the drums ceased and there was only wind and eerie silence. The bristling sea of blood-red pikemen and their needles of steel parted on two sides, and from the center rolled a regal carriage trimmed in gold, driven by beautiful white horses that were decidedly alive. It was followed by an honor guard of high-ranking mounted knights.

The carriage stopped, and the footman hanging on to the back ran to open the doors and pull out the retractable stair.

The doors parted, and there was a shimmer of glorious black sable, and a delicate booted foot appeared, followed by the rest of *her*.

The Sovereign of the Domain, Rumanar Avalais, stood up on the step and then descended to the beaten snow, adjusting her stylish fur hat with her slender black-gloved fingers. Her wrists were draped in ropes of diamond bracelets over the kid gloves, like constellations of stars over a night sky. Underneath the sable cape, its nether side lined with ermine, peeked a pomegranate velvet riding habit.

The Sovereign was a true beauty. Her platinum wig ringlets framed a perfect oval face with impossible blue eyes. And Hoarfrost met the look of those eyes with a stunned glare, and a jaw that would have fallen slack had not his frozen facial muscles held it fixed in place.

At Hoarfrost's side, Lady Ignacia Chitain of Balmue

dropped into a deep curtsy.

The Sovereign took a step toward Hoarfrost, and then slowly strolled around him, examining him up and down with a close scrutiny and a perfectly unreadable countenance.

It occurred to Hoarfrost that he was being appraised like an expensive thoroughbred stallion, before a purchase decision was to be made. And so he towered over her, a giant of frozen lake debris and snow and old blood, a wild briar thicket of hair frosted with crystalline ice. And he observed her in turn out of his fixed round marbles of eyes, daring her not to cower from his terrifying round-eyed glare.

At last, the remarkable sky-blue eyes blinked, and a faint smile gathered on her lips. "Hoarfrost," she said, and her features came alive. "You are a splendid creature! You will do very well."

Duke Hoarfrost gaped. "Oh, is that so? I will do well, you say? *I?* And what of *you?* Your Royal—what does she call you, Shininess?" and he turned to Lady Ignacia who gave him a quick, disturbed glance, before muttering softly, "Her Brilliance. . . ."

"Yes, yes, that's right, *Her Brilliance!*" Hoarfrost picked up, and again trained his face upon the Sovereign. "We'll just have to see how truly Brilliant you are, in your fancy carriage and with your Army of pretty boy tin soldiers, all lined up in rows!"

"Ah, and do you approve?" said the Sovereign, completely disregarding his tone and looking around them lightheartedly, as though they were out on a picnic. She moved, hands lightly spread outward at her sides, almost whirling in place like a girl, and her sable and ermine cape whirled around her, lighter than snow. Another moment, and she would be laughing, it seemed to Hoarfrost, and her laughing voice would sound precisely like a tinkling spring, soft and crisp and sparkling like bubbly wine that some of the fancy sops at Court so loved to drink. . . .

He forcibly made himself stop thinking along those lines, because it was almost a strange thing, an unnatural thing, that his thoughts were suddenly so buoyant and lighthearted, at the mere sight of her, this strange woman who appeared out of nowhere in his presence and made his usually sluggish thoughts gallop like rabbits that needed skinning—

Damn, there he was doing it again.

Or maybe, it was all *her* doing. . . .

And Duke Ian Chidair, known as Hoarfrost, made himself stop and look at her closely, with a measure of caution, in an attempt to understand who and what she really was.

There had to be a good reason why this foreign queen held such a great influence over so many. He was going to find out.

"Hoarfrost!" The Sovereign stopped circling him and looked up at the distant battlements of Letheburg, where the dead were packed tight as fish, straining against the invisible warding barrier. "Why are you and your army still out here, and not *in* there, within those walls?"

"Your Brilliance," Lady Ignacia spoke up, curtsying again. "Your command has been to surround the city and to *wait* for Your Brilliance's arrival. . . ."

"Ah yes, my dear Lady Ignacia, yes, of course," Her Brilliance replied, glancing once in her direction. "It had certainly been the command *given*, and yes, you have done well and entirely as directed in *conveying* it, dear girl, and you have certainly earned your Eternity. But the assumption had always been that our delightful Chidair Ally would eventually lose patience with such a silly thing as a *command* and merely enact the inevitable. Therefore, why has this city not been taken yet?"

And with that, the Sovereign turned to look directly at the Duke, and had he been alive, he would have flinched from her gaze.

"Well, well," he replied, the first thing blurting out of him on the remaining exhalation of air before he decided to pull in more to fill his inner bellows. "And what if I tell you, Your pretty Brilliance, that I have been trying to get in there since day one, and your command be damned?"

"To that I would say, *well, well done*, Duke Hoarfrost! So, what has kept you from succeeding?" Her words, her countenance—all of her was mocking him.

Hoarfrost's eyes bulged in their sockets. The thick tree trunk limbs that were his beefy arms moved and he flexed his elbow joints with effort and then put hands on hips. "What has kept me? Why, damned *sorcery!*" he roared. "Look up there, pretty queen! See all my boys pressing at nothing but air? They've got some kind of witchy ward put on those walls, and the old coward King Osenni hides behind it, and peeks around the skirts of his women, like that little slip of a Grand Princess he's got hidden away there, little Claere, the Emperor's daughter! She's a dead little thing, but at least was plucky enough to talk to me from the walls above, while the old King won't even show himself much less parlay! First they had the fires burning two stories tall all around, and now this infernal magic, as of yesterday!"

The Sovereign watched him calmly without a blink of her perfectly blue eyes. "Have you tried passing through the city gates?" she asked.

"What?" Hoarfrost felt the crush of new breaking ice in his lungs from the brutal effort of his roaring speech. "Are you listening to me, girlie queen? Did you just hear anything I said to you, or do you take me for a daft man? The gates are *closed!* What, you think they'd leave them open? Maybe open 'em wide for us, like a whore? I've got me a good mind to wring your pretty little neck and have you try for yourself to open the damn gates!"

"Would you like to try?" she asked, smiling softly.

"Try what?"

"Come, Hoarfrost . . . come and wring my neck." And suddenly she pulled the ties of her sable cape and let them fall open, reveling pomegranate velvet underneath and a pearl-encrusted grand collar of lace gracing her swan neck. She swept her collar apart, revealing even more of her alabaster skin.

"Come, my creature . . ." she said, and her voice mesmerized. "Come and break me and make me like yourself, neither alive nor dead, but this strange wonderful offspring of both that has filled the land around us."

Hoarfrost reacted instinctively, fury driving him to motion, and he raised one giant hand and reached for her, since it was high time *she* was taught a lesson indeed. . . .

He moved his hand—rather, tried to move it, and grunted with the effort of doing so, but to his disbelief, he was held motionless by an inexplicable *force* over which he had no control. His hand remained at his side, frozen in a new kind of metaphysical rigor mortis.

And Hoarfrost realized in that instant that she was holding him, holding him fixed with the mere blink of her eyes, a flutter of her eyelids, the curve of her lips. He was fixed within a new prison—not of his pitiful dead corpse, but in a prison of *her*.

"What are you waiting for?" she taunted, laughing like the tinkling stream that he had imagined before he even knew the sound of her laughter.

"So you're a witch too, is that it?" Hoarfrost said at last, ceasing to force his limbs, ceasing to fight her, and relaxing in her invisible hold. And he glared at her with his marbles of eyes.

"No, unfortunately she is far worse—she is a goddess!"

A new voice sounded just behind him. Lady Ignacia made a stifled exclamation, while the Sovereign released the monstrous Duke from her gaze and slowly looked in the direction of the voice, coming directly from his back.

Hoarfrost slowly turned his barrel torso around.

A woman stood there, having appeared out of nowhere.

A woman—and yet, she was *not*. For she was a golden torch in female form, a bright source of radiance that spilled over at the snowed ground, turning it to shimmering honey for ten feet around her. Even the air seemed to become brighter, and daylight grew vibrant in contrast to the dull monochrome overcast, as though the sun itself had taken residence within her body. So bright it had become that they who stood nearest her cast new shadows behind them.

The golden woman was attired in a long flowing garment of iridescent pallor, with her hair molded in a braided crown of wheat around her noble head. Her bare arms held golden wide braces and bands of molded gold, and a torque studded with jewels was around her throat. Her face exuded warmth and beauty like the late rich days of summer.

Beauty and immortality. . . .

"Hello, Mother—sweet Mother of Bright Harvest," uttered Rumanar Avalais, the Sovereign of the Domain, while Hoarfrost, Ignacia, and the dead multitudes stared at her.

"Hello, Persephone, my beloved daughter," gently replied Demeter, the Goddess of Tradition, of the harvest and the fruits of the earth.

"What?" Duke Hoarfrost said. "What is going on here? Who are you—both of you? What manner of madness or new sorcery is this?"

Lady Ignacia Chitain made another small stifled sound, and this time it was not to be mistaken for anything but terror.

But the two goddesses had eyes for none but each other.

"Why have you come here, Mother of mine—or am I the mother of you, now?" said the Sovereign who was Persephone. "I thought you had no taste for war or blood? Or have you changed your mind and would join me now and *serve* me?"

"Ah, Persephone, my poor child, I am here to remind you of what you have lost." And the golden Goddess approached and drew her hand forward, reaching for her daughter's black-gloved hand. "Come, child, accept my love and try to remember your true self and your place in the scheme of the world. . . ."

But Persephone drew her hand away. And suddenly, she

started to change before their eyes. Her imperial garments of the Domain were replaced with a timeless antique chiton of silver fabric with an ebony shadow hue defining the folds. Persephone's stylish fur hat and platinum wig faded, and in their place her natural hair streamed down her shoulders in rich flame-gold bounty. The winter boots about her feet had disappeared to be replaced by metal-trimmed sandals.

Persephone's pale arms were bare despite the winter cold, and they were bound in braces of braided red and white gold. On her fingers sat rings with great, deep, light-hoarding gems— obsidian, agate, carnelian, rubies, black diamonds from the bowels of the earth, mined in the Underworld and given her many times over by her dark lover. . . .

"No, Mother," Persephone said, her face expressionless stone, her voice issuing out of her in the slithering manner of a serpent, echoing in the silence of the expanse. With each moment, the quality of the light around her seemed to grow dim, while shadows congealed. "I refuse to accept my place in the old scheme of the world. For the old world is no longer!"

As she spoke, the sky overhead seemed to convulse, and slate clouds started to roll in and deepen the overcast, so that there was now an infinity of cotton layers of grey darkness above them, and the sun hidden deep somewhere beyond, had no hope of ever shining again. . . .

"Oh, Persephone. . . . Will you allow your grief to rule you thus and abandon the world entirely? Open your heart! Have pity for them, for these mortals who need you!" Demeter's words sounded like warm balm in the freezing air, and her light grew to extend even farther around her in a radius of many feet. But her soothing golden light had no effect upon the cluster of shadows that stood about Persephone, or the thickness of the cloud cover overhead.

"Grief?" Persephone laughed. "Grief is far behind me, for I no longer waste my time on futile things when there is so much *else* to be done."

"Is there no compassion within you who is Compassion Incarnate?"

"Come, Mother, enough of your sentimental nonsense!" the dark daughter cried suddenly, and turned her back on Demeter. With an empty face she looked up at Letheburg and its high walls and the tiny figures of the dead, and beyond the boundary all the living ones looking down at them, no doubt in disbelief and confusion and curiosity.

"Persephone! I beg you to cease this! You do not need to harm any more—"

"Be *silent*, Mother of Bright Harvest! If you choose to remain here, then you will stand witness to the last hours of this city!"

A sharp wind arose, tearing in gusts at everything around in the vicinity, sending clothing to billowing, and the Trovadii banners snapping wildly.

They who stood high above on the parapets of Letheburg were also buffeted by the onslaught.

Persephone, her orange-gold hair floating in the ice wind, observed everything around her with a faint smile.

Duke Hoarfrost was like a frost giant, motionless and stunned, unsure of what to do next, of how to proceed, of what to do with himself, for the balance of power had shifted entirely, casting him completely out of the running. . . .

"I have just come from Ulpheo," Demeter said unexpectedly, her voice the only ray of warmth in this winter hellscape. "I have taken it back, you know. It is no longer fixed in your hold, my daughter, no longer bound between Above and Below. Ulpheo is once again fully mine, and Above it remains, with all the citizens and my shrine."

At this, Persephone gifted her with a mocking look. "And what makes you think, Mother of mine, that I care? I've touched Ulpheo only because it pleased me to make you struggle after it. There is nothing there that I want—not any longer."

"And you think Letheburg is yours for the taking?" Demeter's compassionate demeanor hardened suddenly. "The city is warded, and none shall enter it, not even you."

Persephone's smile deepened, and her blue eyes were as cold as the edge of a knife. "I shall enter it within the hour."

"No," Demeter said. "Hecate will not allow it. None can enter where the Goddess of Passages and Entrances has shut the door."

"Maybe not in the old world. . . . But it is broken now, the old world and its framework. It is shattered and it is shrinking and fading quicker than a passing dream. In this new pattern, I shall do as I please, for I alone will rule it, Heaven and Sea and Underworld. Even *he*, my beloved dark lover, my sweet Black Husband, even *he* will cede to me the greater measure of his power, so that, even as my Consort, he will sit below me, and not as an equal at my side. . . . And thus, think you that if My Lord Hades will not stand against me that Hecate's feeble ministrations on these walls can hold me back?"

The winter wind now howled around them in madness.

"Whatever will happen, the old world still stands, no matter how much damage it had incurred," Demeter spoke, raising her powerful glorious voice through the wind. "And with it stands the old order, according to which, Hecate still rules all *exit* and *entrance*. You shall not pass beyond the walls or the gates, my poor broken daughter."

In response, Persephone laughed. "Broken? You think I am broken? I am *remade!* Mother of mine, I am strong and new! But, very well!" she cried through the gale, in a manic parody of joy. "For the moment the old way is still here, but even the old way can be made to serve me now! A mortal or a god might not pass the boundary, but the wind can! And so can winter itself!"

And saying these words, Persephone approached the motionless shape of the Duke, and she reached out and touched him on the forehead. "Hoarfrost!" she cried, "Had I not promised you Eternity?"

Duke Hoarfrost had not expected to be noticed at all in this manner, and he could only reply gruffly, "Aye! Eternity, you say? You—whatever you are, Sovereign, Persephone Goddess— you have promised it indeed! For I have been robbed of my life, and it has been taken from me before my time! What will you do now to make it up to me?"

"This!" she replied. "Serve me, and you shall have it!"

"I serve you, strange Goddess!" Hoarfrost nodded, feeling the touch of her cold immortal fingers upon his brow—a touch more corporeal than anything he had felt in quite some time, since he had been made numb to all sensation by death.

"Give me your knife," said the dark Goddess, keeping her hand upon him.

"Ah, no, do not do it—" Demeter spoke, to no avail.

The long dagger was produced from Hoarfrost's belt. "If you must know, I have no blood, Goddess," he remarked. "None left in this rotting corpse. So if you would have me pledge you an oath of service—"

"It is not *your* blood that is required." Persephone laughed again, and aimed the point of the blade at herself and pricked her own finger, pale and perfect. Immediately a deep red bead welled, sweet immortal ambrosia, and she placed the droplet of blood upon the giant's frozen lips, smearing it across his mouth, then held the finger against him.

"Breathe," she said.

And as he inhaled the usual bellows-breath of broken ice and freezing air, the dark Goddess Persephone suddenly struck him on his chest with her fist, directly in the spot where was his stilled heart.

Duke Ian Chidair, known as Hoarfrost, dead for days, was struck by lightning.

The world faded in and out of focus, went dark, and then returned. And then, his heart was *beating* once again, and there was movement, strange, foreign movement that he had long forgotten, in every fiber of his flesh, every tiny cell, filling with energy, indeed pulling it forth from the air, from the snow and the wind and the cold earth below.

All of it, the living power of the world, passed through him, filling him to overflowing, and then it receded. . . . And he felt the pull of growing muscle and skin as his old wounds drew together and closed up and his damaged organs healed themselves and the cells renewed. . . .

When it was over, Duke Hoarfrost had grown warm for the first time in days, and there was sensation in all his limbs. But then the *mortal* warmth receded also, and a new brazen liquid coursed though his thawed veins.

He looked down at himself, at his own hale limbs and he was sparkling white. . . . His filthy knight's armor and blue Chidair surcoat had been replaced by a long winter coat of magnificent white brocade lined with mink, embroidered in pale silver and encrusted with clear crystals of ice-diamonds. His matted hair, bushy brows, and beard were now grown long and smooth and flowing, sprinkled like sugar with snow radiance, and a lordly mink-trimmed hat covered his head, while his feet were shod in white leather boots with fur trim.

Persephone observed his transformation, and also his bewildered face—alive, and furthermore, immortal—and she clapped her hands and laughed.

"Ah, what a fine sight you are, Hoarfrost! Or should I call you something else now, Old Man Winter?"

"What in Heaven's name is happening down there?" the King of Lethe was saying, still holding up the spyglass trained upon the scene below the walls of Letheburg.

Vlau Fiomarre watched him from the corner of his stilled eye, standing next to Claere, and they were both well away from the group of guards surrounding the King up on his precarious lookout post on the raised portion of the bulwark.

Many of the officer captains were using their own

telescopes to peer over and beyond the outer battlement walls as best they could, for whatever was taking place down there was indeed remarkable.

In the last quarter of an hour there had been the Sovereign newly arrived, emerging from her carriage and meeting Hoarfrost, then the mysterious appearance out of thin air of a golden female figure who was apparently a goddess, and then an exchange between her and the Sovereign.

This is when things became even more strange—Rumanar Avalais, the Sovereign, *transformed*. She was no longer attired in ordinary clothing, and she now resembled the golden woman in appearance, except that she was her antithesis—she was dark and a source of shadow, in direct contrast to the golden goddess with her radiant aura of light.

"Is the Sovereign not human?" someone among the garrison soldiers asked. "Look at that! What is happening to her? And now, may the Lord protect us, look at the sky! The racing clouds, the wind—is she doing this?"

As the baffled defenders of Letheburg crowded to stare beyond the walls—while taking care not to pass the safe warded boundary—there were more peculiar occurrences below. Flashes of lighting came, and a single particularly powerful strike, and then the figure of Hoarfrost was imbued with impossible whiteness. . . .

"Grial!" the King exclaimed from his tall vantage point, gesturing to the middle-aged woman standing nearby and fiddling with the brim of her floppy winter hat. "Come, quickly, woman, tell me what is happening there! You, if anyone, should know what it is, with your sorceries and magics—"

Fiomarre looked at Claere meanwhile, at her dear gentle face turned in profile, and then it was as if she felt the force of his gaze upon her, for she turned and looked at him. There were her eyes . . . great, beautiful, innocent, haunted with the sunken grey shadow of untimely death.

What must I *look like now, to her?* it occurred to Vlau. *For I am pale and cold and frightful, and my blood has frozen to ice in my veins. . . . At last she may look upon me and know justice. Oh, how she looks upon me! And yet, there is only sorrow there.*

The last day and night had been a dream. Vlau recalled what happened after he had died—after he *knew* himself to be dead—for in truth the precise instant it happened was the instant of time that he had *lost*. Just as his life had passed from him unto eternity, so had the moment itself.

He recalled in snatches the floating sense of wild exhilaration from the cold wind, and then no sense at all—he had been exultant and buoyant in the last moments before his death, light as a feather, a snowflake, rising up in spirit with every gust, inhaling the scalding cold air with agony in his lungs. . . . For the ice wind battered at him, and all his extremities were set to pins and needles, and the part of his face bared to the wind was riddled with the acute sharpness. . . . And then it all faded and his skin was numb, his limbs were numb, and his lungs were sluggish, as he momentarily felt the inability to draw breath, and drowned in an excess of air. . . .

It was the moment he had died. He never knew the last spasm of his lungs, the final convulsion of his heart, for death had drawn a vacuum upon him, softly blanketed his mind, and took him, then released, so that he came back and he was already beyond mortal reach, but locked in the prison of his newly dead body.

When it happened, Claere had known it instinctively. She asked him a question, told him to get back indoors and rest, to warm himself—without actually saying it, she told him to *live*.

But it was too late. And he told her he would never leave her again.

For the first few moments, he was triumphant, gloating at his own self-inflicted just punishment, and his guilt at having killed her was only momentarily lessened—or rather, brought into balance, for nothing could ameliorate it, not ever.

Then the rest of the afternoon and the encroaching evening he spent next to her, while the wind died also, while the snow fell, while she spoke to him in an endless stream of sorrow. He saw anguish in her dead eyes, peeking through the still, glassy pupils and irises, deep inside where her soul was beating against the flesh prison. There were many gentle words of regret, and if she had had any tears left in her, she would have wept for him. Instead, she could only look. And her gaze wounded him with its impossible love and regret.

It was then he realized far too late that by dying, he had hurt her yet again, caused her yet another wound, this one intangible, and marked only by things under the surface.

Thus, Claere Liguon not only had to stand a whole day and night with torches upheld, while she cemented the magic barrier of safety around Letheburg, but she also had to stand in new abysmal grief for him, and to see him thus, at her side.

"What have you done, my love . . ." she had said at one point as the night deepened and the faint circular shadow of the moon sailed though the thick overcast. "Oh, what have you done!"

"I have merely let go," he said, while snowflakes crystallized on his brow and eyelashes and his nose and chin, dusted his lips, marking every protrusion and hollow of his lean handsome face, and he had become a creature of snowfall . . . just as she was. "I let go of what mockery of a life I had left, and to which I had no moral right, in having taken yours."

"But I have told you many times over, that I've long since forgiven you!"

"That may be, unearthly angel. . . . But I have not forgiven myself."

"Oh, Vlau, you are a fool!"

Thus they were submerged in an interplay of their mutual love and bitterness, for many long hours of darkness, and somehow Claere managed to keep her mind on the task at hand

and to forge the boundary of sorcery to protect the city.

At the first glimmerings of dawn, the torches had sputtered and gone out. And Claere set them down on the floor of the snow-covered parapet walkway. With the gutting of the torchlight, the sorcery was complete. Vlau hungrily watched her every movement, even then. . . .

There had been few soldiers up on the battlements in that early hour, for the day before they were told to go home and rest, at least for the moment of blessed relief that the barrier granted the city. However, some had been posted just in case, and they passed Vlau and Claere's spot on the bulwark occasionally, patrolling the walls, the blades of their edged weapons held at ready and pikes glinting faintly, and they all inclined their heads deeply in greeting to the Infanta. As the dawn grew brighter, and Claere kindly acknowledged yet another soldier or two making the rounds, there was Grial.

Grial had appeared out of nowhere, it seemed, for one moment there was no one in the spot, and the next, there she was. It was almost uncanny, for neither Vlau nor Claere had seen her approach.

"A very nice job, Your Imperial Highness!" Grial peeked at the spot a couple of steps away where a few enemy dead milled, striking themselves relentlessly against the invisible barrier. She then rubbed her mittened hands together, stomping her feet in the newly fallen fresh powder, and saying "Br-r-r!"

Claere's permanently grieving expression attained a degree of relief at the sight of the familiar eccentric woman. "Grial! I did it, Grial. . . ."

"You certainly have, my dear! Very well done! Indeed, the best job of its kind that I've seen in a long time—and when I say 'a long time,' you genuinely have no idea how long I really mean—"

"Is there anything else that must be done to keep the city safe?"

"Well, you've done all you could for the moment. As for

later—it never hurts to pray. . . ."

Grial glanced from Claere to Vlau, with an astute gaze of her very dark eyes. As her gaze rested for a moment upon Vlau, it appeared particularly somber.

"Ah, young man . . ." Grial said to him, shaking her head from side to side. And then she placed a mittened hand on his shoulder, seemingly in order to brush off a bit of snow, even though the hand lingered a bit in compassion. "I see it has been a very cold night. And I am so very sorry it has been thus . . . for *you*."

But whether or not there was indeed a strange glint in her eyes—a moment of profound, unearthly wisdom—Vlau could not be certain.

"Well, my dears," Grial said then. "You have certainly earned a rest. No need for you to stay up here for the time being, unless you absolutely want to. I would suggest you go someplace warm—not necessarily warm for fingers and toes but warm enough to lighten spirits!"

"Ah, Grial," Claere said. "I would prefer not to go back inside the gilded prison of his Majesty's Winter Palace. And as for Vlau—"

"I will go or stay as you wish . . . and wherever it may be," Vlau uttered slowly, belatedly recalling to draw in a breath of air in order to speak—for he was still learning the ways of the dead.

"Then, might as well stay up here, Your Imperial Highness, and this fine young gentleman will keep you company. Mark my words, this is the place to be, for excitement! As for me, off I go for a little while, but I promise you, I will return in an hour or two!" And with those words, Grial hastily waved at them, patted down her hat, and then started to make her way along the deep new snow of the parapets.

Vlau looked at Claere, and the next time he glanced at Grial's retreating back, she was already gone.

That had been hours ago. . . .

And now, Vlau and Claere stood witness to inexplicable events below the outer walls, and the reaction to them up here on the city battlements.

"Grial!" King Roland Osenni exclaimed, having just seen Duke Hoarfrost consumed by a lighting strike and a blinding flash of white. "What kind of foul sorcery or magics are these? You're a witch, so you must have some dark notion—"

The wind started rising, and it source appeared to be the white figure on the ground below, outside the city walls—the entity who used to be Duke Hoarfrost, and now was *something else*. Gusts of angry freezing air stirred the fresh powder into rapid funnels, so that it swept up in flurries all around them, rising from the field of battle and obscuring the pomegranate color of the newly arrived army that stretched from horizon to horizon. Up on the city battlements the wind picked up also, and its scalding ice fingers were felt, as it agitated the powder that had fallen overnight into a churning chaos of winter.

Within seconds, there was almost no visibility, only swirling *whiteness*.

And none of it was coming down from the sky, but *rising up* from what already lay upon the ground.

Men huddled in their coats or hauberks and chain mail, capes were raised as many hunched over to keep the white stuff from their eyes. . . .

King Roland Osenni himself held on to his fur-lined hat and squinted, raising up his fur collar.

The only ones seeming unaffected by this bizarre onslaught were Claere, Vlau, and . . . Grial.

"Well, I suppose this is as good a time as any," said Grial, taking a step forward.

And as she moved, she *flowed*, she transformed.

Instead of a funny-looking middle-aged woman in a frumpy plain coat and winter hat with floppy scarf flaps and old woolen mittens, an unearthly silver-dark figure emerged, the whirling snow retreating from her in a circle of ten feet.

The woman who had been Grial wore an iridescent garment, ancient, Grecian, noble. The chiton flowed like liquid moonlight around her statuesque form, and her arms were bare, their skin both dark and light at the same time as only night can be when the moon passes through clouds and reveals various depths of shadow and glimmer. Sandals of silver were on her feet, and bands of cool nameless metal circled her wrists, arms, and throat. Her hair—no longer a kinky, frizzled mess—was now a smoothly flowing river of silk gathered upward in a braided crown, and it appeared that snakes lay twining around her brow and their eyes blinked like stars.

The whirling snow retreated from her, and the immortal one took another step forward, while the soldiers and the King gaped at her . . . and Vlau and Claere gazed at her with wonder.

"Grial?" said Claere softly.

"Yes, I am Grial, dear child. . . . But I am also someone else. You are not afraid?"

"No!" replied Claere, with intensity in her yes. "Not afraid of you, how can I be? Oh, Grial! I am—"

"No, indeed, it cannot be happening! Grial? *Grial?* Who or what are you?" the King exclaimed meanwhile, holding his hand up over his eyes to keep away the onslaught of raging snow. "Dear God, are you—immortal? Bah! I knew there was something unnatural, something wrong with you, I *knew* it—"

Grial who was Hecate smiled. She then raised her arms high overhead and threw her head back, and suddenly a *blast* of power came from her, shattering the air, and the wind and snow retreated into a strange calm, like the eye of the storm.

The weather raged beyond them, but at least on the battlements it was suddenly still and peaceful, with not a breeze blowing.

However, the King of Lethe was now suspended at least ten feet over the bulwark, hanging like a sack in mid-air, grasped by an invisible divine hand.

The King struggled and lost his fur-trimmed hat, followed by the powdered wig, revealing his dark hair graying at the temples. He grunted and exclaimed, and then went entirely still in paralyzed terror.

"You said you wanted a better view over the walls, Your Majesty," said the dark Goddess with amusement, and then lowered her arms, and His Majesty came down, directly into the crowd of his guards, so that they caught him in a pile of arms and hands.

"What manner of *insanity* is going on!" the King cried, as the soldiers helped him back on his feet, and one of the guards went chasing after his ignobly fallen wig and hat.

And in the next instant an impossible gale wind struck at them once more from outside the city walls. It was so loud now that it was almost impossible to hear over the screeching wind, and everything went flying—all small unattached objects, barrels of black powder rolled and tumbled, supply carts were being upturned, and even the men in heavy armor felt themselves nearly airborne.

"Whoever you are, Goddess—*Hecate*, as you say—help us now!"

Hecate, pallid and dark at the same time, was still and composed within the eye of the storm. At the edges of the periphery, the air was thick with funnels of white, while the two closest persons to her, the Infanta and the marquis, were also within a sphere of calm.

"I can help you hold this city, but it may not be for long," Hecate said in a voice that was heard above the storm. "There is so much more than Letheburg at stake, mortal King. So much more than your Realm and their Domain. This is a war of the gods."

"Who is our enemy? Who is down there? Who is she, this Sovereign? And what has become of him, the dead madman Duke who was besieging us—" King Roland Osenni struggled to stand while the soldiers around him were all being buffeted with the impossible pressure of the maddened air.

Hecate continued looking beyond the outer walls, and did not reply immediately.

"I beg your mercy, Hecate! In particular I beg forgiveness for any offenses I might have made, or if I questioned your wisdom—" The King was speaking hurriedly. "Please! Have mercy!"

"So many questions, even now, Your Majesty. . . ." Hecate turned her immortal visage at him, and the King recognized the same very dark eyes that he was used to seeing in Grial the witch woman. . . . And for the first time he understood their occult nature, and their otherworldly pitch-black color, its weight like an anvil, and knew exactly why the sight of her always made him shudder—the eyes beckoned with their utter *unknown*, the transition and the ephemera, the boundary and the doorway.

"The one whom you know as the Sovereign is the Goddess of the Underworld, of Life and Death, and Resurrection. She is Persephone, and her coming has been precipitated by grief and madness. She is now the greatest misfortune your mortal world can ever know."

"What does she want here?" Claere asked in that moment.

"She wants to enter and take what she thinks is hers— which in fact is something of *mine*. I will not allow it," Hecate said. "You, my Claere, have warded the city. And without my will, no other entrance or exit will be made. However, I am not able to contain all of the onslaught."

Hecate pointed at the storm around them. "See this, mortals? While men and gods may not enter past the boundary, other more insidious things can. Persephone knows she may not pass, and thus she has made someone who can. Behold, the Goddess of the Underworld has *deified* winter itself."

"Is it he, the Blue Duke?" Vlau Fiomarre asked.

"Yes, Hoarfrost, your enemy so aptly named, is no longer a dead man, but an elemental creature of Eternity—a new god and something more. For nothing can stop winter, no god, no magical ward can stand against it. Only spring can come and bring the thaw. . . . And spring is never again to be, for *she*, Persephone, is spring . . . and she is now *something else*."

The gale-force wind raged, and soldiers held on to the stones of the bulwark and parapets for dear life.

"What of that golden woman?" the King cried through the wind. "Is she a goddess too? Can she do nothing with her warm light?"

"Alas! Demeter is her mother. And she is also the Mother of Bright Harvest and the queen of summer and autumn. . . . Even now she stands below, trying to convince her daughter to give up this madness, but she loves Persephone too much, and can never use force against her. Nor can Demeter summon summer or her favorite rich autumnal season to confront the winter, for it stands out of order, and may not come before spring."

Hecate sighed, for a moment sounding very ordinary, and very much like Grial in her less raucous moments. "And now—I cannot spend more time here, for I must return within the city and protect that which is most precious from Persephone," she said, looking around them from her center of calm. And then her impossible dark eyes attained a spark of living energy.

"Not all is lost, mortals!" said the dark Goddess with sudden inspiration. "For even though we do not have spring, summer, or autumn, we can use winter against itself!"

And with those strange words she turned to Claere and Vlau and she smiled at them. "It is time," she said. "Time to make things right, at least in a very small way. . . ."

Hecate beckoned the nearest garrison soldier to her, having to literally pull him into the sphere of calm, as he was clutching the parapet wall to keep himself upright.

"Now, my good man, have you a sharp knife on you? Any small blade will do."

The soldier, a musketeer, stared at the goddess in awe and

started digging through the inner sewn pockets of his hauberk, and then finding nothing in a hurry, offered her the sharp slim bayonet from the end of his gun barrel.

Hecate took the sharp blade and pricked her index finger, so that a small droplet of blood welled on the tip. "Come to me, Claere . . ." she said.

And when the girl complied, Hecate lovingly placed the blood upon Claere's pale lips, turning them for the first time in days a living shade of rose.

"Breathe, child! Breathe!" the Goddess said, and then struck the maiden in the chest, directly over her dead heart.

While Claere was gasping in terror and wonder, suddenly doubled over, suddenly feeling a strange *impossibility* begin inside her, Hecate pricked the index finger on her other hand and turned to Vlau. "And now, you, young man, come!"

Vlau took a step toward her in utter disbelief, and felt the taste of divine ambrosia on his lips. In the next instant, the Goddess whispered, "Breathe!" and struck him in the chest also, and he grunted, and then spasmed, and the next few seconds were vertigo and agony and intensity. . . .

Lightning struck twice, up on the battlements. The world was suddenly brought into razor-focus and perfect contrast of light and dark. Claere felt a jolt of electricity enter her and she was filled with a river of white *fire* that blasted through her every point and cell, pulling her inside-out and then back again—or so it seemed for a split second. Next to her, Vlau was now doubled over from the same shock, and the two of them were incandescent, luminous, radiant with white light, while inside them the world was turning. . . .

Two hearts pumped, strong and hale and *perfect*, as they had never been in life. Two sets of lungs inhaled air and allowed its life-giving oxygen to enter the bloodstream—for yes, there was living joyous blood again, new fiery liquid in their veins, pulled in and gathered from the air and the sky and the white snow, and transformed into the burning wine of life. . . . Frozen organs came to life, and all wounds closed up, especially the wound in *her* heart that had been made by *him*.

Claere exhaled a shuddering fierce sigh, and she could feel every smallest tingle in her body, every extremity, every tiny hair rise along her skin. . . . Her ears, that had seemed to be full of thick cotton for days, deadening all sound, remote and distant, could suddenly hear and *separate* the different sounds of the storm around them in minute detail, every harmonic whistle of snow crystal against stone, every particle striking another in its frenzied dance. . . .

She blinked, and her eyes focused differently, with infinite perfect sharpness, so that not only could she now see every facet of each tiny snowflake whirling in the storm beyond, but she could also see for leagues forward . . . and she could see *around* the curvature of the earth, see the chiseled rune lines upon the face of the sleeping moon that had not risen yet and hung far below the horizon . . . and she could see the radiant glory of the sun in full force, *through* the overcast.

Claere blinked again, turning her eyes away from the occluded sun's unreal *brightness* that seared her now-immortal eyes. And then she laughed!

Next to her, Vlau was staring around him in equal wonder, listening to the song of the snowflakes striking each other like tiny bells, and observing the dust motes in the distant layer of clouds.

As Claere looked at him, she realized that he was no longer swarthy dark and olive-skinned, but now his darkness had turned to silken gloss of bluish silver, and his skin now reflected like snow and metal, while his hair, still ebony like a raven's wing, was also like black diamonds . . . or like ice encrusting stark branches silhouetted against the pale forest wilderness.

Vlau's simple jacket and trousers were now resplendent white brocade embroidered with silver and pale blue thread and trimmed with white fur, with similar white boots, and a rakishly angled hat of fur and silver sat over his shimmering locks of twilight.

But oh, Vlau's eyes were still the same soulful darkness and complexity—warm like living breath upon a wintry day, and yet cold and eternal like the heart of winter.

And he was looking at her. . . . Oh, how he was looking at her!

Claere looked down at herself then, first at her own fingers, examining their elegant Dresden porcelain delicacy and their slim shimmering surfaces. And if she could only observe herself through Vlau's eyes, then she would have seen a glorious vision of crystalline perfection in female form.

She was a maiden of dream pallor—her skin like the first frost upon which a rainbow had capsized and crumbled into shards; her delicate brows and flowing hair of an immortal hue that changed constantly from silver to lavender to blue, and then to white.

Her eyes were great smoke-colored jewels of introspective innocence. Her lips, a winter rose.

She wore a long dress of white brocade and silver thread to match that of her love, and a fur-trimmed ethereal cape flowed from her sloping shoulders. Tiny perfect white boots warmed her feet, and a hat with a coronet of ice diamonds sat upon her hair, far more splendid than the Imperial Crown of the Realm that she had left behind at Silver Court.

"Oh!" Claere exclaimed, then turned around and spun in place, and her dress and cape and glorious hair spun around her like a flurry of snowflakes.

Vlau looked at her with a hungry gaze of intensity and amazement, and he whispered, "Claere . . . you are *alive!* You are exactly as I have seen you in my impossible dream. . . ."

"And you!" she cried, laughing, weeping with joy. "Oh, *you* are alive also!"

Hecate watched them with a look of amusement and

compassion and wisdom. And the King and all the soldiers on the parapets, and the storm itself, witnessed them thus.

"Yes, yes, enough with the maudlin foolery! You are *both* alive!" Hecate exclaimed, her hands outstretched in an embrace to both. "Blessed be my immortal children! Welcome to the world, immortal Jack Frost! Welcome, thou most beloved Snow Maiden!"

D uke Ian Chidair, who was once Hoarfrost, and now had become Old Man Winter, stood at the gates of Letheburg.

Persephone, the dark, glorious, utterly insane Goddess of the Underworld, had just given him life and immortality—the two things he could never have imagined, yet the two things of which he secretly dreamed.

He stood, still a barrel-chested giant, but now also pristine white and deadly cold and perfect, as the storm he himself had called forth, raged about him.

"Go into the city," Persephone had told him. "Go inside and make them cower, until they open the gates of their own accord."

Do what you must, drive them to insanity, drive them to turn on each other and to open themselves to you. . . .

"Gladly!" Winter replied, with a deep rumbling laugh of crackling ice—for though his lungs were no longer lifeless bags collecting an inner rime of frost, he enjoyed the terrible sound they made as he crushed ice crystals on purpose with the immense force of his own innards. "I will thrust them into madness of freezing wind and snow and ice! And once their fragile mortal flesh dies, they will come forth as undead and open the gates and weaken the wards of sorcery, for it will matter no longer!"

"Good!" she replied. "Let them all die, and let the world fill with the animated dead. For life gives one that unfortunate tedious thing called 'purpose,' while the dead are made docile and ultimately indifferent by their loss of fullness of being. In the end they will surrender most of their free will in order to exist and serve me. And I will take them all unto me, their energy and the immortal power that lies within their souls. For these new creatures are *my* domain."

"I will lay waste to Letheburg, to its puny King and all the mortals!" he roared, and the wind started to gather and thicken, and the fallen snow began to rise from the earth.

"Do it swiftly, Old Man, for now I must be gone, and I leave you to it. . . . But take not too long in your pleasure. For I will return shortly, and when I do, my Trovadii army must be ready to enter the gates."

She stood before him, her form perfection, an animate statue of silver and mercury, flowing in place like an eternal fountain fixed in supernatural motion.

"Where will you go now, dark Goddess?" Old Man Winter asked, adjusting his glorious fur cape, as the aerial turbulence increased. "Must you go and miss all the sporting delights, the fun of it?"

"Ah . . ." the Goddess of the Underworld said. "But I go to see my love! It is what awaits me now, what I've been waiting for, and what must be done, first! Thus, I go to *him!*"

"Persephone! Do not go, my daughter!" Demeter's voice, like a strange unseasonable breath of summer, sounded from beyond. The golden form of the harvest goddess stood just behind them, relentless in her persistence.

But now Demeter was like a faintly glowing weak candle in the dark maelstrom.

"Begone, Mother of mine!" Persephone said, pointing her hand at Demeter.

And the golden Goddess winked out of existence, cast out *elsewhere*.

A few feet behind them, Lady Ignacia Chitain cowered, finding herself surrounded by the dead, their bodies suspended motionless and their limbs creaking while they stood at attention in ranks and formation, Trovadii army divisions next to the original Hoarfrost's men.

"Your Brilliance!" Ignacia cried, in sudden terror. "What of me? You promised me Eternity for my service!"

Persephone's laughter sounded like a rolling spring brook, and she glanced at Ignacia once, briefly, with her impossible blue eyes. "Why, of course, my dear girl—only, I've decided to give you instead an Eternity of Service, for you 'weasel' a bit too much—"

Persephone clapped her hands, and Lady Ignacia found herself suddenly squeezed for breath, and then shrinking and *transforming*. Seconds later, a small furry creature crawled out of a fallen sage green cape—the only thing that remained of Lady Ignacia Chitain of Balmue.

The little beast—a polecat—made a small angry sound, and then it scampered away, narrowly avoiding the legs and other dangerous limbs of the dead soldiers and headed in the general direction of the city of Letheburg.

Persephone laughed again, and then she *disappeared*.

Old Man Winter remained at the city gates, and he raised his hands eagerly, calling the winds to him, and directing the clouds above to thicken into deep grey darkness.

Ah, the winter party was long overdue!

Chapter 12

She had so many names.

Dark Goddess . . . Lady of the Underworld . . . Bringer of Spring . . . the Sovereign of the Domain . . . Her Brilliance . . . beloved charming queen . . . occult seductress . . . savior . . . Rumanar Avalais . . . Kore . . . Despoina . . . Praxidike . . . Proserpina . . . Melinoë—*no!*

Dark lover . . . Black Wife.

Persephone.

The Hall of shadows and bones stood in silence. Not a whisper here, only somnolent repose and softly wafting cobwebs.

She emerged from the fabric of shadows, forming out of a single sigh of emptiness—a sigh that air itself made as it let go to make room for *her*, displacing nothing else. As she arrived, dust barely shifted on the granite stones underfoot.

Here she stood, perfect and fully formed, her skin a shimmer of achromatic grey and iridescent ebony and mother-of-pearl.

Perfect, and yet broken.

The soles of her metal sandals alighted upon the stone floor of the Hall in material silence, which however sent forth a psychic resonance that echoed through Death's Hall.

Hades, Lord Death, watched her coming from a great

distance, attuned to her every movement, every temperature, even to the faint cobweb shadow cast by her thought.

For the thoughts of gods cast shadows. So much existential weight do they bear that they mark the ether ... and this otherwise intangible gravitas is felt metaphysically by other gods in the form of a fine gossamer trail, like cobwebs. ...

No mortals can detect this shadow-thought trail. But sometimes, cobwebs are left behind as tangible proof in the physical world.

Cobwebs.

There was an infinity of them in this Hall, and hence, so many ancient thoughts solidified. Was it Death himself who had thought them, over the ages?

Hades, Lord Death, the shadowed one, sat on the Throne of Bones, waiting.

He heard her every footfall, felt the rustle of the fabric of her chiton against her smooth legs and thighs . . . how it slithered against the curving pear lobes of her hips . . . how it flowed with every loose, gentle swing of her arrow-tipped protruding breasts.

His skin immediately went several degrees darker, deepened into a rich hue, was now pitch-black. . . . His powerful sculpted fingers clenched, sharp nails dug into the armrests of the throne, leaving deep marks in the hard ivory.

Otherwise, he did not move a muscle. Neither did he raise or turn his head.

Another breath, and she was before him.

Persephone.

Then, her voice sounded.

"My love. . . . I am here at last."

He did not answer; did not look.

Moments flowed or fell or flashed—it was impossible to know what manner of *discreteness* happened to time.

"My sweet Lord. . . . Hades, my deep, coal-dark, pitch-black, shadow lover. . . . Oh, how I've needed you, my one profound love. . . ."

No answer.

"My Black Husband."

Her words were *thought* soft, yet came out hard, violent, each one a thrown anvil.

And he could not resist any longer, could not hold himself from looking.

Hades shuddered and lifted his beautiful immortal face, and the long flowing locks of his midnight hair were now true snakes come to life, stirring.

Persephone—demoness, seductress, goddess, soulless broken one—stood before him, beautiful as hell and smiling at him.

Her eyes . . . her beloved blue eyes were vacant, empty as the winter skies of the mortal realm. And yet, the simmering need was there, *something* was there, corresponding to his own.

Hades looked at her, allowed the gaze of his eyes to lock with hers. And one instant was sufficient. He was incapacitated, struck with sacred rage and sweet weakness, falling in his mind. . . .

And so was *she*.

Desire flared. Not shadow, not darkness, but true abysmal pitch-black. It struck, it leached, it sucked the air out of the Hall, and the cobwebs and the dust motes and the fragments of bone crumpled and contorted with infernal dissolution of their fundamental structure.

All matter collapsed for one infinite moment, then spasmed back into being in an involuntary precursor of divine orgasm. . . .

No!

Hades closed his eyelids and exhaled, as control returned to him, a mere flimsy illusion, yes, but still it held him.

She in turn blinked also, and her succulent lips parted in a silent exhalation that transformed into a gentle moan—

No!

"Persephone, we may not—it must *not be!*" His voice rang

in his own Hall, crumpling stone and sending ancient bones to warping, and making the shadows convulse.

"Ah! My sweet Hades! My lover speaks!"

Her breathy laughter issued forth, its sonorous sound caressing him along every point on his flesh, vibrating in his immortal bones. The snakes at the tips of his silken locks opened their jaws and hissed, sharp fangs protruding, lascivious. . . .

And again, a flare of infernal *sacred desire*.

With a hard snap he cast it off, and it simmered wickedly nearby, just nearby, just under the surface of thought.

Hades looked at her with a blank unreadable countenance, and he said, "Why have you come to torment me? Do you not know that I will not allow you to enter Below, no matter what you do, no matter what is done in this shadowed Hall?"

"Oh, my beautiful dark one," she said, coming a step closer, sauntering toward the dais of the throne, with her body trained toward him. "Of course I know! Just as well as I know that this is not real—none of it, *nothing* here is real—and that *you are not really here*. But oh, what sweet torment indeed, to tease and caress your poor shadow-self, your mortal aspect here Above. Poor, poor Lord Death! Ah, how much you need me, admit it my love!"

"It is self-evident that I need you, as much as you need me, Persephone," the dark God replied in a voice of perfect control, never averting his gaze, never blinking. "So what will we achieve in this stalemate, except for undue pain?"

She took the first step upon the dais. The cobwebs near the throne parted before her of their own accord. "Ah, but deep, *bone-deep* pain of this kind is such sweetness, like the scent of the narcissus and the asphodel, and the bitter taste of crushed pomegranate seeds upon the tongue. . . . Besides, why must it be a stalemate? You are growing weaker with every moment that we do not consummate our Longest Night. While I—I am now able to take unto me the life force of the dead mortals who cannot pass on. . . . This life force, it gives me strength, just enough to blunt the edge of my need for you. . . . If I persist, you will fall before me, and you will flee back down Below, and I promise you, My Lord Hades, you *will* vacate this Throne. And the moment you do, I will come to you, and it will be over. Why resist the inevitable?"

"Because what you call *inevitable* is impossible. If you come to me in the Underworld, as you *are* now, the resulting union will destroy this mortal world, corrupt its nature according to your own damaged self. Water would burn, earth would press down from on-high, and the skies would form mountains—"

"Yes, and fire would pour like the tears of those who are lost!" She took another slow step on the dais. "Ah, but would it be such a bad thing, really? Old, worn-out, tired rules crumbling, a new order coming to light, a new fresh pattern. We will still rule this new mortal pattern together, my love! Only it will be of my own making! Come, you know you want to have this pleasure with me, for it will be infinitely more delightful—"

"It will not bring back Melinoë."

For the first time he saw her falter. The *name* still had the effect upon her, even after all that had come to pass.

"How cruel you are, Husband! Do not speak thus of our child who will be made again! Melinoë will be the first new issue of our union, only this time she will be perfect and immortal, and she will be a queen of all places, Above and Below. Death will not be her flaw. And indeed death will be no longer, I've decided, for the mortal world can exist quite well without it, fixed in its own moment Between, as it is now. . . ."

"Have you no pity for these mortals, then? No mercy or allowance for the exercise of free choices in the course of their own fates?" he said, looking at her with liquid eyes of truth.

"None whatsoever," she replied, taking yet another step toward him, so that only a few paces remained.

"Oh, Persephone. . . ." So sorrowful his voice had become, losing its veneer of control. "What has become of you? Your heart, so full of compassion for the world that you die for it, twice every season! Do you remember, gentle beloved, how it comes to you, the gentle choice of sacrifice, the decision, and the act of letting go, the perfect *dissolution of divine will* that recreates the universe?"

"I remember enough to know I will never make that idiot choice again!" she cried then, and her bright voice struck the stones and rebounded in his heart like a dagger of agony.

He said nothing, averting his face slightly, a mere-quarter turn, so that he could gaze elsewhere and not at her, but his own flesh betrayed him, responding with a shudder. His hair-snakes hissed again, undulating in barely leashed desire. Already, beads of divine venom gathered like pearls at the fang tips, quivering. . . .

"My beautiful, beautiful love," said Persephone soothingly in a mesmerizing voice, and then she was up one more stair, and standing directly before him, eye-level, with only one stair remaining.

He observed her indirectly, from the corner of one eye, like a hawk fixing its wild stare, and saw the pulse in her throat and the shadowed deep cleft between her breasts, their softness pressing at the bodice of her chiton. There was a blood-black cabochon jewel nestled there, filled with miniscule golden embers of captured light, mocking him.

Oh, how he wanted to be that jewel, to rest upon her thus, between the rotund flesh, inside—

No!

Hades turned his face directly at her once more and he said, "I have her ashes, you know. Hecate has given me the jar. And it is hidden out of your reach."

But Persephone turned her head slowly sideways and back again, looking at him still, straining toward him. And then she took the last stair between them.

"Foolish love . . . Melinoë's ashes are not there—they have never been within that jar of blue clay." Her lips curved into a mocking smile. "Hecate was given a jar of ordinary mortal earth, to deceive her. Instead, I took Melinoë's beloved ashes to Ulpheo, hiding it in my mother's shrine while she was under the influence of the water of Lethe. Only—only—" And a strange petulant expression came to replace the smile, which then became, in a manner of the insane, a look of horror.

"Only what?" he asked.

"Nothing!" the dark Goddess screamed suddenly, and the Hall of bones was filled with a new degree of darkness. . . . It came pouring out of her, and she was suddenly pitch-black with grief, with fury, and to this complex mixture was added a strange sensual dimension of desire.

"Ah, My Lord . . . sweet, *lusty* . . . Hades . . ." she modulated her voice again so that now she was whispering, leaning her beautiful ebony-black form over him. And as she did thus, her ruddy-gold hair transformed and deepened into earthy brown and then a midnight hue as it cascaded forward to sweep along his skin, while she hovered inches away. "Why not let go and let me in? Receive me . . . sweet and deep . . . down Below. We both know how it will end—"

"Do we?" Hades said in a hard voice and then suddenly took her by the hair and pulled her to him and brought her face down to his with one muscular hand. His sharp claws dug into her scalp, and beads of immortal blood welled on her head under her glorious mane of midnight-ruddy hair.

At the feel of his claws she moaned and her eyelids fluttered, but it was with dark pleasure. He held her thus in a vice of iron, lips almost touching, *breathing* her. She floated over him in lassitude, turned to flowing honey, shuddering with exultation.

And then he placed his lips upon her brow in a strange chaste kiss. "My sweet *Black Wife*," he said, and let her go, harshly.

She staggered back, stunned by the sensual perversity of

such a death-cold touch.

"Now, begone," he said, his visage blank and timeless, for he was Lord Death indeed. "Begone, my sweet love. You may not come near me, not ever again. *I do not allow it*."

And suddenly a dark vortex of wind came sweeping into the Hall, dispelling her added layers of darkness, and turning everything into the same homogeneous pallor as had ruled here for ages untold.

When the maelstrom receded, Persephone was cast out *elsewhere*.

Lord Death, Lord Hades, beautiful, terrible dark God of the Underworld, was once again alone.

And he wept.

Old Man Winter lifted his arms covered in white sleeves and he threw his head back, calling to him the winds, the winter skies, the cold, and the cinereal storm clouds. As the elements raged around him, wind screeching in fury, and the world blurred with whiteness of whirling snow, he rose above the earth, hovering, lifting more than fifty feet, more than a hundred, and then sailing over the walls of Letheburg.

A strange panorama of chaos met him from below. At his back, the Trovadii armies and Hoarfrost's dead men—*Hoarfrost, it was his old nickname*, he remembered. *Ian Chidair, he was Duke Ian Chidair, Duke Hoarfrost, he was—no, not "he," I was that mortal, back then I was a dead man—*

And at his front, lying before him, was the city of Letheburg. He soared, passing thirty feet over the battlements and seeing puny figures of the dead crawling over the outer walls, and then along the inner walls the toy soldiers—garrison soldiers on patrol with their muskets and pikes and halberds, their helms fastened tight against the wind, visors lowered, while they held on to the parapets for dear life . . . and some looked up and stared and *saw* him.

Directly ahead was the invisible barrier, the sorcerous ward of safety upon the city.

Old Man Winter perceived it with his immortal sense as a shimmering curtain of silver light, the thickness of a single cobweb, reaching down below into the earth and high up above, both directions into infinity.

A perfect barrier.

He came to it, and he touched it with the tip of his great gloved finger, and it rang. Had he been a mortal or a mere god, he would not have been able to pass.

But he was *winter*. He was elemental, and the curtain parted before him as cobwebs part before a breeze.

And Winter entered the city. He sailed through the barrier and over the inner battlements, and was now above the rooftops, floating like a low-hanging cloud. He saw the snow-capped roofs of wood and plaster and shingles, the cathedral spires, the twisting streets far below like loosened ribbons, turning into themselves and crisscrossing. He saw the tiny carriages and pedestrians, and the formations of soldiers making their way past the city blocks and landmarks, its still-smoking ruins closest the walls, and its more distant interior that fared better against the catapults, with the great Lethe Square and the Winter Palace in the center, like a jeweled dollhouse toy.

Old Man Winter clapped his hands and the wind redoubled, and it was now gale-force. In a few breaths the snow was being swept clean off the roofs, while citizens ran for shelter like ants below. He snapped his fingers, and the cloud cover overhead thickened, and came down, so that the sky was an achromatic morass of cotton—slate and dun and ashes and smoke.

It was mid afternoon, but it felt like dusk had come down early, so dreary it had become.

And Winter was excessively pleased with the results of his handiwork, and so he alighted upon a tall roof and sat down upon a chimney which immediately stopped smoking and froze. He stroked his long white beard, chuckling deeply, making icicles crack along the eaves, and then folded his great white arms and exhaled a satiated breath of arctic *cold*.

Soon, the city of Letheburg was going to freeze, all living things would die, and their wills will become not their own, ripe for the picking. . . .

Ah, it was good to wield such immortal power!

"Old Man!"

A bright insolent voice sounded from across the rooftop nearby. A young man in sparkling white and shimmering blue, with hair like a raven's wing, sat on top of another chimney, dangling his elegant booted feet, arms folded in the same confident manner as Winter. "Allow me to introduce myself, I am Jack." The rakish hat was lifted then carelessly tossed back to cover his shimmering locks, and he inclined his head very lightly in greeting, and continued to stare with intense dark eyes. A mocking smile played across his lips.

Old Man Winter raised one thick white brow and boomed back across the rooftop. "What's this? A young popinjay? What makes you think you can speak to me, boy?"

"Old Man!"

From the opposite direction in back of him, from an even higher rooftop, another voice sounded, this one female, brash, and even more insolent.

Winter turned his head and there was a young girl, balanced upon the very ridge, walking like a dancer. She was also glittering white, a butterfly of crystalline delicacy. Her dress and cape floated behind her in snow flurries. Her perfectly beautiful face was framed by iridescent flowing tresses, and her haunting eyes of soft smoke-grey watched him intently and mischievously.

"And who are you, pretty poppet?" said Old Man Winter.

But the girl laughed in a silvery chime. She then jumped clear across the ridge and then floated weightlessly like a snowflake, landing directly before him on his own roof. She stood, boots planted firmly, and folded her arms in direct parody of the Old Man.

"Don't you remember me?" she said. "The last time you and I have spoken we were both mortal and merely dead."

"What? Ah, yes . . . I do remember you!" Old Man Winter exclaimed. "Why, you were the little princess—the Emperor's daughter, sent to talk me down—sent by that old fool who thinks he is King of this city!"

"Apparently there is more than one. So, do you think *you* can take Letheburg?" she asked in a voice both soft as snow and hard as ice, turning her head to the side slowly, so that her hair streamed lavender and mother-of-pearl over her one shoulder.

"Hah!" Old Man Winter said, his voice deepening, and the wind and the overcast echoing his tone. "And what can you do to stop me, little maiden of spun sugar and candied snow? *Parlay* me to death?"

"Considering that I've already placed a safety ward around Letheburg when merely a dead little princess, there is likely a thing or two I can do now that I am immortal."

"Indeed, there is plenty to be done here, Old Man," added Jack, and he was suddenly at the Snow Maiden's side. Jack took a step forward and leaned to stare the Old Man directly in the cold pale eyes. He did not blink, and neither did Winter . . . until suddenly Jack reached out like lighting and he pulled Winter by the nose, turning it a deep veiny blue with frost at his brief touch.

"Argh!" Old Man Winter exclaimed, and then reacted by swinging his great beefy hand forward to strike the young man . . . who was suddenly not there, but several feet away, on the end of the roof, laughing. In moments the Snow Maiden's crystalline peals of laughter joined his.

"You missed, Old Man!" said Jack, shaking his head. He then bent down and picked up a handful of snow from the rooftop and started rolling it into a ball with both his gloved hands. A blink, and the hefty snowball sailed, despite the gale force wind, cutting through it like butter, and it smashed against the side of Winter's head, splattering in the fur lining of his hat.

Winter roared. His gloved hands made fists, and he slammed them down on the chimney, and the storm exploded around them.

But the Snow Maiden soared up ten feet above the roof, and then she lifted her arms and spun. . . . Quicker and quicker she spun, with a force stronger than the storm wind, until a flurry formed around her, then a vortex, and all the airborne snow seemed to be sucked into it. The spinning tornado that was the Snow Maiden, raced up into the heavens and she moved like a comet, taking all the snowflakes unto her, and then releasing them to fall down and lie on the ground and the rooftops, adhering as if by magic to the surfaces. No matter how much the wind blew, the snow was no longer to be disturbed. It lay, pristine and sparkling everywhere, and there was crystal-clear visibility in the air for miles.

"What in blazes? You think you can best *me?* I am Winter Itself!" Old Man Winter frowned a deep hoary frown, and he narrowed his eyes. As he did thus, the cold in the air heightened as the temperature plummeted. Whorls of hard frost appeared on glass windows, followed by hairline fractures in some spots because of the intensity of the freeze. Instants more of this and windows would implode all across the city, glass shattering, residences filling with deadly cold. . . .

"Oh, no, you don't . . ." Jack Frost said. "This one is all mine!"

Jack Frost took off his fine gloves and he snapped his powerful elegant fingers. In an instant the cold spell lessened, and started to dissipate, absorbed into the white figure of Jack. The more cold disappeared, the bluer Jack's skin became, until he sparkled like a hard, deep-blue diamond.

At this, the entire city of Letheburg seemed to breathe with ease. All hardened, brittle, vulnerable, cold-stiffened things softened, to the point that the icicles hanging from the gutters and the eaves started to melt, and the wind lost all its chill and was decidedly lukewarm.

Winter wind still raged through the city but it was simply air, without snow or cold, and the deep grey overcast alone seemed to reflect the force of Old Man Winter's anger.

The Snow Maiden and Jack Frost jumped from roof to roof, laughing. And in seconds they were clear across the city, soaring, spinning, walking along narrow poles and lines strung across rooftops, like aerial trapeze artists, and then racing each other to the tallest ridge of the gilded roof of the Winter Palace, with its fancy baroque cornices and dipping sides.

Here, the Snow Maiden paused, for there was a niche spot where the tedious winter wind did not reach, and she sat down upon the edge of the roof, with her tiny booted legs swinging. Jack Frost paused beside her. He hopped up to the nearest ridge and did a fancy stomp and twirl and then stood along the razor-edge of the apex and pretended to be losing his balance, swinging his hands at his sides.

"Come, silly man," she said softly. "Sit beside me."

"Yes, Your Imperial Highness."

"No, please stop. That is all behind us. My father the Emperor, my family, yours—"

And immediately he was right there, having forgotten his foolery, seated alongside her, swinging his own feet off the roof.

"Jack," she said. "*Vlau* . . ."

He turned his face to her at that name, starting slightly. And then he was inches away, looking into her soul with his dark immortal eyes.

"Claere. . . ."

Her strong beating heart contracted in her breast at his proximity, but it was the pain of a pure unconditional love for which there were no mortal words, and not even immortal ones—such a pang of joy that it *hurt*.

"Claere," he said again, having grown almost timid, in a

way she had never seen him before, not ever. And then she felt the gentle touch of his hand against hers, skin sliding against skin, and its strange immortal warmth seared her. . . .

Vlau, who was now Jack, leaned in and he pressed his lips against hers, shaking slightly with impossible wonder.

She felt the touch, surprisingly warm, and then his lips were devouring her, and she could feel it, every hungry point along her living flesh awakened, as he consumed her. His hands were at the back of her head and he pressed himself closer, closer yet, and held her, strong fingers tangling in her long iridescent hair, pushing her backward, sideways, and burying himself in her throat, as a desperate madness came upon him—

The next instant they had fallen off the roof.

They were airborne, and Claere's light cry of surprise and his involuntary exclamation were muffled by his mouth upon hers, and her lips upon his, as they took each other's voices away . . . and then they soared upward, willing themselves simply to fly, and up they went, high into the clouds, still holding each other in a twisting tumble of limbs and bodies, having long given up their breaths to each other.

The sky was below and the city of Letheburg spun above, then things righted eventually, and they slipped past the thick vaporous clouds and started sinking, floating down like snowflakes through the lukewarm winds, and remembering Old Man Winter, started again laughing.

They landed feet first on the Palace rooftop. Then, still holding hands, they scrambled back into the small nook that was safe from the impotent wind. Claere rested her head against Vlau's chest.

"The armies clamor at the gates, and the dead are all around. Even if this mortal world falls," said Vlau suddenly, "we are here together, you and I."

"Always," she said, looking out from the roof at the panorama below.

And then Jack Frost snapped his fingers, and far away

against the grey dreary sky, a tiny shooting star appeared. It fell like a firefly and landed on a small snow-covered frozen fountain pond inside someone's garden. As the light struck the surface of the ice, it shattered and reformed, and to Claere's delight, a tiny ice sculpture appeared, a petite maiden of ice, and next to her, a tiny young man, perfect replicas of themselves, fixed in transparent ice.

"There we are!" the Snow Maiden exclaimed. "How did you do that?"

"Art, my dear!" he replied in a parody of a courtier's nasal tone.

She laughed. "Will I be spending eternity with a court jester? Little did I know! It is lovely. But it will melt, eventually, you do realize. . . . That is, if sorrowful spring will ever come."

"Of course, just as all things eventually do. With or without armies to expedite the dreaded end."

"Then why put such glorious effort into something so ephemeral?"

"Beauty, my dear!" Again, his mocking nasal tone.

"So is beauty and art the justifying purpose of all things?"

"What else is there?"

"Love," she said.

"Stories!" he replied.

"Ah, such is to be our tedious eternity, filled with Beauty, Art, Love, and Stories!" She gazed at him with a mocking smile of mischief.

"We'll have children . . ." he whispered suddenly, his eyes becoming serious and his pupils widened with desire.

"They will be flurries of girl snowflakes and little frost boys with ruddy noses and blue cheeks!"

But he was still serious, gazing at her, and his carnal desire was submerged, made secondary somehow. It was transformed, replaced with divine *love*.

Far below them, Letheburg, with its sorrowful reality,

receded. Or at least so it seemed. It too was ephemeral, for the time being. And with it, was the mortal world.

Chapter 13

Percy moved into the mist and emerged on the other side . . . into bitter cold.

No, this was not Death's Keep.

Instead, a stark winter forest stood around her, sparse trees drawn black in hairline-sharp contrast upon whiteness of snow. She inhaled scalding cold air, and was immediately grateful for her usual winter coat and mittens, and pulled her woolen shawl up from her shoulders and over her hair.

The sound of many horses neighing and various human speech came from about fifty feet away, and Percy turned, seeing the site of a camp being made, and the familiar figures of the people of the town of San Quellenne now shivering in their somewhat meager winter clothing, and no doubt glad that they had listened to her and dressed warmly.

But as the full range of sound made itself known to her from all directions, she realized these were not only the people she had helped transport through the shadows—this was a large camp, and it had soldiers and knights, and some ordinary people who looked very much like residents of Lethe. There were many fires burning among the trees, and stacks of grey smoke rising up into the frigid air. Clanging metal, military commands being given, messages conveyed, even occasional banter and the mewling cries of infants and the barking of dogs.

"Percy!"

Beltain was approaching her.

The black knight in his full plate armor walked effortlessly through the snow, his tall imposing figure sending a jolt of wordless joy and relief through Percy. In that instant she saw him, she knew once and for all that *he* was the essence of *homecoming*. Wherever he was for her, it was the place she recognized as home.

"Are you all right?" he asked, looking at her closely. Vapor curled from his breath in the icy air. His slate-blue eyes—indeed, a single deep glance from them—caused warmth to rise in her cheeks.

"What is going on?" she said, "I am not sure what happened! Did all the people and you come through here, and not in Death's Keep?"

"Apparently so."

"And where is 'here?' Where are we?"

He glanced around, pointed to the trees. "The forest looks familiar. If I did not know better I would say it is the Chidair part of the northern forest. We are on my own land. However—" He paused and pointed again, through the trees, in the direction of the camp. "These men over there are Goraque soldiers. Which means that either there is a whole lot of land missing, or they are here on other business. But to complicate things even more, there are all manner of others here too. Women and children, ordinary country folk—"

While Beltain was speaking, Percy noticed the energetic figure of Lady Jelavie in her knight's armor, approaching with a few other San Quellenne townsmen at her side. Little Flavio ran beside her, kicking up snow with enthusiasm.

"You, girl! Where is my mother?" Jelavie said in a bright commanding voice. "And where in Heaven's name are we?"

Percy felt a pang of sorrow, and for a moment it was difficult to meet the lady's eyes. "The Lady Calliope chose to stay behind. I am very sorry."

"What?" Jelavie San Quellenne's expression was furious and tragic. And then she turned on Percy. "You *killed* her, didn't you? You left her behind on purpose! You left my mother all alone to die in that awful, cursed, fading place! You—"

"Enough!" Beltain interrupted in a hard voice. "Whatever Percy Ayren has done on behalf of your mother and indeed all your people, is something to be thankful for—*My Lady*."

"I am truly sorry. She was already dead," Percy said. "I simply helped her to pass on with the dignity that she had wanted—that she *chose* for herself. When I left her body, it was in a spot she selected for herself. She was looking at the sea . . . in the direction of the island which is now gone. . . . She told me of Saga Mountain, where your father is buried. . . ."

"No!" Lady Jelavie San Quellenne burst into hard sobs.

Flavio San Quellenne came up to his sister and tugged her by the hand. "Jelavie!" he said. "What's wrong? Is mother gone to Saga Mountain?"

"Yes . . . yes she is!" And Jelavie wept even harder, with ragged gasps. Then just as forcefully she quieted herself, wiping her face and nose violently against her gauntlet and took a deep gulp of air. In seconds her face was back to being stony and proud, only the smear of tears remained, freezing on her ruddy skin in a manner of seconds.

The townspeople of San Quellenne approached their group, one by one, and there were many questions as they stood around together with their belongings. The Count D'Arvu and his wife and daughter, were among them.

"You are our Lady now," many of the townspeople spoke. "What should we do?"

At the sound of their general noise and voices, the Tanathe newcomers were noticed at last by the denizens of the camp beyond the trees. Soon, there were several figures approaching from the encampment behind them. They were armed.

"Wait here," Beltain said calmly, with authority, "while I

go speak with them." And he turned back and went to meet the
soldiers of the camp. His great sword was prominent at his side,
but it was sheathed and he made a point of showing that his
gauntleted hands carried no hidden weapons. After a few
minutes of conversation in muted voices with what appeared to
be a Goraque knight, Beltain nodded, then returned to Percy and
the group of refugees from San Quellenne.

"All is well," he said. "These people are not only Goraque
soldiers, but apparently there are villagers from all around the
countryside, including Chidair, and the towns of Duarden,
Fioren, your own Oarclaven, Tussecan, and quite a few
stragglers from outside the Kingdom of Lethe. As I stood
speaking to that knight, I could recognize Styx dialects coming
from beyond the copse of trees. And there are quite a few very
tired, battle-worn Morphaea soldiers from the Balmue border
battlefields."

"What does that mean?" the new Lady San Quellenne
asked. "We are in your Realm, I can see, but do they know who
we are? Did you tell them we are Tanathe? What will they do
with us?"

"Nothing," the black knight replied mildly. "They know
you are from the Domain, just as they know that I am the son of
the Duke Chidair who only a few weeks ago was their prime
enemy. However, the feud lines have been redrawn. This strange
war and this world fading around us have changed all that. It is
now a conflict between the living and the dead—and between
the *gods*."

Lady Jelavie stared at him with a frown. "What gods?"

"Your Sovereign," Percy replied softly. "She is the Goddess
Persephone."

"Who?" There was a look of complete confusion on
Jelavie's face.

"Throughout the course of your noble education, have you
not had the fortune to read the Ancient Greeks?" Beltain said
with an edge.

"I beg you not to insult my family's ability to educate our children! I assure you, we of Tanathe are not savages! And ah, you mean to say, *classical* Persephone of the Greek Underworld? But it is a silly old myth, a *story!* We were told it by our tutors, and they made us read histories mixed in with mythic fabrications—Hesiod and Ovid, Pindar and Aristophanes, Virgil and of course the lofty verses of Homer in the original, which indeed I much prefer for its heroic splendor to the other less valiant histories and myths—But, *Persephone?*" Lady Jelavie appeared stunned.

"Yes, that same Persephone. It seems the fabled stories are histories after all."

"So you say," Jelavie continued, "that the Sovereign of the Domain—*our* Sovereign—is in fact Persephone, out of old classical texts? She is immortal?"

"It is exactly so. And had you been so fortunate as to have ended up in Death's Keep, you would've had the pleasure of meeting her immortal consort, Lord Hades."

"If this is a joke—"

"Unfortunately, Lord Beltain speaks the truth," the Count D'Arvu put in, coming closer through the crowd of San Quellenne refugees. "My Lady San Quellenne, we have not had the pleasure yet, but allow me to introduce myself and my noble family, I am Count Lecrant D'Arvu of Balmue, your countryman, and we have only recently arrived from the Sapphire Court, and had every intention of settling in your delightful spot of paradise that had been San Quellenne."

And then the Count related to Lady Jelavie some of the events of the past days and weeks at Court. "And thus," he concluded, "as you can see, the Sovereign is the enemy now, of all of us. Indeed, she is the enemy of the mortal world."

"Now you have a choice to make, Lady San Quellenne. Are you willing to fight for your Sovereign, and fight all these people in that camp? No? If not, then they have no interest in fighting you," said the black knight.

"We do not wish to fight them, no," said Lady Jelavie, with a proud look. "But we will not stand and be slaughtered. However, I am willing to take your noble word as a Peer of the Realm that we shall not be harmed."

"And much relief be to that," said Beltain.

"Are you a real Peer of the Realm?" said the boy Flavio suddenly. He neared the black knight and tapped a plate of his dark metal armor with the palm of his hand, making it ring, and then stared at the sheathed great sword, mesmerized. "Can I see your sword?"

"Flavio!" Lady Jelavie exclaimed. "Stand back from the Lord, immediately. Keep away from underfoot now—really, now is hardly the time. And put those mittens on, your hands are turning blue!"

But Beltain gave the boy an amused look and raised one brow. "Maybe later, little man," he said.

"Here, child, come with me." It was the Countess Arabella D'Arvu, and she took the boy gently by the hand, the same way she had when they were about to cross the curtain of grey mist and he was about to lose his mother.

"Thank you. . . ." Jelavie gave the Countess a grateful look.

Percy meanwhile watched the young lady who stood next to the Countess D'Arvu.

Lady Leonora, the Cobweb Bride, and her death shadow, were right here, before her.

"My Lady . . ." Percy said.

Leonora inclined her head in a slight nod. And then, saying nothing, she retreated behind her mother.

The group from Tanathe entered the large Goraque camp slowly, taking care not to provoke any hostility, but soon realized that they were received as fellow refugees in an amicable manner. They walked past endless fire pits, small tents and holes dug in the snow and lined with wooden thatch and canvas tarp. Food was being rationed, but for the moment a smell of cooking smoked sausage and salted pork hung in the air. There were little children running everywhere, and there were soldiers of all ranks, attending to weapons and horses.

Looks were exchanged, but friendly casual ones for the most part.

The sight of Lord Beltain Chidair seemed to make more of an impression upon the military men than the appearance of refugees from the Domain. All the Goraque knights and soldiers knew him, the "invincible Black Knight," from years of armed conflict with Chidair—and in many cases from the wounds he had dealt them personally—and he was given quite a few hard stares as he walked near the front, leading his great black warhorse behind him.

They walked deeper into the camp, following a large bearded knight wearing a red surcoat with the Goraque crest. He introduced himself to Lord Beltain as Baron Gundar Dureval, saying that fortunately he had not had the pleasure of meeting the black knight in battle, unlike most of the men here, and hence was quite free of grudges.

"Fear not," Baron Dureval added for the sake of the Lady San Quellenne and her people, and the Count D'Arvu. "You will be perfectly safe here, for you are merely foreigners of the Domain and not Chidair." And then he gave a wink to Beltain, who took the minor jab as well as possible under the circumstances, keeping a composed face.

"Where are you taking us?" asked Lady Jelavie, walking in front in a confident manner.

"The Duke would like to see you first, before you join the camp."

"It is understandable." The young lady nodded with a stonelike face.

They arrived before a modestly large tent, flying the red-and-gold pennants and crest of Goraque. While the bulk of the newcomers remained outside, Beltain, Percy, the Lady San Quellenne, and the Count D'Arvu followed by Countess Arabella and Lady Leonora, all entered the tent, past the guards.

Duke Vitalio Goraque was hunched over a table covered with a large detailed map that took up most of the room in the tent, and next to him were several Goraque knights, commanding officers, and advisors. Vitalio Goraque was a middle-aged man of medium built, with a well-groomed small sharp beard and stylish wavy brown hair, and rather nondescript but generally pleasing features. He had the look and smooth manners of a courtier, as was reflected in the softly erudite and composed cadence of his voice, as he discussed the map with his advisors.

The Duke looked up and the arrivals were introduced. At the sight of Lord Beltain Chidair, Duke Goraque paled slightly, but then recovered his composure, while Beltain nodded curtly, maintaining a very closed and bland expression.

"So the Black Knight has broken with his father," said Goraque. "Well, this should be interesting."

"My father is dead," replied Beltain. "I have broken with a madman to whom I cannot owe allegiance."

"And so you think you can just march in here, into *my* camp, and all will be forgiven? All years of grievances forgotten? Do you know, Chidair whelp, that I still have an old, poorly healed cut on my thigh that you have delivered unto me three years ago?"

"Is that so, Your Grace?" Beltain's countenance was granite. "I do believe my own arm has a scratch from you, and all other parts of me can thank quite a few of your men for their well-placed favors. We are as even as can be."

The Duke maintained a stare, and then he exhaled wearily. "No doubt, you are right, Lord Beltain," he said, giving up any more pretence of posturing, for he was more tired than he let on. "And apparently our differences have now become secondary. We are at war with things we cannot explain, forces that are unnatural. . . . Now, who are all these people with you, Chidair?"

The introductions were made, and Duke Vitalio Goraque politely acknowledged the newcomers. He gave a slightly longer glance to the new Lady Jelavie San Quellenne, no doubt noticing her youth, and then upon learning the circumstances, expressed his condolences on the recent loss of her mother. He then introduced the knights present in the room, including a high ranking operative of the Emperor, a well-composed handsome man with raven-dark hair and fierce aquiline features, by the name of Ebrai Fiomarre.

Percy started at the name and immediately understood why the man looked so familiar. Beltain mentioned that he knew a "Marquis Vlau Fiomarre."

A notable change came to Ebrai's features, a complete closing off, so that he was an impenetrable blank. "Yes," he replied in a neutral tone. "It is my brother." And then he said nothing else.

At one point, Goraque's gaze rested upon Percy.

Percy, in her ordinary peasant attire and poor coat, looked out of place in this gathering of nobles, and was originally assumed to be someone's attending servant or lady's maid— something she did not mind perpetuating. But seeing the Duke's attention upon her, Lady Jelavie pronounced: "And this girl has some kind of sorcerous ability with the dead. However she has served my people well in leading us through the mist and here into your Realm—"

Beltain paled slightly, for he had hoped to keep Percy and her role as quiet as possible, considering Goraque's general intentions were still unclear—but it was too late.

"I am Percy Ayren, Your Grace," she said, with a modest curtsey.

"And she is under my protection," Beltain added in a forceful voice, glancing at the Duke point-blank, and then at all the rest of the men in the room.

Duke Goraque raised one brow, noting Beltain's agitated forcefulness. But then he examined Percy with renewed interest and an evaluating stare. "So, who are you exactly, girl? Sorcery over the dead? Ah! Are you by any chance that girl they talk about who can kill the dead? What is it they call you—Death's Champion?"

Ebrai Fiomarre immediately turned and was staring at her with dark-eyed intensity.

"Yes," Percy said, since there was no avoiding it.

"Very interesting!" The Duke gave her his full attention. "So is it true what they say you do?"

"I have no notion what it is they say," Percy replied, looking up at His Grace to stare directly in his eyes. "I put the dead to rest. That part is true."

"And what of your ability to find passageways through shadows?" Lady Jelavie persisted. "Whatever you did, did not take us to Death's Keep, but it did bring us here to relative safety."

Percy nodded, but did not elaborate.

"Well, well," said Goraque. "If this is indeed true, then it can make a great difference in our favor."

"It must be repeated that this girl is under *my protection*," said the black knight again, angry heat flooding his cheeks.

Goraque glanced again at Beltain, noting his high color. "Yes, I understand what you said the first time, Lord Beltain. If she is also your bedwarmer, have no fear, you have made it abundantly clear that your claim of that nature is made. However, since you and she are availing yourselves of our hospitality, then it might be expected that a little accommodation on her part might be expected in return. If she can put the dead enemy to rest when we are attacked, as I've heard it was done at Letheburg, then it will go a long way toward smoothing the differences between Goraque and Chidair—"

Before Beltain uttered anything he might regret, Percy interrupted them both. "Thank you for your hospitality, Your

Grace. I will endeavor to do what I can to help—to the best of my ability."

Beltain stared at her with earnest agitated eyes, and once more her heart felt a sharp pang of impossible affection.

"I am glad, girl, that you are so accommodating," Duke Goraque said with an exhalation of relief. "We are all fortunate to have you among us—indeed, all of you, Ladies and Gentlemen." He nodded to the room in general. "Now, if I can have you join us, let my men show you to a favorable place where you and your people can set up your own area within our camp. Because we are about to attempt an approach to Letheburg. And a good rest can do everyone some good before we march."

"With all due respect to Your Grace, and frankly our gratitude for your exceedingly kind hospitality, but we are not interested in a war," Count Lecrant D'Arvu spoke up. "We have worked very hard to escape as far as possible from the centers of conflict. Indeed, many of the people of the Lady San Quellenne's party are simple townsmen and peasants with their families and children and beasts of burden, looking to settle down somewhere safe, and they have no knowledge of arms or fighting—"

Vitalio Goraque raised one hand to interrupt. "My Lord D'Arvu—"

But the Count went on, "Furthermore, if we might be allowed to rest overnight, we would happily proceed on our way and not inconvenience you any further, as we seek a peaceful spot in your Realm, or for that matter *anywhere* as far as possible from Her Brilliance, the Sovereign—"

"My Lord D'Arvu. I see you have no notion of what is happening here. No notion at all. . . ." The Duke rubbed his forehead tiredly. He then pointed to the map on the table before him, and beckoned with his finger, motioning for the Count to approach.

Frowning nervously, Count Lecrant stepped up to the table, followed by Beltain and the others.

"See this?" Goraque pressed with his finger a portion on the map marked as Letheburg. "Do you know where this is?"

"I am assuming, a number of miles south of here," Beltain spoke up in the Count's place. "We are about a mile north of Lake Merlait on Chidair land, if I suppose correctly."

"No," said the Duke. "We are not."

Beltain frowned. "Then where are we?"

The Duke pointed at the entirety of the map of the Realm, waving his hand from one edge to the other. "Most of what is shown here, most of the landmarks depicted on this map *no longer exist*. What still exists as far as I know is this—" he pointed to Letheburg—"and I am assuming, this—" he pointed to the Silver Court—"and possibly a small part of this—" and he pointed to the northern portion of the Kingdom of Styx. "Morphaea is gone, most of Lethe is gone—"

"So then where are we, if not in Chidair?"

"Right here." And Goraque pointed to a spot on the map just north of Letheburg. "Except that all this part is gone and this is where the Chidair northern forest is now—four miles away from Letheburg! We can see the Trovadii red through the trees if we go out a bit of distance past the next rise! They surround the city, and we are just hiding here a couple of miles away, biding our time."

"Impossible!" Beltain exclaimed.

"So then what is Your Grace's point?" Count D'Arvu observed in some confusion.

"My point is, you have nowhere to go! You and your family and your people cannot escape this war, nor can you keep running, because the land—*this* land, any land—is likely going to disappear tomorrow!"

"Dear God . . ." The Count paled.

"Then we are not going to run!" Lady Jelavie San Quellenne slapped her elegant gauntleted palm on the map, right in the center of Letheburg. "We will stay and we will fight. Because one way or another we will die anyway. Or should I say, *not* die. We will remain in this horrible world—unless this girl Percy sends us off—and we might as well try to make something of it while we rot!"

It was late afternoon, and the Goraque campsite had swallowed up the newcomers with the ease that comes from an excess of difference. It was composed of so many other refugees that it welcomed all.

Percy sat before a small tent, warming her feet near a fire, next to Beltain and the family D'Arvu. The Count had generously invited them to share his tent for the night, since the cold was rising, and it was likely to snow later.

Percy had a flash of memory of just a few days ago, of sitting in Grial's cart, with Betsy hitched before her, huddling against the wind, pressing herself against Beltain's sleeping body—at that point he was still a stranger, unfamiliar to her, and yet already there was something so wondrous—the other potential Cobweb Bride girls curled in lumps. . . . And then she remembered that Grial was Hecate . . . and that the real Cobweb Bride was found, and that she was right here, sitting not more than two feet away from her, silent, dead, and entirely unwilling to die or even meet her immortal bridegroom.

Percy turned to stare at Beltain as he held a hot mug of tea, the vapor from it curling in the air, and brought it to his lips. She watched the lean lines of his stubbed jaw, the comely profile as he turned slightly to pick up something, a chunk of bread and cheese, then turned, as if sensing her gaze . . . and her heart danced at the look of his beautiful eyes, and his immediate smile. He offered it to her.

"Beltain," she said softly. "As soon as the evening comes—the twilight—I will go to see Death in his Keep."

He immediately set down the food and the smile left him,

replaced by a grave expression.

"I have to try to see him, Lord Hades, and find out what has happened and why we did not end up in his Hall this last time, and also, to find out what is to be done."

"I am going with you," Beltain said.

But Percy shook her head. "No, my beloved, I must speak to him myself."

"There is no way I am letting you be alone with *him!* Not ever again!"

"Why?" she said.

"Because of what *he* is. Because of what he can *do*—to you. I *know* him now." Beltain's face was a mask of intensity.

"He showed you something, did he not?" she guessed astutely. "That last time when you followed me on your own?"

"Yes. . . ."

"What was it?"

But Beltain shook his head. "No," he whispered, "I cannot."

Percy had no chance to say anything else because a familiar girlish voice sounded right behind her. *"Percy Ayren!"*

Percy turned, and there was Jenna Doneil clambering toward her through the snowy campsite. "Percy! Oh, Lordy Lord, it's you! Oh, Percy, am I glad to see you!"

"Jenna? Oh my Lord! What are you doing here?" Percy was amazed and she sprang up, seeing the familiar twelve-year-old girl from her home village. She rushed to embrace her, but Jenna was there first, and she bodily hurled herself at Percy, hugging her so tight that they almost collapsed, and burying her little red-nosed face against the front of Percy's coat.

"Oh, you are here, Percy! Thanks be to the Lord Almighty! I just knew it! Now that you're here, everything's gonna be all right!"

"How did you get here? And who else is here?"

"Oh, lots of folks from Oarclaven! We're way back thataway!" and Jenna pointed behind her at a distant smoking fire.

Percy's heart lurched with sudden hope. "Are my folks here? Ma and Pa, and Belle and Patty?"

Jenna's wildly joyful face lost some of its enthusiasm. "Oh, no, I'm sorry, Percy, I don't think they made it out. . . . At least I don't remember! When things started fading on our street, I just went a little crazy! I was running and screaming, cause I been through all that awful shadow stuff with Death's Keep already, and I knew it when I saw it! So I was screaming my head off, and some people came out and started running too, and all the streets and houses were getting all transparent and horrid, and you could see right through them, and then I just ran and ran and ran!"

And Jenna began bawling, and wiping her face against Percy's coat.

Percy held the girl, gently stroking her head covered by a poor, much-worn shawl, from under which wisps of flaxen hair were sticking out.

Moments later, Jenna quieted and she looked up, and her eyes again brightened. "You know, Flor Murel and Gloria Libbin made it out! They're back there! And so did old Martha Poiron, cause I dragged her by the hand, as soon as she came out the door—"

"Well done, Jen!" Percy patted her again, and pressed her in another hug, while her heart slowly started to ache, thinking of her parents and sisters in their suddenly transparent hovel with its badly thatched roof, all fading away. . . .

Jenna turned around and for the first time noticed Beltain, sitting right near the fire. "Oh!" she said. "The Black Knight!"

"And hello to you too, Jenna," he replied with a light smile, at which Jenna almost shrieked.

"Lordy Lord! He knows my *name!*"

"Well of course he knows your name, Jen, what do you think he is, a dolt? He's been in our company for days."

"Oh, Percy! You ain't afraid of calling the fearsome Black

Knight a *dolt?*"

"She's called me far worse," Beltain said, taking a swig from the hot mug.

Jenna raised the back of her hand to her mouth.

At which both Percy and Beltain laughed. It was good to laugh innocently, even for a moment, and when it was over, their faces sobered, both of them remembering what was being discussed before Jenna's untimely interruption.

"It's so odd, isn't it!" Jenna said meanwhile, not seeing their darkened mood. "How we all went to be Cobweb Brides, and then none of us turned out to be, and then no one ever found her! Wonder where she is, that dratted Cobweb Bride? It would sure be nice to finally find her and make the world all right again!"

Across the fire, Lady Leonora was watching Jenna speak, staring with her glassy dead eyes. Her expression was unreadable.

Percy threw her one tentative brief glance, then looked away again, not wanting to put her on the spot.

Jenna continued chattering, and wanted to drag Percy with her back the Oarclaven fire, but Percy gently disengaged herself and promised to come by and visit them later.

Eventually Jenna ran off, and went back to her Oarclaven group, frequently turning around and stumbling in the snow, and waving to Percy all the way.

Before they realized it, dusk was here, an early evening in this thick winter overcast.

When the shadows started to coalesce on the other side of the tent, and between the sparse stands of trees, Percy stood up from the fire. Beltain had been holding her hands, warming them both between his large palms, rubbing them to get the blood flowing.

But now she pulled away and she said, "I must go."

"Percy!" he started to rise after her, but she put her hand on his shoulder gently, pushing in vain against the hard metal armor.

"Beltain, please wait here," she said. "I promise I will not be gone for long. But I must do this alone."

There was pain in his eyes. A moment of hard decision.

And then he nodded and sat back and watched her go, with an impassive face.

Percy did not look back because she could not bear to see his eyes. She approached the nearest shadow, and reached out with her death sense.

Immediately there was the familiar grey mist.

She stepped through it.

Percy found herself inside Death's Hall of bones. But immediately she realized that something was wrong.

There was a new quality to the light here, a deepening of dusk. The illumination was low enough that the shadows appeared longer, the dark places pitch-black between the columns stretching in rows unto infinity, and the cobwebs cast a forest of secondary shadows of their own—something that had never been seen in the Hall before.

Cobwebs casting shadows, she thought.

And where it had been neutral pallor, the dusk hung deep and oppressive.

"Lord Death!" Percy said loudly, suddenly feeling the beginnings of fear. "I am here, Lord Hades!"

For a long time there was no answer. The silence was so thick that Percy could hear the pounding of her own temples.

And then a familiar deep voice replied, only this time he spoke soft as a whisper. His voice failed to raise even a single echo.

"Come to me. . . ."

Percy blinked, and she saw the faintest stirring of dust at her feet, as a weak breeze rifled the cobwebs and pointed her in the direction she had to go.

She emerged into the great portion of the Hall, with the ribcage structures rising to the ceiling, the dais in the center, and upon it the great Throne of Ivory.

Percy strained to look at the throne and see *him*, the one who was Death, Lord Hades. She blinked repeatedly, willing her eyes to perceive, and only after several long moments could she see a translucent figure of the one she knew to be Hades, seated in a slouching form upon the chair, hands grasping the armrests in weakness, his head bent forward. There was a look of *mortal* illness about him—which was surely impossible. He exuded abysmal weariness and infirmity of limbs, in the way his hands lay passive, and the head was motionless, fixed in vulnerability. For the first time, the infinite compounded ages of men and gods weighed heavily upon him, wearing down his immortality into a brittle husk.

"My Lord Hades!" Percy exclaimed. And then she rushed forward, forgetting for once the repulsive obstacle of the cobwebs. She stopped before him, having climbed up all the steps of the dais, and he was only a foot away.

My Lord . . . what has become of you?

Her thought was unvoiced, but as always, there was no need for speech.

The dark God was within her mind. Had always been.

My Champion. . . .

Percy reached out and placed her fingers upon the great swarthy hand with sharp-clawed nails—his supple ethereal skin no longer had the skeletal pallor of Lord Death, but the deeper black hue of Lord Hades.

And immediately she was transported into a serene place without a frame of reference. No up, no down, only unrelieved grey.

It was here she had seen him once as the glorious White Bridegroom, and he had given her a bit of his own heart and his power through a kiss. . . .

But there was no White Bridegroom now.

Hades stood before her, a mere shadow of himself. Wan and sickly dark he was, like coals that had partially burned down and had a veneer of white ashes coating them.

"What has happened here, My Lord? What happened to *you?*" Percy said.

"*She* has happened," the God replied softly. "My love was here and she tried to pass through to the Underworld, and she did not succeed."

"You stopped Persephone!" Percy exclaimed, hope surging inside her. "It is a good thing, is it not?"

But the dark God's lips barely moved into a bitter shadow of a smile. "I merely delayed her entry. She will persist and she will enter my kingdom eventually and come unto me, and together she and I will bring this mortal world to its final destruction. But for now—yes, a reprieve. . . . Only, it has cost me, dearly. I am weak, as you can see. And—"

Hades grew silent, watching her with eyes of despair.

"Was this why we ended up in Lethe instead of coming here, all those Tanathe people and Beltain and I? Was your Persephone here at that exact time?"

"Yes. I could not have her see you . . . and thus I simply gave all of you passage directly to where you had to go."

Percy felt the burden of sorrow come upon her like a soft blanket that begins with the illusion of comfort and then weighs more and more with each breath, stifling her.

"Would it help," she said, "if I brought the Cobweb Bride here *now*, if I *forced* her against her will to come before you? It pains me to think this way, but—I have already forced so many dead to pass on in the battlefields. . . . What is but one more already dead person? Indeed, if her death might restart the normal process of dying in the mortal world, one more normal thing, maybe it might help somehow—"

And Percy grew silent, horrified at her own ruthless thoughts in this grey monochromatic place of serenity.

But Hades continued watching her, and he slowly shook his head with its dark locks and the faint shadows of snakes. "It is too late now. . . . I can no longer *take* the Cobweb Bride in the proper way that would restart the cycle of death in the mortal world."

"What?" Percy stared in disbelief, while despair was suddenly all around, thick and palpable.

"Look at me," said the Lord of the Underworld. "I myself am fading from your world Above. Soon, Death, my mortal aspect will be no longer, and I will only be present Below in my darkest aspect."

"But how?"

"Do you see the White Bridegroom? He is gone now, quenched by the unfulfilled, unrelieved dark stage of my divine function, swallowed up by my immortal need, *darkened* out of existence. Without the White Bridegroom, other mortals can still be put to rest. But the sacred light that is the White Bridegroom is required in order to re-ignite the complete cycle of death."

"Then there is nothing that can be done?"

Hades fixed a stare of grim intensity upon Percy, and he said, "*You* can still do something. . . . My Champion, it is only *you* alone now who can put the Cobweb Bride to final rest. For you have glimpsed me as I have been once, a pure *white light* that no mortal might see without passing on—you are the only mortal who have seen me thus and have not died. You carry it inside you now, together with my power. And you can *show* her the White Bridegroom in the moment of passing."

"But—but what if I cannot do it properly?" Percy was numb with cold at the implications of what she had just heard. "What if I do it *wrong?*"

"Then she will simply be put to rest as all the others. And the natural divine function that is the cycle of death in your mortal world will still be *frozen in place*, stuck because of a small cog stopping the great machine, with nothing ever to restart it—not even all the gods put together, myself included."

"How is that possible?" Percy exclaimed in sudden anger. "Holy Lord! What manner of bizarre, idiotic world order and Divine Scheme this is, that a single act of one puny mortal such as myself can determine the fate of the rest of the world?"

At this Hades smiled. "Ah, but such is the intricacy, the complexity of the divine mystery that each *act* of each tiny *being* determines the direction and fortune of the *many*, and indeed the *all*. It is rather a perfect Divine Scheme actually, for it guarantees that nothing is ever insignificant, and everything has consequences. Every tiny motion of the tiniest mote in the infinite sea of celestial spheres and here on earth affects the rest of the universe. Some acts and motions are puny in the greater scheme of things and appear to be swallowed by the sheer size of the universe even though they ultimately affect the balance, while others—such as this one possible act set before you, Percy—might be the most important act of all. Make the choice, and you might restart death. Do nothing, and nothing will be the end result—for all."

"My mother once told me and Belle and Patty the story of Atlas who carried the Heavenly Sphere upon his shoulders," Percy mused. "And there was the hero Hercules who briefly relieved him. If I might remind you, My Lord, that while *you* might be akin to Atlas, I am definitely not Hercules—"

"I *knew* both Atlas and Hercules. And no, you're not, and neither am I," the dark God replied. "Indeed, you are yourself, and it makes you the best one to do what must be done."

"Since I am once again talking inside my own head, and all of this is not real, would you mind humoring me a bit more? Tell me where my mother is now. And my sisters, and my father! Where do the pieces of the world go when they fade and disappear?"

"Where do you think? Ah, but you know already. . . . Everything has gone to *me*. It is here, Below."

"In the Underworld? But you have told me once, Lord

Hades, that the Underworld is but a small place consisting of a house with seven rooms!"

The gaze of his eyes was causing her to experience a new vertigo. Was it his hair or snakes undulating lightly around him? Percy was quickly losing the last of her sense of reference.

"The Underworld *was* a small place, before. And now— now it has been *changed* by all the events of the mortal world. It holds more than you can imagine. And it holds less—for it too has been transformed by Persephone, my *changed* love."

Percy was blinking hard, for everything was starting to turn, and the already translucent form of Hades was fading rapidly into the universal grey.

"Go and do what you must, My Champion," he whispered. "The Cobweb Bride is your task now."

"But my mother and father are in the Underworld! And my sisters—"

"Go!"

Percy closed her eyes, feeling herself losing consciousness, and was cast out *elsewhere*.

Chapter 14

Percy came to, and saw the evening sky overhead, a tumultuous slate-blue haze through endless layers of overcast. Or maybe it was *his* eyes, the same color as the falling twilight. Everything was mixed up, her vision blurred. Beltain was holding her up to his chest, looking down at her with concern. She was lying in the snow, a few steps away from the tent, and she was so cold. . . .

"Percy!" he said, seeing her stir and open her eyes. "Oh, Percy, you are back, my girl! What happened? You stepped out of the shadows and fell down immediately!"

Percy sighed and put her hand up to Beltain's rough cheek. "I am fine," she said. "I was there—I saw him, Lord Hades."

"And?"

Percy started to rise and he assisted her gently. They stood then approached the fire.

"And . . . nothing much," she replied, sitting down in the same spot she had sat before she left to see Lord Death. She glanced around them and saw that the Count and Countess D'Arvu had already retreated inside their tent to rest. Lady Leonora however remained outside, seated not too far from the fire where their servants were having a meal. She sat, solitary, motionless, staring into the flames, or possibly beyond them.

Beltain noticed the direction of Percy's gaze. "Tell me what was said? What did the dark God tell you?"

And Percy selectively told him some of it, about
Persephone and how Hades was weakened by her. Beltain's
expression became intense and somber.

The fire crackled loudly, hissed, scattering sparks and one
of the D'Arvu servants added kindling to it.

They both looked in the direction of the noise. But in that
same moment a man soundlessly emerged from the other side of
the fire, coming from someplace in the camp.

Percy looked up and the man was familiar—raven hair,
intense features, dark eyes, demonic, in the flickering light of the
flames.

Fiomarre.

"Good evening to you," he said, standing over them.

"Vlau's brother," said Beltain. "Good evening, though to be
honest, I did not expect to see you for any reason, My Lord—or
should I call you Marquis? Considering your brother's crimes
toward the Liguon Emperor, I am not certain what salutations
apply—"

"Yes, tragic, regrettable things have been done by my poor
misguided brother, for all the right reasons," said Ebrai
Fiomarre. "May I join you?" And without waiting for an
invitation he sat down near the fire across from them, not far
from Leonora.

"My Lady." He nodded to her with courtly politeness but
Leonora did not turn her head or acknowledge him. She was a
frozen creature, and her death shadow, Percy saw, billowed
nearby like the fire's residue, an echo of vestigial smoke from
the living flames.

"So, what brings you to our fire, Lord Fiomarre?" Beltain
watched him.

Ebrai did not respond immediately. "I admit to a bit of
curiosity—this girl—" and he glanced at Percy Ayren. "I would
like to know if what the rumors say is true. Are you truly able to
put the dead to rest? Or is it a clever trick?"

"Why?" Percy was genuinely getting tired of this same question posed to her and phrased a dozen different ways, so she was rather blunt. "Why do you want to know this, My Lord? What would you have of me?"

"For myself, nothing," he replied, again after the briefest of pauses. "However, I do have someone in mind who might have need of your unusual services."

Lady Leonora flinched.

"Who?" Percy was staring at him.

Fiomarre raised one brow. "For a girl from a small village, you are very direct," he said. "Is it confidence or a bit of show? If you don't mind me asking, how old are you, Percy?"

"She may not mind, but I do." Beltain interrupted, and his face was a controlled mask that was an indicator of his anger. "What do you want, Fiomarre? If you are such a man of court, I suggest you employ some of those courtly manners about now."

"Ah, forgive me." Ebrai Fiomarre smiled, meeting Beltain's gaze without blinking. "Let me start over. *My Lady Percy*, if I might inquire—"

"And now Your Lordship is mocking me." Percy bit her lips.

"Not at all," replied Ebrai. "For if you are truly able to do what you supposedly do, then you are indeed a Lady of the noblest rank imaginable. Allow me to explain. What I have in mind, noble Percy is a task that might change the course of this war entirely."

Beltain relaxed slightly, seeing the other man's serious demeanor. "Go on."

And Fiomarre told them the truth. "Officially, in the Realm I am a dead man. Not many know this, especially here in this camp, but I have been working clandestinely on behalf of the Liguon Emperor, installed in a high position at the Sapphire Court of the Domain. In order to achieve my position near the Sovereign, and obtain a modicum of her trust, a complicated fabrication had to be perpetrated—indeed a process of many dire years, during which my family had slowly come under a semblance of disgrace, and then my Father, the real Marquis Micul Fiomarre, and I were publicly condemned as traitors by the Emperor of the Realm, sent to execution, and then discreetly exiled, so that we could flee into the arms of the enemy under the guise of political treachery. To achieve this end, the deception had to be impeccable—so much so that none of the members of our own family could be told the truth, not even my poor mother or my younger brother Vlau who decided that we had been unjustly condemned and martyred by the Emperor. No one expected such a wild act of retribution from my passionate but mild-mannered brother, but he proved us tragically wrong and killed the Emperor's own daughter."

"So that is what happened!" Percy said, remembering the strange relationship between the Infanta and Vlau.

"He has certainly changed his hatred into something else," Beltain remarked. "Your brother Vlau is now a loyal servant of Claere Liguon, indeed, her shadow."

"I think that he—*cares* about her very deeply," Percy said. "And I believe she cares about him."

"Thank you for telling me this," Ebrai's expression was hard to define. "I am somewhat relieved. But now, let me finish what must be said. As I mentioned, I have been at the Sovereign's side for months now. And I have been in her confidence—*somewhat*, for I know it is in part an overall test of my loyalty. To that order she has given me the following task. I am to deliver to her a certain girl who can put the dead to rest—*you*, Percy."

Percy felt a wash of cold come over her. She went very still.

"Yes," Ebrai continued. "The Sovereign, Rumanar Avalais, wants you for her own, Percy, and to be honest I am not clear why, unless it might mean a mark of greater power for Her Brilliance to exercise your abilities selectively over the dead of her own choosing—to be used as a threat or ultimate punishment for insubordination. She expects me to bring you to her, alive. And here is where my own clandestine layer of orders comes in—most recently the Emperor commanded me that I am no longer to bide my time, but to strike as soon as the opportunity presents itself. However, to simply assassinate the Sovereign now that all death has ceased, will do us no good. We must have her *dead* completely, and out of the game. And thus, I wanted to employ your abilities, Percy. Once I have delivered you to her under a pretence of having captured you, I would be close enough to her to strike her a mortal blow, and you would finish her off with your powers—"

"The Sovereign is *immortal*." Percy interrupted his speech and single-handedly destroyed his carefully formulated perfect assassination plan.

"What?" Ebrai sat back, stunned.

"She is the Goddess Persephone and she cannot be killed." With a tired sigh, Percy told him what they knew.

Ebrai listened, and he did not say anything for a long time. At last he whispered in a dead voice, "Well, then . . . apparently all is lost." And he simply got up, and left their fire, striding darkly into the night.

Beltain and Percy stared in his wake. Even the D'Arvu servants cast discreet stares, and Lady Leonora raised her face and looked at Percy.

There was silence and the ardor of flames.

"I have . . . decided," Leonora said softly, drawing in air for speech and crackling ice in her long unused lungs.

"My Lady Leonora, what is it?" Percy looked at her gently.

Leonora's pale lovely face was bathed by the golden reflections of firelight. "Take me to Death's side and let him have me for his Cobweb Bride!"

"My Lady!" Percy got up from her place and approached Leonora. She crouched down and took Leonora's cold hands in hers, feeling the death shadow respond by flickering wildly at her touch, like a candle flame in the wind.

"I—I can *feel* you!" Leonora said in wonder. "It is true, for oh, I feel *something* when you hold my hands! When you touched me that first time, back in San Quellenne, I pretended to myself that it was nothing, but even then, I *felt* your strange power calling me—"

"My Lady, I am afraid I can no longer take you to Lord Death. . . . But he has instructed me on how to do it properly—"

"Then *you* put me to rest, Percy Ayren. But—do it so that I do not know. Can you do it without touching me? From a distance?"

"Yes. . . ."

"Then do it!" Leonora said, and if she had not been fixed in place by the cold, her form would have been trembling. "Only, please, not tonight. . . . Allow me to have this one final night to think. And then, after the dawn comes, do it any time, at any moment, and I shall be ready for you, nor shall I begrudge you the taking of my life."

"I am so sorry," Percy looked into her eyes with compassion. "So truly sorry it has to be done—and I am *not* glad to do it, ever—but it *must* be done—"

"Yes, I know now. The world is in desperate times, and if there is anything that can make things right, even a *little*, then it is to be done." For the first time Leonora D'Arvu met Percy's eyes unflinchingly. "Please do not tell my parents we have agreed to this. And you also, I beg you to speak nothing—" and she glanced at the servants who were watching. "Let my poor parents not torture themselves with the knowledge and the waiting. When it happens, it happens."

"I promise." Percy released her hand, for the death shadow was swaying wildly, and the temptation to exercise death's power was great even in that moment. . . .

"Then it is decided and done." Lady Leonora turned her face back to stare into the fire. "Thank you, Percy Ayren," she said. "For your patience with me all these days, and for your mercy."

"And thank you, My Lady," said Percy, "for the gift of your life."

When the dawn came, they were wakened by the activity in the camp, as the Goraque soldiers were getting ready to march to the aid of Letheburg.

Percy awoke in the corner of the tent with a queasy feeling in her gut, for she had not eaten last night, having forgotten because of all the events, and now there was only the cold dawn. If not for the warm pressure of Beltain's arms around her, she would have been shivering with cold. Snow had come down overnight, almost half a foot, and it weighted down the flimsy roof of the fabric tent, so that it hung low and bumped their heads.

Percy crawled outside carefully so as not to wake anyone, and then went searching for some shrubbery to answer the call of nature. There had been no time to dig camp latrines, so most everyone had the same idea as her, and the hedgerows were busy with women and children and the elderly.

When she got back, Beltain was waiting for her, looking worried that he had somehow slept through her getting up once more, and she would now slip away from him again. At the sight of her, relief came to him like soothing balm, and he smiled at her with his eyes and his mouth.

"Go on! Take care of Jack and yourself, Beltain," she said, knowing his routine with the great warhorse.

In reply, Beltain bent to her with a quick kiss on the side of her cheek that managed to graze her lips and send a pang of electricity through her. And then he went to groom his horse and take care of personal business.

While waiting for him to return, Percy hastily chewed some hard bread and cheese and watched the camp being packed up. It was absolute chaos. About fifty feet away the refugees from San

Quellenne were getting ready to move also, and everyone rushed about, overloaded donkeys unused to the cold stumbled in the snow, while tanned peasants swaddled in several layers of far-too-thin fabric looked miserable.

Would they have been any more miserable, it occurred to Percy, had they simply stayed behind in their homeland and disappeared into the Underworld?

She glanced about and saw formations of infantry lining up, mail-clad cavalry knights mounting on their armored horses, and hastily eaten dry meals gulped down at all the campfires, washed down by weak bark tea.

Where are we going? she thought. *Are these poor people going to be fighting the Trovadii? It will be slaughter. . . .*

And then she thought, *Will I have strength enough to put down so many dead to their final rest, in order to give these living men a fighting chance?*

The next moment she saw Lady Leonora.

Or I can simply take care of the Cobweb Bride. Do it now, swiftly. . . . If I take her—right now—will all those who are dead already fall like dominoes? With one single act that restarts death, would it put them all to rest? Or would it still require a great mass effort of will to kill them, each one by one—

"Percy Ayren!"

Lady Jelavie San Quellenne approached, wearing her full suit of armor, and her sword. Her helm was held in the crook of one arm, but her bronze-red head of hair was covered by a tightly-fitting coif hood of chain mail. The oval of her face that was bared to the elements was already reddened from the cold, and the expression of her brown eyes, sharp as daggers.

Percy turned to her. "Good morning, My Lady—"

"It is a foul morning. Where is he?"

"Who?"

"Your fearsome knave, paramour—whatever you would have me call it—the Black Knight! He is wanted by the Duke in the main tent, for they are discussing last minute field assignments—"

"He is tending his warhorse, Jack, right over there—"

Suddenly there were screams coming from beyond the trees to the south. Screams, followed by running men, women and children, and harsh cries of soldiers, and the clanging of steel . . . and the beat of approaching drums.

"Trovadii! We have been seen! They are coming!"

Lady Jelavie whirled around and drew steel. She held a long powerful sword in both hands, balancing with her feet in the snow, and took a graceful step forward to shield Percy.

"To Arms! To Arms!" the cries of Goraque sergeants and commanders echoed throughout the campsite. "Goraque, to Arms!"

There were flashes of pomegranate red up ahead, and bristling long pikes moving relentlessly forward.

Percy stood in place, staring. She saw the running women and the ground churning underneath their feet, the crawling dead. . . .

In the next instant, Beltain was there, his own great sword drawn, and Jack on a lead behind him.

"Percy!" he exclaimed, and then seeing her safe, his face showed relief. Seeing the Lady San Quellenne with her sword bared, he gave her a quick nod of gratitude.

"The Duke wanted to see you . . . in the war tent, My Lord!" Jelavie blurted. "But now, now it matters no longer, for the fight is upon us!"

"Mount up!" Beltain exclaimed, and in the next moment he was in the saddle, and then pulling up Percy before him.

Lady Jelavie nodded, then ran for her own grey warhorse a few feet away. She flew up into the saddle with the lightness of an experienced rider, and then she was away toward the Tanathe fires to assist her people.

Percy was squeezed against Beltain's chest, and he was hastily moving his vambrace-clad arms, adjusting his armor plates and pulling his shield up, while the flashes of red in the sparse trees drew nearer.

"Percy, hang on . . . yes, hold your hands here on the armor rings—"

And then they were galloping.

"Fall back!" A small group of Goraque knights, about half a dozen, came bursting through past a snowy rise, from the other side of the camp, kicking up snow, and then one warhorse stumbled, screaming, almost falling over the moving limbs of the dead that emerged from the snow. The knight hung on, but just barely. . . .

Percy reached out with her death sense, and the forest rang in her mind, and everything was familiar tolling darkness. She could feel them, individual deaths of the oncoming Trovadii, and the ones crawling underneath the snow.

She plucked them, like strings, testing them, in the vicinity of about thirty feet around them. And then a thought came to her—now would be a good time to try the act of granting death, only accompanied with the vision of white light and the White Bridegroom. Indeed, why did she not think of it before? Here was a chance to test her ability to do it correctly, before she tried it upon the Cobweb Bride. . . .

Percy reached for a random dead man, a foot soldier wearing the red of blood, and she took his death shadow, and as she guided it into his corpse she visualized Lord Death in blinding white—

There was a strange retinal flash in her own vision, and for a moment Percy was *blinded*, both physically and on the inside, in her death sense.

It flared and sputtered, and instead of putting the dead man to his final rest, he was released from her mind's grasp like a wooden puppet and then continued exactly as he was, moving forward in formation, holding his long heavy pike before him. . . .

It was not working!

Percy's heart began to pound in her temples.

Beltain noticed her intent stare, noticed there was something wrong, because she almost ceased breathing.

"Are you all right? What happened?" he spoke in her ear, while directing Jack over craggy areas covered with snow and shrubbery.

"I—" Percy could not speak.

People in the camp were running, foot soldiers and villagers, and dogs scrambling from underfoot, away from the great warhorse. A woman holding up her old mother stumbled, and was lifted up by two Goraque infantrymen, and then they pushed past the women, onward.

Beltain carefully circled back about a hundred feet, taking them to the original place they had camped, and just in time, for the Count D'Arvu and his family were in danger from an approaching tight formation of the enemy.

"What now?" Percy managed to speak, her head reeling. "Oh, Beltain, we need to make sure of Leonora's safety! Nothing must happen to her, not until I can put her to rest properly! She must not be harmed!"

And then she blurted out to him the rest of what had happened at Death's Keep, and how Death was too week to do the deed and it was up to her.

Beltain listened grimly then nodded, saying, "Fear not, we'll look after her. . . ."

He stopped Jack before the Count and Countess and Leonora, who were huddled together with their servants and a small group of the San Quellenne.

"Set me down . . ." whispered Percy. "I'll only be in your way as you fight."

"But I cannot protect you if you—"

"Set me down, Beltain! I'll protect them my own way, and I'll protect *you* also!"

"Damn it to Hell!" Beltain exhaled in grim intensity. And

then he looked at Percy with a hard impossible gaze, and he gently helped her down from the saddle.

"Be careful! Stay together, all of you! Do not move from this spot!" His baritone rang, and he turned to face the oncoming Trovadii.

Percy stumbled slightly in the snow, then came to stand before Leonora and her parents, and she gave them a brief reassuring smile. "The Black Knight has never been beaten in battle . . ." she said. "He will protect us all!"

While I will protect him. . . .

Count Lecrant was not a fighting man, but he drew out a short gentleman's sword. "If it comes to it, I will try to do my best to protect you also."

But Percy was barely listening. She tentatively reached out with her death sense, for she could feel them all around, encroaching, the thousands upon thousands and more beyond the trees. She had to make sure she still had the means to do what had to be done, with or without the white light searing her mind.

A dead man's arm burst through the snow directly at their feet, and Lady Arabella stifled a cry.

Percy reached for him in her old way, and she easily plucked the death shadow and stuffed it into the cold dead flesh.

The dead man ceased moving, was a cold lifeless thing.

But in that same instant she felt someone reach out to her from a distance, in the same manner as she reached out to the dead.

Only this was a living touch, and one she had known once before.

Persephone!

The dark Goddess was inside her mind.

All morning and afternoon Letheburg was besieged by the forces of winter, heavy relentless storm winds and overcast dark grey skies—although it was notably odd that the cold had lessened almost overnight, and the snow started melting all along the rooftops, clinging impossibly to all surfaces despite the gale force wind blowing upon it. . . .

Whatever it was, King Roland Osenni of Lethe had had quite enough.

After what had transpired on the battlements, and the other impossible strange events still happening below—massing armies, goddesses out of classical mythology, flashes of lighting, light-radiating golden figures, darkness-exuding shadowed figures, inexplicable elemental weather patterns and—and, oh yes indeed, the revelation of that flibbertigibbet and meddler Grial as the Goddess Hecate, followed by *his own* magical ascension up into the air like one of the blessed angels—His Majesty swiftly ordered his guards to get him "as far away as possible from the unnatural sorcery and madness" as he called it.

Thus he hastily left the large bulwark where he had seen Grial, or, blast her, Hecate, *create* two new deities out of the Infanta of the Realm and that infernal marquis who had killed her and now followed her around like a lovelorn hound—for yes, the King had his suspicions in that direction. . . . And then the two of them, all sparkling white and very much immortal, disappeared somewhere, while Grial—that is, Hecate—gave the King a nod and told him to have a lovely afternoon, and then disappeared also. . . .

King Roland Osenni moved carefully along the parapet walkway, keeping to the inside of the safety barrier, and was about to start his careful descent from the walls along the snowed-over slippery stairs (with a guard directly behind and two in front in case he fell) when a strange deep rumble sounded for leagues around.

The deep bass sound was so low that it felt as if a mountain had scraped its foundation against rock and had shifted and settled into a new location. It sent up black specks of winter birds screaming up into the skies.

At the same time, the heavens overhead—late afternoon,

but already as dark as evening—seemed to reflect the passing of a great sky-sized shadow sweeping across its cloud-covered sphere. For a few moments the layers of storm cloud thick as cotton shimmered with an unnatural chromatic iridescence, and then it was gone.

Alarmed exclamations of patrolling soldiers resounded all around the battlements.

"Your Majesty!" One of his captains was on the top of the stair, and he was pointing outside the walls. "Wait, Your Majesty! You might want to see this!"

The King grunted, and then turned around with a sinking feeling in his gut, and started back up the few slippery stairs that he had descended. A soldier offered him the spyglass, and the King was assisted onto another raised spot on the walkway that was higher up, so that he could look out without crossing the magical safety barrier in the middle. "What is it that I am looking at? What was that horrendous sound?"

But he peered through the telescope lens, and he stopped breathing.

Beyond the outer walls of Letheburg, where moments ago had been a plain covered with Trovadii pomegranate color and endless enemy army formations unto the horizon, only about two hundred feet away now hulked a strange massive shape cast in shadow, vaguely granite or possibly cream-yellow chalk slate. It resembled a mountain in the mist, a mountain with its top flattened or cut off to form a plateau, which—as he swept the spyglass across—seemed to have strange regular man-made demarcations on the top, that very much resembled crenels and merlons of a great city bulwark and battlements similar to those of Letheburg itself. . . .

Roland Osenni's mind attempted to process the sensory information that his eyes provided, but frankly it was incomprehensible. "What is it?" he muttered. "That thing! What is it that I see? A mirage? A reflection of our own walls? Would someone tell me *what is out there?* And where did it come from?" His voice ended in a yell.

A soldier nearby, also peering through a spyglass, said, "This is very hard to believe, Your Majesty, but I think that's the actual outer walls of the citadel at Silver Court. I recognize the shape of the parapets and beyond it some of the interior landmarks in the distance. . . . There's the dome of the Basilica Dei Coello—"

"What?" the King roared. "Are you telling me that's *Silver Court* out there? That His Imperial Majesty's Silver Court is sitting right outside the walls of Letheburg, together with our blessed Emperor of the Realm?"

"It appears so, Your Majesty."

"What in Hell or Heaven is going on? How? How did it get here?"

"Well, Majesty, considering that the city streets and other parts of the world have been disappearing everywhere, maybe the land between here and there has simply . . . faded away."

The King set down the spyglass, then turned around, and climbed back down from the raised part of the walls. "All right. Put an additional patrol on watch duty, and observe this— whatever the hell it is," he muttered. "Meanwhile, I need to go lie down for a while and think. . . . And have a few glasses of brandy and whisky and maybe top it off with cream liqueur, and then maybe whatever in blazes the Palace cooks have made for supper." He started walking back down the parapet stairs again. Then added loudly, without turning, "But do keep me informed. If anything *else* happens."

The peculiar lukewarm storm winter winds continued blowing through Letheburg well into the evening and night, interrupted at some point by a soft lovely snowfall, then resumed again. And then, about four hours after midnight and very close to dawn, another horrific grating *noise* was heard, and this time it felt like an earthquake had quaked the firmament and the ground all around the city. Or possibly, it felt as if a very large object *collided* with Letheburg.

It was unclear what had happened, but the source of the disturbance came from the direction of the southern walls. Garrison soldiers ran to investigate and report back, but in the ensuing confusion they were distracted by yet a *second* horrendous noise, a true sonic boom, that not only quaked the earth for leagues all around, but seemed to have originated slightly southeast of the city walls.

In the windy darkness of the night, spyglasses were nearly useless, but they were trained in all directions nevertheless, by ranking officers, while frantically confused soldiers stood ready with bared blades, muskets, pikes, tar and pitch and torches ready to be lit, and whatever else was at hand.

After straining their telescopes into the darkness, they noticed small flickering lights of torches a few hundred feet away, strung out across horizontally like beads on a necklace. And as the thick cloud cover was unrelieved, it was impossible to verify whether or not another large hulking shape had grown out of nowhere just outside the walls.

"Ahoy there!" someone from the Letheburg battlements finally cried out.

"Ahoy yourself!" came from about a hundred feet away. "Identify yourselves!"

"You identify yourselves, villain! Are ye dead men?"

"Do I sound like a dead man, sirrah?" came from the south.

"How the hell different does a dead man sound?"

Across the black expanse of night, pinpoints of lights that were distant torches flickered, at approximate eye-level of the soldiers on top of the city walls. The lights seemed to be spread in dots all across the south and southeast, suggesting other walls where earlier in the day there had been only sky.

"Well?" the Letheburg soldier persisted. "Answer now, ye flaming whoreson!"

"I bite my thumb at you!" came from the south.

"What foul-mouthed magic is this?" came another voice, even more distant, this one about a hundred-fifty feet away from the southwest. "Who *are* you people?"

But before anyone could reply, in the pre-dawn murk, another terrifying scrape and boom sounded, and this time the walls of Letheburg shook from the impact.

Patrol soldiers up on the battlements witnessed an unbelievable moment of translucence and dissolution along a portion of the parapets walkway for about thirty feet, as the walkway was swept away from under their feet—and a few misfortunate men stumbled and fell, both from the outer and inner walls like tiny toy soldiers. And then, as they rushed back from the place that was collapsing, dissolving, in the same spot they saw new walls rise—walls a few feet taller than the level of the Letheburg parapets—and these were wrought of a different kind of stone.

There was a godawful scrape, as the strange walls wedged themselves in a circular manner into the break of the Letheburg walls, settling with a deep rumble, sending up snow powder raining from all the tops of the nearby merlons.

And then there was abysmal silence.

Soldiers wearing the cobalt blue uniforms of Letheburg stared up in horrified disbelief, as just a few feet before them, along the newly formed section of wall, a patrol of Silver Court guards wearing the Imperial black and silver with a fine trim of red and gold pointed muzzles of their muskets directly down at them.

But that was not the worst of it.

"The safety barrier!" a Letheburg soldier cried, as several lurching dead figures moved in at him from the outside walls, unhindered by any protective wards of sorcery. "It appears to be gone!"

Percy felt the dark Goddess Persephone inside her mind. It was an intimate touch that held the innermost part of her like a vulnerable living marionette, within the cruel hand of the Goddess. The thing that held her was a terrible dark *intelligence*.

You are mine.

What will you do now, mortal girl child?

Percy knew pressure, overwhelming, stifling, followed by a burst of panic. Her spirit struggled, for the psychic touch surrounding her was full of numbing cold and grating corrosion and there was an even deeper layer of pain beyond, and its color was pitch-black. . . .

Indeed, pain was *her* domain—pain strung along a continuum leading to dark pleasure—and deeper yet, empty hollow silence within walls of sociopath logic and hard soulless reason. No mercy or compassion. . . . No awe or wonder.

Negation of all.

The Goddess was the sickness of grief interspersed with fury at *something* inexplicable. She was hatred and disdain for *all else* that was not herself.

"I am not yours!" Percy cried in the desperate quicksand of her mind, feeling herself choking on the claustrophobic oppression pressing in around her . . . and suddenly she was falling deep. . . .

It was completely unlike Lord Death's serene grey place that was separate unto itself. This was not a separate realm but a translucent *layer* of internal corruption superimposed upon her present field of vision—shadow detritus, tangled, twisted threads turning aimlessly upon themselves in futility, and filaments of befouled silk.

Cobwebs of despair. . . .

Percy had not been transported into another place. Rather, she was still present in the mortal world—standing in the snow-covered forest in the middle of the Goraque camp and surrounded by the chaos of the Trovadii attack.

But she now observed the world though a decadent filter of

depression and corruption, an overlay of *wrongness* that was the dark inverted Goddess, taking residence inside her.

You are mine, little girl. For you bear a mark bestowed by my dark love, and you bear my own name. All that has been his is now mine. You are mine completely. . . .

"No," Percy said, "I am not. Get out of my mind!" And she struggled with white-hot passion, but it was like moving through molasses that thickened with every step.

You will be my instrument in the new mortal world when this one falls. I shall forge it with him who now waits Below, and I shall rise Above, bringing him up, and you will rise with me, my priestess.

"You will not succeed," said Percy, "because your will is an aberration, and you do not command me." And then she saw, through the overlay of wrongness, two beautiful sky-blue eyes that resided in her inner field of vision, as though she was looking at Persephone eye-to-eye, inches away, and the other was looking at her, both of them poised upon the brink of the other like drops upon the surface of a mirror.

I have succeeded already, said the broken Goddess. *For now you may not use the power given you by Death without my will. Every death you take, you will regret. For every act of putting dead mortal things to final rest, I will take mortal lives and grant them death.*

"No! You are lying."

Disobey me and see. Oh, but do come, test me, little mortal who bears my name and boasts of free will! For oh, even now, how I long to add to the ranks of my dead armies. . . .

Percy felt her mind resound with the echo of despair and joyful rage that rang through her like distorted bells, dissonant tolls of discord.

It was the Goddess laughing.

I will take everything from you, mortal child. Everything that is you, and everything that you love. Give me a reason!

"You have are already taken away most of my world . . ." Percy said softly in her mind.

Ah, but it is only the beginning! I will break you and reforge you into my instrument, and you will be sharp and ruthless and you will cut like the edge of a blade.

You will be my *Champion.*

And the next instant Percy was free—free of the hold, and back inside her own mind's walls, and Persephone's presence was gone, for the moment.

"Percy! Bless you, girl, you did it!"

The Count and Countess were calling her name, for the burly dead man who had come through the snow at them was now a true fallen corpse. "Thank goodness!" Countess Arabella exclaimed. "For the dead soldier was about to turn on us. . . . Are you all right, dear child?"

"I—I just saw *her*," Percy said, blinking, breathing hard, yet leaden with despair. "I saw Persephone, or the one you know as the Sovereign. She spoke horrible things in my head. And now—now I am afraid—I cannot do this thing again now, not until I know—"

"What thing? What do you mean, Percy?" They stared at her, fear in their eyes.

"It means, I cannot put the dead to rest, I cannot defend you!" Percy said bitterly. "Not any of you! Else she will take other lives in exchange!"

Chapter 15

Winter dawn came over Letheburg, sweeping softly from the east, and the winds did not abate, and neither did the overcast.

From the thicket of infinite layers of grey, the dome of sky pressed down upon a strange scene of mortal battle below.

Three citadels stood in the plain. Three great walled cities, each framed in invincible stone.

Letheburg was now physically wedded to the Silver Court—the grand citadel that was the heart of the Realm—jammed stone into stone. And the closed circle of Letheburg's walls, and its supernatural safety ward, was thus broken.

Just to the east, beyond these two, stood a third city, a mere hundred feet away, its own magnificent walls rising eye-level to the other two. This was the Sapphire Court of the Domain, standing flush next to the heart of the Realm, having arrived deep in the night, just before dawn. . . .

All that was left of both countries now was but the sparse northern Lethe forest just a handful of miles north, a tiny sliver of the River Styx to the west, no more than three miles away . . . and less than a league south, was the encroaching sea.

Inside Letheburg, snow was melting, for the winter was mild near the Mediterranean, and the weather that had spanned the former Realm and Domain lands closest to it was a wide contrast of mild and continental climates. Winter had nowhere to go, and yet, here it had to stay. . . .

Outside the walls of the three cities, on the plain below, the Trovadii armies of the dead stormed Letheburg, for it had no more defenses left. Men were fighting in chaotic melees and once again the great siege machines of war went to work, catapults hurling boulders and flaming pitch into the city.

In less than an hour after the fall of the magical barrier, the gates of Letheburg were forced open.

When the First Army of the Trovadii under the leadership of Field Marshal Claude Maetra poured into the open gates after the battering ram, rivers of blood flowed, as the living soldiers fiercely defended their city.

In the wake of the First Army, came the dark Goddess.

She walked on foot, wearing her silver-steel immortal aspect, and her sandals left red bloody marks upon the snow as she passed the open gates. . . .

And then, Persephone faded into thin air, for now she could move as swiftly as she pleased.

She was gone in the blink of an eye, hurtling toward the heart of the city.

Hecate sat in her rocking chair in the front parlor of Grial's living room with its cheerful chintz curtains. The windows outside were bluish with dawn.

The girls had just finished rolling the dough for the latest batch of "military pies" as Lizabette was starting to call the apple tarts they made for the city soldiers. Marie and Catrine were cutting apples and stirring the cinnamon sauce for the filling, while Niosta washed a pile of dishes from their hasty breakfast, in a large washing cauldron. Faeline had set the teakettle to boiling, for the fire was cheerful and everyone could use a second cup on this chilly morning.

At some point, as the distant noises from the outer portions of the city grew prominent, Hecate stopped rocking. She then sighed and listened, and then she transformed from comfortable dingy Grial to her divine goddess aspect.

"Ladies!" Hecate said in her sonorous loud voice. "Stop doing everything and anything you are doing and come here! Quickly now, pumpkins!"

Hearing her voice, the girls obeyed instantly, and Lizabette came running first, with flour in her hair and on the tip of her nose. "Yes, Your Divine—I mean, Grial?"

Hecate, seated very still in the rocking chair, hands on the wooden armrests, turned her very dark gaze upon Lizabette and the others as they came into the parlor one by one. All except for Catrine, who was still in the kitchen, wiping apple and cinnamon off her face with a wet towel and scrubbing her forehead.

"Catrine! Get your skinny arse here, sis!" Niosta hollered then cleared her throat in mild embarrassment before the Grecian Goddess, of whom, to be honest, she was no longer as particularly frightened as she ought to have been.

"All here, girlies?" Hecate was looking at them with her wise Grial eyes. "Now then. This is very important. . . . Listen to me very carefully. I want you to put your warm winter clothes on as quickly as you can, all of you. And then, take a few baskets of pies and cheese, load 'em up with whatever's easiest—"

"Are we going to feed the soldiers at the walls now, Grial?" Marie asked.

"No, duckie, unfortunately not this time. Once you are ready, I want you to go outside this house . . . and then I want you to *run* as fast and as far as you can. Run, and do not look back! And do not return here! Not unless I come and get you, wherever you might be. And no, do *not* tell me!"

"Oh! But why?" The girls began speaking in troubled voices.

"Because, my dears, *she* is coming. The one who is Persephone."

"You mean she's coming *here?*" Niosta's eyes got very big.

"Yes."

The room became chaos. Squealing girls went running all over, gathering clothes, pulling on scarves and coats and snow shoes, and Lizabette fled to the kitchen to throw random pantry food items into baskets. In a few minutes they were ready, and Hecate, still seated in her chair, nodded to them as they headed for the front door.

Marie paused at the door and threw her a frightened glance. "Grial . . . will *you* be all right?"

Hecate looked at her with a gaze of wisdom, and her dark eyes suddenly seemed very warm. "Don't you worry about me, sweetie, you just stay safe and out of the way! Promise me!"

Marie nodded, and Catrine and the others stared in awe-filled wonder at Hecate from the door.

"Would—would you like me to bank the fire for you, Hec—Grial? And take the kettle off, so that it doesn't boil over? Since you, well, you may not get up from that rocking chair—I know you may not—" Lizabette was looking at Grial with liquid eyes.

"Yes, dear girl. That would be very kind of you." Hecate nodded to Lizabette, and a faint shadow of a smile came to her immortal face.

Lizabette rushed to the kitchen to do the tasks, hastily wiping her nose and the single wet trail on her cheek.

When she was done, the girls rushed outside, and they heard Hecate say, "Shut the door, but don't lock it, my dears. And oh, if you need any help out there, be sure to call upon the Snow Maiden and Jack Frost! Now, off you go, with all my love!"

The light turned pale blue and the icicles were melting on all the buildings on Rollins Way when Persephone, dark Goddess, stepped out of the shadows and into being before a freshly painted red door underneath a cheerful crooked shingle.

Persephone stood before the red door and opened it with a mere look.

The door swung open with a creak, and the Goddess of the Underworld entered the slightly warmer interior, stepping past a window dressed with chintz curtains and through the entrance into Hecate's house.

Hecate sat rocking in the wooden chair.

Persephone heard the regular creak-creak sound from the parlor as her metal sandals stepped in silence upon the floorboards and the parlor rug. She paused only a moment, then approached.

"Hecate, my sister . . ." Persephone said. "What a quaint little home you have among the mortals."

"Good morning, Persephone, my sister." From her seat in the corner, Hecate raised her serene face at the dark Goddess. "It serves me well. And I rather like it."

"What have you been doing since the time that I've seen you last? When I gave you a little glazed blue jar and told you to hold on to it with all your being?"

"I am afraid I no longer have the glazed blue jar," said Hecate. "But then you don't really mind, do you?"

Persephone smiled. "No," she said, "No, I don't."

Hecate continued rocking in the chair.

"Will you not ask me, sister dear, what brings me here?"

"From the sounds outside, I can hear the city being sacked. No need to ask, though I would be remiss in my hospitality if I did not offer you a cup of tea. It is my favorite of all the mortal brews, almost as cheerful as a drop of ambrosia."

"I believe I will abstain," Persephone said, taking a step closer and looking down into Hecate's very dark, very wise eyes.

"Your Trovadii are very thorough, especially now that they are dead. Tell me, do you plan to leave anything unturned, or will you raze Letheburg to the ground?"

"I have not decided yet. It depends—on you."

"How so, my immortal sister?"

A strange expression replaced Persephone's neutral gaze. Her eyes, blue as summer skies, darkened several shades and changed hue to a deep brown with a shadow of black, the color of rich fallow earth and occult colorless places underneath the roots of ancient trees. At the same time the shadows in the corners of the room seemed to acquire more dimensions and solidity.

But Hecate turned her head slightly to the side, and there was a bloom of radiance in the parlor, as though the moon showed its face indoors and painted the walls with a brief ethereal glimmer.

"Do not tarry with me, Lady of the Crossroads." Persephone's gaze was black fire. "You will *rise* from the Throne upon which you sit, and you will surrender it to my will. Do it willingly, and I shall spare you and favor you in the new mortal world order that comes soon after. . . ."

"Is that so?" Hecate's immortal lips moved into a light smile. "Would you perchance like a freshly baked apple tart to go with it?"

Thunder struck indoors, and it was the *voice* of the dark Goddess.

"Rise before me now!"

"Not a chance, dumpling. You always had a bit of a temper in you, as the Mother of Bright Harvest likes to call it."

Persephone's rage was the force of a storm. The room began to shake, and the furniture and all the objects within it rumbled, as though in an earthquake, jumping and sliding along the flat surfaces, while knick-knacks trembled on shelves and the chintz curtains shook, flapping wildly, in a rising indoor wind.

The wind was gale-force and the objects were soon airborne, hurling themselves at Hecate who was still seated in the rocking chair that had now gone very still. Nothing seemed to land on her or hit her, but the tendrils of her shadow-silver hair escaped from her neatly braided crown, and her eyes were fixed with effort.

"Get up!" Persephone shrieked and leaned forward, reaching with her hands for Hecate, in an attempt to pull her out of her chair.

"Sit down!" Hecate said suddenly in her ringing sonorous voice. And in the next blink Persephone found herself picked up by an invisible force and slammed bodily against the nearest sofa and forced in a reclining position against the chintz pillows—and Hecate did not move an inch from her spot.

In response Persephone clutched the pillows around her and laughed. "Ah, Hecate, but you are so much weaker than I am! You cannot keep this up, not for much longer."

"Well, we'll just have to hope that your mother arrives before anything else is broken, and we can all have a civilized conversation." Hecate again raised her voice and called, "Demeter! Come, O Thesmos, Mother of Bright Harvest!"

The room filled with golden light, and in the next breath Demeter, statuesque and warm like the harvest sun stood in the middle of the front parlor. Demeter's countenance however was grave with sorrow. The flying objects in the room momentarily settled back down, many of the fragile items crashing hard against the floor and shattering into shards of broken china.

Hecate shook her head in regret at the mess in the room. "Ah, there you are," she addressed Demeter, as though Persephone was not present. "Where have you been, blessed sister?"

Demeter glanced bitterly at her daughter, seated on the sofa in a fixed posture. "I have been consulting with the other gods in Olympus," she said. "And our worst fears are justified. Because of what my daughter has *become*, the mortal world, as it is, is irrevocably broken. Even if, or when, the cycle of death resumes, the cycle of new life and resurrection cannot be reinstated."

"Then why let any of it bother you, Mother of mine?" Persephone said from her reclined position. "Let this mortal world fall, and we will make another—or *I* will make another according to how I please. For you know that in this present scheme of things not even Olympus can stand against me. Indeed, I should thank all of you for it—for it is *you*, infinitely blessed immortals, who have assigned to me this accursed divine function and hence given me this ultimate power over all of you. And now, you have only yourselves to blame. Come, laugh with me, for I find it rather amusing."

"Ah, Persephone, my poor daughter. I can only weep."

"Well then, weep, Mother of mine. But do sit down at my side, and let us be 'civilized,' as Hecate would like us to be— that is, while we wait long enough for Hecate's strength to fail her so that I might get up and proceed with my business here."

Demeter sighed and sat down next to Persephone, casting her gilded aura against the upholstery.

From the outside came the noise of soldiers running through the streets and the clash of metal and the screams of the mortally wounded who now could not die.

"Can you not remember what it was like to feel compassion?" Demeter said.

"I remember being miserable." Persephone stretched luxuriously. "And now, I feel delightful because I feel *nothing*."

There was liquid brimming in Demeter's eyes. "What of the ashes of your own shadow child? Does the memory of Melinoë bring anything to you? Does it not touch your heart?"

Persephone slowly turned her head to look at Demeter and the room started to darken once again. "Speak not, Mother, else I will once again cover you with cobwebs of mortality and you will sleep a long sleep filled with endless dreams, while you grow brittle and diminish—"

"Is that what you've done to me the last time? Why, child? What kind of hatred can you bear that would cause you to do this dark thing to me, alongside those poor mortal maidens?"

"Ah, but you do not remember now, Mother of mine. . . . No, you do not. . . . In the same way you have wanted to take away my memory of *her*—how does it feel, not to *remember?*"

"But it was done only to ease your grief! Hades and I and all the gods could not bear to see you thus any longer, not after a hundred mortal years of grief—for that is how long it has been— and you were neglecting your divine function—not willingly, for you were always true, but your creative strength of life and regeneration was failing you. . . . And the vitality of the mortal world was poorer for it. It was best for you to forget—"

"Let me tell you a secret—I have not been *grieving*—I've been gathering power for a hundred years, taking the life force of so many, reaping my own Spring Harvest from the maidens whom I've visited since their childhood . . . softly, gently, taking a tiny droplet from them every time . . . a ghostly kiss, a faint breath . . . weaving it into filaments of power, draining their mortal flesh of every last spark of energy over the years. . . . Oh, the sweetness of the life force! This same life force that I've been bringing into the world every time I arrived Above, why, it is only right that it is mine to do with as I please! Indeed, I have learned so much over these hundred years, Mother! So much of what I can really *do!*"

"And yet you cannot do the one thing you want, which is to resurrect your daughter in the world Above, for it is against the fundamental laws of being! Had we but known you were doing this, working on such an abomination, we might have stopped you earlier!"

Persephone gazed at her divine mother with intense hatred. "Ah, but you never could stop me! For instead I have made the Cobweb Bride! Now death itself is bound to my whim, and all the souls that cannot pass on are fixed in the mortal world, and with them is the life energy! It stays here at my disposal, no longer to be dissipated and recycled—instead it is all mine!"

Demeter looked at her with horror. "Is that what your really want, daughter? You want to wield your own power of life and death and reject your divine function?"

"I want to rule life and death, yes—without the *sacrifice*."

"But it is impossible! You know it cannot be done!"

Persephone smiled a fey smile. "It is done already."

Demeter shook her head in disbelief. "We wanted to heal you gently by making you forget, by taking away your pain and grief. Instead you have spread your soul's contagion into the fabric of the mortal world. . . ."

"You had *no right!* No right to take away the only thing I had left of her!" Persephone's face of perfect beauty was despoiled by a twisted expression of agony. "But oh, I speak not only of my memories of my sweet shadow child—I speak of what was done to her *ashes!*"

"Persephone . . ." said Hecate from her rocking chair. "It is time you tell us what has happened really. "What is it that you speak of? Where are Melinoë's ashes?"

But Persephone raised her hand and pointed it at her mother. "She! She has taken them!"

Demeter looked back at her without comprehension. "My child, as far as I recall, I merely took the real box of ashes from my shrine at Ulpheo where you hid them away for a hundred years, but only to keep them safe—"

"*No!* You took them and you—"

Persephone's anguished voice failed, and instead there was again a storm in the room, and everything started flying.

"What?" Hecate said loudly above the wind. "What has happened? What has the Mother of Bright Harvest done?"

"Tell me!" Demeter uttered, tears streaking the curves of her face. "Once and for all, tell me what it is that I have done that I do not remember and for which you hate and punish me so!"

"You took Melinoë's ashes and you scattered them . . . to the four winds . . . in the world Above."

And then there was absolute silence.

Persephone sat with her hands folded, and her face was dead.

Demeter's lips parted and then trembled. "No . . ." she said. "I could not have done such a thing. No. . . . for I know better than to bring *something* from Below into the world Above and permanently leave it there—thus, no! It is impossible!"

"But you *didn't* know better, Mother of mine . . ." Persephone continued in a voice of driftwood and fallen leaves. "You have just drank the water of Lethe, and you were fresh-minded and clean as a slate and innocent of the many truths of the immortal world just yet, as you were slowly recovering the knowledge of your divine function and little else. . . . It was then that I had taken you swiftly from Ulpheo to the Palace of the Sun—while you were still innocent enough not to resist or protest my will—and I made you sit on the Sapphire Throne and use your powers of the Bright Harvest to attempt to revive Melinoë. You focused your golden radiance upon the ashes, filling the Hall with impossible light, but even so the effort failed . . . Melinoë remained dead. Instead, this attempt of yours broke the Sapphire Throne completely!

"For yes, when I first brought Melinoë to the world Above, killing her in the process, the Throne attained its first hairline crack. . . . But it still worked to transport me to the Underworld and back for a hundred years, each time, admittedly, making me less of myself, leaching me of the fullness of my true being. Even before I decided to drink the three swallows of the cursed water of Lethe just this season, I was already *different*, much reshaped. I have been transformed enough, over the decades of repeatedly using the imperfect Sapphire Throne, to already be *someone else*. But then you broke the Throne completely, and it infuriated me. Furthermore, you were going to try again with Melinoë—or so you told me—and when next I turned to look, you were gone!

"I should forgive you for your innocence alone, back then,

only I cannot. For you knew enough to know how much it meant to me—the very sight of those ashes was precious to me, and yet you took them away, and you stole from me the only means of recreating my daughter!"

"No!"

"In an act of rash folly, from the loftiest vantage point of the city of Ulpheo, you have cast her to the winds—first calling upon the golden force of the sun and your own divine power to imbue the ashes with life. And when it failed to work yet again, you were taken with unholy exuberance. This time you called upon the winds, telling them to carry her as far as the ends of the Realm and the Domain in both directions, as you stood up on the tallest roof in Ulpheo, reveling in your newly rediscovered immortal powers, as you commanded the winds to obey! I had arrived too late to prevent you but not too late to witness the beloved ashes floating like black snow in the wind. . . ."

"And thus," Hecate mused, "it explains why the mortal world is fading. . . . An atrocity against the world has been committed inadvertently. A thing of Below forced to remain Above. Melinoë is a child of the Underworld, and neither she nor her remains are permitted Above—they cannot be stored or left upon the earth. And now—"

"And now the earth itself is being pulled down, taken Below, heavy with the weight of her subterranean ashes that have covered every place that the wind flies, within the borders of these Kingdoms." Demeter spoke in despair. "And I have done this thing!"

"Yes, Mother. *You* have done it all yourself, and the blame rests upon your pretty golden head. But not all is lost! As soon as all the earth laden with her ashes and all the incidental mortal refuse that it contains returns to the Underworld, I will gather them from Below and recreate her, my beloved child."

"It is why you wish to return to the Underworld!"

"It is one of several reasons."

"No," Hecate mused, "there is something wrong here in

what you say, something else you have not yet admitted—"

"Enough!" And with that Persephone stood up suddenly, and Hecate felt herself frozen in place, while a powerful force was directed at her, and she had to put all of her immortal strength into remaining seated upon the wooden chair.

Persephone turned to Demeter with a countenance of immortal evil—so empty, so dark and cold that no ice in the world could match it, no light could ever escape its gaping maw. "It is best that you leave now, Mother of mine."

And she gestured forcefully with her right hand, sending a bolt of power at Demeter, which then cast her out *elsewhere.*

"Now, sister Hecate." Persephone returned her attention to the other goddess, for they were alone in the room. "Now you will stand and give up your Throne."

Persephone turned her palm up, and upon it grew a soft shimmer of life energy. It thickened within a span of moments, took on physical shape, and became . . . cobwebs.

Chapter 16

Percy Ayren stood in the snow-covered forest, holding a farmer's pitchfork. Her mind was crawling with the corruption and darkness that was the dark Goddess, always at the edge of her mind now, whispering, whispering. . . .

They had fallen back, in a large group of ordinary peasants and townsmen, a mixture of San Quellenne Tanathe and Goraque and Lethe and Styx and Morphaea and heaven only knows what other peoples, the children and the elderly herded in a central part, while around them the able-bodied adults stood, men and women armed with clubs and sticks and farm implements.

"Remember, cut off their limbs, or use fire to burn them down—it's the only way to protect yourself," the civilians were told by the soldiers. "And stay low, keep safe from musket fire. For unlike them, if they put holes in you, you die. . . ."

Beyond them, the formations of Goraque cavalry knights, the columns of pikemen infantry, and stragglers from the Morphaean divisions had finally organized in a phalanx and were holding off the streaming mass of the dead Trovadii. . . .

Just a little beyond the trees in the clearing, began the plain around Letheburg. However they could see, even from their position at the outskirts of the forest, that something was significantly wrong. Instead of the walls of *one* city, there were now *three*—three cities clustered together in an unnatural placement right next to each other, and one of them was literally jammed into Letheburg, so that their walls were touching, and in places intersecting.

Civilians and soldiers crossed themselves at the sight, for in their wildest imaginings this was not something anyone would choose to see. And to many it signified, truly and completely, the end of the world. . . .

Lord Beltain Chidair had been asked by the Duke to lead a vanguard formation, but he refused, falling to the back with a smaller troop of knights placed under his command to protect the flanks and the ordinary people.

"I forgive you for striking me down last year, Chidair," said one Goraque knight, Sir Marlon Wedeis, saluting him with his sword. "For I know you will lead us well and true in this fight."

"I am honored, and my thanks," replied the black knight, closing his visor. He threw one secret intense look at Percy, only a hundred feet back with the others, for he knew now that she could no longer help with the dead, and she was vulnerable, and it terrified him.

"The Goddess Persephone has forced herself inside my mind," Percy had confessed to him minutes earlier. "She seems to know all I think, and she will not allow me to put the dead to rest, oh, I am so sorry!"

It had happened only a few moments ago. They were fighting to come to order within the trees, and Percy had granted the final death to one dead man. And then she was somehow . . . *changed.*

"Percy, what is to be done?" he said uselessly. "I need to protect you, then! Come, let me get you back up into my saddle and—"

But she shook her head negatively and her ordinary eyes

wore the most extraordinary expression of all ... and it broke him right through to the heart. She looked at him with intense love and despair, and then she went and got herself a pitchfork from a nearby peasant, and she said, "See, I am armed and all is well! Go, my love! Defend us all!"

"But what of the Cobweb Bride?" he whispered. "What will you do now?"

But she exclaimed, "Go!" And her eyes brimmed with water.

And now, there was no more time to think, not for any of them. . . .

The dead were relentless in their attack, yet this was only a lesser Trovadii battalion sent to the edge of the forest, while the bulk of them, in their trademark pomegranate, were in the great plain, and they were attacking Letheburg. Soldiers of Goraque could not comprehend why only Letheburg was being taken and swallowed by the Sovereign's armies and the volleys of catapults, while the other two walled cities—identified soon enough by disbelieving soldiers as the Silver Court of the Realm and the enemy Sapphire Court of the Domain—remained uninvolved in the battle.

Garrison soldiers of these two enemy citadels stared out in confusion from the walls of their respective cities, armed to the teeth. Yet the Imperial Silver Court waited, not engaging the dead enemy. And the Sapphire Court, for whom the Trovadii forces were native sons, ignored for the time being the Silver Court muskets and cannons aimed in their directions.

Meanwhile, the dead were not the only enemy on the plain. Duke Vitalio Goraque's vanguard officers spied an approaching enemy line on the southwestern horizon, and it signified another enemy army—this one, as they were later to discover—were the Domain troops from Solemnis, consisting of living men, the same armies who had been camped out on the western shore of the River Styx and watched the City of Charonne disappear into the shadows at dawn. . . .

"There is little here that makes sense, and very little hope," the Duke spoke to his captain knights. "But we will fight on nevertheless, and we will try to hold our ground at least, and protect the last of our people, here where we now stand—for as long as there is any familiar land beneath our feet. As for Letheburg—God be with it. For to come to the aid of Letheburg now, to break through these thousands of Trovadii up ahead, would be an impossibility."

Ebrai Fiomarre was with the group of knights in one of the central portions of the phalanx, as the Trovadii broke through their ranks at last and the fight had come to him.

Armored in light chain mail only, he nevertheless fought well, being a hardy soldier, and his sword arm slashed though dead limbs all around, while his shield had been battered with so many blunt and sharp impacts that it was barely holding up.

Their formation was soon cast into a disordered melee, and they had to fall back, together with the vanguard knights and infantry foot soldiers, and they slowly retreated deeper into the forest, holding back the flanks. Their horses kicked up snow and trampled occasional dead rising from the whiteness of the drifts.

Relentless pops of musket fire sounded, and everywhere, the stench of black powder. Startled birds screeched and circled overhead. The dead who had been formerly musketeer corps had no qualm about using firearms to kill the living who could not return the favor, since shooting the dead was useless. And now the Trovadii were decimating the Goraque cavalry knights whose plate armor was poor protection against gunshots. Ebrai Fiomarre thought bitterly that he would have preferred to remain one of the living for just a few hours longer—for once a dead man, few things seemed to matter any longer, loyalties became uncertain (though not necessarily so, since quite a few recently dead Goraque were still fighting loyally at his side), and all the physical senses were compromised. . . .

A few dozen feet behind him, Fiomarre saw a young brash knight fighting like a madman with his longsword, and cutting down the dead as only youthful zeal can justify. Soon, however, he would tire, and there were none in his vicinity to come to his aid. A far more jaded and hence careful combatant, Ebrai steered his mount to assist the young knight.

A flash of movement, tree branches in the way, then he saw the knight's visor lift for better air, and an exertion-reddened young face, that of a pretty youth, breathing hard. Ebrai looked onward and saw a small group of peasants behind him, including children, and understood why the knight fought so hard in that one place—there was nowhere for the people to retreat, and beyond them were more Trovadii, coming.

Ebrai flew into the fight, bringing his sword down skillfully to sever arms and hands of the nearest dead, and then called out, "Watch your back!"

"My thanks!" responded a young voice in a higher register, and Fiomarre suddenly recognized it as the voice of the lady from Tanathe, one of the San Quellenne. "And you, Sir, watch yours—to the left!"

Ebrai redoubled his defense, and in moments a few more knights joined them, while the peasants used scythes and pitchforks to cut up the dead fallen on the ground.

"Get them back in the center with the others," Ebrai said to the lady knight.

She nodded, again raising her helm's visor to breathe easier, and a grin bared her perfect white teeth. Her horse attempted to rear, but she held it down skillfully with one gauntlet sharply on the reins.

She was fierce, electric, like lightning. . . .

Ebrai momentarily thought it, and he said, "Well fought, My Lady San Quellenne!"

"Ah, you recognize me!" She nodded, and her face became proud, and then she once more lowered the visor. Seconds later, the peasants ran, and she followed them, in the direction of relative safety.

Ebrai followed after, making sure to protect their flank.

Percy was next to the D'Arvu family, as they kept to a copse of trees, together with several other townspeople of San Quellenne. The clashing of steel was everywhere, harsh metal-on-metal sounds, and the beating of Trovadii drums was relentlessly ringing from the plain.

The pitchfork weighted heavily in her mittened hand. Percy was no stranger to it, but holding up the farm implement as a vertical weapon was an entirely different kind of fieldwork, and her wrist ached from relentlessly gripping it.

Next to her, the Countess Arabella D'Arvu kept a tight hold on little Flavio's hand. She showed brave composure, but her eyelids fluttered in involuntarily response every time there was the sound of musket fire, especially when the ball projectiles struck the nearby trees. The Lady San Quellenne and she had an unspoken agreement that at present the boy needed a mother more than he needed a sister, and so he was left in the matron's care.

The Count himself stood beside them, his sword ready, and a few other peasants had staffs or pitchforks like Percy. So far they had been fortunate that no new enemy breach had occurred in their immediate vicinity.

Lady Leonora stood motionless, behind her mother, and her eyes had become glassy in the cold, while a thin rime of frost started to sheen her pale cheeks. There was little doubt in anyone's mind now that she was well and truly dead.

Percy cast occasional glances her way, and every time she did, the crawling sense in her mind thickened, as though *Persephone* was watching her every thought, precipitating her every act.

My Champion. . . .

Percy blinked, forcing herself to shut off this dark perverse layer of her mind, to close herself off from the goddess.

There was a small noise to the left, and Percy turned in alarm to find two dead men who had emerged with otherwise uncanny silence from lord knows where, and were upon them.

The first was a burly foot soldier who had been slain in the head, for his one eye-socket was a frozen mess of spilled grey matter, but all his heavily muscled limbs were intact. And he had a musket slung to one shoulder and a sizeable sword in his hand. He must have been one of Hoarfrost's Lethe rabble for he wore no Trovadii colors. His death shadow was a thick smokestack behind him.

The other soldier was also one of the unaffiliated of Hoarfrost's army, and he sported a fixed villainous grin, mercenary unmarked clothing, and a thick club in one hand while in the other a long serrated knife. This one's death shadow also billowed at his side, in an ugly parody of the human body it flanked.

Both of them headed straight for Percy and Countess Arabella with the boy Flavio.

Percy grabbed the pitchfork with both hands and she shoved with all her strength at the burly musketeer. It felt like she was trying to move a side of beef . . . and temples pounding, everything suddenly became very sharp . . . slate-grey sky, black branches, white snow.

She heard Countess Arabella's small cry behind her, and then the grunts of the Count as he swung his sword awkwardly in an attempt to sever the arms of the attackers.

Percy saw violent movements in her peripheral vision, but did not know what was happening, was not sure. . . . She maintained an unwavering grip on the pitchfork handle with both hands, and it was still lodged in the soldier in front of her, keeping him out of arms reach, but he was pushing back, advancing upon her, relentless like a mountain of cold meat and torn armor.

God help me . . . she thought, numb and at the same time

bright and reeling with the terrible inevitability of what was before her. *Lord Hades, help me. Angels in Heaven help me. Anyone . . . help me . . .*

And then she felt her, the dark Goddess, stirring.

Do it! the perverse thoughts slithered. *Do it and test me!*

At the same time, from very far away, Percy felt the distant echo of a vast grey Hall and the sweeping motion of silent cobwebs, and the voice of Lord Death, faded almost completely. *Make your choice. . . .*

Champion. . . .

The God and the Goddess were both speaking now, and the word rang with impossible duality.

Champion!

My Champion!

But Percy heard the little boy, Flavio San Quellenne cry out in pain and fear. And her decision was made.

Percy reached out to the two death shadows and took them desperately in the grip of her mind, and then she forced them into the two corpses, while the so familiar deep sound of cathedral bells filled her head and the expanse of forest. . . .

The dead men collapsed like pieces of wood, with Percy's pitchfork still lodged inside one of them.

Percy turned around and glanced behind her, too terrified to imagine what awful sight to expect.

Little Flavio was crying but unharmed, and Countess Arabella held him shielded behind her, while a deep bleeding gash disfigured the sleeve over her arm. Her husband was pale but unscathed, and so were two of their servants.

Lady Leonora was watching it all with horror in her glassy eyes.

"Take me!" she said suddenly to Percy. "Nothing matters any more, do it now!"

But all hell broke loose as the clearing was suddenly filled with advancing Trovadii from one side, and from the other flew

Goraque cavalry knights, including Baron Gundar Dureval, and at his side, the beloved black knight atop his monstrous black warhorse.

"Percy!" Beltain cried. "Are you all right?"

He had lifted his visor for a moment and Percy saw a flash of his lean comely face and his slate-blue eyes locked with hers in intensity, as he hurtled right at her, intercepting two enemy cavalrymen and engaging them in fierce hand combat, while the other knights mingled all through the clearing. In seconds, Beltain had disabled the nearest enemy, and he came upon Percy and the D'Arvu, reining in Jack with one easy pull of a powerful gauntlet.

"Are you unharmed?" He pointed at the Countess who was bleeding from the arm. And then he saw the two fallen dead men.

"And you, Percy?" He rode closer.

Percy nodded in relief. She saw the concern in his eyes, and for a moment she was taken out of the scene, remembering the soft look of his, the way Beltain looked at her each time with wonder—

Somewhere nearby a musket pop sounded.

The black knight went very still.

Nearby, black birds screeched, rising up from the shrubbery.

Lord Beltain Chidair looked down at himself, and the front of his breastplate was pierced with a round hole, slightly to the left.

Just over his heart.

He stared at himself, and there was again wonder on his features, but wonder of a different kind.

"Percy . . ." he said. And then he exhaled for the last time.

Inside her mind, Percy heard the laughter of the dark Goddess.

Percy looked up at him, and she saw the round hole in his metal plate armor, and it was so small, just a tiny little thing. . . .

There was no blood, really, nothing that could be seen. And Beltain still sat firmly in the saddle, and Jack was stirring restless underneath him, powerful haunches moving, hooves stomping the snow. . . .

And then Percy saw it, the gentle *doubling* of her other vision, the billowing death shadow, gathering itself out of nothing, and materializing at *his* side.

No.

Percy stood like stone, looking up at them both.

No.

"Percy . . ." he said again. But this time it was a strange different sound, for he was speaking on the exhale, and his voice was now *not his own.* "I am so *sorry* . . . Percy."

"Beltain . . ." she said. *"Beltain."*

There was no sound in the world. A perfect, serene silence.

Somewhere out there, there was fighting, and the cries of the wounded, and the slash of steel and the bludgeon of wood, and there were flashes of motion, and more musket fire and distant drums, while something was being perpetrated.

Something. . . .

The Count and Countess and Lady Leonora stared at them in horrified silence and little Flavio had stopped crying.

Percy slowly put her hand up to Beltain, and she touched his gauntlet. She took it off, and his hand was bared—large, capable fingers, still warm. . . . She held them, squeezing, and he did not squeeze back at first, and then there was *something*, a thick awkward movement of a *thing* flexing a wooden limb . . . the response through layers of great distance.

A few knights had noticed something had happened, and two of them approached, then a third, but he as soon had to be pulled back into the fight.

Beltain Chidair carefully moved his wooden limbs, and then he dismounted, and stood before Percy while Jack made terrified noises but stood his ground at his master's side.

Something was pooling at his feet, seeping through the armor plates, from the inside . . . so much crimson staining the snow.

Percy was a numb thing of wood. No breath, no movement. No thought.

But something was happening to her face, and she did not really know, except there was something wet pouring out of her, and she did not know what it was. . . . And she did not, *did not know* anything.

Beltain was looking at her, and he took off his helm completely, dropping it to the snow, and then pulled back the coif hood of chain mail from his head, and his brown hair spilled in wavy soft locks around his face, familiar and beloved.

The black knight spoke nothing, only took her face in his hands and he brought his own face down over hers . . . and the cooling lips pressed against her own, light as a feather and then hard as a dream, holding her for a few moments.

No breath between them.

His *eyes* were so close, stilled in serenity, and she momentarily drowned in them.

He moved away, and then he said softly, "Put us all to rest, my love. . . ."

And Percy cried a rending scream.

She screamed in a horrible broken voice, choking on the wet stuff coming out of her, and screamed, and screamed . . . and the forest echoed, and the full, loud sounds of battle were again all around, while she put white-knuckled hands up to her face . . . and her head was tolling with *the sound of her own voice*, and then the voice of the dark Goddess, laughing.

"Do it now," said the Cobweb Bride, standing right behind her.

Percy reached out with her death sense, and with all of her stupid, useless mortal being. . . .

Beltain was before her, and his eyes—oh, his eyes were gazing into hers with endless quiet love.

She reached out, and out, and out. . . .

The world around her widened. . . . It was deep and fathomless in all directions, forest and plain and somewhere beyond, the lapping sea . . . and it was all filling with roiling darkness, as though the overcast skies had fallen down into her, were being pulled into her shell of a mortal body. . . . She was pulling all of it inside, like a hungry maw, a pitch-black void.

A forest of anemic cobwebs filled her mind. And then she saw searing brightness, and radiant white—a flash—and it was Beltain himself, looking at her . . . only now he was the White Bridegroom, and he was dressed in Lord Death's clothing, and he wore a smile, beckoning.

Gentle, serene love.

Percy saw him thus, his image seared into her permanently, as she held the death-shadows all around—all the infinity of them, for leagues in every direction, human, animal, insect—and she held the death shadow of the Cobweb Bride . . . and Beltain's shadow also, his beloved own.

The dark Goddess stirred. *Do not do it, foolish mortal! I have already taken what you love most! Think you not that I will take from you again?*

"You cannot take anything else from me," Percy said.

And then she took hold of the death shadow of the Cobweb Bride, sensing the physical presence of the maiden's upright dead body from the back—for Leonora stood directly behind her, looking at her with serene, accepting eyes—and she held it long enough to show Leonora the glorious sight of the White Bridegroom with Beltain's eyes.

And then she gently pushed the death inside the maiden.

There was nothing—no great blinding light, no trembling earth, no falling sphere of heaven.

Only a soft, serene exhalation of the soul of the world. . . .

Dissolution of will.

Gentle fading.

The wind still blew in gusts, and the white and black forest still rang with war.

And then Percy felt—knew for certain—that the Cobweb Bride was *gone*.

Behind her, Lady Leonora had collapsed softly, falling upon the snow at the feet of her parents.

Immediately after, Beltain's form was suddenly void of presence. His beloved soul had gone. His eyes had never blinked, but now he was a thing malleable. And the body of the black knight fell down at Percy's feet.

It was happening all over the forest. Soldiers were collapsing, coming down one after another, falling in droves, in columns and formations, men and horses and abandoned sharp steel.

Far in the distance on the battle plain, the sound of drums had stopped. Indeed, the clash and roar was replaced by suddenly growing pockets of silence. The winter landscape had swallowed the last of the sound in its quiet snow-padded maw, and now only the pale boundless sky streamed outward, bearing witness to the last of the dissipating motion.

"Leonora, my child!" Countess Arabella was weeping loudly, hunched over the body of her daughter.

Percy did not notice it, but she herself had come down on her knees in the snow, before Beltain. She felt her knees buckling, and there she was. . . . *He* lay on his back, facing the sky. She looked at him, and it was strange to see his eyes like that, open, but stilled, not looking at her.

A beautiful dead man.

No!

She wanted to touch him, to rock him in her arms, but she could not move. Her limbs. . . . They were not her own.

All she could do now was stay like this, hunched over him, and watch over him. *Someone* had to watch over him, as he lay in the snow. . . .

"Good God! What is happening?" Baron Dureval was one of the two knights who had ceased fighting when the black knight was shot, and stopped at their side. He now dismounted from his horse and came up to Percy, and stood over her and the fallen black knight.

A sharp screech of a bird sounded, and it made Percy suddenly aware of her limbs, her knees, as though her soul had been temporarily disembodied and now she could inhabit the mortal coat of useless flesh.

He lay before her in the snow.

And she made the incomprehensible effort with her limbs and took off her woolen shawl. She folded it, and then she gently placed her fingers underneath his head, feeling the softness of his hair, and the searing touch of snow. And she lifted his head slightly and put the shawl underneath, then lowered him again. She adjusted a few tendrils of his hair, smoothing them over his cool forehead. But she could not bring herself to close his *eyes. . . .*

She stood up.

Percy was light as a feather. She was lightheaded, but quite unlike what had happened to her before when she put large numbers of the dead to rest.

This time she was strong and light as a feather. Feeling nothing.

Nothing at all.

. . . at her feet in the snow . . .

"Look at them! The Trovadii are falling down all over!" Sir Marlon Wedeis who had fought at the black knight's side, exclaimed, riding up hard. But now he dismounted and stood silently when he saw who lay on the ground.

Ebrai Fiomarre also approached and stood nearby, looking at Percy intently, glancing back and forth from her to the fallen great figure in black armor.

"Percy . . . Percy Ayren," Fiomarre said gently. "I am so sorry . . . for your loss."

But Percy said nothing. She continued standing like a pillar, looking down at *him* who lay at her feet.

"Well, I'll be damned," said Baron Dureval. "The Black Knight is down. . . ." And he took off his helm in respect.

"Not just Trovadii falling, but all the dead are going down!" cried another knight, approaching their group on horseback. "All our boys too. What in blazes is going on now? They are all dead! *Really dead!*"

"So, you think death is back in business again?" Baron Dureval said, wiping his clammy forehead with the back of his gauntlet. And then he pointed to Beltain's body and he said gruffly to Percy, "Is he gone, for certain? Maybe we ought to check? Take those plates off, look at the wound. . . . Though, no, I can tell, the poor fellow's got the open-eyed stare, he's gone for sure—"

"Be silent." Percy slowly turned her face around, and the look on it was hard, terrifying, dead. So much power there was in her gaze that the baron did not question the fact that a peasant girl was speaking to him in such a manner.

She looked around her then, seeing the D'Arvu family gathered around Leonora's body, and she saw Ebrai Fiomarre, behind her.

"You," said Percy Ayren, looking at him with a vacant stare. "You, who are Lord Fiomarre, Vlau's brother. I can feel *her* presence inside me even now, even after what has come to pass. She *just will not go away*—the one who is the Sovereign. . . . The one who is the Goddess. You said before you wanted to try—to take me to her."

"What do you mean, girl?"

"I mean, let's go. *Take me to her now.* I know exactly where she is, but I would like you to come along—and do what you had planned to do."

"But if she is immortal," Ebrai said, "and she cannot be killed—"

"Let's go."

And then Percy turned around and she said to Count

D'Arvu, "My Lord, please watch over Beltain, for he lies in the snow. . . . For—I must go and do something. I must do something. But—someone must watch over *him*, as he lies in the snow. . . ."

Chapter 17

Percy rode with Ebrai Fiomarre, awkwardly seated in the saddle before him, as they moved through the forest filled with fallen dead and loudly energetic living. Some of the folk were rejoicing, and the mixed groups of peasants and townspeople cheered the nearby infantrymen and cavalry knights as they rode over piles of fallen dead bodies. A few more feet of forest and they had reached the wide clearing before the plain upon which three cities stood next to each other.

The plain was a sea of pomegranate-red, silent fallen men, all Three Armies of the Trovadii. But the battle had not ended, and indeed the war was far from over, because the living soldiers of Solemnis of the Domain were present and they still had their orders, and they now engaged the Goraque soldiers of the Realm.

However the odds were now mortal, *human*—at least here on this battlefield. Those who were mortally wounded, fell and did not rise again. And for some strange reason, it served to invigorate *both* sides, so that now the battle raged fiercely in the field and around Letheburg. And this time, the garrison soldiers of the Silver Court and Sapphire Court joined the battle. Fresh formations in Imperial colors joined the fray, while on the other side, the Domain garrison came out in a lesser force.

Ebrai Fiomarre rode carefully and swiftly, not engaging in

any skirmishes. And because the distance was short, they had remained lucky enough to approach within a hundred feet of Letheburg's open gates that has been damaged by a battering ram, together with the adjacent section of wall that had come down in coarse granite boulders and lay in pieces on the snowy ground.

"I do hope you know what you're doing," Ebrai said to her through gritted teeth, as he had to draw his sword and ready his shield arm for military contact. "I understand the tragic loss you've had, Percy, and it might have affected you somewhat—"

"Get me into the city, My Lord," she said in a dead voice. "Get me through the gates."

"And then what?"

In Percy's mind the dark Goddess laughed.

Come to me, my Champion, and watch me make another Cobweb Bride! I will stop the cycle of death yet again, for it is as easy as your next breath!

Percy was numb. Her next breath did not rise inside her, for she was suddenly choking, being stifled by an invisible hand . . . her lungs could not move in natural reflex and she was drowning.

See how easy it is, how I hold you, my Champion!

Percy did not struggle. Ebrai saw how she was suddenly sliding limp against his chest. "Percy! Are you well? What is it! What is wrong?"

And then the Goddess released her. And Percy gasped and coughed and took in a deep shuddering breath of air.

"I am—it is nothing," she said to him. "*She* is toying with me. Keep going."

Up ahead, only fifty feet, was the breach of the gates. Musket and arquebus fire volleys came loud and with it the stench of black powder. Solemnis troops were here in force, and they were holding the passage into the city.

"There is no way to get through!" Ebrai exclaimed, pulling

up his horse short.

Mother! Percy thought. *Mother, help me!* And her briefest thought was of Niobea, followed by overwhelming golden light.

Help me, Mother of Bright Harvest, you who are Thesmos, who have come to me in dreams. . . .

And before them, out of the grey smoke and grime, hanging like a curtain before the gates, arose a golden light.

It bloomed forth in a warm radiance against the polluted sludge of snow and the fallen Trovadii corpses and the roiling mess of fallen bricks and sections of city walls and running foot soldiers. . . .

Demeter, golden Goddess of plenty and the riches of the harvest, rose before them out of the icy ground, and she was growing, and she was twenty, then a hundred feet tall.

Help me do this one last thing! Percy thought with all the force of her being. *Take me to her!*

"Come, dear child!" boomed the voice of Demeter the golden-tressed, as her immortal shape towered like a colossus before the gates of Letheburg. "I may not take you through shadows, but I will take you through light! Enter me and ride!"

And the next moment the figure of the goddess blended with pure light and she became a shimmering curtain, a portal into another place.

"Ride!" exclaimed Percy.

Immediately Ebrai spurred his horse and they flew forward into the curtain of golden light. . . .

. . . And they emerged on the other side.

It was a small street in Letheburg, claustrophobic, snow-covered, with narrow buildings nestled together with second story overhangs, away from the clamor of the fighting.

It was Rollins Way.

Percy opened the red door of Grial's house and it creaked gently. And she stepped inside, while her mind was empty and numb. Ebrai Fiomarre came after her.

Grial, or Hecate's parlor was a mess of broken furniture, pulled chintz curtains and smashed knick-knacks, all except for the sofa, upon which Persephone sat, humming to herself and examining her nails, long delicate claws of glossy ivory, reminiscent of those of her consort, Lord Hades. She was dressed in her silvery-metal chiton and her succulent skin was rich bronze and her hair the deepest pitch-black mahogany. An erotic scent of musk filled the room . . . stifling reek of barely repressed immortal *desire*.

In the corner, seated upon her wooden rocking chair, was Hecate.

Hecate was in her immortal form, rigid and motionless. But she was no longer fashioned of silvery-moonlight. Instead, all her surfaces had a strange matte pallor, like a rime of frost. Only her eyes remained unaffected, familiar, warm, and very, very dark, watching Percy with wisdom.

It took a second for Percy to recognize the fine layer of cobwebs starting to cover her from head to toe, and frosting her noble braided crown of hair with whiteness.

Persephone stopped humming.

"My Champion!" she said. "And my dear Ebrai. How good of you to deliver my Percy to me. I suspected you would prove loyal, from the very first instant you looked into my eyes. Although, I must say at first you struggled so hard to maintain your tedious façade of deception that I came to pity you. Such a clever ruthless boy you thought yourself to be—it made you a delicious curiosity, and yes, it kept you alive. Ah, my poor Ebrai. . . . What—did you think I did not *know* you and your father were sent to spy on me?"

Ebrai Fiomarre went very still. He was gripped with the charismatic slithering force of her gaze—eyes that were no longer sky-blue, but sensuous ripe earth and upturned soil, and the sweet, deep burrowing riches of its fertile darkness.

She was his Sovereign, now as much as ever, as she had

been before, undeniably, when last he saw her in the splendor of the Palace of the Sun at the Sapphire Court . . . just before she gave him her last task to carry out.

"It is done," he had told her then. And these same words he spoke again now, even though this time the words were formed in grim resignation.

She knew everything.

"You have done well, my Ebrai—*despite* yourself."

Fiomarre felt cobwebs and darkness suddenly crawling through his mind, and he struggled in despair, for he knew that he could never deny her, not in the very end. . . .

He stood very still, his mind in ruthless turmoil, while Persephone stood up suddenly, ignoring Percy for the moment, and she strode up to him, and placed her nude sensuous bronzed arms around the raven-haired man's neck. She then pushed back his chain mail and the armor gorget round his neck, and her slim fingers stroked the column of his muscled throat, right over the pulse point, and up over the Adam's apple.

Ebrai's eyelids flickered but he held himself steady and he somehow managed to meet the direct look of her eyes.

And then slowly his right hand moved down to his side. With a quick practiced move he took out his short secret dagger, and he plunged it directly into the chest of the dark Goddess.

He had nothing to lose.

She made a small stifled sound. A light, sweet gasp.

Or maybe it was Percy, standing nearby in numb silence. . . .

He drew back violently, and watched silvery-red immortal blood run down and stain the front of her iridescent chiton.

Persephone looked down at her chest and the wound, and then looked up at him. Her lips curved into a smile.

She reached down to touch her blood with her fingertips and brought it up to her lips, and tasted it.

"Sweet ambrosia . . ." she whispered. "Do you know that I used to cut myself and drink from my own wrists?" She put her fingertip directly into her wound, and she offered it to Ebrai. "Would you like a taste of immortality, foolish mortal? But no, you may not have my sweet blood, for you have not earned it. Far from it—now you have displeased me. Whatever shall I do with you?"

Ebrai's lean face was a lifeless mask.

But Persephone already turned her back on him and now she gave her full attention to Percy.

"You are here just in time, my priestess and my Champion," said the dark Goddess, standing before Percy and looking into her eyes. "But oh, you have restarted the tedious grand process of death, releasing so much of that wonderful life energy back into the cycle—so many souls set free and cast back into the universal ocean! I must say I am not pleased. Now I have to start all over again with another little Cobweb Bride— maybe a comely youth this time—"

"What have you done to Hecate?" Percy spoke in a numb wooden voice, not her own.

"My sister is merely indisposed," Persephone cast a brief glance at Hecate in her wooden chair. "You might say I am gently divesting her of all that immortal *gravitas*. Soon she will be light enough that I will move her to this nice spot on the sofa upon which she can recline for all eternity."

"You require the use of this rocking chair?"

"I require the use of this Throne to the Underworld."

Percy stared at Hecate, covered in cobwebs and motionless, and the realization of the magnitude of it all came to her with a blow that was almost tangible.

Thoughts raced within Percy, and connections were made.

"You will sit upon this Throne and you will die, and you will dissolve and fall Below and come into the Underworld . . ." Percy mused, and her voice was cold, remote; someone else was speaking in her stead.

"Precisely, my Champion."

Percy bit her lips. "Ebrai and I will help you move Hecate from the chair. Will you have mercy upon us and the rest of mortal kind, if we help you now do this one thing?"

"Will I?" Persephone laughed, a soft silvery laugh, like the sound of a running spring brook over stones. "But lo! What's this? You have given up—or so you want me to believe—and now you offer your will to me? Not much of a sport, are you, my girl? No fun at all! I'd hoped for more of a passionate struggle and existential flailing, raw mortal anguish on your part, maybe even a few choice curses aimed at the gods, especially after I had slain your true love. What, you would serve me now, and be my priestess and my Champion, while *he* lies in the snow?"

Sharp serrated blades and razors bit into Percy, cutting her in her mind, ripping off slices from her spirit . . . and the room turned and there was vertigo.

"Yes."

Persephone laughed again, and Percy saw her hard, empty evil eyes.

"Ah, but you are lying to me, sweet little Percy, and doing it rather terribly. You always were such an awkward liar, and you can never lie to me. . . ."

"All right, I am lying," Percy said. "I hate and despise you with every fiber of my being—or what's left of it. But we *will* help you to relocate Hecate nevertheless. I don't want her harmed any more than she already is."

Ebrai nodded silently, still stunned from his own failed act of assassination, and grimly stepped forward. "What must we do?"

"Simply lift her up enough that she is not touching the wood of the chair with any portion of her body . . . not even a single hair must touch it, for it keeps her in control of the Throne. That should be enough. I myself cannot do this, for her power still rejects me and my slightest touch, even though she has grown very weak."

Percy approached Hecate, and she put her hand upon the

arm of the Goddess of the Crossroads, feeling the cobweb crystalline layer of energy covering every point of her surface. "I am so sorry, Grial," she whispered, looking into the familiar wise eyes, liquid in the shadows. "But I must do this thing now."

The eyes watched her with infinite understanding, without judgment.

Ebrai approached from the other side, and together Percy and he raised Hecate from her seat, gently, unfolding her stiff figure, a lovely silvery statue . . . and the moment she was no longer in contact with the rocking chair, Persephone gave a gasp of delight.

Ebrai carried Hecate and placed her still form gently on the sofa, while Persephone spun in a circle and then landed neatly in the rocking chair, so that it was immediately set in motion, creak-creak. . . .

"Well done, my priestess and my priest!" Persephone trained upon them her smiling face and her perfectly vacant, soulless eyes. "And now I only need to die one more time, for this ridiculous scheme of things to end. Never again will I endure the agony of complete dissolution and pointless sacrifice for this mortal refuse that you call your world. . . ."

Persephone sighed in contentment and closed her eyes.

Percy watched her with her own blank gaze, saw the exhalation of the last living breath from the lips of the dark Goddess, and heard her startled soft cry of immortal agony in the throes of the paradox that was her impossible death of passing Below—

"Die!" Percy said suddenly, in a voice that rang through the room, while at the same time there came the deep cathedral tolling of bells that were grand and measureless, the size of worlds . . . and the spheres rang with the rising cloak of darkness that was within Percy's mind, pouring into her the infinity of Lord Death's power.

The room filled with broken things began to shake, while a

wind gathered. . . .

Die, you who are dead already! You are a dead goddess, for your soul has been cast asunder, and instead a death shadow haunts you, and her energy form is pallor and cobwebs.

She too is the Cobweb Bride. She is your divine aspect and she is your death shadow and she is subject to my will.

For I am Death's Champion.

And you are an evil dead thing . . . you are nothing and you are now all mine.

With a flick of her mind, Percy struck the cobwebs that surrounded Hecate, and they shattered into a million invisible shards, motes of psychic dust. . . . She gathered them to her like glittering white ashes of crystalline force, and she shaped them into a female form, a ghostly shape of Persephone.

The Bride made of Cobwebs stood up billowing and translucent at the side of the seated dark Goddess.

So perfectly still, the Goddess's dead face, just before its final dissolution and passing. So serene and lovely, like an unfulfilled promise of spring. . . .

And Percy took the glittering death shadow and she pushed it with all her will, and all her passion and all her despair and loss and hope, inside the corporeal body of the Goddess.

She pushed it inward, and into the brightest white light . . . *and she followed after.* She did not let go, not for a moment, for there was nothing for her to do here any longer, and Percy was *done.* . . .

The White Bridegroom stood before them, dressed for the Wedding, and he wore the smile of Hades and Beltain's beloved eyes.

There came a glorious incandescent white flash, like staring into the face of a blinding white sun.

Finally there was nothing at all.

Percy opened her eyes to soft silvery lavender. The illumination came from far overhead, or possibly it came from all around her, for Percy was lying on her back upon a soft blanket of snow and her face was staring up, gaze trained overhead, facing an infinite dome of deep black sky, littered with a sugar sparkle of stars.

Everywhere, serenity and silence. . . . And the same strange muted light. Percy took in a deep breath, feeling her lungs working to inhale the sweet air, with a strange hint of exotic perfume, as though the wind swept here from a remote field of flowers.

Flowers in the snow? Night? Where was she?

Percy sat up, using her hands for leverage, then stood. She wiped the snow off her knees and skirts and slapped her mittens together and stomped her shoes.

She was bareheaded, so there was a bit of loose crystalline powder in her hair, and she shook it out with her mittens, and then glanced around.

She was in her own backyard at home in Oarclaven. There was the side of their house, and in the opposite direction, the barn, and off to the side the ancient elm tree bare of leaves. . . .

Percy blinked, and turned to walk a few steps through the deep drifts that piled over the spot where had been her vegetable patch.

The front door of their house opened, and there were voices, and then someone came through the snow, and it was the familiar tall shape of her sister, Belle.

"Belle!" Percy exclaimed.

Parabelle Ayren, wearing her coat and threadbare headscarf, holding a bucket in her hand, stopped. She looked in the direction of Percy and then froze.

"Percy!" she exclaimed. "Oh dear Lord, Percy!"

And Belle dropped the bucket and ran toward her younger sister.

Percy was enveloped in a great but gentle hug—for Belle always had a light touch, and even her fiercest affections were expressed in delicate grace. "Percy, how did you get here? Oh, my dear Percy!"

"I—I don't know. Where is 'here?'"

"I mean, home, silly! What else would it be?"

Percy grinned at her sister, her face slightly ruddy from the chill air, and she bit her lip then rubbed her nose with the back of her mitten.

And then Belle bit her lip too—it was a family habit. "Well, that is, I suppose it is not entirely what it is, because we are home, yes, but we are also . . . in the Underworld."

Percy stared. "What?"

"Well, it happened a few days ago, and no one is really sure, but we all ended up here—the whole village, and I have a feeling that the whole world did too! Everything started fading, and we were indoors and I don't think we realized what had happened, until some neighbors told us, and Uncle Roald was on his porch too so he saw everything but was too surprised to run—but the fading was just us being picked up by some kind of divine magic and *moved* down here! Houses and people and animals and even the land and the trees—everything!"

"But how do you know it's the Underworld?"

"Well, it just is!" Belle turned and gestured all around her and then up at the sky. "Just look at it!" She swung her hands. "See that huge beautiful moon? It's always like that, and it is very bright, and it never sets, only *fades!* And those tiny bright lights? You think those are stars? No, it's actually a very high ceiling of ebony rock, and those are diamonds stuck up there! Every single one of them, a huge light-reflecting diamond the size of a goose egg!"

"No . . ." said Percy. "Now you're just jesting with me."

"Not at all! Am I the kind of person who jests? That would be something *you* would naturally do, Percy, not, me. You always say I have no sense of humor, only a sense of worry." Belle shook her head and then smiled at Percy and pursed her lips.

"I suppose, you're right, Belle." Percy smiled back.

"Oh, and then there's the strange daytime!" Belle resumed with excitement. "It's not a normal sun, but a very odd and peculiar sun that rises every morning. Its light does not burn the eyes, so you can stare at it directly for hours. It is bright golden like a lemon and at sunset it is cheerful orange like an egg yolk! The sky suddenly turns from black like it is now, to pretty cornflower blue, because all those diamonds and ebony rocks in the ceiling light up! They are sharp and polished like mirrors, so they shine the light back and forth . . . and it's like blue rainbows!"

"I suppose it doesn't rain or snow here either." Percy wiped her forehead with her mitten.

"Of course it does, silly, how else would there be all this snow on the ground?" And then Belle paused, thinking. "Well, actually, there was already snow on the ground when we all arrived here, backyard and houses and streets and all. So then, I suppose, I don't really know. . . . I could ask Gerard, he might know—"

"Who's Gerard?" Percy asked.

Belle suddenly blushed—it was visible even in the moonlight. "Oh," she said. "I guess you don't know about Gerard Sorven. He is a very nice young man, from Fioren. He has been coming by our house, since he did some work with Pa. He likes to talk about all kinds of things and seems so very knowledgeable—"

"Belle, are you two *courting?*" Percy exclaimed with a sudden grin.

Belle continued to blush furiously. "I think so. . . . Ma and Pa like him very much too."

"Good heavens! What other great things did I miss?"

Belle smiled and patted Percy's cheek.

"Is Pa and Ma and Patty in there now?" Percy said, somewhat shyly.

"Oh, yes!" Belle turned to look at the house. "They're all inside, and we've just had supper, and Pa is telling Patty a story, and Ma and I are making dough for Mid-Winter Holiday bread. I just came out here to get a bucket of snow—"

"Since when can we afford Holiday bread?"

"Percy, you're not going to believe this, but a large sack of flour, a basket of eggs, a pot of freshly churned butter, several juicy pomegranates, and jars of milk, honey, brown sugar and satchels of cloves and cinnamon appeared in the pantry, just a little while ago! And they are all *fresh!* As if the milk was just taken from a cow's udder this morning! And the eggs were laid a few hours ago!"

"You're right, I don't believe it."

"Well, come on in and see for yourself! Oh, they'll be so happy to see you! Ma has been really worried that she treated you badly, and she regrets all those times terribly, especially now that you're all famous and a heroine! Let's hurry and go inside before we wake up Uncle Roald and the neighborhood dogs—"

"Wait," Percy said. *"A heroine?"*

"Well, of course!"

"Being Death's Champion was more of a horrible burden. All I did was make people *die.* Good people, bad people, little innocent kids, everyone."

And then Percy again rubbed her forehead and her nose with the back of her mitten, because something was itching there. "Belle, this may be a weird question, but—am I *dead?* Are *you* dead?"

"Of course not!" Belle sputtered in her usual serious manner, with that gentle humorless worry. . . . "I mean, I don't think so. I don't feel dead. You'd think a person would know when they died, right? We've seen enough of those poor undead to know what that's like. And Gran. . . ."

"Aye, there was that," Percy said. "But now that Death has his Cobweb Bride, and the world is back to dying like normal, maybe we all died and came down here. I suppose you might say it makes me a heroine, though, one would think, a lousy one. I put the Cobweb Bride to her final rest, and it was no different than putting Gran to rest, and it took me most of forever to get to it too."

"Oh, Percy, what are you nattering on about?" Belle put her hand on her sister's shoulder and patted her lightly, then tweaked her round cheek. "You're a heroine because Persephone, Goddess of the Underworld has awakened here tonight, as she always does, on the Black Throne—and somehow, *thanks to you*, she is her own proper self again—gentle, compassionate, glorious, and full of spring. I know that Lord Hades is now with Lady Persephone, and tonight is the Longest Night. And that's why we're making Holiday bread!"

And then Belle laughed with joy, and she pointed up at the diamond stars again. "Look, oh, there is one great bright star there, and it just appeared! It is like the rainbow! Look up, Percy, it's just directly overhead, where the North Star used to be, near the Little Dipper! The constellations are a bit different here. . . ."

Percy's mind was reeling with the news, and she threw her head back and stared together with Belle, directly up, seeing indeed a very distinct looking bright star, larger than the others around it.

Belle put her arm around her, and they gazed together, like they used to do so many nights before. Percy put her head on Belle's shoulder, smelling the sweet familiar scent of her sister, and Belle ruffled Percy's hair that had many loose tendrils and was starting to fall out of its braid. "Why are you bareheaded in the cold, girl?" Belle said suddenly, picking snow out of Percy's hair. "Where is your nice big woolen shawl?"

Percy thought about it, and wondered too. . . .

And then it came to her, and she remembered.

Suddenly everything was twisting, churning, her gut, her

innards, her lungs were being torn out of her, and the lump in her throat came to choke like a boulder, and tears and snot and shuddering sobs came, and Percy opened her mouth and screamed and *wailed* . . . while the bright star started to fall from overhead, like a meteor, directly onto Percy.

A bright flash . . . then only white light.

Chapter 18

Percy awoke with a shuddering breath, and she was lying on the floor in Grial's parlor. Ebrai Fiomarre was bending over her with concern, while Hecate, free of cobwebs or any other binding sorcery, stood nearby. Percy could see the sheen of her immortal feet and the metallic sandals, just out of the corner of her eye, on the edge of the rug.

Percy groaned then turned her head, feeling her face strangely wet, her eyes salty and her nose swollen, and she started to get up.

"Careful, do not move too quickly," Ebrai said. And then he gave Hecate a very strange look.

Hecate was gazing down at her with a look that was truly hard to describe—a mixture of wonder, awe, and exultation. It was a look usually reserved for beholding the gods, not for the gods themselves at the sight of mortals.

"Where is she?" said Percy, with a glance at the empty rocking chair.

"She is where she should be," Hecate said serenely. "And she is once more the *true* Goddess of dark and light."

"What happened?"

"My dear girl, you put her to rest."

"What? What does that mean?" Percy's mind was a mess. Indeed, she had difficulty gathering her awareness enough to know where she was, or what day it was, and how much time had passed. Everything felt extremely hazy and fuzzy. Edges blurred . . . in her mind.

Hecate smiled gently, and then reached down and took Percy's hand, and pulled her up with the ease of a feather. "Your instincts were true. At the point of Persephone's immortal death, you, as Death's Champion had dominion over her, and you did the one and only thing that could have enacted the healing change in her—you showed her the White Bridegroom who is indeed the gentle Mortal Aspect of her one true love. It is an aspect of him that she *never* sees—indeed, it is but a counterpart of her own loving nature, and thus there is no need. But now—now it was the only thing that could cleanse her broken soul and restore her compassionate vision of mortality. For the White Bridegroom conducts your mortal kind in unconditional love to the next *stage*, that which you may know only as the Final Mystery. Through *him* and his light Persephone glimpsed it and was thus reminded of her original nature. Then, as she was resurrected Below, the Immortal Scheme—the so-called order of the world—came into play, and it restored her in the process of her own divine function."

"So—she is a monster no longer?"

"Blessed be the dark Goddess—no, she is not."

"Ah-h-h . . ." Percy groaned, as a phantom spasm gripped her head.

"And you," Hecate continued, speaking in Grial's sonorous voice, "you, my dumpling in apple sauce, have done something that not even the Olympians could imagine, nor the Angels of the One God could conceive, nor the celestial spheres could sing about! For nothing such as this has ever been done before! There simply is no precedent! Admittedly, divine rebellions are not all that common, although they do happen—as witness the Angel Lucifer and his Fallen Host—but in the case of our poor broken Persephone, she was the crux and anchor of the whole mortal world, the *one* goddess whose corruption would affect the very life process.

"Persephone had been gradually growing ill in her soul for far longer than we imagined—even before she was damaged completely by drinking too much water of Lethe. And her present course was fatal for the mortal world. Had you not *changed* her just as she died to enter Below, inducing her to conform to the divine function and rebirth in the *white light*, she would have done even more damage in the Underworld. And that would have meant that the whole universal scheme would fall apart and naturally, everyone would have to start over! And really, the planning and making of a new mortal scheme is such a horrible, usually tragic hassle for the gods, with all manner of repercussions and needless futility—"

"Grial . . ." said Percy. "That is, Hecate. I need to go to *him*. . . . Now."

Hecate observed her with compassion.

There was a pause of silence, and Ebrai stared also, grim and somber.

"Very well," Hecate said. "I will take you to your true love. This fine gentleman can come separately, on his horse. While you and I, we will walk through the shadows of daytime."

Percy nodded, and Hecate pointed to a corner of the room, where the pale daylight from the window did not reach. As she watched it, a soft silvery shimmer began to appear, as an *entrance* formed, akin to the twilight shadow curtain of mist that led to Death's Keep, but not precisely the same.

"Take my hand," Hecate said with a solemn face. "I give shape to entrances and exits where none are found. Come, child."

And Percy took a step, and placed her hand in the warm powerful hand of the Goddess, feeling a jolt of power.

She walked after Hecate into *silver*.

They emerged in a white snow-filled forest. It was the same familiar spot where Percy had vaguely remembered was the scene of battle, and where *it* happened.

Percy's heart was pounding. Her breath caught, and there was a lump in her throat, as she glanced around them, at the sparse trees and graphic black branches laden with snow, the various rises and shrubbery, and the spots where bodies of the dead had lain, bright pomegranate. . . .

She saw groups of people, mostly collecting the dead and piling them into carts. Others were dealing with the wounded. Occasional weary Goraque soldiers walked around the former campsite, but there was a noticeable absence of the sound of gunfire.

Percy glanced up past the trees toward the clearing and she saw that here was the portion of the plain that she remembered. But ahead there was no longer the cluster of three walled cities. The only thing remaining was the southwestern portion of the walls of Letheburg, silhouetted against the anemic pallor of the winter sky, while both the capital citadels—the Silver Court and the Sapphire Court—were gone.

The plain itself had shrunk to the size of a small square. The Trovadii bodies still littered whatever was left, and there were only a handful of living troops of the Emperor and the Sovereign, but they did not appear to be fighting.

But Percy did not care about any of it. . . .

She turned around, her eyes boring into the nearest groups of people in the forest, looking for a frame of reference.

Suddenly she spotted a familiar mounted knight, slim and elegant, with helm off and a mass of brazen red hair flowing down her back. It was the Lady San Quellenne.

"My Lady!" Percy cried in a hoarse voice.

Lady Jelavie turned and then came riding toward her.

"Where is Lord Beltain Chidair?" said Percy, looking up into the lady's dark brown eyes.

Immediately a somber look came to Jelavie. "Percy

Ayren!" she said. "I am—so sorry—"

"Where is he?"

The lady pointed with her gauntlet to a spot about fifty feet away where was a mid-sized tent. "In there," she said. "They laid him out with the other ranking dead."

Percy did not hear or see what else Lady Jelavie was saying, because she ran, stumbling through the snow.

Hecate walked slowly after.

In the tent, there were many rows of tarp spread out to cover the ice ground, and upon it lay motionless figures, many of them in armor, some not. A soldier stepped from the entrance with a kind look, and asked her whom she sought.

"Lord Beltain Chidair!"

"Ah, the Black Knight. . . . there he is. What a great loss." And the man pointed toward the back in one of the central rows.

Percy pushed past him, and she walked inside, head pounding, and right then she could see *his* distinctive black armor plates from many feet away.

Beltain's body was placed in a row of three other men.

"They did not touch him, any of them yet," said the man, trailing her. "They still have to break ground to dig, and there will be burial likely tomorrow, or the day after. So many good, brave men to bury—"

Percy was not listening. She came up to *him* and stopped. And then her knees again buckled, and she collapsed, and then as she crawled to him, she saw that his arms had been folded on his chest, both gauntlets back on—even that one had removed for a moment to touch his warm hand for the last time—with the length of sword now resting in noble honor underneath the gauntlets. The chain mail coif hood was pulled back up over his hair and his eyes had been closed.

"His *eyes!*" she said with accusation, looking up at the man. "Who closed his eyes? Who *touched* him?"

The man stood awkwardly, then mumbled, "Not sure,

lass.... It is a common thing that is done, generally, with the dead—"

"No!"

And then she wept, in deep shuddering sobs.

"No," she cried, "I am Death's Champion! He is *not* dead!"

A small crowd had gathered, including several of the San Quellenne, and a few familiar folk from Oarclaven.

"Percy!" Flor Murel, a slim, pretty blonde, came rushing forward, and she put her arms around Percy from the back, and started to rock her—or at least it might have been so, but there was only numbness, and Percy did not know or hear or *feel*. And then Jenna came running, and she was bawling too, and Gloria Libbin stepped forward, stocky and quietly comforting.

Hecate approached, clad in her mortal Grial aspect, and the crowd parted for her, for even though they were unsure who it was, there was an aura of great power about her.

"Here he is, your true love...." Hecate's resonant voice came softly.

Flor and Gloria and Jenna turned their heads and a burst of hope came to their eyes, "Grial!" they whispered.

"Hecate!" Percy blurted fiercely—and all the girls stared in confusion at the use of the different *name*, for none of them of course had known yet about Grial's true nature. "Hecate! You too are of the Underworld! Can you do something?"

"I am so sorry," the Goddess said gently. "But he is gone too far into the *otherplace* even for me and the other immortals to remedy. Not even my divine blood can bring him back—unlike the dead who were still with us when death was stopped. I could bring them back by making them immortal, as I did for Claere and Vlau, for they were merely suspended between worlds, and their souls were still within reach of this world—"

"You brought back Claere?" Flor said in amazement, wiping her nose from weeping. "She lives?"

"And Vlau died? Oh no! But you brought him back too?" Gloria muttered.

Percy stood up. She pushed past them all, choking, needing air, and she stumbled outside the tent.

The cold forest was all around. People moved, horses made sounds. Carts creaked.

Percy stood and she looked up at the monochrome grey skies, all the many infinite layers. . . .

God in Heaven! The One God who rules them all. . . .

Take my life and give him his life back!

There was no answer.

"God in Heaven!" This time she cried the words out loud, and people turned and stared, in passing.

"He cannot," said Hecate, standing behind her.

"Then who can?"

Hecate advanced forward and gazed into Percy's eyes. "Know, child, that the One God—He is so vast that He *cannot be moved*, else the Universe falls. Nor can He answer, for the very act of opening His Mouth is Movement, indeed the greatest Act of all, for it is the Word. And this is precisely why He has made an infinity of lesser gods, creating them in His own image, so that we can do the lesser things on His behalf. We are His hands and arms and feet and mouths. We are His answers to your prayers, enacted along the great Framework of Being."

"But—you said that no immortal can bring my love back!"

There is one who can.

The words fell softly, reaching Percy from a distance, like the soft flutter of verdant leaves in the trees and the warm mellifluous flow of the surf, foaming in the southern sea. . . .

Persephone.

The Goddess of Resurrection walked through the cobweb forest toward them.

She was bright and glorious, as though the sun had broken through the overcast and cast its rays upon her immortal form— the deep hues of profundity and darkness of the Underworld had been leached from her, for she was pregnant with light. And thus her colors were luminous pastels and warmth, her chiton pure white, her skin alabaster and her hair a mass of burnished gold and ripe persimmons. Wherever her golden sandals stepped, the snow parted to reveal peat moss and soil and eager breathing earth. . . . She cast her gaze upon Percy, and her eyes were soft blue as summer skies.

And all her visage, her exultant face—it was gloriously *alive*.

She was bursting with life, filled to the brim with the energy of renewal, carrying inside her the pure joy of being.

The Goddess of Resurrection approached, and everyone in the forest and the surroundings turned in her direction, sensing her approach. People stopped whatever they were doing and came forth from the trees and the shrubbery and the makeshift tents. Weary soldiers, wounded or hale, moved closer, elderly and young, peasants and townspeople and country folk, and even those from the city—for there were people coming from the plain, from the direction of what remained of Letheburg and the other citadels. . . .

Persephone the Goddess stood before Persephone the peasant girl.

Eye to eye they stood, and Percy found that she was no taller and no shorter than the Goddess.

"You . . ." Percy said, and there was anguish in that one word.

"I have wronged you greatly," said the bright Goddess. And her eyes, filled with infinite compassion, were liquid with moisture.

"Bring him back," Percy said in a hard voice. "Take me if needed, but bring him back."

The Goddess said nothing, only looked at Percy.

"I owe you a life, Persephone Ayren," Persephone said. "And I owe you another, for having taken away your true love."

"What do you mean?" Percy was breathing hard.

"You have died when you put me to rest, Percy Ayren."

Percy felt hot and very cold at the same time. There was vertigo and there was ringing in her ears. "But of what do you speak? I am here! I am unharmed! I am crying, look! Tears, snot! And for Heaven's sake, there is no death shadow at my side, for I myself would see it! And all of you here can see me!"

Persephone sighed gently. "It is your spirit that stands now before me. Your body lies on the floor in Hecate's house, before the Throne. You had died in that moment when you healed me with your own sacrifice, and you refused to come forth from the Underworld where your soul went hiding in despair . . . for you did not want to live in a world where your true love died."

"But—" Percy said, flexing her hands in confusion.

"Hecate pulled you forth, coaxed you back to the world Above—remember the bright star?"

"So what nonsense is this? I am solid flesh!"

"It is an illusion. You are a *Miracle*."

"But Flor and Gloria just hugged me!"

But Flor Murel and Gloria Libbin, standing nearby shook their heads negatively. "I touched you, Percy, or I thought I did, but you felt odd, like thin air . . . and then I wasn't sure. Since I *can* see you, after all," Flor mumbled. "It is all very strange, but then everything has been so strange, the whole world. . . ."

"So. I am dead." Percy stood like a dolt.

"I will bring you back," said the Goddess.

"Bring *him* back!"

Persephone slowly inclined her radiant head. "I will restore you *both*. But it is a thing most difficult, and the balance of the world itself might suffer. Thus, I need a life for a life. To restore the two of you, two others must die."

There was perfect silence in the forest.

"It will be an easy, gentle death, like the breath of spring, the falling of a single leaf, and the plucking of a flower," said the Goddess. "Two will die such deaths, the gentlest deaths of all. But it must be done willingly. For there can be no new life without self-sacrifice."

Silence was replaced with murmurs, stirring speech.

"Come, friends!" said Hecate in the shape of Grial, using her comfortable raucous voice to be heard above the crowds. "Who among you is loving enough to grant *the Soteira*—the maiden who is your latest savior—and her true love, their lives? For they have already given theirs on your behalf!"

Percy stared, stunned, numb, disbelieving.

"I'll do it—for Percy!" a familiar young voice cried, teeny and cracking and childish. It was Jenna Doneil.

"Oh, no! No, Jen, no!" Percy was horrified.

There was a pause.

And then, "All right, I'll do it." An old limping soldier said loudly. "Might as well, since a gentle death at my age would be a blessing."

"Take my life, Percy Ayren!" cried a young new widow from the crowd of San Quellenne.

"And aye, you can have mine for the Black Knight!" a burly musketeer exclaimed.

"And mine, for the Chidair bastard, since he spared me once in battle, bless him!" another wizened soldier cried out, wearing Goraque colors.

More and more voices sounded, until the crowd roared, "For Percy! For the Black Knight!"

Suddenly two elegantly dressed aristocrats pushed their way through the group of those who had come from the plain where had stood the cities.

Lady Amaryllis Roulle was dressed in a lovely blue winter coat, with a jaunty plumed hat and great rubies along the brim and at her throat, while at her side was Lord Nathan Woult, clean-shaven and elegant in a fine black greatcoat and starched lace at his throat.

"Enough! This noblest and fairest of Ladies from the Silver Court and I have decided!" exclaimed Lord Nathan in a loud commanding voice that carried over others and effectively silenced the crowd. "We hereby volunteer our lives in this worthy endeavor!"

"Damned aristos . . ." someone muttered. "Even now they won't let us have our chance at peaceful deaths, blast 'em."

Percy gazed in absolute astonishment, not only at the outpouring of the crowd, but now at these two familiar nobles, appearing out of nowhere and offering so much.

Persephone meanwhile appraised them with a wise gaze, and she said, "It is good. I will take what you believe to be your trite and humdrum lives and imbue them with meaning."

"My ennui is hereby banished!" Lady Amaryllis exclaimed, and glanced at Nathan with her dark eyes that were suddenly sparkling with vivacity.

"We are absolutely stark mad, but oh, what an adventure awaits!" he replied, looking at her intently.

Persephone looked at Percy. "Now, my child, are you ready to live again?" And then she glanced at Hecate.

"I am," Percy whispered. "But only if I can also love."

They had returned to Letheburg—or what remained of it, a portion of wall and a handful of streets, including Rollins Way.

Lord Beltain Chidair's body was placed in a covered wagon and driven the distance of less than a mile from the forest into Letheburg. Percy walked alongside it—even though she was *in spirit*—of which she was unconvinced, even now.

Lord Nathan and Amaryllis walked behind them, choosing to take a stroll as their last outing. And at one point Nathan took the Lady's slim gloved hand and he pressed it to his lips. "For courage . . ." he whispered.

"I need none!" she replied.

"I do . . ." And Nathan's handsome face appeared vulnerable for a moment. "What are we doing, Amaryllis, love?"

She glanced at him, dark and beautiful and fey. "We are

doing something *worthwhile*."

"But—what of the rest of our lives? Maybe at some wiser, more rational point we might choose to do something else?"

"Such as what?"

"Oh, I don't know, perchance, dearest, I might venture one of these days to ask you to marry me?"

"What?" Amaryllis stopped walking. "Fie!" she said. "Nathan! I thought we've agreed never to speak of such odious matters! We are the League of Folly, after all, a pair of delightful friends forever linked in wit, intellect, and perfect camaraderie! Why bring odious love and romance into it and spoil everything?"

"You are right," he said with a tiny smile, and then a laugh. And they resumed walking.

At some point, just as they were entering the city, a tiny furry creature raced underfoot, then turned its long, whiskered muzzle to stare.

"Look, a polecat!" Amaryllis exclaimed. "Such a furry, wily little red thing, it reminds me of someone, though I cannot recall—"

They moved on. But Hecate, glancing with mercy at the tiny creature who for some reason paused to observe them all with very astute, almost *human* eyes, said to the little beast, "Come, dumpling, fear not. . . . It is not so bad, being a polecat, is it? Quite a change of pace for you, wouldn't you say. . . . From now on, you will serve me."

And the polecat sniffed the air and followed at a safe distance.

The wagon turned into Rollins Way, and then the Black Knight's body was carried gently through the red door and into Grial's house.

"Stay out here for a moment, dearie," Hecate said to Percy. "I asked Ebrai to stay behind to watch over your body, and now we'll put your dear Beltain inside also, and I want to make sure everything is presentable."

Percy stood patiently, waiting, during the strangest moments of her *conscious existence*—for surely this was not her *life*.

When she was finally beckoned inside, gently, by Hecate, Percy saw that the large kitchen table had been pulled out and brought into the front parlor.

Upon it lay two people.

The first was Beltain, free of his black armor plates and his chain mail, and now clad in a clean white linen shirt. Pale and gaunt and suddenly *different*-looking from himself, he lay— inexplicable, in the way of death that makes dolls of all of us. Not a trace of blood anywhere, and Percy's non-existent heart raced like mad nevertheless, seeing him thus. For the shirt covered the hole in his chest. . . .

The second person was—

Percy blinked.

It was *herself*.

Percy stared, frozen, stilled, never in her wildest nightmares imagining that she would one day have the privilege of looking down at her own body from the outside perspective of *another*.

Lord, she was fat! Pudgy and fat and awkward, and her hair was of a dull color in its messy braid, and her round face seemed utterly bland. Thank goodness her eyes were closed, because Percy really did not want to look at herself that way, eye-to-eye.

In moments, Persephone walked into the room. And suddenly light was cast everywhere, bright, joyful, redolent of youth and spring-blooming flowers.

Lady Amaryllis and Lord Nathan sat down on the sofa. "What should we do?" the lady exclaimed, nearly hyperventilating. "Should we lie down or sit or stand? What is the best, most artful and aesthetic posture to assume for eternity? That is of course for about five minutes, until they fold us up and put us in long boxes?"

Lord Nathan clutched her hand. And suddenly he leaned in and took Amaryllis's beautiful face in both his hands and he pressed his mouth against hers in a hard kiss.

She sputtered, and then suddenly she was pliant and her lips parted briefly and she kissed him back with one gasp of secret hunger. They looked into each other's eyes. And both of them smiled.

"What greatest mystery awaits on the other side!" Nathan whispered.

"Nathan!" the lady said suddenly, gripping his hand tight. "I am glad—I am *fortunate* that I will be discovering it with *you.* . . ."

"Are you ready, my beloved?" Persephone said in that instant, speaking to Percy, and also to all the others present.

Percy nodded and again felt spectral, unreal liquid come to her eyes.

Then close your eyes now, child, and remember the spring.

She looked at the two bodies lying motionless on the table. And she looked at the two living, suddenly very real people who were about to take their place.

Amaryllis, Nathan.

Thank you.

And Percy Ayren shut her eyes.

Chapter 19

It hurt! Oh, it hurt!

Percy gasped, deeply inhaled air into strangely atrophied lungs, and then she felt her entire body tingling sharply, with renewed circulation.

Everything ached and hurt!

She was lying on the surface of the table, staring at the ceiling. And at her side—

At her side, suddenly she could hear *him* breathing!

Beltain!

The face of the Goddess Persephone was hovering over them both, and then Percy could hear Beltain coughing, and shifting, which made the table creak under his weight.

She stirred, and turned her head, and there he was!

Lord Beltain Chidair sat up on his elbows, and he looked an awful fright, his face gaunt, unshaven, and almost bluish, with sharp prominent angles of jaw, cheekbones.

But it lasted only for a moment, for even as Percy looked, the Goddess of Resurrection placed her hands upon his forehead and her own, and there was a brilliant white flash of lightning inside Percy's mind.

She blinked again, seeing the electric flare on her retina when the lids came down. And then she suddenly felt perfectly normal. Her body was warm, and she moved and easily sat up.

Beltain turned around, and he was still unshaven, but there was a warm healthy color on his cheeks and his skin was rich living bronze. And his eyes—oh, his beautiful, kind, blue eyes, they looked upon her with such awed wonder, and he said, "*Percy!* Are you a fair dream? Am I dead in Heaven? Or the Underworld?"

"Beltain!" Percy simply fell upon him full-body, and she clutched him with both her arms and cradled him against her, and she started to weep uncontrollably, her face hidden against his chest.

And it was then, wonder of wonders, that she heard his strongly beating, living *heart*.

Beltain awoke, pulled from somewhere indescribable—a place, a state of being, for which there were no words, and which was already receding from memory like a distant dream—but its afterflash seared his eyes with blinding whiteness.

He shuddered and he sucked in air hungrily with atrophied lungs, and he breathed, and felt the entirety of his body burn with fire, as blood returned to movement within his veins, and his chest hurt like Hades and Tartarus and hell all put together. . . .

He heard voices, some strange, some beatific, and he was aware that he lay on something hard. He opened his eyes, and there was a ceiling, vaguely familiar . . . Grial's house?

Beltain breathed and breathed some more, and stirred and groaned and flexed his hands and fingers, and—

With a jolt, it came to him—the last thing he remembered, before all *this*, was the horror of Percy screaming, standing in the snowy woods at a chaotic scene of battle, while he had just been shot by a musket round, and he knew he had died, but . . . because death was stopped, he transitioned to the strange un-death, and he was still *there*.

Beltain remembered that moment, sharp and clear. . . . The agonizing shock to his heart, and then his body had suddenly receded from him, and he was like a bird trapped in a cage of thick walls of unresponsive flesh, and everything was so remote. . . . And then—because he knew there was no certain time left for anything, not ever again—he got down from Jack, and stood before Percy and took her beloved face to him, barely feeling its sweet dear softness through the thickness of his dead fingers, and kissed her . . . again, barely feeling her lips with his own—*hurry, hurry, while you still remember how it feels*. . . .

Something serene had come to him then, at the end. "Put us all to rest, my love . . ." he had said.

And then Percy screamed and screamed. . . .

Beltain blinked, and he felt a bout of dizziness, and his head was still thick and fuzzy. But he felt surprisingly strong, and then he could prop himself up on his elbows, and he turned his head to the side and saw . . . Percy!

She lay at his side, and his heart gave a healthy jolt and was pounding with joy.

"Percy!" he exclaimed, and he mumbled something else, some nonsense about dreaming, and then all he could see were her hauntingly beautiful eyes, her rosy face, for some reason wet with tears, and the reddened nose and the lips that were full and ripe. . . .

And the next instant she was embracing him, hugging him with the raw force of a berserker warrior, and her arms were fiercely strong and warm, and he was holding her, stroking her hair as she pressed herself tighter and sobbed into his chest . . . and then overwhelming sweet heat came to him, a vigor born of flaming impossible joy . . . and his body was suddenly fierce and virile and he was scalding hot, burning like the first sun of spring. . . .

"Percy, oh my Percy!" he said, his voice cracking. But her soft lips were upon his, drinking his living breath, and he was now gasping in divine madness, pressing his mouth over hers like a drowning man, *breathing* through her. . . .

"That would be quite enough for now, pumpkins, else you break my lovely kitchen table!" Grial's voice sounded, familiar, loud and sonorous as always. *Grial—she is Hecate, the Goddess,* it occurred to him. Her voice—such a human, brash, ringing sound. For some reason it was possibly the most wonderful sound in the world.

Percy tore away her face from his, and she grasped his coarse, stubble-covered cheeks with both her hands like the most precious thing. She glanced into his eyes with wildness and she laughed! She laughed, open-mouthed, gulping, nose-snorting, horsey sounds, loud and brash and mindless of anything in complete joyful delight.

Ah, thought Beltain. *But it is* this *sound, this is the most wonderful sound in the world.*

Percy and Beltain, hands still twined around each other, limbs touching, unable to let go even for a moment, got down from the table, and looked around.

This was Grial's front parlor, but what a horrible mess of broken things and upturned furniture. There were also people present, familiar faces—Hecate the Goddess herself, and Ebrai Fiomarre stood off to the side and a few girls were peeking from the back . . . and there was Persephone, radiant Goddess of Spring, standing before them.

Percy turned to the sofa, clutching Beltain's hand, and she quieted. . . .

Two still figures were seated there. Heads leaning toward the other, hands placed together. Amaryllis and Nathan.

They were *gone.*

A sharp jolt of awe came to Percy, and her eyes burned.

"They have given their lives for our own, Beltain," she whispered. "I don't even know how to begin to honor them. . . ." And Percy told Beltain what had come to pass—not all of it, for that would require long evenings and intimate words—but enough.

"Honor them by living your lives and loving one another as was your life's desire," said the Goddess Persephone.

Percy stared at her, willing herself to remember even a

moment of former hatred, of bitterness, of accusation for all that had come to pass. But there was none. . . . It had been washed away in the sacrifice.

As they spoke thus, more people came through the red door into Grial's house.

Lady Jelavie San Quellenne stepped within, and Ebrai Fiomarre gave her a long glance and a brief smile. She in turn, nodded proudly, and then announced: "My people of San Quellenne and I are leaving. Where to, it is uncertain, but it might be France—that is, if it still stands! This insane war is over, for blessedly there is no one left to fight, and no land to be fought over. Have you looked outside? Your city, Letheburg is no more, and there are some other strange streets with signs in a foreign language! I asked a man where were was the last remaining wall of Letheburg and he looked at me as if I were mad. He spoke words I could not understand! He pointed at the streets and said, 'Luxembourg, Luxembourg!'"

There were many looks of confusion.

"It is true, your entire Realm and Domain are no more," Hecate spoke gently. "What remains of the city you once knew as Letheburg is this little house, and it alone shall stand thus, even though no one will ever remember where it had stood before."

"But, Grial! Oh dear, I mean, Hecate!" Flor Murel spoke up from the back. "What has happened to all of it? Where is Oarclaven and the rest of Lethe? And all the rest of it?"

"It is all with us now, in the Underworld." Persephone lifted up her hand, palm up and on her palm a silvery lavender light appeared, blooming like a great lotus.

They looked, and it was like a window into another place. They could see a distant soft sun illuminating a vast familiar expanse, and below it a swiftly flying bird's eye view of golden palace roofs, streets and gardens, and then more cities and a sweet rolling countryside. Faster the panorama swept by them, tall fields of flowers and pastures and then snow-tipped mountains, and snaking rivers reflecting like mirrors the gentle sun. . . .

"That is Charonne, the great city of Styx!" Ebrai said in wonder. "And the Elysian Fields of Balmue, at the foot of the Aepiennes!"

"And there, I see the warm sea lapping, it is surely Tanathe, our Rivereal, and look, that was the Island, and oh, Saga Mountain!" Tears welled in Jelavie's eyes.

A blink, and there was Lake Merlait, frozen and snow-filled, and then expanses of evergreens and then a rich forest of bare branches, twisted and graphic-fine like cobwebs.

"Those are Chidair northern forests . . ." Beltain whispered.

"And look, I see my beautiful Serenoa!" suddenly exclaimed little Marie. "Look how beautiful flows the river Eridanos!" Marie had come into the house followed by Lizabette and Faeline and Catrine and Niosta, for they had found their way back here somehow.

They continued looking, and at last the vision faded.

"I will treasure your Realm and your Domain with all my heart," Persephone said. "For they are now my dominion, and that of my sweet love."

"But what of all those people? Are they dead?"

"Our families, friends? Can we not visit them? Can they come forth and come here?"

"No mortal can come Below while living, or return Above," Persephone said with sorrow. "They came to be with us through a miracle that may never be replicated. But I promise you they are not dead, and they will live out their lives just as they have always, and new generations will be born in joy, and old will pass on. They are a special people now, belonging to both worlds, mortal and divine, and their fate is a sacred mystery. Never before had there been such a place, for the Underworld is now a great world unto itself."

"And now," Hecate said to them, "it is time for all of you to go. Choose a direction into the winds, for the greatest Crossroads stands before you, the Crossroads of the rest of your lives. There are many lands left standing, for the World itself has been healed, and no more places will disappear into the Underworld, since it has now collected that which belonged to it, in full."

"We will bury our dead with honor first, however we may," said Beltain.

"It shall be done," Persephone said. And then she glanced at Percy with a strange intimate glance. "Percy, you must speak to *him* one last time, child. My dark immortal love waits outside these walls, only steps away through the shadow."

Percy paused for a moment, but Beltain took her hand firmly, and together they and the others followed Persephone into the daylight outside.

The streets were narrow, quaint, curving, snow covered cobblestones and bright cheerful shingles in a language that was unfamiliar to Percy. Overhead, grey wintry sky.

They took a few steps, waiting for a donkey driven cart to rattle by, and then directly overhead there was soft crystal laughter.

Everyone looked up, wondering.

Up on the roof sat two figures dressed in brilliant white, their feet dangling. The beautiful young man wore a jaunty hat, and the young woman was like a snowflake.

Suddenly they both jumped . . . and then floated down softly, and they stood before the people on the street.

"Jack Frost! And the Snow Maiden!" someone exclaimed, and it was Jenna Doneil, clapping her hands together in absolute wonder. "Oh, I *knew* it!"

"Your Imperial Highness? *Claere?*" Lizabette said. "And the Marquis Vlau Fiomarre? What has happened to you, you both look beastly *white!*"

The Snow Maiden laughed and raised a hand, and suddenly

a flurry of snowflakes came down upon their heads, raining from heaven like white flower blossoms. "Claere would be my one and only true name. As for 'Imperial Highness,' let someone else have that dubious honor in the Underworld. My dear Father and Mother reign there now, and it is well enough with me!"

But Jack Frost was staring at a raven-haired handsome man before him, with a strong family resemblance. And Ebrai Fiomarre stared back with strange, intense, haunted eyes.

"Ebrai!" said Vlau. "My brother! Oh, my *brother!* You are alive!"

The older Fiomarre approached him, and reached out his hand. There was an instant of pause, and suddenly they came together in a tight embrace.

"Br-r-r!" Ebrai exclaimed. "You are so damn cold, little Vlau! But yes, both Father and I are blessedly alive, and have been working for the Liguon Emperor all this time, you sorry fool, so no dishonor stains our ancient family name. Father is well enough, although he has aged quite a bit, though now I believe he is in the Underworld along with the entire rest of the Sapphire Court. He will have a time of it, with all the political factions and clandestine machinations, now that they no longer have the Sovereign to plot against, whatever shall they do?"

But Jack Frost laughed, and suddenly he turned slightly blue—while all the chill seemed to be sucked out of the air around them—then he paled again, and kissed his brother on the cheek with as warm a kiss as could be. They stepped off to the side and started whispering, raven heads close together. Oh, the stories they had to tell!

"Beltain Chidair!" exclaimed the Snow Maiden, folding her arms. "Beltain, your father is well also, though you would not know it from the amount of huffing and puffing he does, blowing this winter air all about, thickening the overcast, and still furious at us for taking away some of his fun."

"What of my father?" Beltain looked at the Maiden with bitterness. "What has befallen the madman who was Duke Ian

Chidair, known as Hoarfrost?"

"You might be happy to know he is no longer a dead bitter old fool, but an immortal one. He is Old Man Winter himself, terrifying, bleak, and as vicious as is the nature of the season, and he will hold a grudge against you for some time, but not forever, this I promise."

"What? What does that mean?"

"Your father is an elemental now, just as we are. He is Winter, and thus, you might beware some of the chillier northern climes, wherever you make your new home. However, do not let fear keep you away from us entirely. For I promise," said the Snow Maiden, "I will always keep the snows away from you."

"And I promise," said Jack Frost, looking away briefly from his brother, "I will always keep the cold at bay, and the wicked bite of frost shall never harm you."

"Then let my Father Winter blow and frown," Beltain said with a smile, exchanging glances with Percy. "I think we will choose warmer lands for now, though in time we will visit you."

They stood thus outside the house with the freshly painted red door on a street of Luxembourg, speaking with hope and energy and making choices. At last Persephone, bright Goddess, motioned to Percy and Beltain, and they took a few steps after her, toward the shadowed spot at the corner between two houses.

Hecate threw Percy a warm glance from her very, very dark eyes, and she waived and nodded.

Percy glanced at her, saw her gaze of wisdom and love, and then she turned and followed Persephone into the sudden gathering of mist. Beltain stepped in right behind her.

They emerged into a Hall of bones and fluttering cobwebs, and immediately a serene sense of eternity came to them. The lighting in the Hall was once more somnolent soft dusk, and only a few steps before them was the dais and upon it Death's Throne.

Hades, Lord Death Himself stood before it, on the top stair. He was in his silver Shadow aspect, harboring the White Bridegroom and the Black Husband in equal measure.

He was strong and hale and his handsome face wore a light, slightly sardonic smile.

It was a smile that touched Percy, for there was the wanton simmer of desire underneath, at the same time as there was compassion.

Persephone stepped aside and she pointed Percy toward the Lord of the Underworld.

"My Champion," Death uttered. "Come!"

With a look at Beltain, Percy approached the dais.

Hades, great dark God, stood looking down at Percy as she climbed each step.

At last she stopped before him.

"My Lord Hades," she said. "Here I am."

"And here you are." His fathomless eyes surrounded her. "You have done well, sweet Persephone Ayren, and you have done even more than I asked of you. You have restored to me my Cobweb Bride, and my one true love, and the mortal world persists because of you."

Percy gazed into his eyes and she asked. "Might I ask a boon of you, My Lord? Since I have done all I can for Death, will you now take the dark power of death away from me? For in this world I want to never again lay anyone to rest."

Hades smiled.

He neared Percy and he placed his clawed hand upon her cheek, drawing it down softly. Where he touched, a chill ran through her, and Percy shivered, feeling the chill of the grave.

"Regretfully, I can never take the reality of death and dying from you, Persephone. You are mine ultimately, as is all your kind. However, I will ease this burden from you for the rest of your days."

Hades bent his head, and he placed a light kiss upon her forehead, a touch that left no sensation at all, but in that moment

Percy felt something profound—a darkness—leave her, and in its place entered a measure of light.

Such a strange relief came to her, that Percy wanted to cavort like a silly goose and spread her arms and dance. Instead she smiled at Lord Hades and she said, "Please take care of my parents and my sisters, for they are now of your Kingdom and you are their King. Oh, if only I could visit them!"

King Death nodded at her and he said, "I shall care for them as my own children, of which I had none before and now I have as many as there are diamond stars upon the roof of my subterranean heaven. As for visiting them, know you not, child that you can visit them every night in your dreams? Simply ask Queen Mab before you sleep, and she will grant you dreams of your loved ones in the Underworld."

Percy glanced behind her where Persephone stood like the essence of spring, bringing a living glow to the shadowed Hall.

"What of Melinoë?" she dared to ask softly.

For a moment, Persephone and Hades both remained silent.

And then Persephone raised her gentle gaze at her. "My child Melinoë is already with us, in the realm Below. Her memory is sweet, and I have shaped her beloved ashes into a luminary upon the sphere of subterranean heaven, and she shines brightly there, one of the stars—but nothing more."

Persephone paused then, gathering herself, and she continued, "There is one secret that I had not admitted to anyone before all this, a secret which I have never spoken but which I can now divulge at last, for I am renewed and healed and made strong enough to bear the revelation—all because of your own act of sacrifice.

"Truth is, I had taken Melinoë my child up with me to the world Above, knowing very well that it would destroy her, because I *wanted* her to die. . . . I knew that Melinoë was a vaporous thing of shadows, and she was made wrong and incomplete, a mistake of my own creation. She could neither have a true life nor a true death, all because of my own selfish hubris—for I birthed her Below in a moment of anger and pique.

"And thus I, who regularly give birth to so many—indeed to all in your mortal world—I made the terrible decision to end her existence. I was a murderess mother! And it was the guilt at what I had done—her creation and her destruction—that broke me. As my mind went darker with despair and self-hatred, I blamed Demeter the Bright Mother of Harvest, but it was I who sat Melinoë on my lap and together we rose Above, and in the doing I shattered the Sapphire Throne.

"For as soon as we went through the rebirth, and Melinoë fell apart, the Sapphire Throne received a hairline crack, and thus the sickness of *instability* was initiated. Guilt drove me for a hundred years, together with self-hatred. I was rid of her who was 'my mistake' and in doing so I myself became the greater mistake, the instrument of the end. For you cannot escape yourself, especially if you are immortal."

Persephone sighed, then a bittersweet light came to her. "But enough, it is now behind us. For to dwell on evil is to call it into being, and I call only the spring and joyful life force."

"And thus," Hades spoke in a ringing voice of power, to dispel the sorrow, "it is time to live, and to love, Percy Ayren. You are no longer my Champion, for you are now *your own*. You have done your duty to the divine and now all the freedom of mortal choices is before you. Take your human lover and live your lives in joy and mortal wonder—a thing that even the gods envy you who see all things of the world with innocent eyes."

"The Gods," Percy said softly. "What strange creatures you are! Indeed, knowing now all that I know, whom shall we mortals pray to? To you, Grecian gods? Perchance to other gods of ancient times and distant lands? To angels? Or to the One God?"

"Pray to One, pray to many, pray to none," the dark God replied. "The world turns regardless. What matters any of it, as long as a true prayer is forged in your heart and it calls for a true answer? Sometimes, the only true answer is nothing at all, for there can be none. But it is always *heard* by at least one of us—the one who can make a difference."

Hades turned to Persephone then, and he held out his hand. "Come, fair Goddess Persephone, my only love! We have come to the end of speeches and farewells here. And while spring comes to reawaken the land, you and I shall tarry and bide our ghostly time here Above, in my shadow Hall—You in your Bright Aspect, and I as a mere shadow, the Lord Death—until next season when you again return to me Below in the flesh!"

Persephone strode forward with a light step, and approached her immortal lover and husband.

Percy meanwhile descended the dais, and took Beltain's hand. They stood watching while Hades took Persephone to him in an ethereal embrace, and the snakes around his hair stood up, while a strong wind arose through the Hall, sending up dust and cobwebs in a silver funnel about them. Faster and faster the maelstrom spun, while the immortal forms of the God and Goddess blurred, and soon there was only dusk and light.

Fare thee well, and blessed be, beloved! sounded both their voices.

Percy and Beltain had no time to blink, for they were back in the mortal world.

The ship sailing from the busy port of Marseille left the harbor and entered the balmy waters of the Mediterranean, with a fair wind and a cargo of goods and passengers.

Percy and Beltain stood on deck, watching the foam and the strange greenish-blue rich waters. Catrine and Niosta were somewhere below deck, together with their father who had arranged everyone's passage, including a number of former Goraque soldiers and civilians, half the town of San Quellenne and various other stragglers from Lethe, Styx, Morphaea, Balmue, Solemnis, Serenoa, and Tanathe. They were all seen as harmless but incomprehensible foreigners by the ship's crew of Frenchmen, who could not understand—no matter how much they tried—who the devil these people were and where on earth they had all come from.

"Might they be those wandering Romany folk?" muttered an old sailor.

"Maybe Egyptians?" another said, biting into a knot of rope he was tying.

"I think that tall knight, the one who stands with the pretty round-cheeked lass, is a Norse Dutchman. . . . He has the look of a fighting man, and a great built on him, well muscled. Those arms, *tres magnifique!* No wonder the *mademoiselle* is sweet on him."

"About as much as he is on her. It's a pleasure to watch the young lovers, eh? *Vive l'amour!*"

The shores of France were receding and Percy cast a soft glance at the misty morning haze and then at Beltain.

The young man was looking down at her with a frankly enamored soft gaze of his slate blue eyes. His arm was about her, and Percy leaned into him, and saw underneath the smooth linen of his shirt, open at the neck, the bronze planes of his chest with its light sprinkling of brown hair. She was staring at the spot right above his heart. The skin was pristine, smooth, with not a trace of an old mortal wound—as if it had never happened.

Percy breathed a sigh of infinite relief as yet again she placed her fingers upon his chest and felt its strong heart beating. "Promise me," she said, "you will not die!"

"I promise," he said with a smile. "Not for a very long time. Not until you are so sick of me that you send me packing as a ninety year old man. And now you must promise the same."

"Do not die! Not ever!" she said. "Do not even jest, for I cannot bear it, this much I know now. I will end the world myself if anything happens to you, Beltain!"

"But, sweet Percy," he whispered in her ear. "You are no longer Death's Champion."

"I am my own Champion and yours."

"Will you then wed me, a poor landless knight, with only a good name of Chidair that no one on this earth remembers, duke of a long-gone land, and no fortune except my great black horse, my retired suit of armor, and my sword? Will you give me sweet fat children? Will you strike me lovingly with a skillet once a year in memory of all good things?"

"Yes," she said, "Sir Knight, ninny fool, love of my life."

He pressed his lips against her forehead and held her very tight. "Then I think we will do very well together, you and I . . . My Lady Persephone Chidair."

The ship was only a few hundred feet from the harbor when a strange light seemed to shine from the waters, from the hazy greenish depths below.

"Oh look! What is that?" Percy pointed to some strange fluid shape of translucence that passed beneath them as they moved through the occasional foaming swells.

Or rather, they passed over *it*.

Whatever it was, it suddenly caught the light of the sun like a prism, and it seemed to reflect a thousand tiny colored stars like a rainbow of fractured shards, a thing of molten blue and heliotrope and lavender and liquid sky. . . .

Sapphire blue.

Percy and Beltain looked overboard and gazed with wonder at what was surely a splendid chair, made of translucent glass . . . as though the wind had stolen itself underwater and taken the fluid form of a throne.

It was the *Sapphire Throne* of the Domain.

The only remainder of the past, it would thus grace the dreamland of the Mediterranean waters, and one day, a goddess might reawaken upon it and rise forth, bursting in delight, to play upon the waves.

The Beginning

Author's Note:
Imaginary History, Mythology and Cosmology

If you've made it this far, you are probably wondering about some of the liberties taken with history, in particular the fantasy version of the Renaissance, and the unusual European geography and mythical topology and mindset in this alternate universe.

The *Cobweb Bride* trilogy takes place in an imaginary "pocket" of Europe sometime in an alternate version of the 17th century Renaissance. I've modified the continent of Europe by inserting a significant wedge of land between France and Italy, dissolving Austria and Hungary into Germany and pushing the whole thing up north, shifting Spain halfway to the east and lowering the northern shores of the Mediterranean by pushing the southern portion of the continental landmass further down south so that the French Riviera is now where the sea is in our own reality.

Imagine a cross, with Germany up north, Spain to the south, France to the west, and Italy to the East. In the heart of the cross lies the imaginary land that comprises the Realm and the Domain.

Now that you've read the third and final book, you see that this is really an origin myth about the creation of the Underworld. It is also a myth of the grand scheme of things—the cycle of life and death (as they are inseparably linked together) and the cosmology involved, based on ancient Greek traditions. Persephone and Hades take center stage in this worldview, and I think they fit remarkably well into the sensibilities of the Renaissance. Indeed many of the Renaissance ideals evolved from the classical world, so this is truly a "marriage made on Olympus."

According to Greek myth, Hecate took responsibility for the polecat. Pomegranates are really an Underworld "thing." What happened at the original Eleusinian Mysteries remains a mystery, but I choose to think that it could very well be the pantomime of the Longest Night. Of course, in the language of modern science, it is also the metaphor for the Big Bang.

The culture of the mythical Realm and the Domain is an uneven mixture of French, Italian, Spanish, and German influences of the late Middle Ages and early Renaissance. The language spoken is Latin-based "Romance," and the linguistics are also a mixture of the same.

Other minor liberties taken include the referral to some physical parcels of land as "Dukedom" as opposed to the correct term "Duchy." Royal and noble titles, ranks, and their terminology are similar, but not the exact equivalents of our own historical reality.

I hope you enjoyed spending time with Percy, Beltain, Claere, Vlau, and all the other curious mortals and gods in this mythic tapestry of story.

May Queen Mab herself bring you the sweetest dreams of airy wonder and delight!

And now, please see the next page for a list of all the character names with a pronunciation key.

List of Characters
(Dramatis Personae)

With Pronunciation Key

Death, Lord of the Keep of the Northern Forest

Village of Oarclaven (Lethe) (Oh-ahr-CLAY-ven)
Persephone (Per-SEH-pho-nee) or **Percy** (PUR-see) **Ayren** (EYE-Ren), middle daughter
Parabelle (Pah-rah-BELL) or **Belle** (Bell) **Ayren**, eldest daughter
Patriciana (Pah-tree-see-AHNA) or **Patty** (PEH-dee) **Ayren**, youngest daughter
Niobea (Nee-oh-BEH-ah) **Ayren**, their mother
Alann (Ah-LAHN) **Ayren**, their father
Bethesia (Beth-EH-zee-ah) **Ayren**, their grandmother
Johuan (Joh-HWAN) **Ayren**, their grandfather
Guel (Goo-EHL) **Ayren**, their uncle from Fioren (south of Letheburg)
Jack Rosten (ROS-ten), villager
Jules (JOOL-z), Jack's second son, promised to Jenna Doneil
Father **Dibue** (Dee-B'YOU), village priest
Nicholas (NIH-koh-luss) **Doneil** (Doh-NEYL), village butcher
Marie (Muh-REE) **Doneil**, his wife
Faith Groaden (GROW-den), village girl
Mister **Jaquard** (Zhah-KARD), villager
Uncle **Roald** (ROH-uld), villager, the Ayrens' neighbor across the street.
Bettie (BEH-tee), village girl

Kingdom of Lethe (LEH-thee) *(Realm)*
The Prince Heir **Roland** (Roh-LUND) **Osenni** (Oh-SYEN-nee) of Lethe
The Princess **Lucia** (Liu-SEE-ah) **Osenni** of Lethe
Queen Mother **Andrelise** (Un-dreh-LEEZ) **Osenni**
Prince **John-Meryl** (JON MEH-reel) **Osenni**, son and heir of the Prince.

Dukedom of Chidair (Chee-DEHR) *(Lethe)*
Duke **Hoarfrost, Ian Chidair** of Lethe
Lord **Beltain** (Bell-TEYN) **Chidair** of Lethe, his son, the black knight
Rivour (Ree-VOOR), Beltain's old valet
Father **Orweil** (Or-WAIL), Chidair family chapel priest
Riquar (Reek-WAHR), Beltain's man-a-arms
Laurent (Loh-RENT), pennant bearer of Chidair
Annie, girl in the forest

Dukedom of Goraque (Gor-AH-k) *(Lethe)*
Duke **Vitalio** (Vee-TAH-lee-oh) **Goraque** of Lethe

The Silver Court (Realm)

The Emperor **Josephuste** (Jo-zeh-FOOS-teh) **Liguon** (Lee-G'WON) **II** of the Realm
The Empress **Justinia** (Joo-STEE-nee-ah) **Liguon**
The Infanta **Claere** (KLEH-r) **Liguon,** the Grand Princess
Lady **Milagra** (Mee-LAH-grah) **Rinon** (Ree-NOHN), the Infanta's First Lady-in-Attendance
Marquis **Rinon** of Morphaea, her father
Lady **Selene** (Seh-LEHN) **Jenevais** (Zheh-neh-VAH-is), Lady-in-Attendance, of Lethe
Lady **Floricca** (FLOH-ree-kah) **Grati** (GRAH-tee), Lady-in-Attendance, of Styx
Lady **Liana** (Lee-AH-nah) **Crusait** (Kroo-SAH-eet), Lady-in-Attendance, of Morphaea
Lady **Alis** (Ah-LEE-s) **Denear** (Deh-ne-AHR), Lady-in-Attendance, of Lethe
Baron **Carlo** (KAR-loh) **Irnolas** (Eer-noh-LAH-s), Imperial knight
Lord **Givard** (Ghee-VAHR-d) **Mariseli** (Mah-ree-SEH-lee), Imperial Knight
Doctor **Belquar** (Behl-KWAH-r), head Imperial physician
Doctor **Hartel** (Hahr-TEH-l), Imperial physician

Kingdom of Styx (STEEK-s) (Realm)

King **Augustus** (Uh-GUS-tus) **Ixion** (EEK-see-ohn) of Styx
King **Claudeis** (Kloh-DEH-ees) **Ixion** of Styx, deceased
Queen **Rea** (REH-ah) **Ixion** of Styx, deceased
Marquis **Vlau** (V'LAH-oo) **Fiomarre** (F'yoh-MAH-r) of Styx
Micul (Mee-KOOL) **Fiomarre** of Styx, Vlau's father
Ebrai (Eh-BRAH-ee) **Fiomarre**, Vlau's older brother
Celen (Seh-LEH-n) **Fiomarre**, Vlau's younger brother
Marquise **Eloise** (Eh-loh-EEZ) **Fiomarre**, Vlau's mother, deceased
Oleandre (Oh-leh-AHN-dr) **Fiomarre**, Vlau's younger sister
Lady **Ignacia** (Eeg-NAY-shuh) **Chitain** (Chee-TAY-n), of Styx/Balmue

Kingdom of Morphaea (Mohr-FEH-ah) (Realm)

King **Orphe** (Or-FEH) **Geroard** (Geh-roh-AHR-d) of Morphaea
Duke **Claude** (KLOH-d) **Rovait** (Roh-VEY-t) of Morphaea
Andre (Ahn-DREH) **Eldon** (Ehl-DOH-n), the Duke of **Plaimes** (PLEY-m's), of Morphaea
Duchess **Christiana** (Khree-stee-AH-nah) **Rovait** of Morphaea
Countess **Jain** (JEY-n) **Lirabeau** (Lee-rah-BOH) of Morphaea
Lady **Amaryllis** (Ah-mah-REE-liss) **Roulle** (ROOL), of Morphaea
Lord **Nathan** (NEY-th'n) **Woult** (WOOL-t), of Morphaea

The Road

Grial (Gree-AHL), witch woman from **Letheburg** (LEH-thee-b'rg)
Ronna (ROHN-nuh) **Liet** (LEE-eh-t), Innkeeper at **Tussecan** (TUSS-see-kahn), Grial's cousin
Mrs. **Beck** (BEH-k), cook at Ronna's Inn
Jenna (JEH-nuh) **Doneil** (Doh-NEY-l), butcher's daughter from Oarclaven
Flor (FLOH-r) **Murel** (M'you-REH-l), baker's daughter from Oarclaven
Gloria (GLOH-ree-ah) **Libbin** (LEE-bin), blacksmith's daughter from Oarclaven

Emilie (Eh-mee-LEE) **Bordon** (Bohr-DOHN), swineherd's daughter from south of Oarclaven
Sibyl (SEE-beel), tailor's daughter from Letheburg
Regata (Reh-GAH-tah), merchant's daughter from Letheburg
Lizabette (Lee-zah-BET) **Crowlé** (Krow-LEH), teacher's daughter from Duarden (Doo-AHR-dehn)
Catrine (Kaht-REEN), sister of Niosta, from south of Letheburg
Niosta (Nee-OHS-tuh), sister of Catrine, from south of Letheburg
Marie (Mah-REE), girl from **Fioren** (F'YOH-rehn), originally from the Kingdom of **Serenoa** (Seh-REH-noh-ah) (Domain)

The Sapphire Court (Domain)
The Sovereign, **Rumanar** (Roo-mah-NAH-r) **Avalais** (Ah-vah-LAH-ees) of the Domain

Kingdom of Balmue (Bahl-MOO) *(Domain)*
King **Clavian** (Klah-vee-AHN) **Sestial** (Ses-tee-AH-l) of Balmue
Marquis **Nuor** (Noo-OHR) **Alfre** (Ahl-FREH), ambassador of Balmue, Peer of the Domain
Viscount **Halronne** (Hal-RONN) **Deupris** (Deh-oo-PREE), Peer of the Domain

New Characters Introduced in Cobweb Empire

Kingdom of Lethe (Realm)
Carlinne (Kahr-LEEN) **Ayren**, wife of Guel, in Fioren
Martin (MAHR-tin) **Ayren**, Percy's cousin in Fioren
Mistress **Saronne** (Sah-RONN), tavern proprietress in Duarden
André (Ahn-DREH) **Saronne**, young boy, her son, dead, in Duarden
Jared (JEH-red) **Gaisse** (Gah-EESS), dead man in Duarden
Hendrick (HEN-drik), dead man in Duarden
Faeline (Fey-LEEN), girl in Chidair Keep
Jacques (ZHAHK) / **Jack**, the black knight's horse

Village of Oarclaven (Lethe)
Martha (MAR-thuh) **Poiron** (Poy-ROHN), old village woman
Rosaide (Ro-ZAH-eed) **Vellerin** (Vel-leh-REEN), village gossip

Kingdom of Tanathe (Tah-nah-theh) *(Domain)*
Flavio (FLAH-vee-oh) **San Quellenne** (SAHN Kweh-LENN), young boy on the beach
Jelavie (Zhe-lah-VEE) **San Quellenne**, his older sister on the beach

Kingdom of Solemnis (Soh-LEM-niss) *(Domain)*
King **Frederick** (Freh-deh-REEK) **Ourin** (Oo-REEN) of Solemnis
Duke **Raulle** (Rah-UHL) **Deotetti** (Deh-oh-TET-tee) of Solemnis
Duchess **Beatrice** (Beh-ah-TRISS) **Deotetti** (deceased, undead), wife of the Duke Deotetti

Kingdom of Balmue (Domain)
Count **Lecrant** (Leh-CRAH-nt) **D'Arvu** (D'AHR-voo) of Balmue
Countess **Arabella** (Ah-rah-BEL-lah) **D'Arvu** of Balmue
Lady **Leonora** (Leh-oh-NOH-rah) **D'Arvu** of Balmue, their daughter
Lady **Sidonie** (See-doh-NEE), young lady playing in the fields in Elysium
Valentio (Vah-LEN-tee-oh), young gentleman in the fields in Elysium

The Sapphire Court (Domain)
Quentin (KWEN-tin) **Loirre** (Looh-AHR), spy in the service of the Sovereign
Marie-Louise (Mah-REE-Loo-EEZ), maiden in the cobweb chamber
Lily (LEE-lee), maiden in the cobweb chamber
Beatrice (Beh-ah-TRISS), maiden in the cobweb chamber
Lady **Melinoë** (Meh-lee-NOH-eh) **Avalais**, daughter of the Sovereign
Thesmos (THES-moss), the Goddess of Tradition
Trovadii (Troh-VAH-dee-ee), the loyal special army of the Sovereign
Field Marshal **Claude** (CLOD) **Maetra** (Mah-EH-trah) from Tanathe, commanding the First Army of the Trovadii
Field Marshal **Matteas** (Maht-TEH-ahs) **Quara** (Koo-AH-ruh) from Balmue, commanding the Second Army
Field Marshal **Edmunde** (Ehd-MOOND) **Vaccio** (VAH-chee-oh) from Solemnis, commanding the Third Army
Graccia (GRAH-chee-ah), personal maidservant of the Sovereign
Diril (DEE-rihl), secret surveillance agent, of unknown affiliation

New Characters Introduced in Cobweb Forest

Hades (HAY-dees), God of the Underworld
Persephone (Per-SEH-pho-nee), Goddess of the Underworld
Hecate (HEH-kah-tee), Goddess of the Crossroads

Kingdom of Styx
Bruno (BRU-noh) **Melograno** (Meh-loh-GRAH-noh), officer of Charonne garrison at Styx

Kingdom of Lethe
Lord **Granwell** (GRAN-well), advisor to the King of Lethe
Captain **Brandeis** (Brahn-DEIS), officer of Letheburg garrison
Gerard (Jeh-RAHRD) **Sorven** (SOHR-ven), Belle's beau from Fioren.
Baron **Gundar** (GUHN-dahr) **Dureval** (Duh-reh-VAHL), Goraque knight
Sir **Marlon** (MAHR-luhn) **Wedeis** (Weh-DEIS), Goraque knight

Kingdom of Tanathe
Lady **Calliope** (Cah-LAH-yo-peh) **San Quellenne**, liege lady of the region of San Quellenne
Father **Suell** (Sue-EHL), parish priest at San Quellenne

About the Author

Vera Nazarian immigrated to the USA from the former USSR as a kid, sold her first story at the age of 17, and since then has published numerous works in anthologies and magazines, and has seen her fiction translated into eight languages.

She made her novelist debut with the critically acclaimed arabesque "collage" novel *Dreams of the Compass Rose*, followed by epic fantasy about a world without color, *Lords of Rainbow*. Her novella *The Clock King and the Queen of the Hourglass* from PS Publishing (UK) with an introduction by **Charles de Lint** made the *Locus* Recommended Reading List for 2005. Her debut short fiction collection *Salt of the Air*, with an introduction by **Gene Wolfe**, contains the 2007 Nebula Award-nominated "The Story of Love." Other work includes the 2008 Nebula Award-nominated, self-illustrated baroque fantasy novella *The Duke in His Castle*, science fiction collection *After the Sundial* (2010), self-illustrated Supernatural **Jane Austen** Series parodies *Mansfield Park and Mummies* (2009), *Northanger Abbey and Angels and Dragons* (2010), *Pride and Platypus: Mr. Darcy's Dreadful Secret* (2012), *The Perpetual Calendar of Inspiration* (2010), and a parody of paranormal love and relationships advice *Vampires are from Venus, Werewolves are from Mars* (2012).

Vera recently relocated from Los Angeles to the East Coast. She lives in a small town in Vermont, and uses her Armenian sense of humor and her Russian sense of suffering to bake conflicted pirozhki and make art.

In addition to being a writer and award-winning artist, she is also the publisher of Norilana Books.

Official website:
www.veranazarian.com

www.ingramcontent.com/pod-product-compliance
Lightning Source LLC
Chambersburg PA
CBHW020419030726
47495CB00006B/1579